ENIGMA OF LOVE

A Novel By Divine G

Also by Divine G

Novels:

Baby Doll

Money-Grip

Money-Grip 2

The Canarsie Connection

No Other Love

Short Stories:

Averted Hearts (appearing in *The Game*)

Stage Plays:

Peak-Zone (appearing in the anthology, *Exiled Voices, Portals of Discovery*)

ENIGMA OF LOVE ®

ISBN-10: 1940765080
ISBN-13: 978-1-940765-08-2
Createspace Edition

Published by: Divine G Entertainment

Written by: Divine G

Edited by: Divine G

Cover Design by: MjStudios

For information contact:

Divine G Entertainment

Website: http://www.divinegentertainment.com

Email: divinegentertainment@gmail.com

Dedication

This novel is dedicated to the numerous family members, friends and associates who were very instrumental in helping me to get this novel written, edited and published. The list of supporters is so huge and extensive, I am very apprehensive about attempting to mention names, because from past experience, if anyone is inadvertently left out and feels he or she should have been mentioned, it creates a lot of bad feelings. So, this time, I am taking the safe road by sending out a universal dedication to all those who played a part in the success of this novel, without itemizing each individual name. If you were there, by my side, had my back, and was supportive, then you are the person I am referring to when I send out this dedication. This novel is dedicated to you for being there when times got extremely rough, rocky and raw. Once again, thanks for all the support, love and understanding.

CHAPTER # 1

Danielle was in the passenger seat of the cream colored Lexus, watching the late night deserted Bronx streets scroll across her vision. She was contemplating her answer to Jamil's question. After he made a right turn onto Kingsbridge Road, with the ghettoized Tenement buildings sliding across her vision, she said, "It's a surprise."

Jamil Nevez momentarily took his eyes off the road, glancing over at Danielle. His golden brown skin, strong baby face features, hard brown eyes, and that contagious smile made him look like a cross between the ultimate choirboy and an urban ruffian. Expertly concealing his dislike of surprises, with humorous vigor, Jamil said. "I see you gettin' ready to take me on one of them mind rides again."

"Believe me, this ain't a head game," She said softly, her voice matching her extraordinarily exotic features. "You know I don't get down like that." Her flawless maple syrup colored complexion, sleek brown bedroom eyes, and long shoulder length hair took on a special glow tonight and was in syche with her mood. She was seconds from blurting out the news, but quickly contained the urge. "I just wanna check out a few things before I jump to conclusions."

"Well, maybe you should've waited until you had all the facts. I hate being left--" Jamil saw two men walking down the street up ahead. One of them looked like Joe Rock-head he realized. He took his foot off the gas pedal, and slowed down the Lexus to an inconspicuous crawl.

"What's wrong, Jamil?" Danielle followed Jamil's stare that was locked on the two approaching men.

"It's nothin', Boo," Jamil said without blinking once. Through the heavily tinted window, he scrutinized the two men as he cruised pass them. *Yeap, it's him.* Jamil smiled inwardly. *Thought you was gonna sneak in and sneak out, huh, motherfucker!?* His adrenaline kicked in; the epinephrine made him feel light headed.

Danielle's heart flickered in her chest as Jamil killed the headlights and made a U turn. Her nervousness caused her to unconsciously turn the gold ring on her pinkie finger. She sensed something real crazy was about to happen.

Jamil doubled parked the Lexus as he observed the two men turn down an alleyway. "I'll be right back, Danielle." He got out of the car, quietly closed the door behind him and walked very fast after the two. His black leather jacket flapped in the early March breeze.

When Jamil turned into the alleyway, he quietly kneeled behind a bunch of garbage cans. The wretched odors struck his senses like a slap to the face with a shit covered glove. It smelled like a conglomeration of shitty diapers, decayed fruits, rotting fish and God only knows what else. With squinted eyes, while breathing very lightly, Jamil pulled his 9mm from the back waist of his pants, reached in his jacket pocket for the silencer, and rapidly screwed it onto the 16 shot automatic.

Peering around the trash cans, Jamil saw a third man approaching Joe and his side kick, Baltimore. The newcomer came from the back of the dead-end alley and stopped in front of the two, talking. The situation was developing so perfectly in his favor, Jamil wondered was this a set-up or a trap of some kind. These chumps had nowhere to run and he had the element of surprise. Indeed, the circumstances were simply too good to be true. Jamil didn't give a fuck what it was as he flicked the safety button into the off position. He had rage in his eyes, revels of retribution pumping his heart, and murder on his mind.

Jamil rose to his feet and eased towards the trio with his automatic aimed at Joe's back. He was definitely gonna get it first! With his heart rate increasing from the excitement, Jamil smiled when he saw the newcomer's eyes bulge. Just as the three men frantically scrambled for cover, Jamil's trigger finger came to life.

SZK! SZK! SZK!

Silent flames roared from the 9mm. Jamil saw Joe's body convulse when a bullet struck him in the lower back. Joe fell to the ground as two bullets struck Baltimore in the chest when he stupidly turned around to see what was going on. He fell hard to the pavement. Jamil's eyes got wide when the newcomer pulled a gun.

BOW! BOW!

The two ear-shattering 44 magnum explosions vibrated everything in its circumference as Jamil frantically sought refuge behind a huge garbage dumpster. Bullets ricocheted and whizzed pass him. Jamil peeked around the dumpster and saw the newcomer running deeper into the alley. He took aim and carefully squeezed off two shots. The newcomer flinched from the impact of the bullets, then tripped and fell flat on his face. Jamil sprung to his feet and ran towards the newcomer.

As Jamil moved rapidly down the alley, he saw the newcomer had dropped his weapon and was crawling for it. Jamil increased his speed and fired two shots to the man's head. Chunks of flesh and bone were splattered all over the pavement.

Suddenly, Jamil heard a scurrying noise in back of him. He turned and saw Joe stumbling away. Jamil ran over to Baltimore's motionless body and planted two bullets in his head. There wasn't gonna be any survivors of this conflict. *No tales will be told of this night*, he promised as he turned and saw Joe stumbled into a crowd of garbage cans. The noise of the crashing cans seemed to be ear shattering.

Jamil bolted after Joe. With the 9mm aimed, Jamil squeezed off a shot. It missed. Joe made it pass the entrance of the alleyway. *Shit!* Jamil muttered, realizing there could be eyes all over the place because of those two fuckin' loud ass gun shots! Those fuckin' garbage cans didn't help either.

Jamil fired another shot. The impact of the bullet spun Joe around as he crumbled to the ground. He was just beyond the curb and started crawling desperately into the middle of the street. Jamil's speed increased.

Breathing hard, Jamil kicked Joe square in his ass, catapulting him into a two foot slide on his stomach and his chin. With his foot, Jamil flipped Joe over onto his back. He wanted to see this motherfucker's eyes before he let him have it. Staring down at Joe with a warped smile, Jamil slowly raised his 9mm.

"Jamil, please man," Joe Rock-head slurred from the pain. "He came at me first, I ain't have a choice, man--"

SZK! SZK!

The two bullets ripped into Joe's skull, causing his whole body to jerk and flinch with tremendous force.

Jamil turned and quickly walked towards his Lexus. He sighed with anger, realizing Danielle saw him kill Joe Rock-head. *Damn it!* He didn't want her to ever see anything like this! *Shit!* But, it was too late to change all that. Unscrewing the silencer, he hastily scanned the surrounding buildings to see if anyone was looking. He saw nothing out of the norm. Jamil stuffed the silencer in his pocket and tucked the hot automatic in the front waist of his pants.

Jamil snatched open the car door, jumped in, slammed the gear in drive and sped off. He maneuvered the Lexus around Joe's body sprawled in the street.

With excitement still racing through his blood-stream, Jamil said to Danielle, "What did you see?"

Danielle was aghast. "You, you killed him?" When she turned and made eye contact with Jamil, something frightening bubbled inside the pit of her stomach. His expression was scary. It took a fraction of a second for her to catch on. "I ain't see, heard or know a damn thing. Absolutely nothing."

Jamil smiled broadly. He always knew Danielle was a trooper. Now he would find out if she was really built like that. He prayed she didn't fail the test; he sure would hate to kill something as fine and perfectly stacked as Danielle.

£¥♥   £¥♥   £¥♥   £¥♥

Meanwhile, a woman named Debra Holmes crashed from the front door of the tenement building next to the alleyway where the murders occurred, screaming. "Joe! Joe! Oh God, please, Joe!" She hysterically latched onto his dead body, crying profusely. She told him not to fuck with Jamil and them damn drugs. And how the hell could he even think he could come back out here after killing two of Jamil's workers!? *Stupid! Stupid! Stupid! If he had only listened.*

Moments earlier, Debra heard the two shots and rushed to her window. She saw a double parked Lexus with a woman in the passenger seat. The car window was rolled down and the brown skin black woman was smoking a cigarette. Debra almost became frantic when a closer observation revealed it was Jamil's girlfriend.

A few seconds later, Debra saw Joe stumble from the alleyway, fell and started crawling into the middle of the street. Then, right on Joe's heels, she saw Jamil approaching with a gun in his hand. When Jamil stood over Joe pointing the gun, she was seconds from screaming out the window for him to stop, but common sense told her to be easy; real easy. Then silent flames leaped from the gun, Joe's body jerked from the impact. It took every drop of energy for her not to rush out the apartment until Jamil fled the scene.

With blood covering her hands, Debra sprung to her feet and raced back inside her first floor apartment and dialed 911 with trembling fingers. "Hello, is this the police!?" Crying hysterically she said, "Jamil Nevez killed my man!"

CHAPTER # 2

The following morning, Jamil swirled from the deep sleep and slammed the palm of his hand on the buzzing alarm clock. He laid there for an two extra minutes, then rolled out of bed and stumbled to the bathroom. Last night's drama jumped in his head as he brushed his teeth. He was enthralled at the thought he had finally caught up with Joe Rock-head. He'd been trying to track him down for four months, and had even put out a fifty thousand dollar contract on his big ass head.

After taking a shower, Jamil got dressed, fixed himself a protein drink and exited his six million dollar Westchester County mansion in Scarsdale. He was on his way to the stash-house in Tracy Towers to pick up last night's money. As he got inside his sky blue Mercedes-Benz E360, Jamil re-enacted the discussion he had with his big brother, Kilroy, last night after dropping Danielle off at her crib.

Jamil pulled the car onto the road and still couldn't fix his mind to understand why Kilroy hated Danielle so much. She was a hard-core trooper, was easy to get along with, never nagged, complained or whined about anything, the sex was literally off the Richter scale, she wasn't a gold digging hoochie mama, since she wasn't phased by all his money, she was insanely loyal to him, and most of all, his guilty conscience was growing out of control with each moment he spent with her.

In other words, Jamil truly felt Daneille was a dream girl. And from the perspective of one who's life involved ripping, running and mastering the streets, he believed this was the only rational way to view her. Although he had a major beef with her occupation, Jamil did realized it showed just how much she kept it real and funky, and would never be a cross over Negro. After he proudly told Kilroy about the dirty little secret Danielle had lingering in her closet, Jamil couldn't believe Kilroy still wasn't convinced she was beyond snitching on him.

As Jamil drove onto the parkway and saw a black couple in a BMW cruising along side of him, he wondered if he was starting to get soft? After a life time spent being a womanizer, a 'hood rat abuser and the ultimate pimp daddy, this feeling was very threatening. Even he didn't quite understand why he was feeling Danielle so much? Maybe Kilroy was right, maybe he was getting soft. If he believed in witchcraft and voodoo, he would've been convinced she hit his ass with some kind of Moe Joe or something. But when he looked closely at what he was experiencing, he sensed it wasn't a pussy whipped feeling; he was sure of that. He was hoping it wasn't a love thing, but his subconscious was telling him that's exactly what it was.

For the umpteenth time, he wondered if he was allowing his heart to taint the rational part of his mind? Under normal situations, Danielle would have to go and would have been dealt with immediately after witnessing the shooting. Kilroy had vehemently insisted they send a hitter to deal with Danielle, but Jamil made it unequivocally clear he was not going to allow it, and when Kilroy saw Jamil's facial response, he instantly retracted the suggestion.

Twenty minutes later, after entering the Bronx, Jamil started spying his rearview mirror much more frequently. A few minutes later, Jamil noticed a green car behind him containing a white and a black man. It took him ten minutes, and six unintended turns to discover they were definitely tailing him. A small ping of nervousness began beating wildly in his chest as he stopped at a traffic-light on White Plains Road.

When the light turned green, Jamil sped off. He saw the car turn right and sighed with partial relief. He immediately started looking for the new car because it was standard police procedure for several cars to take turns following a target. He was getting far too paranoid to go through with this pick up and decided to head back to his crib.

He made a stop at a red light, looking out his mirrors.

AAARRHHH!!

Suddenly, four unmarked cars came to a screeching stop in front of him. Three similar cars stopped in back of him. All fourteen detectives, sprung out of their vehicles with weapons pointed.

"Put your hands up!--NOW!--Get 'em up!" The detectives screamed.

Jamil put his hands up in the air. He was glad he left his hardware home and hoped they didn't find his secret compartment in the back seat where he hid his back-up 9mm.

The Mercedes' door was snatched open, the heavyset white detective reached over, slammed the gear in park and snatched Jamil from the car, forcing him to lay face down on the pavement.

"You have the right to remain silent . . ."

As the cuffs were slapped on his wrists, and his rights read in full, Jamil forced himself to relax. This was probably just a routine harassment situation. After he paid some extra pay-off funds, everything would be all right.

". . .You're under arrest for murder. . ."

Jamil's heart leaped in his chest. *Murder!?* As Jamil was snatched to his feet and shoved inside the green car that followed him moments ago, his mind was hurling information around in his head. In a restrained panicked state, he was trying to figure out if this arrest was for last night's run? Maybe it was for one of the dozen other runs he'd done in the past decade since becoming involved in the drug game? It couldn't be for any of those previous runs, he easily concluded, because he wore a mask, all those runs were well thought out and he kept his business to himself. The only person who knew of his past exploits was his brother, Kilroy, and he obviously wouldn't flip out.

His inner voice assured him that he was being arrested for last night's run. In a state of dread, he realized there was no one else besides Danielle who saw the incident. She had to be responsible for this! Naw, it can't be! Danielle would never do some shit like that! Kilroy's statement jumped in his mind as the car sped off: "She's even more dangerous to you because of all that shit she got in her closet, fool!"

Jamil gritted his teeth so hard, he heard ringing in his ears. His mind refused to believe Danielle was responsible for this because he felt it in his heart she was built to endure such an incident, and most of all, he realized he loved her. He repeatedly told himself, *it can't be Danielle! It can't be!*

£¥♥   £¥♥   £¥♥   £¥♥

Danielle sat staring at her make-up laden image in the mirror. The thunderous bass coming from the club dance floor made her shabby, small dressing room tremble and shiver. With the exception of a gee-string and a tiny bra that covered only her nipples, Danielle was naked. She wore a ton of elegant perfume that could clearly be smelled twenty feet away.

She gazed into her brown eyes. In a semi-trance like state, her mind was somewhere else. Even her inner voice was screaming at her, telling her something was terribly wrong. She sighed hard, fighting to stay focused, since she was on deck next. From past experience, she knew she couldn't perform her routine effectively without being totally in the mood and focused.

Danielle reached over and sparked up a cigarette. She cursed at herself because this was the fourth one within a half hour. She wanted to stop this nasty habit, and even tried twice, but there was just too much stress and frustration going on in her life. Plus, her discipline was shot when it came to controlling her habits; especially the bad ones. In between drags on the cancer stick, she rotated the ring on her pinkie finger without realizing what she was doing.   Her subconscious was telling her something real bad happened to Jamil. He didn't showed up at the club or called her in two whole days. This was the first time he'd ever failed to pick her up and bring her home after work without calling to let her know he couldn't make it. She beeped him over and over again and got no response. When she called his crib, she got no answer.

Her intuition told her that his current missing in action status had something to do with the shooting the other night. Every bad thing her pessimistic mind could conjure up, took full control of her imagination. Is he laying dead somewhere? What if he was shot and killed by the peoples of the man he smoked the other night? Maybe he had to skip town in a hurry?

She sighed with angry force. This was extremely bad timing. Her surprise was confirmed yesterday, and instead of being a moment of joy and happiness, it was now transformed into a moment of sadness and deep depression. When would anything, even the most simplest thing, ever go right for her? Just when she started to think her bad luck was about to ease up just a little bit, now this had to happen.

That night of the shooting stayed in her thoughts. It wasn't because of the death of that man Jamil killed. She had seen so much death during her 31 years on this planet, she long since recognized death was absolutely an indispensable part of life. Everybody lived in order to die; some simply died a little quicker than others, and often had a helping hand to assist them with the trip. Indeed, it was nothing short of a miracle she could still feel distressed when death occurred in her midst. But, thanks to the massive number of trials and tribulations she underwent, Danielle was far from one of those sensitive, unblemished, stuck in the house type of women, who would have been shattered by the shooting.

Put another way, she was a gruff woman of the world, who'd been hurt, disrespected, abandoned, beaten down physically, psychologically, spiritually, and emotionally, and had developed an impenetrable shield that could put Teflon and Titanium out of business. The story of her life read like an urban horror tale; tragedy after tragedy was all that life seemed to offer Danielle. She was a loner, and because of her past, she had no choice in this matter. Even her girlfriend and co-worker, Brenda "Sweet Cheeks" Taylor, was not as close as Brenda preferred. As far as Danielle was concerned, Brenda was more or less someone to talk to in order not to go completely insane from loneliness and boredom when Jamil wasn't around.

Danielle's intense, long-standing pain, suffering, alienation and self-inflicted ostracism caused her to hate people; they always seemed to be the root of so much unnecessary heartaches. But, her bitterness and anger was non-toxic to others in the sense that she never wanted to see other people in the same state of turmoil she was in. The saying, misery loves company was totally inapplicable to Danielle. She attributed this humanity component in her heart to her loving and caring zodiac sign, Sagittarius. But despite all the outer images, the callused coverings and the protective shields, Danielle wanted what most women wanted--a family.

She sighed angrily as the cloud of Newport smoke swirled from her mouth. Her plans for the future were rapidly unraveling before her eyes. Danielle started mentally beating up herself because she should have known getting too deeply involved with a bad boy, sophisticated rough neck type, was not a wise move. After all the madness all the previous 'hood-minded brothers put her through, one would think she had learned her lesson by now. But, she had no control over the way her feelings reacted to matters of the heart.

Plus, Jamil was uniquely different from most men from the 'hood. He was like some kind of character right out of an intriguing romance novel. His amazing sense of humor was a tremendously big thumbs up; she always enjoyed the company of a man who could make her laugh. He was rich, he was feared and respected, and most of all, he wasn't afraid to show his affection in public. If a man was uncomfortable around her when in the presence of others, he had no business with Danielle. She definitely sensed he loved her; he never said it straight out, but his ways and actions spoke volumes.

Danielle always wondered what in the hell did Jamil see in her? Why was he attracted to a strip-tease dancing 'hood rat who was running from her past and had a bad attitude as big as a bazooka blast? At first, she always thought it was because of her big round ass; all black men loved big butt women, and she knew she had plenty junk in her trunk. But, as time went on and the relationship slowly grew, it became self evident her body wasn't what Jamil was out to get. He sincerely seemed to be after her heart. That day she first met Jamil, about a year ago, when he entered the club and walked over to her, introduced himself and started cracking jokes on Big Pete, the bouncer, would live in her mind for eternity. The vibe he gave off made her feel like she knew him all her life.

There was only one other man in her life who made her feel as good as Jamil did, but the harm he inflicted on her heart and mental well-being caused her to literally hate him with an unmitigating passion. There was indeed a very thin line between love and hate, and when he crossed that line,

Danielle developed an aversion for him that was so profound there was no word in the English language to describe the hate she felt. She despised the ground he walked on.

There was a sudden knock on the door.

"Come in!" Danielle shouted.

The bouncer, Big Pete, opened the door, and stuck his high yellow fat face inside the room. "It's time, baby girl." He smiled, showing off his gold plated front tooth.

"I'm on my way," Danielle snuffed out her cigarette as she rose to her feet. She didn't hear the door close and turned. "I said I'm comin', Pete."

Pete was smiling broadly, enjoying the view. He closed the door and headed down the corridor towards the dance floor.

Danielle checked herself in the mirror one last time and pranced out of her dressing room. The song, Slam it and Jam it, was booming through the speakers, which was Sweet Cheeks' finish-line song, indicating she was whining down her routine. Danielle stood near the dance floor entrance for the DJ to see her. She saw the house was almost full, with the exception of four tables.

She shook loose of the stress and started tapping her foot, allowing the bass to draw her into dance mode. The electrical vibe struck and started with her foot and moved upwards. Her hips started moving to the beat, then her shoulders, and before she knew it, her whole body was bouncing to the beat.

A minute later, the music was slowly turned down. When the music was just above a mellow level, DJ Freaky Frukwan said into the microphone. "Come on! Let's show my girl Sweet Cheeks some love my brothers! Yeah!"

There was a huge round of applauds accompanied with whistles and heckling comments of pleasure and delight.

Frukwan continued. "Our next dancer needs no introduction. With the biggest butt in the Bronx, and the sweetest smile you ever did see, please welcome and show some heavy love for the one and only Danielle, AKA Midnight Flower!"

Danielle strutted seductively towards the two foot platform. Her song, Swing Those Things, lit up the club. There were hoots and hollers of joy and happiness as she mounted the stage and went into her routine.

Twenty minutes later, sweat was oozing from her pores and her gee-string and bra strap was littered with bills of all denominations from her regular horny old customers. Her whine down song came on and she sighed with relief. All throughout her routine, Danielle was looking into the sea of faces, searching and hoping Jamil's face would pop-up, but in accordance with her bad luck, that didn't happen.

Danielle rhythmically pranced off the stage, across the dance floor, and down the corridor to her dressing room. She opened the door and was surprised when she saw Sweet Cheeks in her dressing room. She was a light skinned, petite sister with real reddish brown hair and aqua green eyes. Her unusually large and shapely hips and thighs with a tiny waist were her best features. However, she was twisted in the breast department.

Danielle saw the troubled expression on her face. "What's wrong, Brenda?"

Brenda excitedly grabbed Danielle's hands, and pulled her over to the chair. "Girl, I think you should have a seat before I tell you this."

Danielle's heart dropped to her pelvic bone. She struggled to keep her eyes from taking on a terrified look. "What is it!?" She sat down.

Brenda stretched out the torturous suspense for as long as possible. She enjoyed teasing people in this fashion. "You know that cat who got all them spots in Bronx River Projects locked down? I think his name is BJ? He works for Jamil?"

"Yeah, yeah, I know him." She just knew Jamil was dead.

"He told me Jamil got arrested for a triple homicide the other day. That's why he ain't been around here."

Triple homicide!? She whistled. That night of the shooting flashed across her mind. She felt a stabbing sensation in her chest. "Did he say where the homicides happened?"

"Naw, he ain't go into all that."

Danielle stared at her image in the mirror for a moment. "I gotta go see him. He should be on Rikers Island, right?"

"Danielle, I know you ain't gonna start runnin' this nigga down, now that he's on lock down?"

Danielle screwed up her face. Brenda was the epitome of a gold digger and had no shame in her game when it came to jumping from man to man as long as it worked to her advantage. "I ain't flippin' on Jamil 'cause of this. I'm gonna go see him tomorrow morning."

"And how you plan on doing that?" Brenda said matter of factly as she propped her soft, plump behind on the counter. "We gotta do that Wall Street job tomorrow."

"Shit!" Danielle muttered. "Yeah, you right." She quickly analyzed her schedule inside her head.

"And don't forget the day after tomorrow we supposed to go to Long Island to Jason's mansion. I heard that party supposed to be the bomb. He wants us to get there before noon so we can rehearse. This is the biggest week we gonna see for a good while."

Danielle gritted her teeth. Brenda was right; they were going to be busy most of the week. But, she had to make a sacrifice. "I ain't gonna be able to go to Long Island. You gotta do that one without me."

"Naw, Danielle, you know we roll as a team, girl. Jamil can wait until the weekend. Business before bullshit is the rule in this--"

"What the hell are you talkin' about!? This is business. Keepin' it real is all about the business. This ain't open for discussion. I'll do the Wall Street gig tomorrow, but the Long Island one is dead."

CHAPTER # 3

The following morning, as Danielle and Brenda were on the #2 train on their way to Wall Street, Jamil entered the visiting room floor of Rikers Island's HDM (House of Detention for Men), dressed in a gray jumpsuit. The huge sliding door gate closed behind him. His eyes scanned the area with smooth precision. The visiting area was filled primarily with women and children. When his eyes landed on Brute and Cleavon, he noticed they stood out like a white speck of lint on a jet black piece of cloth. They had thug written all over them.

As Jamil approached the small plastic table, he realized Kilroy had to be in war mode for him to send these two crazy fools. That was a good thing, since this situation was going to require the use of some very serious measures. They both stood up when they saw Jamil.

Jamil gave them both some dap (striking their clinched fists together) and sat down. "Nigger, you brushed your teeth today?" He said to Cleavon with a crazy smile. "I ain't in the mood to be smellin' no shit."

Brute unleashed a deep baritone chuckle. "That's why I like you, Ja. You crazy as hell, man." The bass in his voice matched his big, burly body.

Jamil continued. "I smell enough foul ass odors in this place, I don't need you comin' in here fuckin' up my breathin' air."

Cleavon smiled. His ruthless persona was turned down two notches. He was in the presence of one of his bosses; the second in command of the Nevez Brothers' drug syndicate and he struggled to act accordingly. "Damn, son! You don't ever take shit serious, do you? This ain't the time for your little ranking games. These crackers are gonna fry your black ass as sure as the white man is the devil."

"They need to fry that shit on top of your head. Maybe a little heat'll straight out that silly ass Wally way back hairline of yours."

Brute laughed harder. He loved when Cleavon got dissed because he was so hard on everybody else it was a relief to see him get a taste of his own medicine.

Cleavon was seething with anger, but didn't reveal it. "You ain't gonna be laughin' when you hear what's up with that fine bitch of yours."

"What? You jealous, motherfucker?" Jamil teased. "I get the fine ones while you get them old busted ass crack smokin', dog dick suckin', crusty ankle havin' ass bitches."

Brute exploded with laughter, drawing attention to their table.

Cleavon laughed as well. "You know I ain't never trusted them fine bitches. They ain't nothing but foul and trifling motherfuckers, out to suck a nigga's pockets bone dry like a Hoover vacuum cleaner. Give me an ugly broad any day."

"Nigger, like you got a choice in the matter. Ain't no fine bitch in their right mind gonna want your twisted ass. Look at you, your furniture is fucked up, you got a ole lumpy ass head, breath smell like buzzard ass, your hairline starts at the top of your head, and you keep a set of black eyes. I'ma start calling you asscoon. You smell like ass and look like a damn raccoon. Asscoon motherfucker! That's you."

They all laughed.

"At least I ain't no pussy whipped, strung out motherfucker, jumpin' through the bra strap, and funky ass G-string of a strip club tramp."

Jamil was smiling, but he didn't find that funny. He locked eyes with Cleavon as the smile disappeared. His face was as blank as a sheet of clean notebook paper and as cold as freon. He deliberately rode the silence.

The silence was long and penetrating.

Cleavon started getting nervous. *Ah, shit!* He done fucked around and crossed the line. It was time to cop a plea. "I'm—I—you--I--" He swallowed hard. "Come on, Jamil, we was jokin', man. You started it first. Now, you gonna spazz out on me!?"

A moment later, Jamil said, "You see, look at him, Brute." He burst out laughing. "He's a bitch. Cold blooded bitch, tremblin' like a Mexican Chihuahua about to get fucked with some horse dick."

Brute laughed, but Cleavon silently sighed with relief.

"All right, all right," Jamil held up both hands. "Rec. time is officially over. The next motherfucker crack another joke from here on end, will feel the wrath. These motherfuckers are about to fry my black ass . . . So, what did Kilroy find out?"

Cleavon spoke enthusiastically. "Kilroy found out the snitch is your girl Danielle."

Jamil put his head down. He was devastated. He sensed it was her, but was hoping and praying it wasn't the case. His eyes started getting misty and he struggled to keep from showing his pain.

Cleavon was staring at Jamil's eyes. He always thought Jamil was pussy whipped; now he knew it was true from the way he responded to this news. "Sorry, Jamil, but she's gotta go."

Brute spoken seriously. "Kilroy wants to send some hitters out tonight. He wanted us to let you know what's going on. This is a triple homicide case and we gotta step to this real quick before they take her to the grand jury." Jamil went into a deep silence. This was strictly survival from here on end. He loved Danielle, but Cleavon was right; she had to go. There was no question about that. Even if she wasn't the snitch there was no time or room to take chances. And it had to be done right. All variables had to be confirmed and neutralized. "Tell Kilroy to keep his eyes and ears open even after we do this run. There could be other witnesses. I ain't takin' no chances."

"He said Danielle was the only one," Cleavon said, "He got his inside peoples to check this shit out."

"I don't give a fuck who he got checking, tell him to stay on this shit." He still had his doubts about Danielle being a snitch, but a triple homicide beef didn't allow him the luxury of permitting his heart to guide his decisions. "Check it out, Brute. You know that hitter named Hair-trigger . . . Tykim?" He saw Brute squint his eyes. "He just came home from up north. He's from Brooklyn."

"Oh, yeah! Yeah, I know him."

"I know him too." Cleavon said, wondering where the hell Jamil was going with this. "I heard he's runnin' around blazin' drug dealers."

"I want him to do this hit," Jamil said, "Tell Kilroy this is gonna be a two man run. He can hire one of his own hitters, and Tykim is gonna be my hired hitter."

"But, but," Brute was bewildered. "Kilroy wants to handle this straight up. He's making plans right now as we speak."

"Yeah, Ja," Cleavon said, "He got Hector and Lunatic on standby, waiting for the green light."

"You tell Kilroy I said this is my black ass on the choppin' block. I'm gonna have some input in this shit, case closed. Any way, Lunatic and Hector are known to get real sloppy when they think shit is in the bag. Tykim is top grade material. Big dog status. He'll organize the hit professionally. Even if the police got her under watch, it'll go down correctly."

"You know how much it's gonna cost to hire this motherfucker?" Cleavon said, "And how the hell do we know he's even gonna take the job?"

"I'm offering him 150 gees for this hit," Jamil said, "Half up-front, the other half upon completion." He smiled when he saw both their wide eyes. "Imagine any 'hood hitter turnin' down that kind of money?"

15

£¥♥   £¥♥   £¥♥   £¥♥

Tykim "Hair-trigger" Hall sat at the poker table staring at the cards in his hands, waiting for Smithy to throw out a card. A rap tune was playing in the background, it was loud enough to be heard clearly, but low enough not to require the four men to shout over the music. The Queens club located on Jamaica Avenue was empty since it was about 5 o'clock in the afternoon.

Tykim's light brown skin and matching brown eyes were as deeply focused as his concentration. His neatly groomed goatee and his head full of corn-row braids made him look like the epitome of a ghettoized brother from the 'hood. "Come on, Smithy, throw a damn card out, man."

Primo, who sat on Tykim's left side, said, "This nigga's procrastinating. He ain't got shit, but he's too scared to turn that fucked up hand in. Come in, bow down gracefully, Smithy."

Smithy looked up smiling. "Patience and contemplation is the mark of a true winner." He tossed a card on the table.

"Hey! Tykim!" A brown skinned woman with big sensuous eyes and finger waves in her hair, shouted from the threshold of the back room door. She was chewing gun with nasty girl vigor.

"What's up, Charmaine?" Tykim said, still thinking about his next move.

"You got a phone call."

"I thought I told you to tell anybody who calls, I'm not--"

"Whoever it is, told me to tell you it's important. He told me to tell you something about a Universal Mathmatic Supreme or something or another."

Tykim's heart started beating faster. That was the code word and it meant this call was confirmation that it was work time. "I'll be right back." He laid his cards down on the table and rose to his feet.

"What are we suppose to do about this hand!?" Smithy was pissed off. "We ain't throwin' this hand in, fuck that!"

As Tykim headed towards the door, he said, "Put the game on pause, I'll be right back." Exiting the room, he heard them bickering over whether or not they should scrap the hand.

Tykim strutted across the empty club dance floor, then down a corridor towards the office. He entered and Charmaine handed him the phone. He took it and waited for Charmaine to leave. When the door closed behind her, Tykim spoke into the phone receiver. "Peace. Tykim speaking." He nodded his head as Intelligence, the person on the other end of the line, spoke.

A few seconds later, he said, "Make knowledge born in mathematics." About thirty seconds later, he said, "That sounds good, but I need a picture of her." He nodded his head, listening intently. "You know I'm a dough-low artist . . . Tell him I'll meet him in about an hour. We can go in-depth then . . . Don't worry, I'll be there." He laid the receiver down in its cradle.

He leaned against the maple oak wood desk and folded his arms, in deep thought. There was something up with this run. But his intuition was telling him to be easy and not to jump to any conclusions. Proceeding with extreme caution was going to be an absolute prerequisite. This was the biggest payment he'd ever been offered. It was so huge it made him nervous because it could be a trap.

Maybe one of the drug gangs he had hit, found out it was him and were tryin' to draw him out into the open? After some deep pondering, Tykim dismissed that possibility since the target was a woman. Whoever this woman was, she had to be dangerous to someone important. Or Intelligence wasn't telling him everything. He sighed, shook loose of the invading doubts and headed back to the card game.

For 150 gees, he didn't give a fuck if it was the daughter of the biggest mobster in the United States, she was going down tonight.

CHAPTER # 4

Tykim sat in the passenger seat of the brown Chevy Trailblazer watching the deserted late night Streets. Hector Ortiz was in the driver's seat. They were parked on 242nd Street near Vancourtland Avenue, about a half block away from the target's building. All the houses in this area had long stairs leading up to the main entrance. Rain was in the forecast all day, but never came to fruition. Even at 2:30 am in the morning, the rain was still held at bay.

Tykim savored the weight of the 9mm tucked in his waist. His pessimism was finally starting to take a back seat. After he received the 75 gees and was allowed to drop it off at his man Kamel's crib, he knew this run was a genuine hit. If it was a set-up, they wouldn't have given him the money and would have made their move by now. He just hoped they didn't have to kill any cops, since they were talking like this woman would be under police protection.

Tykim felt out of place because working with a partner was something new for him, but for the amount of money he was receiving he was willing to break one of his own golden rules. In any event, he liked Hector's style. He was definitely about his business and didn't do a lot of talking. A very critical requirement in this line of work. In this game, loose lips could do a lot more harm than merely sinking a ship.

Like everything else in life, this run had its bad elements. There was no picture of this woman named Danielle Lewis. He also was unable to find out why they wanted her dead. Based on their belief that she might be accompanied by the police, Tykim was able to surmise that the woman might have turned state's evidence on someone important or was about to do so.

Suddenly, the glare of headlights appeared in the back of them.

Tykim watched the green Toyota cruise pass. He smiled; it was his man Kamel. He glanced at his watch. Kamel's rounds were on time. There was no way Tykim was going to walk into a situation without having a set of eyes in the back of his head. Even though he didn't think he would need Kamel's back-up assistance, it couldn't hurt to be over-prepared. Also, taking into consideration Hector's knowledge of the hitter's game, Tykim sensed he might even have his own back-up crew lurking somewhere in the shadows.

Tykim's curiosity was growing larger by the minutes. He wanted to know how this woman looked. They said she was a strip-tease dancer working at the Paradise Lounge over on 177th Street and Southern Blvd., near the Bronx Zoo. In light of this fact, she had to be a dime piece and was holding because that club was a sophisticated joint and didn't hire any hardcore 'hood rats. If a stripper wasn't a dime piece and a half, she wasn't getting any air-play at the Paradise Lounge.

"Yo, Hector, check it, bro," Tykim said, "Ain't nobody tell me how this broad looks. What's the deal man, how she look?"

Hector cleared his throat. "I ain't gonna do it to you, son." He paused. "Put it this way, she's so fine it's a crime we gotta smoke her ass."

"What a waste, huh?" Tykim said, as a set of headlights appeared in front of them.

Hector sat up all the way, looking at his watch. "This should be her." He pulled his 9mm and screwed the silencer onto the barrel.

Tykim nonchalantly did the same thing, keeping his eyes on the car that came to a stop in front of the house they had been watching. He saw a woman get out of the yellow taxi cab, and his eyes grew wide. Shock waves rippled through the pit of this stomach. He blinked his eyes rapidly, but instantly realized there was nothing wrong with his vision.

"That's her." Hector said calmly. "Look for any other cars that might've followed the cab." His eyes darted about. Hector saw she wasn't being followed, and it momentarily threw him off because he was hoping they would get boggled down in a big shoot-out. "After she finish paying the fare, and the cab pulls off, we blaze this bitch."

Tykim was brain-locked with shock; his mind had almost completely froze up. He had to do something and whatever it was he knew he had to do it before Hector got out the vehicle.

£¥♥   £¥♥   £¥♥   £¥♥

Moments earlier, Danielle got out of the yellow cab, paid the fare and headed for her building. As the cab sped off, Danielle suddenly felt like she was being watched, and it gave her the chills. She looked both ways down the empty street, but saw nothing. Danielle shook loose of the sensation and started climbing the stairs.

£¥♥   £¥♥   £¥♥   £¥♥

Tykim's mind was moving at breakneck speed. Do something! Hurry! his mind screamed. "Hector! Wait!"

Hector stopped with one leg out of the Jeep, the 9mm in his left hand, and a perplexed expression on his face. He was becoming enthralled with anger. "What the fuck's wrong!?

19

With flinching speed, Tykim aimed the 9mm at Hector's head and repeatedly pulled the trigger.

SZK! SZK! SZK!

Hector's body jerked violently from the impact of the three shots that tore through his unsuspecting flesh. One of the bullets struck his forehead and the other two hit him in the upper chest. Hector was knocking on the gates of hell as he crumbled to the sidewalk, spilling blood profusely.

Tykim turned his head and saw Daquasha walking up the steps of the building. He bolted out of the Jeep and down the street, screaming. "Daquasha! Wait! Daquasha, hold up!"

£¥♥   £¥♥   £¥♥   £¥♥

Danielle's heart leaped in her chest when she heard her real name being yelled. With her key jammed in the lock, she turned with terror surging through her body. She just knew this man running towards her was an undercover cop, coming to put her under arrest. Her panic and terror drenched mind saw flashing images of prison bars and big bull-dagger bitches beating flames out of her in order to get a juicy lick.

Trembling uncontrollably, Daquasha focused her vision and saw it was Tykim. An avalanche of mixed emotions almost buckled her knees; relieved it wasn't the police, but fuming with debilitating rage because Tykim had apparently found her. This was the man she hated and could have killed him right here on the spot if she had a gun.

Through exhaustion, Tykim spoke excitedly as he climbed the stairs. "Some drug dealers put a hit out on you, they paid me and some other dude to kill you."

"I ain't got time for your fuckin' head games," Daquasha gave him her back and continued unlocking the door. "I told you not to ever--"

"Daquasha!" Tykim grabbed her shoulder and spun her around. The smell of her perfume brought back a flood of memories. "A cat name Kilroy paid me 150 gees to kill you!" He locked eyes with her. "I don't know what you did or what you seen or whose nerves you got on, but I think you better come on with me. I got a place I can hide you out until I can find out what--"

Daquasha violent shoved Tykim in the chest, causing him to stumble backwards. Kilroy had no reason to kill her. Jamil would never tolerate something as outrageous as that.

Tykim almost tumbled down the whole flight of stairs, but grabbed hold of the banister.

"Get the fuck away from me!" Daquasha shouted as she frantically rummaged through her tote bag for her can of mase. "If you think I'm going for that lame ass game, you gotta be the stupidest nigga to walk this planet!" She pulled the small aerosol can and aimed it at Tykim.

With his hands raised in the air to wardoff the mase, Tykim moved slowly down the stairs. He spoke softly. "Please, Daquasha. This is no bullshit. You can't stay here! I was sent here to kill you! They ain't gonna stop coming for you until you're dead. This folks are not fuckin' around at all."

"Oh, so you a hit-man now," Daquasha aimed for his face. "You still love lying about shit, huh? Well, you can hit-man this you bastard!" She hit the button and a huge stream of mist shot from the canister. She saw Tykim jumped backwards, almost losing his footing as he stumbled down to the bottom of the stairs. *Shit! It missed him.* "Leave me the fuck alone, Tykim!"

Tykim stood staring at Daquasha with both hands on his hips as she unfastened the locks. After she entered the building, Tykim ran down the street back to the trailblazer. He saw Kamel was standing near the Jeep. His speed increased. When he arrived, Tykim saw Hector's body was dumped in the back of the Jeep and covered with a blanket. "Thanks, Kamel. That was good thinking, bro."

"What the fuck is this!?" Kamel's brown eyes were wide with confusion. His brown hoodie covered his head, making him look like the ultimate cat burglar. "What part of the plan is this!?"

"It's too complicated to explain right now." Tykim jumped behind the wheel of the trailblazer. "Follow me over to the west side. I gotta get rid of this motherfucker." He turned the ignition and the jeep came to life.

Kamel bolted to his car parked several cars away, jumped inside and started his car.

As Tykim maneuvered the Jeep into the street, his mind was working overtime. *That damn crazy ass Daquasha!* His foot almost got too heavy on the gas pedal, and he had to focus his attention in order not to drive too fast. He started calling Daquasha all sorts of names along the lines of crazy, stupid, hard-headed and foolish. Suddenly, his subconscious reminded him that if he was in her shoes, he would have probably responded in a similar fashion. Indeed, he couldn't blame her for hating his guts.

As he drove through the deserted Bronx streets, Tykim realized he had to work very quickly; once Kilroy found out Hector was dead and Daquasha was still alive, there was going to be plenty violent drama with lots of gunplay. And it didn't take a brain surgeon to figure out both he and Daquasha were going to be the center of attraction.

As Tykim tried to formulate a plan of action, an anxiety ridden realization tickled the back of his mind. He subconsciously knew he couldn't stop them from killing Daquasha, and it scared him. He and Daquasha had major problems between them, but he couldn't bear the thought of seeing her dead. He tried telling himself repeatedly that he could save Daquasha, but the reality of the situation kept entering his thoughts, shattering his optimism.

CHAPTER # 5

Detective Guzmon entered his office on the second floor of the 49th Precinct located on Ryder Avenue, carrying a stack of four huge mug-shot books. His black wavy hair was plastered to his forehead and mingled with sweat. He was a slim Latino man with a thin mustache and a severe case of dandruff. Wherever he went, he left a trail of white flakes of dead skin. His shoulders were covered with the stuff. He sat the books in front of Debra Holmes, who was sitting at a table next to his desk.

Debra sighed tiredly. "I'm tired of looking through all these books. My eyes are about to fall out of my head."

Detective Guzmon took a seat behind his desk. "May I remind you, this is a very serious case. This is a triple homicide. If this woman who was in the car was ever arrested before, she will be in one of those books. You said her name was Danielle, right?"

Debra nodded. "That's the name I heard Jamil call her that time I saw them hanging out at the Red Rooster." She folded her arms.

"Go on, look through them. She's probably in one of those."

"But that's what you said before." Debra pouted. "I looked through dozens of those damn books, and she wasn't in any of them."

"Please, Miss Holmes, look through those books. I understand your frustration, but this woman is a critical element of this prosecution." He waved his hand for Debra to begin looking through the books.

Debra opened the book and began scrutinizing all the faces of the women. She realized some of the women were so rough looking, they literally could pass for clean shaved men. As she scanned over the pictures, she remembered the request she had made to the Assistant District Attorney handling this case, but he suggested she talk to Guzmon about it first. "Hey, Mr. Guzmon, what's up with my request to be relocated out of the Bronx. I think my life is in danger staying around here."

"At this point in the case, you have nothing to worry about. No one knows you saw anything. Isn't that what you told us; that neither Jamil, nor his girlfriend saw you?" He saw Debra nod her head. "So, wouldn't that mean your request is premature?"

Debra turned a photo laden page. "I just don't think you realize how strong Jamil and his brother are. I hear they got all kinds of people working for them. Even the police is down with them, and probably some of them crooked cops are right from this Precinct. If that's the case, then who's to say a cop won't tell them where I've been moved to?"

"Relax, Miss. Holmes," Guzmon said, lying his pen down while leaning back in his chair. She was definitely making a lot of sense. "This case is being handled as a high profile matter. Every precaution in the book is being utilized to insure your safety. I thought a 24 hour watch would be enough to let you see that we are going to great lengths to protect you from any harm."

Debra sighed. "I guess you're right. Maybe I'm just nervous and still shaken up by what I saw." The flames that blazed from Jamil's silenced weapon flashed across her memory bank.

"It's normal to feel the way you do," Guzmon picked up his pen and resumed writing his report. "However, if you need any counseling, it's still available. I really think you should give it a try."

"Naw, I'm okay," Debra continued looking at all the faces. "I'll pass." She completed the first book and slid it to the side. *One down three to go*, she thought as she flipped open the cover on the second book. When she got to the sixth photo laden page, Danielle's face lashed out at her. It was her, no question about it. "I got it!"

Guzmon sprung from his chair and scurried over to Debra.

With her index finger planted on the photo, Debra said, "This is her."

As Guzmon retrieved the book, he spoke. "Miss Holmes, I want to thank you once again for your cooperation." From the way Debra responded, he didn't have to ask her if she was certain. "I'll be right back." As he headed for the door, Guzmon said, "Make yourself comfortable, I'm gonna be a while."

Guzmon felt an excitement racing through his veins. This case was going to catapult him to Lieutenant status, and he was so glad things were falling perfectly in place. Plus, this case might be the one that would quench his personal hard-on he had for Kilroy and Jamil. It might even be the one that would change Jamil's big headed perception that he was untouchable.

Guzmon exited his office and headed straight for the main frame computer located in the Special Investigations Department at the other end of the hall. This computer would provide him access to data from all over the tri-State. He was glad he decided to have Debra look at those out of State mug shots. He entered the room and saw Detective Wyrick on the computer.

Guzmon sighed loudly as he approached. "Excuse me, Wyrick, I got an extreme emergency here. I gotta use this computer like yesterday, if you know what I mean."

"And what do you think, I got here?" Wyrick's striking blue eyes sparkled with sarcasm. "I could've sworn all main frame use required an emergency? I know you can't possibly think I'm over here jerkin' off."

"I get your point." Guzmon folded his arms and started tapping his foot impatiently. After a moment he said, "Just be mindful that I've just found out that there are other eyewitnesses to the Nevez case." He sat in a nearby chair. "I wonder what Captain Fletcher is gonna say if we miss these critical witnesses on account of my not having expeditious access to the main frame?" He squinted his eyes while tilting his head upward as if he was thinking with a struggle.

Wyrick looked over at Guzmon and after a moment said, "All right, all right. I get the message." Wyrick down loaded his file and exited the room.

Guzmon sat behind the computer and his fingers danced across the keyboard. He punched in 4798441; the number that appeared under the mug shot photo of Daquasha Lawrence. After feeding the computer additional information, her file popped open. The 20 inch screen was filled with data. Guzmon began to read.

Guzmon smiled from ear to ear when he saw Daquasha was a fugitive of justice. When he saw what she was running from, he whistled loudly. This information made him feel extremely good because when he got hold of Daquasha, he was convinced he could not only make her talk, sing, flip and snitch, but he could make her beg and plead to let her do it. It wouldn't save her from doing time, but she didn't have to know that.

Guzmon activated the printer. The deskjet spit out a data littered sheet of paper almost instantaneously. With Daquasha's whole criminal history in his hands, Guzmon rushed out of the room. He was on his way to the dispatcher to put out an All Points Bulletin (APB) on Daquasha Lawrence.

CHAPTER # 6

Daquasha was on the stage swinging her hips to the slamming beat. The smoke filled dance floor was hot and steamy; the Paradise Lounge was filled to capacity. The house music song called, Hit the Floor and Let It Loose, had the huge crowd moving lively to the music. Daquasha's G-string was loaded with bills.

Although Daquasha was in full dance mode, her mind was locked on the issues plaguing her life. She was seething with anger because she couldn't go see Jamil earlier. There was a flood in the apartment next door to hers and the water had eased it's way into her apartment. After she awoke from a restless slumber and discovered the mess, she couldn't leave the water as is, since it would have completely destroyed the carpeting throughout her apartment. Every time she found a way to stop the water from rushing into her apartment, the water found another way to evade her endeavors. By the time she was ready to go to work, Daquasha decided she was definitely going to go see Jamil tomorrow and vowed that nothing would stop her.

All day long, Tykim's reappearance into her life was another stress provoking issue. What he told her was stuck in her mind; she knew he was lying about being a hit-man and that Kilroy was trying to kill her. Why would Kilroy want to kill her? She didn't do anything to warrant being killed by him. Even if it was true, Jamil wouldn't allow no shit like that. When Daquasha recalled how Kilroy had boldly displayed his dislike towards her on numerous occasions, she wondered if he was trying to put some shit in the game. She instantly swept those thoughts out of her head because it was obvious Tykim was up to his little head games again; trying to get back with her by concocting a wild story that portaryed him as a hero out to save her.

But something in the back of her mind was eating at her. She didn't know exactly what it was, but it was there. Its aggressive impact on her entire thinking process was like a throbbing toothache demanding to receive the appropriate attention. Maybe it was her intuition telling her danger was close-by.

Prior to getting on stage, Daquasha's eyes had been scanning the sea of faces all night long. There were several new faces, and twice she had to force herself not to let her imagination start running wild. Suddenly, her finish line song came on and Daquasha sighed with relief. She swirled around the pole with her legs thrown up in the air as she slid down the pole.

A minute later, Daquasha was leaving the stage. The cheers from her regular customers were warm and truly heartfelt.

She strutted across the dance floor towards her dressing room. When she reached the corridor, she saw a strange man walking towards her. She slowed her pace substantially. *What the hell is he doing back here!? And where the hell is Big Pete!?* Big Pete didn't allow any customers in this area of the club. The man was huge with a bald head, and had on dark blue clothing that looked black. Hot flashes of anxiety pulsated through her body as the man drew closer. He was staring at her. And as he walked by, she felt the danger resonating off him. She hurried to her dressing room.

Daquasha opened the door and stepped in, breathing hard from exhaustion caused by her dance routine and the terror from the strange man's appearance. From the corner of her eye, she saw movement.

SLAAMM!

The blow to Daquasha's head knocked her silly. She stumbled backwards and fell crashing to the floor. The side of her face was on fire and her ears were ringing. Through a haze of bone crippling terror, Daquasha saw a muscular light skin black man with a huge afro and a gold ear-ring in his left ear, slowly walking towards her. He had a fiendish smile on his face and reached in his pocket and pulled out a piece of rope.

"Let's see you dance your fine ass out of this, Midnight Flower," The man said teasingly, even though his inability to get his 9mm or the knife pass security at the door still had him fuming with anger.

With her hand clapped on her cheek, Daquasha stumbled to her feet. "What the fuck are you doing back here!?" Her eyes scanned his clothing looking to see if he had a gun; she saw all he had was a rope.

The man said, "Before I murder your snitchin' ass, Jamil wanna know why you--"

"Snitchin'!?" Daquasha was aghast. "What the fuck are you--"

The man charged at her and took a wild swing at her head.

Daquasha ducked and kicked him in the stomach. She frantically commenced to punching him in the face with a series of vicious upper-cuts and over-hand rights.

The man stumbled away from Daquasha. He was shocked by the ferocious nature of her blows to his face. *This bitch is rough, huh*, he thought with delight because now he could treat her like a man. He shook his head to regain his senses and spit out a glob of blood from the gash on his bottom lip. He laughed when he saw Daquasha in a boxing stance, bouncing around like she was trying to imitate Sugar Ray Leonard. As he sized up her naked, voluptuous body, the door opened.

"Hey Alley-bush!" Two-face yelled from the threshold. "Hurry up and finished this bitch off! The last dancer's on stage now."

Daquasha saw the man talking to her attacker was the bald headed man she had just walked by moments ago. Dread engulfed her being. Images of caskets scroll across her mind. Panic and desperation eased its way into her cipher when she realized the man was going to strangle her with that rope. He was twice her size, and reality told her it was just a matter of time before he would overpower her.

The man charged at her. She tried to side step his attack while throwing punches, but the room was too small for her to evade him. He tackled her hard, slamming her back into the wall. She tried to punch, scratch and bite him, but he was locked onto her. Daquasha screamed when she realized she was defenseless, and the man was punching her in the face while tossing her around like a rag doll. "Pete! Help! Pete, help m--"

The blow to her right eye cut the shriek clean off. Stars danced across her vision. Her knees gave out, and the fall to the floor knocked the wind out of her lungs. On the verge of losing total consciousness, Daquasha felt her upper body being shoved into a sitting position. When the rope touched her neck, she sprung back into a state of full consciousness. Her fingers dug underneath the rope that suddenly grew tighter and tighter around her neck. Her eyes were seconds from springing from their sockets. Her lungs screamed for air as the rope continued to grow tighter. Thrashing hysterically, flashing images of all her deceased loves ones reverated in her third eye. She didn't want to join them, but she suddenly realized she no longer had any control over that decision. Her inner voice screamed horrifically *No! No! Please! I don't want to die!*

£¥♥   £¥♥   £¥♥   £¥♥

Two-face stood in front of the dressing room rocking impatiently back and forth on his heels. He was enjoying all the explosive commotion going on in the room. His hard-on had finally subsided once he got it in his head that he wasn't going to be able to rape Daquasha. Earlier, upon seeing her get on the stage, and after really checking out the way she was built, Two-face tried to convince Alley-bush to go along with his idea of raping Daquasha, but he shot it down. Two-face truly hated to see good pussy go to waste. They were killing her anyway. Shit, they might as well get their skeet on before they blazed this bitch, he pouted inwardly.

Two-face turned his head and saw a man dressed in a forest green workman's jumpsuit approaching. He moved quickly towards the man to block him from getting too close to the dressing room. The man looked lost and appeared to be looking for the bathroom by the way he was fidgeting while touching his groan.

The man spoke before Two-face was right upon him. "Hey, Bro," The man said, "Where's the bathroom?"

"Listen, man," Two-face said, "Ain't no bathroom back here. It's on the other side of the dance--"

"Oh, shit!" Tykim shouted as he frantically pointed in back of Two-face. "What's that!?" When Two-face fell for the oldest trick in the book, Tykim pulled a hard plastic Rambo style knife from his waist, and stabbed Two-face in the throat. The two acts transpired so remarkably fast, they appeared to have occurred all at the same time. Tykim grabbed Two-face's shoulder with his other hand and drew his body closer as he crammed the knife deeper into Two-face's throat with straining force. The blade struck something hard, apparently the spine cord. Tykim twirled the blade around in a circle, shredding and ripping flesh in the process. Snatching the knife from Two-face's throat, Tykim made certain he severed some more flesh. Sprinkles of blood sprayed the immediate area and saturated the front of Tykim's jumpsuit.

Two-face fell crashing to the floor with both his hands clamped around his neck. Gurgling sounds escaped through his fingers as his body was having convultions. Blood spurted savagely from the gapping wound. Seconds later, his arms lifelessly flopped to the floor.

Tykim hastily dragged Two-face's body over to the door he was standing in front of moments ago. He instantly heard commotion on the other side of the door. Listening carefully to determine the exact location of the noise, Tykim detected it was coming from the right side of the room.

Tykim burst into the room and saw Alley-bush with a rope around Daquasha's limp body. He threw the knife.

"AHHHH!!" Alley-bush hollered as the knife planted itself in his upper chest. The impact jolted him backwards, causing him to crash into the counter. Cosmetics and other items were scattered all over the room.

As Daquasha's lifeless body fell unconsciously to the floor, Tykim retrieved his other knife and pounced upon Alley-bush, stabbing him repeatedly in the chest. After six stabs, Alley-bush stopped thrashing and laid motionless.

Tykim turned and terror gripped him when he saw Daquasha looked like she was dead. He rushed to her, and frantically started checking her pulse. Panic-stricken anxiety raced through his body so intensely, it interfered with his ability to find her pulse.

Daquasha suddenly started coughing.

Tykim sighed with relief. "Can you walk, Daquasha?" He flipped a turned over chair right side up, gently scooped Daquasha up into his arms and sat her in the chair.

Daquasha suddenly felt her mind swirling up from a dark, scary sector within her subconscious. It was a sensation similar to awakening after coming from under heavy exposure to anesthesia. She felt drunk, light-headed, and her throat was extremely sore. The tangy, coppery taste of blood in her mouth was strong. Aching all over, her blurred vision began to come into focus.

When Daquasha realized it was Tykim standing in front of her, she didn't know how to respond. It was evident he saved her life. She suddenly felt embarrassed by her nakedness. "What are you doing here?" She said hoarsely, her throat felt like it was out of order.

Tykim suddenly remembered the other body outside and ran to the door. He snatched it opened and looked both ways down the hallway. The coast was clear. He grabbed Two-face's ankles and dragged him inside the room, leaving a long trail of blood. Tykim cursed profusely because anyone who walked by the room would obviously see the blood. He turned and spoke excitedly to Daquasha. "Get dressed, hurry!"

When Daquasha saw the two dead man, she sprung into action. It took her two minutes flat to get fully dressed.

As Tykim was stuffing the two dead bodies in a small closet, he spoke to Daquasha. "Is there a back door on this side of the club?"

"No," Daquasha said, looking at her bruised face in the mirror. "But there's a room with a window we might be able to use."

"Go look and see if the corridor is clear." Tykim was now trying to soak up some of the blood with napkins and a roll of toilet tissue. He took off his jumpsuit and used it to help wipe up the blood. Tykim had on his Rockawear underneath.

Daquasha limped to the door, noticing the huge trail of blood on the floor was already starting to coagulate. She opened the door and looked down the corridor in the direction opposite the dance floor. Then she turned her head the other way. She frantically pulled back into the room. Terror flared up inside her whole body once again. *Oh, no! Why now, damn it!* she muttered angrily to herself.

Trembling, she peeked out again, and saw the two men were still approaching. What terrified Daquasha out of her mind was the two approaching men were members of Big Pete's security staff; one of them, Keith, was an off-duty Corrections Officer, who carried his gun everywhere he went and thought he was the ultimate super cop.

CHAPTER # 7

Lunatic sat behind the wheel of the red Ranger-rover parked a block away from the Paradise Lounge. His impatient huge brown eyes were locked on the entrance of the club. Due to his naturally wide eyes, the name Lunatic was a well earned appellation. However, maniac might have been a more appropriate name, since it would be more consistent with his way of doing things.

Sitting in the passenger seat was Devil-dog, a medium built brown-skinned black man with noble features that were totally inconsistent with his general behavior. Dressed in basic inner-city hoodlum attire, Devil-dog prided himself on his ability to intimidate others with his well known knack for inflicting extreme pain and suffering and even death upon those that didn't comport with his views and ideologies.

Lunatic sighed, breaking the silence. "I don't know why the fuck we ain't just wait for this bitch to come out to kill her dumb ass."

Devil-dog gave him an impatient look. "You should've said that shit when Kilroy told us he wanted it done this way. Ain't no need in beefin' about the shit now."

"I ain't beefin'," Lunatic reached in his pocket for the pack of cigarettes. "I'm just mad 'cause I wanted to blaze this bitch personally." He struck the match, touched it to the tip of the tobacco stick and drew the smoke into his lungs.

"What we need to be worrying 'bout," Devil-dog said, rolling down the window. "Is Alley-bush and ole tree-jumpin' ass Two-face fuckin' this thing up 'cause they too damn stupid not to mix business with bullshit."

"You know that's why Kilroy wanted them two to go in there; he wanted to make sure they dissed Danielle before they killed her ass. And that little talk you had with Alley-bush before he went in ain't gonna change shit, and you know it. What? You thought I ain't know you was pissing in Alley-bush's ear on the down low?"

Devil-dog didn't care what Lunatic saw or heard, he hated rapists. According to the rules of prison etiquette, they were the worse criminals and were at the lowest level of the totem pole. Devil-dog knew if he was still bidding up north in spots like Clinton, Attica, Comstock, and had ran into a tree-jumper, there would have been plenty knife play with him on the side of inflicting the harm.

Lunatic blew a cloud of smoke from his mouth. "What we really need to be focusing on is that motherfucker Tykim. That nigga killed my man

Hector." Lunatic felt deep pain in his heart, since Hector was his ace running partner. "After this bitch is out the way, I'm personally gonna find that motherfucker, Tykim."

"I still can't understand why he killed Hector," Devil-dog saw a couple exit the club, and continued when he saw it wasn't Danielle. "From what I was told, Tykim was all for this hit. It don't make sense for a hitter to throw away the other half of that 150 gees just to kill Hector. All that money was in the bag for him. All he had to do was smoke the bitch."

"Come on, man," Lunatic sighed with frustration and impatience. "Tykim is that motherfucker running 'round murdering drug dealers in Brooklyn and Staten Island."

Devil-dog was shock. "Get the fuck outta here."

"That's my word is bond, it's him. And to make shit worse, Kilroy knew he was the one and still hired that bitch ass nigga to do this job."

Devil-dog went into a silent cocoon. After a moment he said, "Well, I guess it really don't matter, anyway. We gettin' paid properly." He paused for a moment. "I just think it was real stupid for Cleavon and Brute to kill Tykim's man, Kamel. It was good they got that 75 gees back, but with him alive we could've use him to draw Tykim to a place where we could deal with him. I swear I hate workin' with dumb ass niggas. That's basic one-oh-one shit. Use a love one to bring the target to you." He sighed angrily.

"That's a small thing, son." Lunatic flicked the cigarette butt out the window. "Tracking down Tykim might be fun. It'll let us know if our shit is tight."

"I don't need a test to find out if my shit is tight," Devil-dog said, looking at his watch. It was almost 3 o'clock. "All you gotta do is check my track record. It speaks for itself."

£¥♥   £¥♥   £¥♥   £¥♥

Daquasha was looking around the room nervously, her mind was congested, clustered and clogged up with indecisiveness. The thumping beat of the music from the dance floor only made matters worse. She had to move swiftly, but didn't know what to do. Then, suddenly, an idea jumped in her head. She turned and faced Tykim. "Security's comin', one of them got a gun." She saw Tykim pulled both his knives and moved towards the door. "Wait! I got an idea. Grab those clothes and cover-up the blood on the floor."

"What about the blood out front?" Tykim said.

"I got that," Daquasha ran over to the counter and snatched the pink bath towel lying on top of it. She rushed to the door, opened it ever so slightly, tossed the towel onto the blood and closed the door.

"What the hell are you doing?" Tykim whispered.

She turned with her pointer fingers to her lips and waved Tykim over to her side.

There was a knock on the door.

Daquasha took a few deep breaths and opened the door partially; only her face could be seen. She saw it was Keith and Joseph was standing in back of him. "What's up, Keith?"

Keith squinted his eyes when he saw Daquasha's bruised face. "I came to ask did you see Big Pete." He looked down at the pink towel that was soaked in blood. "What the fuck is all this blood all about?" He suddenly became excited. "You alright in there, Daquasha?" His voice was turned up two notches. He tried to look inside the room while attempting to push the door open.

"I'm okay, Keith," Daquasha held the door in place with her body weight. "Please, give me a break, man. I'm sick; I got my period. That's where all the blood came from. When my period came on, I fell and bumped my face."

Keith gave her a questioning expression. This was a hell of a lot of blood for a woman's period. But who was he to debate an issue concerning a woman's biological workings; he hadn't the slightest clue about women's menstruation cycles. "Girl, I think you better go get yourself checked out. That's sure a lot of blood. You sure you don't need any help in there?"

"I'm all right, Keith," Daquasha said with a attitude. "I gotta finished my business in here." She tried to close the door, but Keith stopped it.

"Hey, did you see Big Pete?"

"No, I ain't seen him. The last time I saw him was earlier this evening when I first got here." She tried to close the door, but Keith stopped the attempt again.

"Whine it down, Midnight Flower," Keith said, "We 'bout to close in another half hour." A smile tugged at his face. "You know you did your thang tonight. I sure like that move you did on the pole."

"Thanks Keith," Daquasha closed the door.

Keith continued down the hall, looking back at all the blood while shaking his head still in shock. He spoke to Joseph. "Don't you think that's a lot of blood for a woman on the rag?"

Joseph had a smirk on his face which clearly said he didn't believe any part of Daquasha's explanation regarding the blood. "Put it this way, if she's leakin' like that from her pussy, she should've been death by now."

Keith continued walking and wondered if he should turn back right now? After a moment of contemplation, he decided to return after he found Big Pete.

Inside the dressing room, Daquasha waited a few seconds and slowly opened the door. She peered down the hall and saw Keith and Joseph turn down the hall towards the back room she was intending to leave through the window. *Shit!* she muttered inwardly as she closed the door, turned and spoke to Tykim. "The back window's out of the question; that's where they went. That means we gotta go out the front door."

"Bad idea," Tykim enthusiastically shook his head no. "In fact, that's a terrible idea. I stashed my guns in the back. My car is that way too. I think these two got some other cats holdin' them down, and if they're out there, they'll probably be out front."

"We gotta leave now," Daquasha was anxious to bolt out the door. "From the way Joseph was looking at all that blood out there, he's gonna convince Keith to come inside here. I don't think we wanna be in here when they find these two."

"Let's go," Tykim said excitedly, remembering this guy Keith was a cop and gave Daquasha a small push towards the door. "We're wasting too much time. When we get out we gotta get to the back."

Daquasha opened the door, looked both ways, saw everything was in order and lead the way. She moved rapidly down the corridor, bouncing to the heavy bass of the music. She struggled not to let her facial expression reveal what she was feeling internally. Moving across the dance floor, she saw Jerry. He was one of her most dedicated fans. She sighed with irritation. He charged at her with a crazy wide eyed smile.

"Midnight Flower!" Jerry shouted over the music. He was rubbing his hands together as if he was cold or was about to receive a pleasant treat. "Please let me buy you a drink."

"Sorry, Jerry, not tonight. I'm in a hurry." She tried to weave pass him, but he blocked her path, not taking no for an answer.

Tykim stepped in front of Daquasha and shoved Jerry out of the way. "You heard what the fuck she said."

Daquasha continued towards the door with Tykim on her heels.

They got pass Barry, the head door man, without any major complications.

When Daquasha stepped out of the club, the late night air touched her face and it made her feel like she had suddenly awakened from a bad dream.

Daquasha turned, heading for the alleyway that would lead them to the back of the club. Tykim was on her side closest to the parked cars. Suddenly, a sensation came over her; she was being watched. It was the same feeling she felt the night Tykim showed up at her doorstep. This time she was listening to her inner voice. Her eyes hastily scanned the empty street and the nearby cars.

A few moments earlier, just as Daquasha and Tykim exited the club, Lunatic was hurled into a full sitting position when he saw them. "Oh, shit!" He frantically pulled his Desert Eagle. "It's them! Both of them!"

Devil-dog looked up and smiled as he hastily pulled his Uzi. "Now, this is some serious shit here. What the fuck are they doing together?"

Lunatic screwed the silencer onto the weapon and was about to rush out the car.

"Hold up!" Devil-dog shouted, still screwing his silencer onto the Uzi. "Let 'em get closer. If you open the door, the inside light'll come on; it'll put 'em on point."

Lunatic was seconds from barking on Devil-dog because his plan was to simply rush out the vehicle and open fire like a true blooded maniac.

"When they get near that green car in front of us," Devil-dog said, "We rush out and do our thang."

They watched as Daquasha and Tykim drew closer. Their trigger fingers itching with anticipation.

£¥♥   £¥♥   £¥♥   £¥♥

Inside the club, Keith and Joseph entered a room and heard noise. It was coming from the closet and they rushed towards the noise. Keith snatched the door open and saw Big Pete tied up with thick tape covering his mouth. Keith pulled the tape off his mouth.

Big Pete screamed in pain. "Them motherfuckers hit me in the damn head!" He hollered in rage. "Untie me, hurry up!"

After Big Pete was untied, he lead the way towards the dance floor. He was about to walk pass Danielle's dressing room, but saw the blood on the floor. He rushed inside. Bloody clothing were dispersed everywhere. "What the fuck is this?! Where's Mid-night Flower?!" He shouted at Keith.

"I don't know," Keith said calmly. "She was just here." All the blood was making his heart thunder in his chest. This wasn't no pussy blood. His eyes followed a trail of blood. Pointing at the closet, he said, "Over there." He rushed to the closet and snatched the door open. "Ah, fuck!"

Big Pete peered over Keith's shoulder and saw his job disappearing right before his eyes. The two dead bodies were neatly stacked, both lying face down. But the sight did make him smile, since the bald headed man was the one who bust him in the head. "You can make that call, Keith. Try to talk to Captain Fletcher." He saw Keith nod his head. "How long ago was Danielle here?"

Joseph spoke excitedly. "It wasn't no more than a few minutes ago. We might be able to catch her if we hurry."

The three raced out of the dressing room, down the corridor, across the dance floor and stopped at the front door. Joseph made the call to the police while it took seconds for Big Pete to explain to the other security staff members what they found in Mid-night Flower's dressing room. He also discovered Danielle had just left with an unknown man.

BOW!--BOW--BOW--BOW--BOW!--BOW!...

Massive machine gunfire was heard right outside the club, causing Keith to pull his weapon. Big Pete ran to the weapons locker a few feet away and started hastily handing his security staff automatic pistols.

£¥♥   £¥♥   £¥♥   £¥♥

Moments ago, Daquasha saw movement inside a red jeep up ahead. It was two men.

"Come on!" Tykim shouted and started running at top speed when he saw the two shadows inside the red vehicle.

They jetted for the corner that was less than a dozens yards away.

Terror-stricken, Daquasha sensed they weren't going to make it. The men were rushing out of their vehicle and they had guns! *Oh, shit!* Her legs were pumping frantically.

Seconds earlier, Devil-dog and Lunatic saw Daquasha and Tykim had suddenly started running. They hastily got out of the jeep, carefully took aim and both squeezed the triggers on the fully automatic weapons almost at the same time.

BOW!--BOW--BOW--BOW--BOW!--BOW!...

CHAPTER # 8

Detective Guzmon was dreaming about an argument he was having with his partner, James. The dream was so vivid, the ringing phone next to him merged itself into the dream with remarkable accuracy. After four rings, Guzmon felt his wife, Katherine shaking him. He heard his name being called and the dream started fading away like a cloud of smoke making contact with a strong gust of wind.

Guzmon opened his eyes and reached over for the phone. "Hello?" He sighed when he heard who's voice it was; this meant he was needed somewhere immediately. "What time is it, Captain? . . . . a quarter to four!? For crying out loud, couldn't it wait about two more hours? . . . Okay, let's hear it . . . The Paradise Lounge? Yeah, I know, it's located near the Bronx Zoo . . . All right, I'm on my way." He hung up the phone.

Guzmon slid out of bed. It took him ten minutes to get dressed. As he exited his two story home that had a two car garage, located on the Westchester County border-line, he was hoping that lead he got yesterday produced something tangible. He discovered the lead from a patrol unit who investigated a large pool of blood on the sidewalk of 242nd street near Vancourtland Avenue. According to the patrol officer, he had interviewed a woman named Mrs. Grenadine Johnson who lived in the nearby apartment closest to the pool of blood. Mrs. Johnson told the officer she heard someone calling a name and when she looked out her window, she saw a man placing an unconscious man inside a brown Jeep. She further went on to say she thought the man was drunk, which was the reason why she didn't call the police. After the cop showed Mrs. Johnson a picture of Daquasha Lawrence, she identified her as a young lady who lived a few apartment buildings down from her. However, she was unable to indicate the exact building in which Daquasha lived.

At this point, Guzmon immediately sent out the night team to go investigate the lead. Since there was no available information regarding Daquasha's exact apartment building, the night team was instructed to canvass the entire block.

As Guzmon pulled his vehicle onto the highway, he retrieved his cellular phone and activated Nathan's number. He was the detective in charge of the night team. "Hello, Nate, anything good?" He nodded his head. "Good. I'm on my way to the Paradise Lounge near the Bronx Zoo. There's two stiffs waiting to see me." There was a moment of silence. "Do me a favor, Nate, see if you can hang out there for another hour. I'll be there within that time." He nodded. "Exactly. I'll see you in a few." He disconnected the line.

Guzmon sighed with a smile on his face because he felt he was only seconds from getting his hands on Daquasha Lawrence, who was going to be his star witness in the Nevez triple homicide case; an event that was destined to jettison him to bigger and better things.

£¥♥   £¥♥   £¥♥   £¥♥

"AHHHHH!" Daquasha screamed with ear-torturous force. Her hand reflectively shot up to her face, and her legs not only continued pumping, but her speed increased two folds. She was just about to turn the corner when the machine gunfire rang out; chunks and chips of pulverized bricks from the bullets hitting the buildings were splattered into her face. Daquasha hit the corner, turning down the alley at break-neck speed and continued running.

Daquasha felt warm liquid on her left cheek as she ran deeper into the alley heading for a fence. She suddenly heard more gunfire as she and Tykim frantically climbed the fence. They made it over. She followed Tykim to a bunch of garbage cans. He dug into the trash and retrieved a brown paper bag.

"Let's go!" Tykim said as he started running towards another fence.

They climbed over it and ran to a shiny black Nissan Maxima. Tykim snatched the driver's door open; he allowed Daquasha to get in first and then got in behind her. He started the car and sped off.

£¥♥   £¥♥   £¥♥   £¥♥

Big Pete, Keith, Joseph and the three security staff members rushed out of the club and saw two man firing Uzi-like weapons. The flicker of machine gunfire coming from down the block looked like a nest of angry fireflies had been violently agitated.

They had just missed Daquasha and Tykim by seconds.

As the security staff all sought cover behind nearby cars, Keith opened fire. He saw the two men sought refuge behind the nearby parked the cars.

Suddenly, a massive barrage of bullets rained upon the area they were located. Two screams were unleashed.

"Shit!" Big Pete shouted when he saw Joseph was down. He rushed to him and saw he was struck in the chest. The machine gunfire was instantly turned on full blast and seemed like it was never going to stop. Bullets ricocheted off of everything in the immediate vicinity they could not penetrate. Glass from car windows rained upon the pavement. Big Pete turned his head and saw another one of his security staff was also shot in the upper chest area.

As the machine gunfire drew closer, Big Pete realized he was unable to squeeze off a shot because there were no intervals between the machine gunfire. His intuition told him he was about to lose his life. It didn't take an intellectual giant to surmise that once the Uzi totting men were upon them, they were going to be loaded up nice and thoroughly with bullets. He wanted to kick Keith in his ass for firing those shots at the two men.

£¥♥　　　　£¥♥　　　　£¥♥　　　　£¥♥

Moments earlier, Devil-dog and Lunatic saw Daquasha and Tykim had made it to an alleyway without being struck by any bullets. They were cursing with intense rage as they ran up the street still firing their weapons. They saw a group of men rush out the club, but paid them no attention until shots were fired at them. They instantly sought cover.

"Oh, so y'all motherfuckers want some drama!" Lunatic shouted down the block as he rose to his feet and began firing the Uzi indiscriminately. He rapidly moved down the street, spitting bullets at the area near the club. Disintegrating car windows sprayed glass all over the place.

Devil-dog joined in the malady.

Lunatic's weapon registered empty, and he hastily reloaded. Devil-dog did the same when his weapon emptied.

Suddenly, police sirens were heard at a distance.

Lunatic and Devil-dog gave each other a calm look as they snapped out of their murderous delirium. They were four cars away from the two bullet ridden cars Big Pete, Keith, Joseph and the others were cowering behind.

Lunatic and Devil-dog scurried to their red jeep and screeched away.

£¥♥　　　　£¥♥　　　　£¥♥　　　　£¥♥

Daquasha sat in the passenger seat watching the streets breeze pass her vision. Her heart-beat and adrenaline slowly began to settle back to their normal levels. In place of these biological workings came the emotional turmoil, the fear of what lay ahead and how was she going to deal with what was going on inside of her body.

Habitually, Daquasha rotated the ring on her pinkie finger. She wanted to cry, but there were no more tears left from all the weeping she'd been doing for a considerable portion of her life. She wanted to lash out at Tykim because he was, in essence, the root of all this misery, pain and suffering, but now that he just saved her life, she was completely stumped.

Tykim cleared his voice, breaking the deafening silence. "I was thinking maybe we should skip town. After what happened back there, I would say the police is gonna be looking for us for murder charges."

"Why did you go and kill them?" Daquasha said seriously. "Don't you think that was a little over-board."

"You can't be serious!?" Tykim started laughing. "I see you ain't change one bit. Them motherfuckers was seconds from murdering your ass, and now you wanna make it look like I was in the wrong for stopping them!? If anything, you should show some gratitude."

Daquasha felt the rage starting to boil. If it wasn't for the intervention of the reality check her subconscious imposed upon her conscious mind, a temper-tangent would have erupted.

The silence held firm for several long seconds.

"We gotta map-out a game plan," Tykim said and waited for her to say something. After a moment he continued. "First I gotta make a stop at my man Kamel's crib, pick up my money, and we can head south. I got family in Georgia. Once we get there, we'll think about our next move."

"I need you to stop at my house," Daquasha stopped toying with her pinkie ring. "I need to pick up a few important things."

Tykim sighed loudly. He didn't know how to break the news to her, but he knew giving it up in the raw was what worked best for Daquasha. "We can't go to your apartment. I drove pass there earlier and I saw mad DT's going in and out that building. Based on the way the police do their thang, and because of all this other shit going on, I would say they're looking for you."

"But, how the hell am I supposed to get my--"

"If we go there, we gonna run into the police. Now, if you think the stuff you're going to get is that important, and it's worth us risking getting caught, then I'll go there."

Daquasha was seething with anger. She hated when he tried to beat her in the head with his logical sarcasm. But, once again, she held her tongue in check. "Well, when you get a chance, I need you to find a phone booth. I gotta call my neighbor."

"No problem. When we're out of this area, I'll make a stop." Tykim made a turn onto a four lane street, heading down town. "Can I ask you something, Mid-night flower?" He said teasingly. His smile was wide and saturated with good natured humor.

Daquasha glanced over, made eye contact and rolled her eyes. She felt two inches small. Tykim was the last person she ever wanted to know she was a stripper. It ate at her pride to let him even think she wasn't on top of her game after they broke up. "I don't give a shit what you ask. I don't know if you'll get an answer."

Tykim brought the car to a stop when the street light turned red. "I know you got a unique way of striking folks' nerves, but what the hell did you do to cause a nigga like Kilroy to wanna kill you?"

Daquasha was about to tell him to kiss her ass, but she knew Tykim might take her up on her offer. But the real deal was, she felt awkward telling an ex-lover that she was dealing with another man. Even though it was obvious, he knew she had to be dealing with someone else since Tykim had been out of her life for five years, but she couldn't help feeling guilty. Why she suddenly felt this way was a complete mystery to her.

The light turned green and Tykim hit the gas pedal.

Daquasha spoke with an attitude. "To be honest with, I really don't know why. But, from what that dude who attacked me said, Jamil thinks I snitched on him." She shook her head in disbelief. She turned and saw Tykim's facial expression, indicating he didn't know who Jamil was. "Jamil is Kilroy's younger brother. He killed three guys the other night, got arrested for it, and he must think I'm the snitch."

The silence returned.

Tykim realized that explained it all. He was shocked a top notch baller would think Daquasha was a snitch. She was a straight up trooper and held firm to the rules of the street. Tykim assumed Jamil was one of those reckless clowns that didn't really know how to read people from the 'hood and was probably living off the clout of his big brother. "So, did you and this cat have a little thing going on?"

Daquasha felt a smile tugging at her lips. This nigga was still jealous; she could hear it in his voice. She wasn't into the tit for tat business, but Tykim had hurt her heart so many times, this opportunity felt irresistible. "Yeah, he was my man. And as good as he used to treat me, I don't understand why he would think something as crazy as me snitchin' on him."

Tykim nodded his head to that. "I guess y'all wasn't clicking too well, otherwise he wouldn't have doubted your realness and loyalty."

"I see you ain't change one bit," Daquasha said, "You just gotta get the last lick in, huh? And if you wanna know, yes he was better than you. In every department."

"Ouch." Tykim felt that one way down below the belt. Why she went there didn't baffle him at all. In fact, he was a little surprise she wasn't trying to tear his head off. He turned and smiled at her. "Yeah, you got that one, ma." Tykim wondered if she realized just how close she came to losing her life? If a man loved a woman, he would never hurt her. He also wondered if she realized what he was doing for her? Did she realize he just put his life on the line in order to save hers? From her response, it was clear she didn't appreciate it. When he went against the grain by taking Kilroy's money and then killing one of his hitters during a hit, Tykim knew he had just signed his own death certificate and he hoped Daquasha realized this. Indeed, Tykim knew wherever he and Daquasha went, Kilroy would track them down. And with all the money and connections he had, finding them was merely a matter of time.

£¥♥   £¥♥   £¥♥   £¥♥

Lunatic and Devil-dog were traveling down the Bronx River Expressway. Lunatic was in the passenger seat spraying coolant on the weapons while Devil-dog was behind the wheel talking to Kilroy on the cell phone.

Devil-dog was struggling to get a word in. "But . . . I know. . . Yeah, they . . . I hear you, Big papa . . . Yeah, I'm sure it was Danielle and Tykim. You can even ask Lunatic, he's right here . . . We did try to blaze them . . . Yeah, we did . . . huh . . . Yeah, we on our way over there right now . . . Okay, talk to you later. Peace out big dog." He barked like a dog into the receiver and hung up.

"So, what's up, man?" Lunatic said with maniac eyes. He had sprayed so much coolant on the weapons, they were dripping with the substance. "What he say?"

"He wants us to go to Kamel's crib. Lay for 'em to show up there. Since Tykim don't know Kamel is dead, and he don't know the money ain't there either, Kilroy thinks Tykim is gonna go there to get that cheddar. Cleavon and Brute and about five other hitters are already there waiting for us."

43

"Well, I think you better straighten out that lazy ass foot of yours. At the speed you going, we might miss all the goddamn fun, son. Now, come on and move this motherfucker."

"What if we get pulled over for speeding? And the police decides to search the car? Huh?"

"Well, I guess the party'll start a little earlier than we expected."

They both laughed.

£¥♥   £¥♥   £¥♥   £¥♥

Tykim pulled the car to the curb when he saw an empty phone booth.

Daquasha got out, entered the booth and dropped a quarter in the slot. She rapidly dialed the number.

After four rings, Kim picked up the phone. "Hello."

"Hey, Kim, this is Daqa--Danielle."

Kim's sleepy voice transformed into one entrenched with urgency. "Danielle are you all right!? The police came to your apartment, girl. Then they went to everyone's apartment on the whole floor asking if any of us know you. They had a picture of you and everything."

Daquasha's heart stopped, even though she knew Tykim wasn't lying. She just didn't want to believe it. "Yeah, I'm okay. I'm all right."

"They told me to tell you to call a Detective Guzmon if I see or speak to you. They gave me a calling card. What happened? What's going on?"

"I can't go into it right now, Kim. It's too much to explain. I'll--I just called to see if they came."

"What happened with that test? Did it come back positive?"

Daquasha was flung into a state of silence. The reminder was as crippling as a blow to the stomach. She wondered for the hundredth time if she had told Jamil she was pregnant with his child, would this have stopped him from trying to kill her. "Yes, Kim, it came back positive. I'm pregnant. I . . . I don't know what I'm gonna do with it, but, I'm . . ." She turned and looked at Tykim in the car. "Listen, Kim. I gotta go now, I'll--"

"Wait! Danielle! I want to help--"

"I gotta go, I'm sorry, I'll talk to you soon." Daquasha hung up. This situation hurt her heart because she now had to cut off all ties once again.

As Daquasha headed back to the car, she forced back the tears with a huge struggle. When she realized she was feeling sorry for herself, the hurt suddenly started to disappear and was replaced with her ever-present friend, anger. She got in the car and Tykim sped off.

"You all right?" Tykim inquired. "You look a little gray around the gills." He proffered her his best smile when she looked at him.

Daquasha rolled her eyes at him so hard, the hatred in the act vibrated the air in the compartment of the car. If it wasn't for him, none of her life-long misery would have occurred!

Tykim glanced at his watch. He hoped Kamel was in the house. Since it was 4:25 in the morning, Tykim concluded there was no reason for Kamel to be running the street. Tykim's foot got just a little heavier on the gas pedal; he sincerely wanted to be on his way out of New York before the sun was up.

CHAPTER # 9

Detective Guzmon maneuvered his car pass the numerous ambulances, patrol cars and Coroner vehicles that littered the street in front of the Paradise Lounge. When he saw the row of about ten bullet-ridden cars with shot-out windows, his anxiety instantly came to life.

Guzmon hastily brought the car to a stop and exited the vehicle. He saw Sgt. Talbert, the current crime site supervisor, rapidly approaching. "What happened here?" Guzmon gestured at the cars.

"The witnesses claim after they called us," Sgt. Talbert's radio was squawking loudly. "Two men with military style weapons opened fire on them when they came out to investigate a series of gunfire. There's two additional DOAs as a result." He pulled Guzmon over to the curb and pointed.

Detective Guzmon sighed angrily when he saw the two black body bags. He headed towards the club, with Sgt. Talbert following suit. "Did you begin procedures inside?"

"Yes, sir," Sgt. Talbert answered. "This is the part I think you're going to find quite interesting. This ordeal has something to do with that material witness you're seeking to apprehend, sir. I believe her name is Daquasha Lawrence."

Detective Guzmon stopped abruptly just as they stepped across the threshold of the door, almost causing Sgt. Talbert to collide into him. Struggling to contain the shock, he turned and faced Talbert. "Was she involved with this?"

"I believe so, sir," Sgt. Talbert nodded his head. "I'll let you talk to the person in charge of the club's security, he'll explain it all to you." He pointed at Big Pete, who was sitting in an aluminum folding chair, sipping from a white Styrofoam cup. "That's him right there, sir."

Detective Guzmon approached Big Pete. "Hi yah doin'? I'm Detective Guzmon." He stuck out his hand.

Big Pete rose to his feet and shook his hand. "Big Pete. AKA Peter Smith."

It took Guzmon five minutes to discover this was Daquasha Lawrence's place of employment, she was a stripper, the two dead bodies were found in her dressing room, she left with an unknown black man, and there were several security staff employees who could identify this man she left with if given the opportunity to view a picture of him.

As Detective Guzmon strutted across the empty dance floor, on his way to Daquasha's dressing room, realization slowly engulfed his mind. All the facts were starting to indicate Jamil and his people were trying to beat him to Daquasha. He was willing to bet his entire pension that the two dead men inside the dressing room were affiliates of Jamil or his brother Kilroy.

Guzmon entered the room and closely examined the two dead men. When he saw Alley-bush's sunken in face, he saw his assumption was correct. This was one of Kilroy's workers and was a well known strong-arm man. Jamil and his brother were sending out hit-men to kill Daquasha. Guzmon felt a nervous tingle in the pit of his stomach because he had to find a way to get hold of Daquasha before they did.

As Guzmon watched the fingerprint technicians powdering the place, a smile appeared on his face because he knew if things got too hot for Daquasha to handle there was a good chance she just might come to him for protection. And even if she didn't, the APB was Statewide with special emphasis placed on all interstate toll-booths. The worse thing she could do was to try to leave the State. Indeed, he believed in his heart it was just a matter of time before she would be caught. But every time he thought about Kilroy and Jamil sending out hit-men, he uttered a silent pray that she was caught before they got to her.

£¥♥   £¥♥   £¥♥   £¥♥

Tykim brought the Maxima to stop in front of the dilapidated Tenement building on 158th Street and Melrose Avenue. He was double parked next to a gray station wagon and an old brown Toyota. "It's that building right there." He pointed at the building across the street.

The streets were deserted except for stray cats, dogs and rats scouring the area for food. An occasional crack-head, in search of a way to find another blast, could be seen shuffling by. Streaks of dawn were beginning to lighten the sky.

Daquasha thoroughly scanned the building Tykim pointed to. Something inside her was telling her something wasn't right. She didn't know if it was because she was becoming scared of her own shadow or her current feeling was a genuine warning of impending danger. "This don't feel right, Tykim."

He stared at her for a moment. "What don't feel right? If you talkin' about this place; don't nobody know about my man Kamel."

47

"I just don't feel right." Daquasha said softly, still staring at the building.

"You wanna stay in the car or come along with me?" Tykim retrieved the brown paper bag from underneath the seat. He spilled the two 9mms and matching silencers into his lap and began getting them ready. "I suggest you come along with me. Since we a team, we should do everything as a team. Plus, you'll be safer with me. Crack-heads at this time of the morning get extremely bold." He finished screwing on the silencers and handed one of the guns to Daquasha. "Go on, take it."

She looked at the gun with a smirk on her face. "Oh, now you think I'm some kind of thug or something. I ain't with that."

Tykim laughed as he tucked both guns in his front waist. "I strongly suggest you learn how to get with this. Now that you got a big ole bad and dangerous dog gunning for you, if you intend on living to see a ripe old age, you ain't got a choice in the matter." He opened the car door. "Come on, let's go."

Daquasha got out of the car and followed Tykim towards the building.

Tykim pulled out a set of keys, unlocked the two locks and entered.

Daquasha followed Tykim up the stairs; they were moving very slowly, listening intently. The smell of marijuana was heavy in the air and she instantly wondered were there any crack-heads nearby. Suddenly, whispering voices were heard. The sounds were coming from upstairs. Tykim pulled out one of the weapons, causing her heart to jump.

They reached the second floor, and Daquasha saw Tykim peering up the next flight of stairs. When the two unknown persons started laughing among themselves, she saw Tykim turned and headed for the apartment across from the staircase. He inserted a key in the lock and suddenly paused. He abruptly pulled away from the door with his gun in the ready. With his foot he pushed the door open. Retrieving his other gun, he slowly entered with both 9mms aimed.

Daquasha wanted to scream, *Let's get the fuck out of here! Can't you see something is wrong! That door ain't supposed to be open, you fuckin' fool!* But, she held her tongue in check and followed Tykim inside. With the exception of the giggling addicts upstairs, the silence was intense.

"Yo, Kamel!" Tykim said in a normal voice. "Where you are at, man?"

There was no response.

Daquasha could feel the tension resonating from Tykim's body as he tensed up and his nervousness started to grow profusely. Tykim peeked around a corner, looking down a small hallway leading to the back rooms. The silence in the apartment was highly irritating to the senses. With both guns carefully trained, Tykim moved down the hallway as Daquasha tip-toed directly behind him. Her heart thundered in her chest at a remarkable speed.

Tykim reached the first room and paused while listening cautiously. After a moment, he held up a hand for Daquasha to wait outside the room. He did a smooth body roll into the room like one of those T.V. cops or something. Springing to his feet, swinging the guns around the room, Daquasha thought Tykim looked truly ridiculous. He waved at her, directing her to entered. Her trembling legs obeyed.

Tykim raced over to the bed and pulled it from the wall. Daquasha's eyes grew wide when she saw the safe built inside the wall. Tykim climbed over the bed, tucked one of the weapons in his waist, knelt and began turning the dial on the safe. Seconds later, she saw him pull the safe door open.

"What the fuck!?" Tykim was aghast. The safe was empty. He climbed back over the bed with a look of desperation on his face and began looking around the room. The anger, rage and confusion was at a boiling point. His mind was struggling not to believe Kamel stole his money. This shit couldn't be happening!

Tykim stomped over to the closet; he knew sometimes Kamel stashed money in the other safe he had in the closet. Tykim snatched the door open. "Ah, shit!" He jumped back and pulled the other gun when he saw Kamel's bullet-ridden body. The safe was open and was empty. Tykim's mind instantly went on a rampage, trying to rapidly piece together what might have happened. But the pain of losing a life long friend, blinded him of the obvious possibility that he had just walked into a deadly trap. He was on the verge of brain locked.

Daquasha was seconds from diving headlong into a state of panic. The sight of Kamel was truly grotesque. Half his face was blown off and his chest was pure red from the coagulated blood that had long since stopped seeping from the seemingly countless bullet wounds. Her mind was telling her to *run like hell! Leave this place right now!* Extreme danger was all her mind seem to be shouting at her. "Let's get out of here--"

A noise came from the front of the apartment.

Daquasha and Tykim looked at each other. Terror jolted them both.

Just as the sound of frantic footsteps of numerous people entering the apartment was recognized, Tykim realized Daquasha was standing far too close to the doorway and screamed. "Daquasha, come over here---"

BOW!--BOW!--BOW!.....
The machine gunfire completely destroyed all traces of early morning tranquillity.

£¥♥   £¥♥   £¥♥   £¥♥

Earlier, at about the moment Daquasha and Tykim were climbing the stairs, slowly moving towards the second floor, Devil-dog and Lunatic were upstairs on the roof waiting patiently. Cleavon and two assistants, Light and Johnny B, were sitting on the third floor steps smoking blunts, pretending to be drug addicts hanging out, kicking the Willie bow-bow.

Outside in the back of the building, Brute and Pepper-P kept their eyes peeled for anyone attempting to use this route as an avenue of escape. In the front, across the street from Kamel's building, Don stood in a vestibule waiting as a back-up in case one of the targets miraculously slipped pass the inside hit team.

Every single hitter was equipped with fully automatic artillery ranging from Uzis to 16 shot 9mms.

Devil-dog waved Lunatic over to him. "They should be inside the crib by now." He quietly opened the roof door and tip-toed down the stairs to Cleavon and his team. Devil-dog whispered to Cleavon. "They went inside yet?"

Cleavon nodded his head as he pulled out a 9mm. "It's show time when you say the word."

Devil-dog pulled his Uzi from the back waist of his pants while heading straight for the apartment. "Well, in that case, say no more."

Lunatic loudly ejected a bullet into the chamber of his Desert-eagle as he followed Devil-dog. "Let the all mighty lead do the talkin'."

Devil-dog entered the apartment, not caring about the noise he was making. Lunatic, Cleavon, Light and Johnny B followed suit and took their predetermined places.

Devil-dog saw Daquasha, took aim and unleashed a fusillade of bullets.

£¥♥   £¥♥   £¥♥   £¥♥

The moment Daquasha heard Tykim shout her name, she frantically rushed further into the room just as a wave of bullets exploded pass her. Had she moved a fraction of a second later, she would have been struck. The bullets hurled chunks of plaster as they ate at the walls.

Daquasha took cover behind the bed, lying flat on the floor. The machine gunfire went on for ten seconds, ripping, tearing and pulverizing the walls and other things inside the room. She saw Tykim lying flat on his stomach with both guns in his hands, looking as if he was secretly enjoying the rapid pounding of the bullets while keeping his eyes locked on the door.

There was a sudden silence.

The silence was so intense, Daquasha's ears were ringing. From down the hall she heard a man say, "I think we got 'em! Light and Johnny B, go check it out!" "But why we gotta go check it out?" "Don't make me repeat myself, motherfucker!"

Daquasha then heard the slowly approaching footsteps. She saw Tykim quietly move to the side of the room, got on one knee with both silencer equipped weapons aimed at the door.

Daquasha's heart-beat increased when she saw the two black men enter the room, looking around. They both had huge weapons in their hands. When the hell was Tykim going to open fire?! She was moments from becoming frantic. *What the hell is he waiting for!?* Terror surged through her veins as the men began searching the room, kicking everything in their path out of the way.

SZK!--SZK!--SZK!--SZK!

The first bullet Tykim fired, hit Light dead in the forehead. The impact shoved him back several feet. Almost simultaneously, Johnny B was struck in the face just below the right eye, splattering blood all over the immediate area. They each received another bullet to the extremities as they collapsed to the floor.

Daquasha saw Tykim rush to the fallen men and retrieved their weapons.

Tykim whispered to Daquasha. "Here, take this." He handed her a 9mm automatic handgun. "I guess you gotta learn this the best way; on the job training."

Daquasha crawled across the floor and took the weapon. She hated guns, but she also hated the thought of dying more than anything else in the world. The gun felt heavy and cumbersome. She caught a flashback of when she was a little girl, no more than nine years old; she was playing with her father's gun she found in the closet. The ass whipping she got when her mother walked in and saw her toying with the gun even though the thing wasn't loaded, made her cringe.

"Yo, Light! Johnny B!" Devil-dog shouted down the hallway as he moved towards the backroom. "What the fuck is up?" He waved for Cleavon to get next to him as they moved down the hallway.

Tykim took two slow, deep breaths and moved to the threshold of the door. When he sensed the remaining men were moving towards the room, Tykim counted to three and pointed a 9mm around the corner.

SZK!--SZK!

Cleavon screamed when the bullet sliced through his right calf. As he fell, Cleavon instantly scrambled back down the hall, seeking refuge. At the moment Cleavon hollered, Lunatic and Devil-dog were already retreating back to safety behind the living room wall.

Tykim looked at the window. In his haste, he was about to instruct Daquasha to go to the window, but his years of knowledge and experience with conducting hits, told him these particular hitters were not stupid enough not to have some folks holding down the front and back of the building. Tykim's mind was racing. They couldn't wait for the police to arrive since that would be suicide. A life sentence would be waiting for Tykim if he was arrested and convicted again. He'd already did two state bids, and a third strike would most definitely get him life.

Tykim realized he had to take a dangerous chance. *Fuck it!* It was better than waiting for the police, who were probably on their way.

As Tykim headed for the windows, he heard the distinct sound of sirens. "Shit! God damn it!" He muttered as he ripped the curtains down, peering down into the backyard of the building. Trash cans, raggedy cloth lines, and decrepit gardens were scattered about.

BOW!--BOW!

The two shots were fired from outside, leaving two bullet holes in the window.

Before pulling away from the view, Tykim was able to see the two men seconds before they fired the shots.

The sirens grew louder.

Tykim peeked out the window again and saw one of the men nervously prancing back and forth, talking to the other. Then, suddenly, he ran off, waving his hands as if to say he was not going to wait until the police got here. *Yes! Leave nigga, leave!* Tykim's anticipation was growing. When the other men followed behind the one who was leaving, Tykim made his move. "Come on, Daquasha, hurry!" He tried to whisper, but the excitement of the moment was simply too intense to permit talking in a low volume. He frantically opened the window.

Daquasha sprung to her feet and rushed to the window. The adrenaline rush made her feel dizzy. She climbed out the window and began racing down the fire escape apparatus.

Just as Tykim was through the window, he heard the approaching footsteps moving rapidly towards the back room. He hid on the side of the window. When he heard the men had reached the room, Tykim took aim, pulling the trigger.

SZK!--SZK!--SZK!

All three of his bullets missed their targets, but he saw the two men had hit the floor and frantically scrambled back out of the room. Tykim raced down the fire escape. He saw Daquasha had already made it down to the ground.

BOW!--BOW!--BOW!

Daquasha fired at one of the men who had returned, causing Tykim to increase his speed down the escape apparatus. The man looked like he was struck as he sought cover.

Just as Tykim jumped from the last step of the fire escape to the ground, the sirens sounded like they were right upon them. When Tykim saw the huge man fleeing with a limp, he followed him. Daquasha followed. This direction was the only way out of this area and they didn't hesitate in deciding to head towards that way.

BOW!--BOW!--BOW!--BOW!--BOW!

Bullets whizzed by Daquasha and Tykim.

From the fire escape, Lunatic and Devil-dog opened fire on Daquasha and Tykim as they fled through the garbage littered backyards.

Devil-dog waved for Lunatic to stop firing. "Man, if we intend on making it out of here to fight another day," The reluctance was noticeable in his voice. "We better cut our loses right now. Five O is almost here."

Lunatic sighed. Devil-dog was right. He ran back to the front of the apartment. He and Devil-dog scooped up Cleavon and rushed out of the building. They jumped in their car and sped away just as the first patrol car turned the corner two blocks away.

As Daquasha approached the fence, she mimicked Tykim by tucking the weapon in the front waist of her pants. "AHHH!!" Daquasha screamed when the scorching hot barrel touched her stomach. She flung the weapon to the ground, sighing and cringing in pain while holding her stomach.

Tykim held back the laugh. He picked up the weapon, tucked it in his waist, easily enduring the burning sensation on his skin and helped Daquasha over the fence.

They made it to the street in back of Kamel's tenement building, and began jogging.

Tykim was thinking strictly about acquiring a quick ride, since his vehicle was history. They headed towards Melrose Avenue. This was a street known to have reasonably moderate traffic. A minute later, they were walking rapidly down Melrose.

Suddenly, Tykim saw an approaching car. "Daquasha, stand over here and pretend your stomach's messed-up. Bend over like this," He demonstrated.

Daquasha obeyed.

As the car approached, Tykim stepped into the middle of the street; excitedly waving both hands in the air. "Help us! Please help us!" He then pointed at Daquasha.

The yellow cab stopped, and the Indian looking man with a beige turban wrapped around his head and a thick beard and mustache, got out of the vehicle. "What's wrong?" His eyes were filled with true concern.

"My wife was stabbed, mister," Tykim moved towards the man. When he was close enough, Tykim pulled one of the guns. "Just be easy and you'll be all right. All we need is a ride, my man, that's all."

The Indian cab driver raised both hands and stepped away from the car.

Daquasha bolted for the passenger side and jumped inside just as Tykim got behind the wheel and screeched off.

Through the rear view mirror Tykim saw the man stomping his feet, cursing and waving his arms in a rage. Suddenly, a police car turned onto Melrose Avenue. It was coming up behind the cab driver. "God damn it! Ain't this a bitch!" Tykim said out loud, causing Daquasha to turn around in her seat to see what was going on.

When Daquasha saw the police car come to a stop, and the officers inside started talking to the taxi driver, who was pointing at them, she turned back around with that all too familiar wave of anxiety swirling through her mid-section. She wondered if all this anxiety and stress was hurting her unborn child? Daquasha tried to conceal her fear as she spoke. "I guess this is the part where we find out if you really about your business."

Tykim smiled as he stomped his foot on the gas pedal. The car jerked into a faster speed. "Well, I ain't never had a problem with showing and proving anything I claim to be about."

The engine on the cab unleashed a deep whining sound as it opened up. Tykim pressed the pedal all the way to the floor board.

The police siren came to life, racing after Daquasha and Tykim.

CHAPTER # 10

Detective Guzmon stood over Light's dead body staring down into his blank, soulless eyes. Standing next to him was his partner, Detective James Armstrong, who was dressed in a cheap Colombo style trench coat. His clean shaved face and striking blue eyes made him look far too young to be a seasoned law enforcement official with well over two decades of experience.

"Yeah, this is one of Kilroy's boys," Guzmon said, scrutinizing the bullet ridden room.

Armstrong walked over to the closet and kneeled. "This one here ain't a drug dealer." He moved Kamel's face to get a closer look at his devastating head wound. "I arrested this guy some years ago for a string of arm robberies. If my memory serves me correctly, he just returned from prison not too long ago."

Guzmon walked over and stood peering over Armstrong's shoulder. "This guy here was probably a friend of this individual traveling with Mrs. Lawrence. Why he ended up like this is a mystery we may never resolve." Guzmon's eyes were pulled to the empty safe. "Now that's odd. What would this guy be doing with a safe like that?"

"Yeah, that's a Seal-Master. A damn good brand." Armstrong rose to his feet. "It was obviously put there to keep something real safe. What would a ex-convict with a arm robbery MO want to keep safe, besides the money he steals?"

Guzmon continued examining the bullet ridden walls. "It's probably not even his."

Armstrong walked over to the window and looked down at the backyard. "This was how they escaped."

Guzmon walked over and looked out the window. He wanted to remind his partner that the apparent use of this escape route was the most obvious of all facts they'd come across so far while at this unique crime scene. There were bullet holes near the surrounding walls and the window. The bed was in disarray. "Here's another safe behind the bed."

Armstrong pulled the bed into the middle of the room. "Well, well, I guess this guy is some kind of safe freak or something, huh?"

Guzmon didn't find the joke funny. "I wonder what was taken from these two safes?" He said more to himself than as a question meant to be answered.

"I think we oughta be more concerned about this woman, Mrs. Lawrence." Armstrong walked over to Johnny B. "With all these bodies piling up all over the county wherever she goes, I believe we better find her quickly. I would say if any more bodies drop, Captain Fletcher is going to blow his top."

"Let's bring in the tech-team." Guzmon headed for the door. Armstrong followed. "That black Nissan out front should give us some leads. The prints we lifted at the club and those found in that vehicle should be a match." He entered the living room and spoke to a red haired white man with freckles. "It's ready. We want every print in that room."

"No problem, sir," The red haired man lead the tech-team down the hall to the back room as Guzmon and Armstrong exited the apartment, descending down the stairs. They exited the building and headed for the black Maxima.

As Guzmon and Armstrong stood by watching the latent technicians lifting prints and other microscopic evidence, a uniformed officer standing near a patrol car shouted. "Excuse me, Detective Guzmon!" He waved at Guzmon when he turned around.

Guzmon approached. "Yeah, what's up officer?" He couldn't remember this officer's name to save his life.

"I think you might want to hear this last transmission." The officer turned a knob on the radio, pressed a button on the device in his hand and spoke into it. "This is seven four one to dispatcher. Please repeat that last transmission."

A woman's nasal voice spewed static laden words from the radio. "High speed vehicular pursuit has ended at Woodlawn Avenue and 243rd Street. Three pursuer patrol vehicles are down. Request immediate back-up from all available patrol units. Ambulance in route. Stolen yellow cab containing suspects has collided into moving truck. Suspects, black male and female, believed to be incapacitated."

Black male and female!? Stolen yellow cab!? Guzmon's eyes lit up. Shock waves of anticipation surged through his body. He turned with flinching speed. "Hey, Armstrong! Let's go!" Guzmon hastily headed for his car. He turned and continued talking to Armstrong as he started jogging towards him. "I think we found them!"

£¥♥   £¥♥   £¥♥   £¥♥

Kilroy Nevez stood staring at Devil-dog, Lunatic and Brute with his arms folded across his chest. His facial expression was so tight jawed it could have detonated a pack of C4. The huge warehouse they were in was filled with boxes of clothing, electrical appliances of all sorts and household furniture. This building, located in Yonkers, along with the several dozen other business structures scattered all throughout the tri-state area were owned and operated by Kilroy. He was a multimillionaire and vowed to become a billionaire by the time he reached his fiftieth birthday, which was thirteen years to go and counting.

With two heavily armed bodyguards close by, both dressed in sleek Gucci suits, Kilroy began to pace. His hard sole Armani shoes scratching upon the pavement. The stylish black Armani double breasted suit made him look like a true CEO. With light brown skin, a flawless complexion, ten percent body fat, and a neatly trimmed short afro, Kilroy could put plenty models to shame had he chose to adventure into that profession. Soft he may have appeared, but pity the fool who judged this book by its cover and made the deadly mistake of reacting in accordance with such misconception.

"I really don't know what the fuck I'm gonna do with you clowns," Kilroy stopped pacing and folded his arms across his chest again. "Now, would I be wrong to spazz out and have all three of you stupid motherfuckers murdered right here on the fuckin' spot?"

The two bodyguards pulled their compact Israeli style Uzis, loudly ejecting bullets into the chambers of their weapons.

"Easy y'all," Kilroy waved for them to put their weapons back in their special made holsters. This little ritual was needed every so often to let them know that games, procrastination and laziness was not tolerated in any way and under no circumstances. "If my brother's case touches a grand jury on account of y'all not seeming to get your shit together, sparks will fly, heads will roll and asses will be set on fire." Kilroy locked eyes with Devil-dog; he was really surprised at him. "So, what's your next move, big dee?"

Devil-dog shifted his weight on to the other foot. He spoke enthusiastically. "We got peoples on the street everywhere looking for him. In Queens, Brooklyn, everywhere. Any where Tykim hangs out or used to hang out, we got eyes on full alert. If he shows his face anywhere in this city, somebody'll see him. I even put out a track on his head; anyone who gives us information that leads to us finding Tykim will get 20 gees."

Kilroy nodded his head. He was impressed by the way Devil-dog used that little money trick. If there was one thing people moved to, it was definitely money. He thought 20 gees was a bit too high, but this did indicate he was taking this situation serious. "That's good, but what if Danielle splits up from Tykim? The way you got this thing mapped out, you're assuming

Tykim is going to remain with her. Be advise, the person we're gunning for here is Danielle."

"We got the word out on her too," Devil-dog felt a sheet of perspiration formulated under his arm pits and on his nose. "I will admit, she's a little harder to track because she ain't got a lot of shit in her jacket like Tykim." He paused for a moment. "I was wondering if you can get Jamil to give us a little more info about this broad. Maybe if we knew where she grew up, some of her family members, you know, shit like that, maybe we can get a good jump start on finding her?"

Kilroy gritted his teeth. He was pissed off with Jamil. *What the fuck did he see in this slut!? And how the fuck could he get strung out on a tramp and don't even know shit about the bitch!?* He already tried to find out what Jamil knew about Danielle, and his fool ass wasn't even able to tell him where she grew up at, whether she had family or what she did before he met her.

Kilroy sighed, feeling slightly embarrassed by what he was about to say. "Jamil don't know much about her." He saw Lunatic squint up his face. "What's your motherfuckin' problem, Lunatic?"

"Ah--I—ah--nothing, Kilroy," Lunatic's eyes were wide with insanity. "I ain't meant no disrespect, but--but we gotta find out some mo' info on this broad, so we's can blaze her ass, man."

Kilroy relaxed. There was no need to get upset with these guys for reacting like anyone else would react. Jamil was making him look bad, and it wasn't their fault. Even when they were young, Jamil was always one of those sensitive ass niggas that got twisted in the head over those pretty bitches. He had told Jamil repeatedly that fine women are usually the subject of too much controversy; especially those 'hood oriented ones. Gold-digger's delight was all their greedy minds could seem to comprehend. But Jamil was never the type to listen to good sound advice; his head was as hard as titanium laced blue steel. They didn't lie when they said, some people just had to learn things their way or no way at all, and Jamil was a classic example of such a person.

Kilroy often tried to present himself as an example for Jamil to follow; he was happily married with three children, never did a state bid before and controlled one third of the drugs in the Bronx, and numerous clusters in every other borough. He never touched the stuff he sold, and was college educated with two bachelor degrees (one in Business Administration and the other in Real Estate). Kilroy even had sixteen completely legitimate businesses. Kilroy also found every way in his power to give back to the

Community, made donations to damn near all Black non-for-profit organizations and knew almost every politician in the State. Staring at his three workers standing in front of him, Kilroy sighed while pulling himself out of the deep thought he was in. If he didn't love his bad ass, troublesome baby brother, he would've thrown the towel in on him a long time ago.

Kilroy cleared his voice. "All right, I guess your plan will have to do for now. I suggest you pull some of those workers from the spots and put them out on the street." He saw Brute was about to make a comment, and cut him off. "I know it's gonna interfere with some of the cash flow. Don't worry, Brute. Right now money don't mean shit to me if my brother is murdered by these Devil's because of some snitchin' ass bitch."

There was a moment of acute silence.

Devil-dog sensed the meeting was over. "We outta here, Big Papa." He headed for the door; Brute and Lunatic were in his tracks. "I'll give you a buzz in another hour and let you know what's going down."

Kilroy gave him a head nod and a raised clenched fist salute.

They vanished out the door.

Kilroy stared at the door, wondering if he should bring in his clean-up crew from Brooklyn? After a moment of contemplation, Kilroy realized that would be a little too extreme for the moment. Patience was always the key to effectiveness, and he'd mastered this skill many years ago. But, he decided if Devil-dog fucked up again, we might have to sic his little back-up team on his reckless ass.

CHAPTER # 11

Daquasha sat in the passenger seat watching the east river down below. The sound of the green Mazda's tires rolling across the steel grate like floor of the Throgs Neck Bridge was steady and rhythmatic. Everything seemed like it was spinning. The pain in the joints all over her body was explicit and pulsated with agonizing strength.

Daquasha was sick. Her stomach was bubbling and she wanted to vomit. Overhead, the sun was creeping across the early morning eastern sky. By the way the sun-rays beamed and bounced upon the land, Mother-Nature promised to produce a day of decent, spring like weather.

The lump on her forehead had grown to the size of a marble and the small cuts and scratches on her face had transmutated into tender scabs. The ring around her eye was now turning blue. She was completely exhausted and wanted to lay her head down to sleep so bad she once contemplated giving herself up to the police. But the fear of losing her liberty for probably the rest of her life was a force far too powerful to compete with. Giving up simply wasn't a rational option, Daquasha repeatedly told herself as she unconsciously twirled the ring on her pinkie finger. Her body felt grimy from all the anxiety induced sweating she'd been doing. Images of a nice smoothing, steaming hot shower was suddenly on her mind.

Daquasha glanced over at Tykim. She wanted to reach across and scratch his eyes out of his head. Every time this bad luck motherfucker popped up in her life, the pain, misery, death, destruction and pure hell started up all over again. She spoke with an attitude. "Where we going?"

Tykim looked at his watch. "It's about time. Twenty minutes it took you to say something. How's that bump on your head?"

She didn't respond.

Tykim saw Daquasha was staring out the window. "Just imagine if you didn't put on that seat beat when I told you to. See, that's why you should listen to a good brother like yours truly. Girl, you would've went straight through the windshield, if you ain't have on that seat beat."

Daquasha's mind flashbacked to the high speed chase and the collision. When the first cop car started chasing them, Daquasha was making plans in her head, trying to sych herself out because she just knew they were going to get caught. Then two additional police cars joined in the chase and that was it. She braced herself psychologically and emotionally for what she thought was inevitable; life imprisonment. Just as Tykim ran a red light at 243rd Street, a huge truck slammed into the back end of the passenger side and hurled the cab into a wild and savage spin. Upon impact, Daquasha's head hit the passenger window, but luckily the glass didn't break. The three cop cars crashed into the truck and a mini-station wagon head on. The yellow cab smashed into a parked car and was totaled. The front end was crunched in like a crumbled up piece of paper. Dazed, she and Tykim fled on foot, running for three blocks. Tykim broke into the green Mazda, hot-wired it and headed towards the Throgs Neck Bridge.

"So, where we going?" Daquasha said, "I hope it's somewhere where we can eat and get some sleep."

"Well, all your wishes won't be coming true," Tykim wondered if she realized there was no place in this city that was safe for them. "The next stop is to get us some money, some food and a legit ride. Then we hit the road. When we're outta this city, then we'll think about sleep."

"How we gonna function without rest!? Do you know how much stuff we might miss and how reckless we can get with a tired mind and a worn out body?" Her mother's intuition for the safety of her child was taking charge. She not only needed rest for herself, but for the life inside her stomach as well.

"You right," Tykim paused for a moment. "Okay, let's say right now we decide to go to a hotel and get some sleep. That cost money. I'm sure we can agree on that. I got about fifty dollars on me. How much money you got on you?"

Daquasha dug into her pants pocket and pulled out a hand full of bills. She counted them. "I got forty dollars."

"The average cheap hotel room costs at least forty dollars for a twenty four hour stay." Tykim brought the car off the ramp of the Bridge and onto the Streets of Queens.

"We can find one for half that price. I say we get us something to eat and then get us some sleep. I'm so tired, I can't even think straight."

"I understand how you feel, Daquasha, but right now we gotta stay ahead of the game. With the police on our ass and Kilroy searching for us, we're in a real fucked up predicament. With that kind of heat on us, it would be dangerous and sheer insanity to hang around here."

"If we got the police looking for us," Daquasha softened her tone some. "Leaving the State could be even more dangerous. The toll booths and highway patrol are all gonna be on point. They got pictures of us, that much we know for sure. Probably all couples that fit our description are gonna be pulled over."

Tykim glanced at Daquasha. "Yeah, you're right. That's why I'm planning to get us some disguises before we hit the highways. After I pick up a couple gees from my, ah, my friend, we'll try to get her to do some shopping for us." Tykim sighed, wondering if what he was about to do was a sane thing to try. He was going to get his girl, Charmaine, to do some costume shopping for him and Daquasha. The sparks and friction was definitely going to fly, but he believed he could talk her into it. He would have done the shopping himself, but running the streets under any circumstances was basically suicide.

"Get me to a Dimes Savings Bank," Daquasha said, knowing what she was suggesting was not possible, but assumed Tykim with his conniving ass mind might be able to find a way to make it happen. "I can get us five gees."

Tykim laughed. "You still full of jokes, huh? You know that money is dead. When the police started snooping around your crib, everything you had in the bank was put on point. With all that drama at your job last night, you about as hot as volcano lava. If you try to touch that doe right about now, you'll go down faster than rain drops falling during a thunderstorm."

There was a moment of silence.

Daquasha unconsciously and habitually pulled the pack of Newport cigarettes from her pocket, pulled a cigarette from the pack and was about to light up. With trembling hands, she'd been thinking about a smoke ever since she'd entered the car, but needed time to let her mind wind down some. She couldn't hold back any longer. Suddenly, a voice in the back of her head spoke. She stopped and looked at the cigarette. All the stuff she'd heard about cigarettes causing cancer and birth defects jumped in her mind again. Now that she knew for certain she was pregnant, she could no longer pretend this wasn't the case.

Her hand containing the cigarette flopped down in her lap. The urge to smoke was as powerful as a heroine craving. Although she had no idea what a heroine craving felt like, she saw the crazy activities of enough dope fiends in her life time to know how wicked that vicious appetite was. She decided to discard the pack of cigarette when they came to a stop. Today she was going to stop. She had to. As she put the cigarette back into the pack, a hundred excuses bum rushed her mind. She struggled to stay strong, but the urge was just too strong. Daquasha sighed in defeat.

Daquasha sparked up the cigarette and drew a huge cloud into her lungs. She decided she would stop tomorrow. Right now, there was too much stress in her life and one more day wasn't going to hurt her unborn child. Plus, smoking soothed her stomach and made her morning sickness go away.

Tykim rolled the window all the way down. "Don't you know smoking is bad for your health?"

"Don't start that bullshit," Daquasha flicked ashes into the tray. "Since when did you stop smoking?"

"Four years ago when I was in Clinton Dannemora." Tykim stopped the car at the red light. "I got up one morning and decided I wasn't gonna smoke anymore. I went cold turkey and was kickin' every step of the way." He really wanted to ask her why she never answered any of his letters, but he subconsciously knew the reason why. Even as he wrote those letters, he knew damn well she wasn't going to write back. But the mere act of writing just seemed to have a therapeutic effect on his well being.

The light turned green and Tykim pulled off. Tykim wondered if the time was right to apologize? It seemed right to his heart, so he went with it. "Daquasha, I never got the chance to tell you I'm sorry." He paused. "I tried writing you, but I guess you never got any of my letters. You never gave me the chance to tell you what really happened. That night wasn't my--"

"I don't wanna hear it!" Daquasha said, her heart sunk just being reminded of that god-awful night. It was the foundation of so much agony and she preferred to leave it buried deep down in the archieves of her subconscious mind.

Tykim realized the time apparently wasn't right. "Sorry, I brought it up." He wanted to spark up some conversation on another issue to regain what little bit of ground he'd acquired thus far. But what could he talk about that wouldn't get her upset? After a moment, he decided to let her do the talking.

The silence held strong until they pulled up in front of Charmaine's house.

Tykim killed the engine. "I'll be right back. Hold tight." He exited the car and headed for the two family home.

Daquasha's stomach was growling so hard, she thought something was wrong with the fetus inside her. She was developing a hungry headache. She watched Tykim walk up the three steps and press the door bell. When a light skin black woman answered the door, Daquasha really took a look at the fact Tykim was going to his woman for help. She couldn't believe how stupid he was. Any fool knew a woman wasn't going to help a man, who was about to run off with another woman, financially or otherwise. She sucked her teeth in disgust. Daquasha saw Charmaine arguing with Tykim while pointing at her in the car.

Suddenly, Daquasha realized this was a very precarious situation. Spiteful woman usually always called the police on their cheating boyfriends. Suddenly, Daquasha saw Charmaine charging at her. *Ah, shit! Here we go!* Daquasha was about to exit the vehicle and step straight to her business, but instead, she pressed down on the lock button and rolled the window up. She was cursing Tykim's ass out. *Why didn't he park the damn car around the corner or something?*

Charmaine banged on the window. "Come out of the car, bitch! You fuckin' tramp! You trying to steal my man! Come on, come out."

"Charmaine! Chill!" Tykim dragged her away. Well, he guessed that killed his costume shopping plan. "It ain't what you think it is I told you!"

"You ain't gonna beat me in the head with that lame ass shit about peoples trying to kill you. You just wanna run off with this bitch!"

Tykim nervously looked at the nearby houses. They were making a scene and that was no good. "Fuck it, believe what you want. Now, let's go in here and get my stash!"

"You ain't gettin' shit!" Charmaine yelled. "If you think I'm gonna give you money to spend on some low life bitch, you outta your fuckin' mind!"

Tykim was seconds from slapping fire out of Charmaine. He didn't believe in beating on women, but he was desperate now, and her talk about not giving him his own money was making him very dangerous. He grabbed her by the throat. "Stop yelling!" He said in a low venomous tone. He saw his aggression instantly calmed her down. Charmaine's eyes were huge and comical. "Don't make me spazz out on you, Charmaine." He pushed her towards the house.

Charmaine stumbled, but maintained her footing. She burst out crying as she entered the house with Tykim on her heels. "Why are you doing this to me?" She wasn't crying because Tykim broke her heart, she was really crying because she was terrified of what Tykim was going to do to her when he found out she spent every dime of his sixteen gees.

As Charmaine slowly climbed the stairs, she realized there were no other ways to stall him. When she reached the second floor, she turned and spoke softly. "Tykim, you picked a bad time to come asking for that money."

Tykim's heart almost stopped. "What the fuck are you talking about, Charmaine!?" He instantly knew she did not have the money. "Don't tell me you fucked up my money!" He balled up his fists and eased towards her, about to pounce on her.

"Tykim, please," She tried to hug him, but was shoved away. "I was gonna replace it this week--"

"How much of it did you fuck up!?"

"Please, Tykim, don't hurt me," Charmaine started crying as she collapsed to her knees and grabbed hold of his pants leg. She strategically placed her face near his groin, looking up at him with pitiful eyes. "I swear I was gonna replace it. I had to use it help my mother with her bills. They was gonna put her out on the street."

Tykim was shattered. His mind was thinking of all the other money he had floating around in the streets, but all of those sources were too dangerous to attempt to retrieve. Kilroy's contract out on his head was probably big enough to make anyone flip.

After a moment, Tykim concluded all debts owed to him were dead. They were as worthless as shitty toilet tissue lying in a garbage dump. "Get up!" He grabbed Charmaine by the collar and hurled her on to her feet. "Let's go." He roughly escorted her to the bedroom. "All the jewelry is history." He went to the jewelry box.

"But I need my--"

"Don't play your motherfuckin' self, Charmaine!" He snatched up the jewelry box and spilled the contents on the bed. "You lucky I don't break you the fuck up for fuckin' up my money." He spoke while scouring through the items. "How the fuck could you mess up a whole sixteen gees!?" He sensed she might be lying, but he didn't have time to waste. Torturing her to find out the truth was an option, but his conscientious wasn't built for inflicting that sort of harm on the opposite sex. In any event, he figured the jewelry might do the trick. He found all the items he was looking for.

With a pocket full of gold and diamond stubbed bracelets, rings, and ear rings, Tykim rushed out the room, down the stairs and out house.

As Tykim entered the car, he made a quick calculation and figured he could get maybe seven gees for the jewelry. He struggled not to take out his anger on the gas pedal. The car eased from the curb.

Inside the house, Charmaine was fuming. She paced back and forth, wondering should she do it. Jealousy and envy started running rampant through her veins. She was seething with hatred. She was a jilted lover with a spiteful and guilty conscientious, and needed a way to vent her rage in order to make her feel vindicated. None of this was her fault! It was all Tykim's fault! *That cheating, two timing motherfucker!* Daquasha's pretty chocolate brown face flashed across her third eye, and in that instance, Charmaine made up her mind. She warned Tykim when he started sticking his dick in her; if he flipped on her, she would flip too.

Charmaine stomped over to the phone, pulled the piece of paper from her pocket and dialed the number she got from this guy named Joker yesterday. He came to the club looking for Tykim and offered her twenty gees if she revealed his whereabouts. Twenty gees was far too much money to let pass her by; especially for a dude she was no longer feeling.

CHAPTER # 12

"Tykim Hall," Detective Guzmon said, reading from the document in his hand. He was standing near his desk while Armstrong sat behind his desk on the other side of the squad room. "Born and raised in Brooklyn. Even committed most of his crimes all throughout Brooklyn. Looking at his and Daquasha's childhood addresses, it's fair to say they know each other quite well. They're about the same age. He's 32; she's 31. They attended the same schools together. From elementary to High School."

The fax machine came to life, and Armstrong went for it. He ripped the sheet of paper from the jaws of the machine when it was finished spitting out the document. He scrutinized the report, humming as he read.

Guzmon's eyes gleamed with anticipation. "What else we got?"

"This guy has been real business since he got out of prison about two years ago," Armstrong took a seat behind his desk. "According to this international tracking report, this guy is wanted for questioning in five contract killings. Three in Brooklyn. Two in Staten Island. All five victims were drug dealers, which tends to explain why not much attention has been placed on these cases."

Guzmon took a seat at his desk. "How did they draw the conclusion that those shootings may be connected to Mr. Hall?" He picked up the rap sheet and viewed it for the third time.

"Eyewitnesses and fingerprints left at the scene of the crime."

"This guy is bold almost to the point of recklessness." Guzmon sat the document down and picked up the cup of coffee. "He left prints at the Paradise Lounge, at the house over on 158th Street, in the black Maxima. All eight eyewitnesses at the Paradise Lounge identified him and so did the woman upstairs over Kamel Ferguson's apartment." He took a sip of coffee. "Thank goodness we're not dealing with a top grade hit man. Otherwise we might be banging our heads on the walls trying to pin point this guy."

"Don't get locked into any hasty assumptions." Armstrong leaned back in his chair. "His involvement with Daquasha seems to me to be the main reason for his current activities." He waved to Guzmon. "Come here, let me show you something."

Guzmon approached. From behind Armstrong, he beamed down at the document.

"This guy's last conviction involved Daquasha Lawrence."

Guzmon read the case summary. When he finished, he was even more perplexed about this case. He squinted his eyes and shook his head to display his confusion. "If he actually did what this report says, I can't see how Ms. Lawrence would even give him the time of day."

"If he's protecting her from being murdered," Armstrong said, "She'd overlook something like that."

Guzmon thought hard about Armstrong's analogy. "Yeah, I guess you're right." He returned to his desk and sat. "I be glad when we get Ms. Holmes to the grand jury. What the hell is taking ADA Flynn so damn long to formulate the case. I made it clear to him we have to at least acquire an indictment and get Ms. Holmes' testimony on record. Waiting to see if we can obtain Ms. Lawrence is not practical."

"The principle of the more, the merrier applies in this case. One eyewitness cases, especially those where the victim is related to the eyewitness, gets shaky when a top notch defense attorney tears into such a witness. If she got a speck of dirt in her closet, it will be aired before the jury."

There was a knock on the door.

"Come in," Guzmon responded.

A detective opened the door and stuck his head in the room. "Captain Fletcher wants to see you two ASAP." He closed the door behind him as he disappeared.

Guzmon spoke as he rose to his feet. "Let the thunderstorm begin."

Guzmon and Armstrong exited the squad room, strutted down the hallway and entered Captain Fletcher's office.

"Come on in and have a seat, gentlemen." Captain Fletcher was a heavy-set white man with a beak of a nose and had thick eyebrows. "Thanks for coming immediately."

Guzmon and Armstrong sat in the two cushioned chairs positioned in front of Fletcher's desk.

"This Nevez case is starting to create a lot of problems. This Domino effect of incident after incident has to come to a stop. The Borough President, Mr. Julian Cruz, is having a shit fit. This is an election year, and if he's not re-elected due to turmoil in the Borough, he vowed to bring all responsible parties down with him. Guzmon, he made it clear your name would be on the top of the list. This is your case. Borough President Cruz and so do I, want these crimes resolved and the killings to stop. Within two weeks from today, if Ms. Lawrence and Mr. Hall are not in custody, you should re-familiarize yourself with how it feels at the starting point on the detective's ladder. I'm sorry this has to be so harsh, but careers are on the line . . . "

£¥♥   £¥♥   £¥♥   £¥♥

"No, you listen to me!" Devil-dog shouted into the cellular phone. He was behind the wheel of a blue Cherokee Jeep with Lunatic in the passenger seat. They were cruising down Castlehill Avenue. "Tell that motherfucker if he don't call me back with a name and address of this bitch, it's coming out of his ass. He got ten minutes and after that, I'm personally gonna pay his ass a visit!" He disconnected the phone and angrily tossed it on the dashboard.

"How could that dumb ass cock sucker forget to get the woman's name and where we can find her?" Lunatic had a cigarette in between his fingers. "We need to beat some common sense into his stupid ass."

"This is the kind of reckless shit that starts happenin' when we start showing these punk motherfuckers too much love."

Five minutes later, the cellular buzzed and Devil-dog snatched it up. "Yeah, what's up?" After a moment, a smile crept onto his face and he nodded his head. "Tell him to tell her, I'm on my way." He disconnected the call and laid the phone next to him.

"So, where we headed?"

"Queens. Some chicken-head named Charmaine claims Tykim was her man. She wants us to meet her on the corner of Liberty Avenue and 236th Street."

"What if this is a set up?" Lunatic pulled on the cigarette and then snuffed it out in the ashtray. "You know Tykim blazed a couple of dealers. He might be setting a trap. Kinda like bringing the noise instead of running away from the drama."

Devil-dog expelled a breath of air, he was in deep thought. "I guess we gotta take that chance. We keep our fingers close to the trigger and our eyes wide open.

"Oh, yeah, that sounds like love to me," Lunatic pulled his trusty old Desert Eagle from under the seat.

"Call Brute. Tell him to meet us there and bring an extra car load with him."

Lunatic pulled his cellular phone and dialed the number.

A half hour later, Devil-dog pulled the jeep into a parking space in the middle of Liberty Avenue. He saw joker, their no common sense having Queens runner, approaching with a high yellow skinned black woman, apparently Charmaine.

70

Lunatic opened the door, got out and let the two get in the back. He was still scanning the streets in all directions and saw everything still looked safe. Lunatic gave a head nod to Brute who was a block away in an old Cadillac. He got back in the jeep and closed the door.

Devil-dog turned in his seat and locked eyes with Charmaine. "So, let's hear it."

It took Charmaine three minutes to tell her story. She paused and then said, "So how we gonna do this reward thing? I figure since you know how the car looks and all the places he'll go to get rid of the jewelry, I should get broke off a little piece of that reward money up front."

Devil-dog started laughing, causing Lunatic and Joker to join in the laughter. Devil-dog wind down enough to speak through his chuckles. "How we know you ain't tryin' to play us?" He knew Charmaine's story was legit, but he had no intentions of paying her or anyone else a damn thing. "I heard about y'all Queens bitches setting up mad brothers."

Charmaine acted like she was shocked. "Set y'all up!? Why would I wanna do somethin' stupid like that--"

BLAAM!

Devil-dog punched Charmaine in the nose with a hard right jab. Her head snapped back and blood oozed from the crevasses of her hands clamped over her face. "Ain't you fuckin' this nigga!?" Devil-dog shouted. "I think your story stinks about as foul as that pussy of yours smells. Don't you know I value my motherfuckin' time. You wasting my precious time with this bullshit!"

Charmaine was about to respond, but Devil-dog's fist connected with her eye.

Charmaine squealed in terror, sounding like a horrified small animal being beaten to death. She squirmed in the seat. Flashing stars and lightning bolts swirled before he eyes, even though they both were closed.

Lunatic looked on with wide-eyed delight. He faced front, opened the glove compartment, retrieved a set of brass knuckles and quickly put them on. He cocked his fist for the knock out blow as he turned and said, "You should've waited until your story checked out first before asking for money, ma." He was itching for her to put her arms down from covering her head and face. "Yo, man!" He shouted at Devil-dog, winking his eye for him to play along. "Yo, motherfucker! Why you hit her like that, nigga! You ain't had to hit her like that."

71

With a fake smile, Devil-dog changed his voice and demeanor. "Ah, come on, man. I ain't hit her all that hard. Hey, Charmaine, listen baby girl, I ain't mean to hit you like that."

Lunatic spoke softly to Charmaine. "You all right now, ma. He ain't gonna hit you no more." He shouted at Devil-dog. "Nigga, you hit her again and I'ma air you the fuck out!" His tone was soft again. "Lemme see what he did to that pretty face of yours. Come on, look at me when I'm talking to you, ma."

Through tears and debilitating fear, Charmaine allowed her arms to slowly ease down to her lap. She realized she played herself totally and was praying they didn't kill her.

BLAAM!

Lunatic's brass knuckled laden fist connected with Charmaine's forehead. She was knocked out cold. Her lifeless body fell into Joker's lap.

The laughter ignited again.

Lunatic spoke while opening and closing his fist with gigantic eyes and a Kool-aid smile. "Cut throat bitch! She suppose to be his girl, and here she is snitchin' him out from hell to high waters." Images of the woman who told on him and cost him seven grueling years in various upstate prisons, tumbled through his mind. "That could be me she snitchin' on."

"Kick that bitch out the ride," Devil-dog turned around in his seat and activated the ignition. The engine jumped to life. "Don't forget to take all her ID. If her lips decide to get loose when she talks to the law, we'll be able to touch that ass."

Joker searched her purse, founded her wallet and handed it to Devil-dog.

Lunatic opened the door, flipped the seat forward as Joker dragged Charmaine's limp body out of the jeep, and tossed her to the pavement. The back of Charmaine's head impacted with the concrete with skull breaking force. Joker nonchalantly got back in the vehicle.

The Jeep sped off.

£¥♥   £¥♥   £¥♥   £¥♥

Charmaine swirled from the pit of a dark hole at the bottom her mind. She heard voices. Through the throbbing pain and the red haze, she opened her eyes. Sporting an outlandish black eye, she saw she was in a hospital bed. She even had on a hospital gown. The smell of antiseptics engulfed her senses. She saw a heavy-set black nurse rapidly approaching.

"Well, good afternoon, child," The nurse said, "Sure glad you could join us. What's your name?"

"Charmaine Wilson," She said through a crackling voice. It all started fading back into her conscious mind. She remembered she was in the Jeep with Joker and his friends from uptown.

"There's someone here to see you, Ms. Wilson." The nurse turned and headed for the door. She stuck her head out the room and said, "She's up."

When Charmaine saw the two police officers walk through the door, her headache throbbed a little harder. It wasn't hard to figure out what they were here for. Hatred and revenge sparkled in her eyes. If Tykim hadn't brought that bitch to her door step, asking for money at the wrong god damn time, this would have never happened!

The two officers stood near her bedside. The tall, linky, clean shaven one said, "We would like to ask you a few questions, Ms, ah . . ."

"Charmaine Wilson."

"Ms. Wilson. Who assaulted you?"

Charmaine's rage was sizzling. Her forehead pulsated with agony. That motherfucker Joker, would die if she could get her hands on him. "It was three men. They drove a blue jeep."

"Did you know these men?"

She thought hard about the answer she was about to give. The code of the street about snitchin' tried to inch its way into her subconscious without much luck. "Yes, one of them. I only know his street name. It's Joker."

"Joker!?" The officer appeared confused. "That's his name?" He wondered what kind of parents would name a child joker?

Charmaine nodded her head.

"Why did they assault you?"

Charmaine let her thirst for revenge and retribution guide her tongue. She told them just about everything, including the circumstances surrounding her relationship with Tykim and the visit she received from Joker yesterday.

The slim officer stared at her with a surprised expression. She said a mouthful. Her mentioning of the name Tykim sparked all sorts of new avenues of concern. He dug in his pocket and pulled the photocopied mug shots of Daquasha Lawrence and Tykim Hall. He showed her Tykim's picture. "Is this the Tykim you're referring to?" He held the picture in front of her.

"Yeah, that's him."

The officer then held the picture of Daquasha in front of her. "Was this the woman with him?"

"Yeah, that's that bitch. They came to my house in a green car, I think it was a Mazda."

The other cop was writing down the information.

The slim cop, tucked the photos back in his shirt pocket. "Thank you, Ms. Wilson. We'll be right back." He turned.

"Hold up! There's more!" Charmaine insisted.

"Relax, ma'am, we'll be right back." The slim officer said, continuing towards the door.

They both exited the room.

The slim cop said to his partner as they headed for the Administrator's office down the hall. "Headquarters will lose their minds if we didn't call this in immediately."

"How right you are. Those Bronx detectives handling that Nevez case are going to enjoy this lead."

CHAPTER # 13

Daquasha was standing next to Tykim as he haggled with the Corona Avenue Junkyard owner named Willie, who had two missing front teeth and his brown skin looked like old dried out leather. Willie's lips were so crusty, it looked like he kissed the flame of a blow torch. His blue jumpsuit was covered with axle grease and other grit and grime.

The three of them were standing near a wooden shack with old cars scattered all over the immediate area. Barking dogs violently rattling their restrictive chains could be heard; they were somewhere behind a pile of old cars in the back. Tykim was trying to get the price of the nearby sky blue 1991 Lincoln Continental down from $2,000 to $1,500.

Daquasha noticed the junkyard owner, Willie, kept looking at her with lust in his eyes and a twisted smile on his beat-up face. She saw Tykim noticed and was struggling not to react in a jealous fashion.

"I can sell this ride for $2,500," Willie insisted. "I dropped it $500 to avoid all this going back and forth in the first place. You ain't gonna find a deal like this in the whole damn city."

"Look at all those dents," Tykim pointed at the door. "And that knocking sound in the engine means there's a problem with the rocker arms. I'll be lucky if I get 2,000 miles out of this ride before I have to get a new engine. This car ain't worth $2,000, man . . ."

As they went back and forth, Daquasha realized those four slices of pizza with extra cheese and olives had made her even more sleepy. She had a huge shopping bag in her hand and thought they were going to look quite ridiculous when they put on the wigs, mustache and beards and the old folks clothing they purchased at a novelty store on Merrick Blvd.

Daquasha's frustration was growing; she was seconds from telling Tykim to just give the man the damn $2,000 so they could get the hell moving. She calmed herself down, realizing Tykim only got close to four gees for the jewelry he sold at a pawnshop over on Linden Blvd. According to their calculations, even if they spent $1,500 on a car, they would still be gambling with catastrophe, but to spend $2,000 would virtually guarantee it.

Daquasha turned and watched the street, Corona Avenue. Cars were cruising by both ways. She could see the front end of the green Mazda they drove here in. About twenty seconds later, she saw a police car cruise by. Her heart picked up speed as she held her breath. She instantly felt the urge to spin the ring on her pinkie finger. Daquasha saw the cop car had kept going and wasn't going to double back. She sighed in relief.

Daquasha was seconds from allowing her frustration to explode; she wanted to get the hell out of this muddy, dirty and filthy junkyard. She sighed out loud, but Tykim and Willie paid her no attention. Suddenly, something blue in her peripheral vision snatched her attention. Her head turned with frantic speed. It was the police car. The officers were looking at the green Mazda. She turned to Tykim. "Do the knowledge! Cee Cipher Power!"

Tykim turned his head and his eyes sprung into a state of shock when he saw the police car.

Daquasha inconspicuously moved further into the junkyard when she saw the two officers got out of their patrol car and began examining the stolen vehicle more closely. She pretended she was looking at a car that was out of the cops eye shot. With her knees knocking with shivering anxiety, Daquasha's eyes were searching for somewhere to run and escape if that time should happen to come.

Tykim also moved out of the officers line of sight.

Willie wondered why Daquasha and Tykim were suddenly acting strange. He started looking around to see what was causing all this tension. When he saw the police, Willie instantly made the connection, but pretended he was still in the dark.

Tykim realized he had to do something quick without inciting any suspicion. "You got a bathroom around here?"

Willie pointed. "It's in the back. Go straight down this aisle and make a right when you pass the second pile of cars." They ain't fooling nobody; these two are running from the police. Willie turned and saw the two police officers entering his junkyard. He headed towards them.

Tykim saw Daquasha peering around an old red Dodge van. He rushed to her while looking in back of him as he moved towards her.

Daquasha whispered excitedly. "We gotta find a back way outta of here. They know that car is stolen by now!"

"Don't panic, Daquasha," Tykim grabbed her by the arm and pulled her down the aisle. "Let's just hope this guy don't flip out. I think he knows what time it is with snitchin'. He might keep it real, he looks like he's from the old school. A lot of them old school cats are serious about that telling business."

"Fuck that might shit," Daquasha stared at Tykim like he had lost his mind when he leaned against a dirty white Volvo and patiently folded his arms. "Let's find a way out of here. We gotta find a back entrance or something. What are we waiting for!?"

Tykim sighed. "There ain't but one way in and one way out. Remember when I drove around this place a couple times before entering? Well, that was to see what we were walking into."

Daquasha stood looking at Tykim with her mouth hung open. After a moment, she leaned against the car next to him, wondering how much time they would give her for all the stuff they was going to charge her with? When she realized she may never see another day as a free woman, Daquasha decided she'd rather try her luck shooting her way out of this trap, than bowing down gracefully.

£¥♥   £¥♥   £¥♥   £¥♥

Devil-dog's head bobbed to the deep, heavy bass coming from the jeep's speakers. GPX was the name of the rap song played and was loud enough to barely be heard. There was no need to draw any unwarranted attention to themselves, Devil-dog decided as he drove down Corona Avenue. He saw a huge Junkyard up ahead. There were auto repair shops, tire shops and a couple of auto parts stores all over the place.

Lunatic was smoking a cigarette while humming along and tapping his foot to the beat.

They had been traveling all around Queens for the pass three hours, checking all the pawnshops, jewelry stores and any place they thought someone would try to sell jewelry. Devil-dog was two seconds from splitting Joker's helmet wide open until the white meat was revealed, since he was no help at all. He wondered how did this imbecile survive this long in the 'hood? Usually, idiots and folks soft in the head either stayed locked up or was six feet under. It was a rare occasion to find such a person running a whole network of players. Devil-dog felt Joker was about as bright as an old rusty set of dumbbells, and that was a gross understatement.

Devil-dog saw the police car up ahead and reflectively reached over and turned the CD player off. He scrutinized the car the two cops were looking at. "Oh, shit! It's a green Mazda."

Lunatic was enthralled. "It's stolen too. The way they checkin' it out, it's hot."

The Jeep slid pass the police car. Devil-dog and Lunatic's eyes absorbed the activities going on inside the junkyard as the police searched the insides of the Mazda. They also saw a black man dressed in mechanic's clothing approaching the police.

Devil-dog drove two blocks down the Avenue and made a U-turn. He double parked the Jeep and watched the police. The black mechanic was talking to the cops. About ten minutes later, Devil-dog saw the police rushed to their patrol car and drove off. He concluded they must have gotta an emergency call.

"This mechanic cat gotta know something," Devil-dog said as he put the Jeep in drive and headed towards the junkyard.

"We going inside there!?" Joker asked stupidly.

"What the fuck you think!?" Lunatic barked. "How the fuck else we supposed to find out what's going on." He turned in the seat. "You ain't no help at all, Joker. You supposed to be here to help us move around Queens. You don't know shit about this borough! Now, would I be wrong for fuckin' you up for that?" He saw Joker shake his head no and then turned back around.

Devil-dog parked the jeep across the street from the entrance of the junkyard. He scanned the area, realizing he had to question the mechanic quickly. As he got out the Jeep, Devil-dog hoped if Tykim purchased a car from here, it wasn't too long ago.

£¥♥   £¥♥   £¥♥   £¥♥

Moments earlier, Daquasha was nervously watching the two police talking to Willie. She was peeking around a Chevy Nova. Tykim was standing next to her. With her heart racing, her knees trembling and the sense of imminent doom dancing through her veins, Daquasha couldn't believe her eyes when she saw the police officers rushing towards their patrol car. They were leaving! When the police car pulled off, she turned and spoke excitedly to Tykim. "Let's go." She was about to take off.

Tykim grabbed her arm. "Wait! The police could be laying in the cut. Just give it a minute or two."

Daquasha instantly realized Tykim made plenty sense. She relaxed and maintained her position. Watching Willie examine the stolen Mazda, she was dying to know what the hell he told the cops. It was apparent he didn't tell the cops about them, otherwise they would have began searching the junkyard. *Or would they? Oh, shit! Maybe the police left to go get back-up!?* Daquasha's mind started running wild.

Suddenly, Daquasha saw a blue Jeep pull up and parked across the street. A black man got out and headed across the street.

"Shit!" Tykim sighed loudly. "That's one of the dudes who was shootin' at us at Kamel's crib." Tykim pulled both silencer equipped 9mms. Mental images of that moment the two men rushed into the back room of Kamel's apartment while he was standing on the fire escape looking inside twirled in his mind.

Daquasha pulled the 9mm from the shopping bag. This was the weapon Tykim gave her at Kamel's apartment. The gun felt heavy and dangerous. She never thought there would come a day when she would wield a weapon that could inflict death and destruction upon other human beings and be anxious to use it, but her survival instinct was turned on full volume.

£¥♥   £¥♥   £¥♥   £¥♥

Devil-dog approached Willie, who was looking inside the Mazda. "Excuse me, Mister, can I have a word with you?"

Willie looked up and pulled a hand-clothe from his pocket, wiping his filthy hands. He said nothing, waiting for Devil-dog to get closer.

"Where's the owner of this car right here?" Devil-dog pointed at the Mazda. His eyes were covertly scanning the interior of the junkyard. He saw movement and honed in on the area it came from. It was a woman. She had pulled back behind a car as if she was hiding. Devil-dog's anxiety revved up.

"A man and a woman drove up, got out and walked in this direction." Willie pointed. "The police were just here and they said this car was stolen. Is it yours?"

"Naw, it ain't mine. I was thinking about buying it for parts. I got one like it that needs some body work." His eyes were still nonchalantly observing the area where he saw movement.

"The police said they're coming right back with a tow truck." Willie sensed this guy was up to no good. His whole persona emanated danger and bloodshed. "They just left a couple of minutes ago. From the way they sounded, they comin' right back."

Devil-dog conducted another observation of the junkyard and shifted his position when he saw the peeking face once again. He locked eyes with whoever it was and the person's head frantically pulled away. Devil-dog held back the smile. "Thank you, mister." He turned and headed for the Jeep. Devil-dog got in and drove off.

"Must be good news in the air," Lunatic said, "Whatever it is, I see the shit got you smiling." He smiled even broader than Devil-dog.

"We gonna post up right here," Devil-dog made a U-turn and double parked. "I think they're inside that junkyard. Call Brute and tell him to get over here immediately."

As Lunatic dialed the number, Devil-dog mumbled to himself. "This shit is gonna be over soon. I can feel it in my bones."

£¥♥   £¥♥   £¥♥   £¥♥

Daquasha's heart pounded as she followed Tykim. They were heading towards Willie, who was re-entering the junkyard. Daquasha saw Willie had that usual smile on his face. She couldn't get Devil-dog's face out of her mind. The urge to get far away from this area grew to monolithic proportions. Devil-dog saw her; she was sure of it. Something in the back of her mind assured her he was either coming back or was out there waiting for them to make their break.

Tykim spoke to Willie in an excited fashion. "What did the police want?"

With a knowing smile, Willie said, "I don't know what y'all up to or what y'all done did, but the police is comin' back to tow that car." He spoke as he headed for the shack. Tykim and Daquasha followed. "They said it's stolen. I ain't tell them about y'all 'cause I would sure hate to see this young lady here, as fine as she is, get into trouble." He stopped at the front door.

"Listen, mister," Tykim pulled the money from his pocket. "All I got is $1,700. Please, Willie, we need that car. If I had the $2,000 I would give it to you. Here, take it all. If I had more, I'm telllin' you, man, I would give it to you. Yo, I appreciate you not puttin' five-oh on us. Thanks, man." He handed him the money.

Willie took the web of bills, counted them, peeled off three hundred dollars and gave it back to Tykim. "Y'all gonna need this more than me." He entered the shack. "This is my good deed for the week." He activated his cash machine.

Daquasha gave Willie her best smile when he looked up. "Thank you, mister."

Ten minutes later, Daquasha and Tykim drove out of the junkyard with temporary license plates on the Lincoln. They turned right and scooted down the Avenue.

Looking out the back windshield, Daquasha was waiting to see the blue Jeep.

"What's wrong, Daquasha?" Tykim said, looking out the rear view mirror.

"I think that dude from the blue jeep saw me when I was peeking around the car," She still maintained her seating arrangement. When she saw the blue Jeep pulled onto the street and began following them, Daquasha faced forward. "Damn it! They're following us!" She dug in the shopping bag, pulled the 9mm and held on to it.

The speed of the Lincoln jumped 15 notches within 10 seconds when Tykim's foot pressed down on the gas pedal.

CHAPTER # 14

Detective Guzmon pulled the two mug shots of Daquasha and Tykim from his pocket and handed them to the pawnshop owner. This particular shop was located on Forest Hill Avenue. "The jewelry they're trying to hack has diamonds chips."

The shopkeeper was a short, chubby white man with a huge forehead and beady eyes. Staring at the photos, he shook his head. "Haven't seen them." He handed the pictures back.

Guzmon reached in his pocket, retrieved one of his calling cards and handed it to the man. "Please give us a call immediately if they re-visit your place of business."

"No problem."

Guzmon and Armstrong exited the shop. The doorbell tingled loudly as the door closed behind them. They entered their vehicle and pulled off. Guzmon was in the passenger seat and Armstrong did the driving.

"Make a right turn on Baisley Blvd," Guzmon said, "The next shop should be about ten blocks down after that turn." After a moment of silence, Guzmon continued. "They're getting desperate. And when desperation rears its ugly head, so does recklessness and carelessness. Mistakes are bound to follow. Hopefully, we'll be close by to monopolize on them. As long as they keep a money problem, they'll have to run the streets."

"From what Ms. Wilson claims, there's a contract on Mr. Hall. If it's large enough, which I would assume it is, their roaming the streets could work to our disadvantage. Ms. Lawrence is worthless to us dead."

Guzmon wanted to tell Armstrong what he was saying was obvious, and his suggesting that he hadn't figured that out was an assault on his intelligence, but instead, he went into a state of deep thought.

Two minutes later, the car's cellular phone buzzed and Guzmon picked up the receiver. "Detective Guzmon speaking." His eyes and facial response showed no emotions. However, what was being told to him was very compelling. Watching the streets, the stores and the pedestrians, Guzmon spoke calmly through his excitement. "Tell the tow trucker to hold fast. We're on our way. Over and out." He sat the receiver back in its tray. "They found the Mazda. It's at a junkyard on Corona Avenue. The occupants of that vehicle, black male and female, are traveling on foot and should still be in the area. Attach that flasher and let's see if you still got that lead in your foot . . ."

£¥♥   £¥♥   £¥♥   £¥♥

Daquasha struggled not to let her panicked state of mind cause her to go overboard and do something stupid, out of haste. She felt the car wasn't moving fast enough, even though common sense told her if they fled in a reckless fashion, they were bound to draw the attention of the police. Cop cars could be anywhere, and all it took was a fast moving vehicle to bring them into this chase. Each time the Jeep got close, Daquasha ducked down into the seat, expecting bullets to start flying.

Daquasha noticed her nervousness was not as intense as it was last night. Maybe she was becoming desensitized to all this drama. She saw Tykim's eyes were practically glued to the rear view mirror. Although he kept his speed at a sensible rate, Tykim never permitted the pace to drop to a speed that would allow the Jeep to get side by side with the Lincoln. It was about high noon, the streets were crowded, and she knew this was probably the only reason those men following them hadn't opened fire.

Tykim's instinct and his knowledge of the hit game were telling him to do something quickly; there was little doubt in his mind more hitters were on the way to assist in this cat and mouse game. He had a plan. Twice Tykim was about to implement it, but the timing of the traffic lights didn't match up.

With his two silenced weapons lying neatly in his lap, Tykim cut his eyes at Daquasha and saw she was finally waking up to the reality of their situation. If they tried to retain a state of non-violent, and a waiting for shit to happen type attitude, they might as well go to the police station, turn themselves in and spend the rest of their lives behind bars. In fact, it would be hazardous to their health to keep running without acquiring a going all out, no non-sense attitude. The way Daquasha was holding the gun in her hand, looked real sexy to him. If it wasn't so much drama in the air, his dick probably would've rose to the occasion and saluted her.

About two minutes later, Tykim saw the traffic lights were in order. The yellow light came on and he slammed his foot on the gas pedal. The Lincoln jerked and its engine roared as it raced towards the four lane cross section.

The light turned red.

The Lincoln barely made it to the first lane as the waiting cars started pulling into the intersection. Running the red light, Tykim whipped the steering wheel, with his hand pressed down on the horn. Two cars in the fourth lane stopped abruptly, missing a collision with the Lincoln by inches. Both cars blew their horns in retaliation and continued on their way.

Looking through the rear view mirror, Tykim saw it worked. "Yes!" He saw the driver of the Jeep tried to ease into the busy traffic, causing screaming tires to be heard. The traffic in all four lanes was now moving with a continuous flow. Tykim instantly realized he had to do something he didn't want to do; he increased his speed ten folds. He made a screeching right turn, raced the car to the next block, and then made a screaming left turn. All the while, Tykim was hoping the traffic light that held their pursuers at bay was a long stop light. He was hoping with equal force that the traffic was thick and continuous enough to prevent the Jeep from running the light.

Daquasha was turned around in the seat, watching the traffic in back of them. "It worked." She said softly. Her position was maintained for two straight minutes. She saw no blue jeep.

"We're out of this city," Tykim said, "We don't stop til New York City is at least twenty miles in back of us."

"That sounds good to me," Daquasha sat forward. She put the gun back in the shopping bag. Their disguises jumped into her attention. Pulling the items out of the bag while lying them next to her, Daquasha said, "It's probably a good time to start puttin' on these disguises. The Belt Parkway is minutes away." She handed Tykim the fake beard and mustache.

Tykim held the items in his hand. With his eyes on the road, Tykim said, "And how am I supposed to drive and put this stuff on?"

Daquasha snatched them back. "I thought you was mister self-contained, I figured that still applied." She peeled the adhesive covering off the back, scooted over towards Tykim and began gently placing the disguise on his face, making sure she didn't interfere with his driving. She felt in the mood to mess with Tykim's head, so she deliberately allowed her breasts and hip to touch him repeatedly.

Tykim felt her soft body touching his and he was bombarded with all sorts of memories. When her breast touched his arm, he felt his blood started racing. His mind flashed back to all those tender moments they had together. He wanted to reach over and kiss her soft lips. Suddenly, he felt himself becoming excited; his penis was coming alive. Quickly clearing his mind of all those explosive sexual memories, he felt the heat downstairs started to fizz out and he returned back to a state of calm.

Daquasha pulled the wig from the shopping bag and put it on. She then retrieved the granny style glasses and put them on. Daquasha turned the rearview mirror in her direction and examined herself. She definitely looked like the person she was trying to become; an old lady. Putting the rear-view mirror back in its original position, she noticed Tykim nodding his head approvingly. After Daquasha put on the big coat, she was set. She sat back comfortable and said nothing for a long while, wondering what lay ahead. Tykim had a plan, that much was certain. "When are we gonna get some sleep?"

"When the sun goes down, I'll start looking for a hotel. By then I think we might be in Delaware. We should be safe then."

"So, where we going after that?" Daquasha said softly. "And how do our future look?"

"As a fugitive to a fellow fugitive," Tykim smiled at her, trying to cater to her well known love for men who had a strong sense of humor. He changed his voice, speaking with a heavy English accent. "I would say our future is bleak, gloomy and filled with much pain, great suffering and plentiful hardship."

Tykim saw Daquasha didn't find his little comic relief humorous, and so he returned to a state of seriousness. "All jokes aside, I think we should make a stop in Atlanta Georgia. I got a cousin down there who might be able to help us. When we get there, we can hustle up some money, get some fake IDs good enough to give us new identities, and head for South America. Then, maybe we could slide over to Cuba or one of those Caribbean Islands where America don't got too much influence over the country."

Daquasha thought about Tykim's proposal. The idea of not being able to settle down somewhere scared her. Tykim's suggestions sounded like they were going to be on the move for quite some time. How was she gonna bear a child while on the run from the law and hit-men? Should she tell Tykim about her condition? That was out of the question. She wasn't going to tell Tykim anything. At least not yet.

The thought of having an abortion entered Daquasha's mind. Her fingers went to work on the ring, rotating it with a smooth unconscious intensity. Murdering a part of her was unspeakable. Killing herself was out of the question. She seen so much death throughout her life, and it terrified her to even consider killing her child.

Daquasha decided conclusively she would have this child. But what kind of mother to this child was she going to be? How could she be a fugitive and raise a child? Wouldn't that be the equivalent of bringing this child into a world of massive chaos, one replete with pain and suffering? Yes, it would.

Of course it would. How could she claim to love this child and knowingly bring it into a world of suffering?

"So, how that plan sound to you?" Tykim inquired.

"It's a plan, that's for sure. I guess I'm in, since you don't have a choice. What's this thing about we gonna hustle up some money. What you got in mind?

Tykim didn't want to break the unfortunate news to her so early, but since she asked, she obviously had a right to know. "Well, first I gotta talk to my cousin, Nuke. But, this much I will say. He's been trying to get me to come down there and do some stick ups with him for a long time. That kind of shit ain't never really been my thing. But, he always made it clear if I changed my mind, I could always come down there and check him out. Now is that time."

"I hope it's not sticking up Banks. That would be a stupid move because we'll be piling on problems. Not to mention, that's federal stuff. I ain't with it, if that's what you planning."

"Calm down," Tykim liked the fact she was smart enough to know the dangers of robbing Banks. "We ain't robbing no Banks. I'm with you on that; it's dangerous and stupid. We probably gonna rob drug dealers, number runners, anyone involved in the underworld. The benefits are obvious, but the downside is also obvious."

Daquasha sighed. "Shit, don't you think that's almost as bad? At least with the Banks, we ain't gotta worry about bullets flying without warning."

"We need money and there ain't a lot of other ways to get it, especially in the amount we're gonna need to get out of the country."

"Like I said, I guess we don't have much of a choice." She went into her personally world of silence.

Daquasha looked down over New York Bay as they rode across the Verrazano-Narrows Bridge. Her anxiety finally disappeared to such an extent, her inquisitivity started setting in. "What you been up to all these years? By the look of your girl, Charmaine, I see you been scrapping the bottom of the barrel."

Tykim glanced over at Daquasha. "You gotta lotta nerve talkin' about scrapping the bottom of the barrel. Stripping butt ass naked and showing off your goods, ain't the most noblest occupation this city has to offer."

"Fuck you, Tykim," She hated his brazen, foul mouth way of responding to everything she shot at him.

"I still can't understand how this clown ass nigga Jamil would let something as fine and gorgeous as you work in a goddamn strip club." He shook his head with a twisted up mouth piece. "That nigga gotta be outta his fuckin' mind."

"Unlike your power struck ass, Jamil has an open mind and respects my choices. Our relationship ain't based on what he feels is appropriate for his ego. I'm a performer. I'm a professional dancer, who makes an honest living." She suddenly remembered why she started working in strip clubs. The anger erupted in an explosive fashion. "And why should it concern you any way! If it wasn't for you . . ." She clamped down on her comment, sizzling with rage.

"I admit, stripping is an honest job. It's far better than selling ass on a street corner or pumping poisons into our community. I just can't see why you, of all people, would settle for such a livelihood. I always saw you as one day becoming an executive of a big-time business or a lawyer or something like that."

"And look at you," Daquasha's snotty attitude was filled with disgust. "You running around killing people for money. Now, that is foul. You can't go no lower than that! So before you start throwing bricks in a glass house, you need to look in the mirror and check ya self."

"Wow! That hurt," Tykim sighed. "Yeah, I do hits every now and then. But all cats that get it from me are drug dealers."

"Bullshit!" Daquasha said through clenched teeth. "I wasn't a fuckin' drug dealer and you came to kill me!"

"In your case it was different. The price on your head was too big to turn down. And they made it look like you was down with drug dealing. Ain't Jamil a drug dealer? Shit, if anything, you should be glad they hired me. If someone else had picked up that contract, your ass would be dead and stink by now."

"After all the shit you put me through, it's about fuckin' time you started paying for the damage you've done."

There was a long moment of silence.

Tykim knew she was right. "I ain't mean nothing by the remark about you're stripping, baby girl."

Daquasha was about to check him about the use of that phase "baby girl", since this was the name he called her when they were dealing with each other years ago.

Tykim continued, "I just expected more from you. But what you're doing is cool. Hey, who am I to judge anyway, right? My shit is definitely twisted. I was just wondering what caused you to get involved in that line of work?"

"Well, put it this way," Daquasha was holding back her explosive anger with everything she had in her. "Thanks to you, I'm who I am."

Tykim was about to respond in his usual sarcastic fashion, but what she said had a tremendous amount of truth to it. He pondered her answer with intense vigor. When Tykim thought about the incident that destroyed their relationship, he did see how his major fuck up could have lead her to this. But, there was something Daquasha wasn't telling him. "Daquasha, I'm sorry for even bringing up your occupation. And you're right, dancing is--"

"Fuck you, Tykim! Don't say shit to me!"

Tykim knew that meant talk time was officially over. He focused his attention on the road in front of him and on what they would do when they got to Atlanta.

Daquasha watched the Staten Island landscape with lock-jawed anger percolating in her heart, mind and soul. Her mother came into her mind and she fought to shift her thoughts to something else. Her baby brother inched his way into her thought process, then her father started fading in and out. If she could have one wish; she wouldn't ask for all the money in the world, nor would she ask to live forever; she would ask that they all be brought back to life. Mom, dad and her baby brother; her whole family, all the loves ones she loved as much as she loved herself. Why did they have to die!? Her mother's words echoed in her head, "Family is everything."

The tears were moments from surfacing, but Daquasha defeated the waterfall by focusing on the good times from her past. She closed her eyes, got in a comfortable position, and propped her head on the car door. Her tiredness was so powerful, it soothed the burning sensation in her heart when she decided to submit to the ravaging force of sleep. With a hidden smile, Daquasha thought back to the time when her whole family were alive and living in Bedstuy Brooklyn.

As Daquasha spiraled downward into a vivid and remarkably realistic dream world, her restless and turmoil stricken soul and inner being were in a state of serenity. She was eight years old and her father, Terrance Lawrence, was playing with her and her four year old brother, Tareek. Her mother, Danielle Lawrence, stood on the sideline looking on with great pleasure regulating her facial expression. Daquasha's joyful laughter and giggles were filled with love and admiration. These wonderful moments re-lived themselves in Daquasha's dreams on a regular basis. Oh, what she wouldn't do to get her family back. Yes, family was everything.

As usual, her dreams progressed into a nightmare. That day when her mother told her, Terrance, her father died at Attica State Prison, was the spark that lit the fuse that blew up the family foundation. Initially, her mother never told her how her daddy died, but it had to be a violent death she surmised because her friends told her men in prison did mean things and that all prisoners had to be mean in order to survive in such a violent and hostile environment.

When Daquasha was twelve years old, she found out her father died during a knife fight with another prisoner. Around that time, she also discovered her father was in prison for shooting and killing a man who killed his brother, her uncle Hakim, over a gambling debt and was serving a five to fifteen year sentence for manslaughter. She often visualized her father being stabbed to death while screaming for help. She would hear her daddy screaming her name.

"Daquasha! Daquasha!"

The name calling was always so vivid and realistic, and filled with great pain. She would scream in desperation, assuring her father she would help him. "I'm here daddy! I'm here for you."

"Okay, okay. You here for your daddy," Tykim saw Daquasha's sleep drenched eyes slowly opened. He killed the ignition. "Wow, that was one mean dream, baby girl. You talk in your sleep like that all the time? 'Cause if you do, we gotta get separate rooms."

With a crackling voice, Daquasha said, "Fuck you, Tykim," She sat up right, feeling embarrassed by her frantic sleep talking. Her granny glasses had fallen off her face and her wig was in disarray. Looking around, she saw it was night outside and they were parked in a parking lot. A white brick building was in front of them. The surrounding grass was neat and everything looked clean and country like. Her neck was throbbing with agonizing soreness. "What time is it?" She pulled her shirt sleeve up and glanced at her watch. It was almost 7 o'clock. She was surprised she slept so long. It felt like only minutes had gone by. "Where are we?" She unleashed a joint snapping stretch.

"Delaware, just like I predicted. Come on now, fix yourself up. We gonna get us a hotel room, eat, and sleep. I'm so tired, I'm gonna need at least twelve hours of sleep in order to get my shit together." Tykim opened his door.

Daquasha fixed herself up and exited the car. Her legs wobbled momentarily as she followed Tykim towards the hotel. After several strides, her legs were operating correctly.

They entered the hotel and Tykim purchased a room on the second floor. The clerk gave him a key, and they went to the restaurant on the first floor. After they each ate a $30 dish consisting of rice, black beans, Salmon, broccoli, fried cabbage, and for dessert, there was sweet potato pie with butter almond ice cream, they entered their room. They both were so full they felt miserable.

Tykim checked out all the rooms thoroughly. The place was real clean and smelled like raspberry and jasmine perfume. The polished wood floors gave the place that elegant and regal type feeling. He entered the bedroom and approached the bed.

Daquasha stopped at the threshold of the bedroom, watching him.

Messaging the soft, but firm mattress, Tykim said with a smile. "I guess one side is your zone, and the other is mine." Pointing at her teasingly, he moved towards Daquasha. "Now, I don't want you crossing my border line."

Daquasha knew this was coming, but she was going to bust his bubble. "I'm using this bed. You can sleep on the sofa, the floor or even the kitchen table, but it won't be in here! I don't sleep with no man, who ain't my man. And we ain't about to start no bad habits. There will never be a you and me, ever again!" She scooted pass Tykim and went to the closet.

"Wait a minute now," Tykim followed in her footsteps. "I should have some say in this shit. That sofa out there looks like it's gonna fuck up my lower back."

Daquasha turned and crossed her arms, tapping her foot impatiently.

"Listen, Daquasha, I ain't tryin' to get in your draws, if that's what you spazzing out about. I need to sleep in a bed. I been up runnin' around tryin' to protect your ass for damn near thirty somethin' hours straight. The last thing I need is my back going out on me."

Daquasha suddenly felt sorry for him. She sighed and was about to give in, but when she locked eyes with Tykim, realizing he was the root of her current misery, she instantly snapped back into reality. She had to be firm. "We ain't sleeping in the same fuckin' bed and that's that." She turned, picked up her shopping bag and headed for the bed. "Now, who's gonna use the shower first, you or me?" She spilled the contents on the bed.

Tykim was about to spazz the fuck out, but his conscious and heart agreed to let her get her shit off. She deserved it and vis-a-versa he deserved it coming from her. "I'll go first, if it's really all right with you." He shuffled out of the room.

Tykim took a twenty minute shower and exited the bathroom.

Daquasha waited ten minutes to make sure he was either dressed or lying down on the sofa before heading for the bathroom. As Daquasha approached the bathroom, she saw Tykim's naked body through her peripheral vision. He was standing near the mini bar, fixing a drink. She wanted to curse his ass out because he was streaking around the damn apartment. If he was planning to get dressed, he apparently would have by now. She pretended she didn't see him as she entered the bathroom.

Twenty five minutes later, she exited the bathroom and saw Tykim was lying on the sofa. A white sheet covered his body, the lights were out and he appeared to be sleep. Daquasha was glad there wasn't going to be any drama. Not that she was worried about Tykim as far as him trying to gorilla her out of a piece of pussy, but she knew he had no problem begging for some. She was still tired and her anger was still at its high point.

Daquasha laid down and got under the covers. Sleep swarmed over her mind almost instantly. Damn, she was tired. She knew all the adrenaline flooding her system along with the ever-present fear, and the over exertion of her body for so many relentless hours was manifesting themselves in the only way they knew how. She faded into a dream-world, and this one was truly painful.

A hour flew by and the sweat eased from the pores all over her body. Another hour after that and she was talking in her sleep. At three o'clock in the morning, she was crying in her sleep like a baby. When she started fighting in her sleep, Daquasha swung and kicked at an imaginary opponent. She sprung up into a sitting position, breathing like she'd just been involved in a real live knuckle thumping brawl.

Daquasha cried even harder; she felt she was losing herself. Her mind was slipping away from her grasp as she was she struggling through the tears. Tykim had to pay for what he did to her. He had to be punished. She had dreamed about this moment for years, and tonight it was going down! Daquasha got out of bed in a state of delirious rage and grabbed the shopping bag. Violently searching the bag, Daquasha found what she was looking for. She held the silencer equipped 9mm with trembling hands. Daquasha was glad Tykim exchanged this weapon with the other one that didn't have a silencer. Making a lot of noise was not going to be a wise move.

Staring at the gun, Daquasha realized it was amazing how fast the heart could change so suddenly. It was even more perplexing how things had a remarkable way of working themselves out. That song, it's a thin line between love and hate, was twinkling through her mind.

Breathing like a ferocious bull, Daquasha stomped out of the room, heading towards the sofa. She positioned herself directly in front of Tykim, beaming down at him with the weapon aimed at his chest. Her tears flowed as freely as the Nile river. She wanted him to be awake when she let him have it.

Daquasha spoke softly. "Tykim, wake up! Wake up, Tykim."

When Daquasha saw his eyes slowly opening, and then sprung into huge round circles upon detecting the gun, she said in a devious manner. "You killed my brother! Now I'm gonna kill you, motherfucker!"

Tykim moved in an hysterical fashion, but the bright flash was far too fast   for   him.

CHAPTER # 15

"Man, I think you fucked up," Lunatic said to Devil-dog, who sat on a sofa in a jazzy living room smoking a blunt. Lunatic was pacing. "You shouldn't of lied to him. Now, if he finds out, I'm gonna be done off along with you." Lunatic took a seat in a matching arm chair across from Devil-dog.

"How they say it?" Devil-dog blew out a cloud of smoke. "Speak now or forever hold your peace. When you ain't say nothin', you basically said you was down with the program." He sat the blunt in the ashtray on the coffee table, got up and headed for the kitchen. He spoke as he searched through the refrigerator. "Relax. How is he gonna find out we lost them during a chase? I ain't gonna say shit, neither is you."

Devil-dog found the can of Old English malt liquor and returned to the living room. "Joker may be a stupid motherfucker, but he ain't got no death wish. Brute ain't gonna say shit 'cause the ax will fall on his ass too." He sat in his original seat on the sofa, opened the can of malt liquor, took a swig, sat the can down, retrieved his blunt, and inhaled a huge cloud of smoke into his lungs. He started coughing and handed it to Lunatic.

Lunatic took the blunt, and held it as he spoke. "You amaze me, you know that. Just that fast you forget that time when those cats from Jersey lied to Kilroy about shuttin' down that spot, and all three of 'em mutha-fuckas disappeared." He sucked on the blunt, savoring the smoke that swirled in his lungs. He released the smoke, and said, "You and I both know Kilroy got crews all over the fuckin' place. That nigga don't trust no goddamn body. He got crews checkin' on one crew while another crew is checkin' that crew, and even then he got another crew checkin' the crew who supposed to be checkin' the other crew." He took another toke.

Devil-dog laughed. "That's a whole lot of checkin' goin' on. Listen, Lunatic, right now Kilroy ain't gonna flip out on us. We about the most loyal hitters he got on this job. He knows this is one of 'em touch and go situations. Plus, as long as the police ain't got Tykim and Danielle, he ain't gonna beef. Shit, man, since Danielle is runnin' the streets, we accomplished a part our mission. Kilroy just wants to keep her from testifying at the grand jury. Now, Tykim, that's something else."

Lunatic nodded his head and then puffed on the blunt. Passing the blunt to Devil-dog, Lunatic looked at his watch. Smoke fumed from his mouth as he spoke. "In about another hour, we gotta go down to Brooklyn. I told you, I got this kid out there who said he grew up with Tykim. He supposed to know all about him. He knows Tykim's family and all that good shit. This cat is looking for money, but I think he's on point. Can't hurt to check this chump out."

"We gotta be back before 6 o'clock." Devil-dog snuffed out the blunt in the ashtray. "Tonight's Johnny B and Light's wake and funeral." He took a huge gulp of the malt liquor and burped loudly.

Lunatic leaned back comfortably in the chair. His heart went out for his comrades. "That mutha-fucka Tykim is gonna pay for this shit. The day before, we went to Hector's funeral. Yesterday we went to Alley-bush and Two-face's, now it's Johnny B and Light." He was seething with anger. "Oh, man, I can't wait to bang out with this mutha-fucka."

Devil-dog's anger rose four levels. Just being reminded of the losses had his head throbbing with rage. "That bitch ass nigga knocked off five of us. He ain't gettin' away with this shit. This ain't business no more, it's personal."

£¥♥   £¥♥   £¥♥   £¥♥

"There's gotta be a way," Jamil was sitting at a table across from his lawyer, Mr. Ron Cody, Esq., who had sandy brown hair, was dressed in a navy blue pinstripe suit, and his face was clean shaved. The HDM attorney/client conference room was about the size of two large housing project closets. The dingy, depressing green colored walls were peeling and chipping from years of neglect.

Shaking his head, Jamil said, "If you was able to find out it's a woman, why can't you go a step further and find out her name?"

"Mr. Nevez," Ron sighed, this topic was making him very uncomfortable. He never trusted jail-house conference rooms, since there was a strong possibility there were hidden microscopic listening devices planted somewhere in this room. Even though the law forbid such activity, when juxtaposed with the fact that this was a high profile case and New York City law enforcement officials had no problem violating black defendants' constitutionally protected rights, unlawful eavesdropping was something that would naturally be expected to occur. He had told Kilroy to make sure Jamil didn't engage him in a discussion on this particular topic when he came to visit.

Ron pulled a pencil and piece of paper from his briefcase and started writing a message down as he spoke. "This is not the appropriate time to discuss that part of the case, Mr. Nevez. I'm here to determine what are the basic facts of this case. No more, no less." There was a short pause as he continued writing. "I understand your concerns, but please bear with me; at least until I have determined the preliminary stuff." He slid the paper to Jamil.

Jamil started reading. It said, "This is not the place for talk of that nature. I have friends who assured me it was a woman. If you like, I'll continue investigating this matter. If you want a name, finding it is considered an unrelated employment endeavor."

Jamil looked up momentarily and spoke as he wrote a message in response. "That night, I was across town." Jamil stopped talking, realized writing and talking wasn't as simple as Ron made it look. "I ain't have shit to do with them murders." He stopped talking again, but continued writing. "I was hanging out at this club called the Paradise Lounge." He slid the paper back to the lawyer.

"I see," Ron said as he speed read the response which said, "If you get me that name, I will personally give you $100,000." He gave Jamil a smile, a head nod and erased the pencil writings. Folding the paper, he tucked it in his pocket, planning to rip it up and flush it down the toilet the first chance he got. "Mr. Nevez, are there any witnesses who can support this alibi of yours?"

"Maybe the people at the club," Jamil was about to say Danielle Lewis, but he knew she might be the police witness. "I need you to explain the entire grand jury process for me."

As Ron Cody explained the process, Jamil was listening intently, but at the same time his mind was thinking about other things. He hated the fact that they weren't 100% certain who this witness was. The word on the street was that Tykim had backed down Kilroy's hit mob and he and Danielle were on the run from both the police and the hitters. He also heard the police were snooping around Danielle's apartment before the hitters were on to her, which made him wonder if she really was the snitch.

Things weren't making sense, Jamil concluded yesterday upon hearing all this information. If Danielle was snitchin', how the hell was the police able to arrest him without her already being totally and completely under their control? He knew they had to have some kind of physical evidence to get an arrest warrant.

After pondering numerous questions along these lines, Jamil decided he had to take matters into his own hands. Kilroy hated Danielle. This was a universal fact no one could deny. The voice in the back of his head was repeatedly telling him something was wrong with this whole situation. His intuition was also telling him that Kilroy might have either prematurely jumped to conclusions or was bent on killing Danielle because of his personal dislike of the woman. This was when he decided he had to get the specific name of this allege female witness.

Ron concluded his explanation with, ". . .as it stands, your case will be presented to the grand jury within the next three days. I suspect it will occur the day after tomorrow. With this in mind, I want to know would you be interested in testifying before the grand jury? Pursuant to CPL 190.25, you have a right to be notified of this right to testify. However, before you answer this question, I advise you not to exercise this right. For strategic purposes, it's never a wise move to lock yourself in a sworn statement so early in the case."

Jamil really didn't need that little extra added piece of advice because he had no intentions of testifying at anybody's grand jury. In fact, he had no intentions of letting anybody else either. "I'll take your advice. I'm not testifying at this grand jury."

"One more thing we need to discuss in depth, Mr. Nevez," Ron pulled several documents from his briefcase. "I need you to fill out these forms. They're background information forms." He slid them over to Jamil. "As you can see, we're gonna need to know everything you've done throughout your life. Since this is a capital punishment case, if we should happen to blow trial, we'll have to present evidence to mitigate a death sentence--"

"Wait a minute, man," Jamil was tight around the collar. "Ain't no need to start planning to blow fuckin' trial. Shit, we should at least get pass this grand jury thing first."

"Mr. Nevez," Ron sighed. "This is not to imply that we're gonna blow trial. I need this information so we can start the process as early as possible." He smiled inwardly because he enjoyed seeing these thugsters sweat and tremble when the reality of the death penalty started to set in. He was tempted to up that price another $50,000. By the look in this guy's eyes, he'd probably give him every single dime he had in exchange for avoiding the wrath of old Sparky. "I didn't mean to upset you, Mr. Nevez. But, we have to develop and maintain a strict policy where we do not wait for the last minute to do things that are crucial to an effective and meaningful defense. Your life is on the line as you know. One foot dragging mistake can cost you the ultimate price."

Jamil nervously swallowed hard, but held firm to his thuggish persona.

Ron gave into the temptation. He pulled the same piece of paper from his pocket and wrote, "However, for an additional $75,000, I'll find a way to get that name by tonight." He slid the paper to Jamil.

Jamil read it. With a smile, he looked up. Jamil suddenly realized he didn't trust this bastard. This red neck cracker was trying to milk him. He wrote the following. "I'll give you a total of $200,000." He showed Ron the response, but instead of giving him the paper, he erased the markings and began ripping the paper into shreds. Then he began tossing the shredded paper into his mouth, chewing and swallowing the paper until it was all gone.

As Jamil sparked up another conversation about the grand jury, he saw the greedy look on the lawyer's face and he wondered if he was going to have to put a hit out on this conniving ass shyster. Jamil instantly sensed that this trifling motherfucker probably already had the name, but was trying to get paid for it. Jamil shifted his thoughts to the matter at hand. All the money he had access to meant nothing to him if he was dead, and if he had to give it all up to save his life, and get his freedom back as a result, then so be it.

But one thing was certain, Jamil decided conclusively; after he sent Brute over with that money, and if Ron didn't produce that name, he would find out how the dark-side, the biggest mystery of all mysteries (otherwise known as death), looked within the next week.

CHAPTER # 16

Daquasha felt strong regret.

She stared at the road in front of her as the Lincoln moved along at a pace well within the 55 miles per hour speed limit. Highway 95 was practically empty and the urge to open up the engine was very tempting. It was a dreary day; the sun was nowhere to be found and the rain clouds hung heavily over the Delaware landscape. The atmosphere was a perfect match with her mood.

She regretted what she did this morning. She felt guilty and was beating herself up inwardly. But the more she thought about the incident, the more she realized she reacted while in a sleep walking state; all induced by her nightmares. She couldn't believe she felt sorry for Tykim. After all the pain he'd caused her, he deserved no pity from her. Slowly her heart, mind and soul were transforming, allowing her to endure and even accept what had happened.

But she did feel good inside because she always knew she could never be a cold-blooded killer and this morning proved it. Glancing over at Tykim, who was behind the wheel of the Lincoln, Daquasha was still trying to determine if Tykim was telling the truth when he insisted he had no control over her baby brother Tareek's death. Her mind flashed back to this morning when she stood over Tykim with the 9mm.

At the moment Daquasha saw Tykim tried to grab the gun, she repositioned her aim and squeezed off a shot into the bathroom door. She fell completely to pieces, crumbling into a heap of tears, moans and sheer heart-shattering distress. As Tykim held her firmly in his arms, Daquasha back tracked their relationship in her sob-stricken mind.

At the tender age of 11, Daquasha met Tykim while they were in public school. Tykim was a year older then her and a grade above her. They initially met on bad terms, and by the time they were in junior high school, they were communicating with each other on a peaceful basis. It obviously wasn't a love at first sight situation, but after clashing with each other at parties and other social events, they started feeling each other and decided to go out on a few dates. Eventually they grew to love each other very dearly and became inseparable.

Although their relationship wasn't unlike all the other ghetto love relationships, but what made theirs different was they both believed they were soul mates. They did a little cheating on the side (experimenting) and got caught a couple of times, but the strength of the relationship was strong enough to withstand such ordeals.

Tykim was deeply caught up in the streets and the fast life, and eventually dropped out in the 10th grade, but Daquasha never abandoned him at times when he needed her most, nor did she give up trying to convince him to go straight. Daquasha's mother hated and liked Tykim. She always said he was like a healthy poison and couldn't understand what Daquasha saw in him because they appeared to be total opposites. Tykim was extremely rambunctious, a high school drop-out, wasteful with money and worked over-time to please people, while Daquasha was the quiet, shy type, very cautious with the way she handled money, completed high school, and didn't give a rat's ass whether people liked her or not. Daquasha's mother also didn't like the fact that Tareek (Daquasha's baby brother) was extremely fond of Tykim and looked at him as a role model and a big brother. There were many times when Mrs. Lawrence had to whip Tareek's behind when he tried to follow Tykim around the neighborhood.

When Tykim caught his first state bid (a four to twelve for assault with a firearm), Daquasha was there with him every step of the way, bringing him drugs and the whole nine yards. Daquasha was surprised by how Tykim was able to support her from behind a prison wall. Every week she would go to a P.O. Box to get checks and money orders ranging in the amount of three to five hundred dollars. The money got her so opened, it made her love Tykim even more. She knew what she was doing was wrong and dangerous, but she told herself the rules of capitalism made it all legitimate. Shit, everybody did a little skimming off the top; Politicians on down to Reverends. Why couldn't she and Tykim do the same?

Mrs. Lawrence didn't approve of her daughter dealing with a jail bird and tried to prevent Daquasha from going up state to see Tykim, without any luck. Mrs. Lawrence blamed her miserable life on Terrance's going back and forth to prison, and didn't want to see her daughter follow in her footsteps.

On almost every visit, Daquasha would constantly try to convince Tykim to go legal when he got out. She brought him information on how to start a small business, stuff on trade schools and colleges and numerous other educational materials. Tykim would simply ignore her. She never threatened to leave him if he didn't change his life because Daquasha knew it would be a bold face lie. She was in love Tykim and would love him no matter what he did for a living. However, after the tragedy, she wished she had put some real pressure on him to clean up his life. Maybe it could've prevented it from happening. It definitely would've made her feel she didn't subliminally contribute to the nightmare.

After graduating from high School, Daquasha took a two year break and then enrolled in a computer trade school where she dropped out without completing the course. Mrs. Lawrence's drinking was getting worse and caused Daquasha to leave home. Daquasha started working in a clothing bouquet store in order to pay her rent and other bills. There was no way she could go to school and maintain an apartment all at the same time. School had to be put on the shelf for a while.

After two months out on her own, Daquasha was forced to return to her mother's apartment. She got into debt way over her head with those credit cards and the rent was too expensive for her from the start. Plus, Tykim was placed in the Box due to an altercation, which cut off a crucial source of income. Mrs. Lawrence welcomed Daquasha back with open arms. An extra income meant extra money for her to drink up.

With her strong morals and principles, Daquasha was probably one of the most faithful girls in the 'hood, and her friends thought she was "crazy as hell" for waiting four years for Tykim to come home, especially when everybody knew Tykim chased pussy like a poverty-stricken kid in a candy factory. But, Daquasha loved him and knew he loved her. And that's all that mattered. But what her friends didn't know is that Daquasha secretly got her groove on regularly with a guy name Dumar from East New York. She kept it so on the down low, nobody in the 'hood knew because she went out of the neighborhood to do her dirt and would never let Dumar come out to Bedstuy with her.

When Tykim got out of prison, it was paradise for the first year. Tykim dove back into the game and started his own little empire. They hung out all the time, went on trips and was planning to get a crib of their own. They even talked about marriage. Then havoc struck. Their mutual love was shattered when Tykim brought death to the Lawrence family's doorstep. One night Tykim arrived at Daquasha's house to wait for her to get home from work. As Tareek was closing the door behind Tykim, two masked men rushed in before the door was locked. In a hail of bullets, Tareek was killed and Tykim was shot in both legs.

Tykim was arrested after receiving surgery to remove the two bullets in his legs. Initially, he was charged with Tareek's death, but when ballistics tests proved the bullets inside of Tareek's body matched one of the bullets in his leg, the charges were dropped. Tykim was convicted of possession of a weapon and reckless endangerment, and sentenced to five to ten years imprisonment.

When Daquasha heard the news, she was shattered. Her pain ran so deep, she couldn't work for two straight months and lost her job at the clothing store. For the first time in her life, she truly hated another human being. Daquasha's mother blamed her for Tereek's death and eventually drank herself into a grave.

When Daquasha's mother died, she lost the apartment and relocated first to New Jersey, where another catastrophe occurred. Then she moved to the Bronx. Alone, angry, scared, depressed, on the run from the law, and as broke as a skid row bum, Daquasha took on a fake name (her mother's maiden name, Danielle Lewis), went underground and was forced to work in strip tease clubs. The owners of such establishments didn't ask questions and paid reasonably well. In light of her unique beauty and meticulously prefect shaped body, Daquasha had no problem staying gainfully employed in this particular business. The shape of her ass literally looked like a fine sculptured upside down St. Valentines Day heart.

She met Jamil Nevez and her life felt like it was beginning to have meaning again. Jamil was a kind, warm and caring man who treated her like a Queen. But he was a bad boy. The thug of all thug type. He was into practically everything: drugs, gaming, strong arm work, racketeering, guns; had an explosive temper mixed with a love for violence, and many other things she couldn't begin to imagine. Daquasha came to accept the fact that she was destine and ordained to be with men of this nature. They were attracted to her, and she to them. Daquasha really didn't mind because she was gradually becoming immune to the pain and suffering that went along with loving bad boys from the 'hood.

Daquasha let go of those past memories as Tykim's embrace relaxed. Her tears subsided enough for her to engage Tykim in a discussion. He let go of the embrace and faced forward. She could tell Tykim was furious, but he spoke softly.

"Daquasha, I know It's hard for you to relive that incident, but if we're gonna survive this situation here, you need to know what happened that night your brother was killed."

Tykim propped his elbows on his knees and spoke while using his hands animatedly. "I love you and the whole nine yards, Daquasha. But if I can't close my eyes without thinking you gonna blow my damn head off, I'm gonna have to let you go your own way and I'll go mine." He knew he was lying, but he had to take a firm stance; she tried to kill him. "You ready to talk about this once and for all?"

Daquasha nodded her head; she wiped the tears from her face.

"I didn't kill your brother." Tykim let those words hang in the air as the shooting re-entered his mind. "I ain't have no control over it."

"So, why did the police arrest you for killing Tareek?"

"Daquasha, no disrespect, baby girl. You been around long enough to know police ain't got no problem with puttin' shit on a black man knowing he ain't the person who did the crime. They dropped those charges after they found the same bullets inside me that was in Tareek." He wanted to tell her if she had read any of his letters, she would have known this.

"But how--how did--why would someone kill Tareek? He was a little kid..." Daquasha wiped away the barrage of tears.

"Shit, to be honest, I don't even know why those two motherfuckers in masks bum rushed your mom's crib. I was--"

"What!?" Daquasha was about to explode. How could he say he didn't know why those men came to her mother's house!? Her tears instantly dribbled away. She sighed angrily. "Listen, Tykim, if we gonna clear the air, don't fuckin' play me like I'm some goddamn idiot! You know them niggas came there looking for you! They told you to close down that drug spot you had, and you didn't! That's why they came there looking for your sorry ass."

Tykim felt like a trapped fool wearing a dunce hat. How the fuck did she knew all that!? He could've sworn nobody knew the underlining facts of that situation. Somebody apparently was running their mouth, who wasn't supposed to. Now, he didn't know how to respond. "Daquasha, I'm sorry. I didn't--"

Daquasha rose to her feet, about to head back to the bedroom, but Tykim grabbed and held on to her arm, stopping her in her tracks.

"Daquasha, please, baby girl, you gotta believe me. I didn't know it was gonna go down the way it did." He pulled her back down into a sitting position on the sofa. "I mean, I knew there was some cats out there hatin' on a brother because of all the cheddar I had comin' in, but they was nobodies. At least that's what I was told."

Tykim stared at the floor, formulating his next words. His anger was growing because he caught a raw deal out of that whole situation, just like Daquasha. "Look at me, I'm all fucked up because of that incident. I was shot in both legs, and now I got a permanent limp. You did hear I got shot?"

Daquasha contorted her face. Of course she heard he was shot, she wanted to say, but locked eyes with him instead.

"Them niggas cost me five years of my life. That was the worst bid I ever did. When I got home from up north on that bid, I started picking up contracts against drug dealers all because of what happened that night. I hate all drug dealers because of what that motherfucker did to Tareek. You know I loved Tareek like he was my little brother." Tykim's eyes started becoming misty. "I vowed I'm gonna find that motherfucker who killed Tareek. He made a statement just before he killed Tareek. It was something like a way of leaving his mark behind." He sniffled, struggling not to cry. "I'll never forget what he said. Somehow, some way, I'm gonna find him."

"Yeah, go on, cry motherfucker!" Daquasha was seconds from picking up the gun and shooting him for real this time. "Cause when you let them kill Tareek, you killed my mother. She died a couple months later because she couldn't deal with it."

Tykim had heard Mrs. Lawrence died, and suspected it was as a result of Tareek's death. She was a heavy drinker before Tareek died, and he could only image how much her drinking increased when Tareek was killed. Tykim was momentarily speechless. He wiped away the run away tears. He picked up the gun. "Listen, Daquasha, I've said I was sorry ten thousand times. In every letter I wrote you from prison I begged and begged for your forgiveness." He handed her the 9mm. "If you believe this will make you whole again, then go ahead and blow my brains out."

She wouldn't take it; his gamble worked as he expected. Tykim sat the gun next to him on the sofa. "If what I'm doing for you right now ain't enough to prove I still love you, always have and always will, then I don't know what to do. I just killed five motherfuckers who was gonna kill you. And now I'm on the run with you! We're both being hunted by a rich nigga with international clout, and by the police. And you know what? I'll do whatever it takes to protect you Daquasha, even if it means I keep puttin' myself in harms way."

He examined her facial expression and knew he had her. Putting his arm around her shoulder, Tykim spoke softly. "We been together since we was in public school. You was my first love and I was yours. I fucked up. I admit it. But, please find it in your heart to forgive me. I ain't perfect and won't pretend I am. But, if I can't close my eyes or turn my back around you because of what happened in the past, something I had no control over, we might as well go our separate ways. The only way we gonna survive this is if you and me work together."

Daquasha was so used to being angry all the time, she was tempted to tell him to go his own way, but she knew Tykim was right. He was putting his life on the line to save hers. And, in any event, what would she do without Tykim? Where would she go? How would she get out of the country? She suddenly regretted her murder attempt on Tykim. Subliminally, she always knew he didn't mean to bring death to her family, but she needed someone to vent her rage upon, and he was the perfect punching bag. If she was going to survive this ordeal, she would have to find a way to re-direct her anger. When she thought about all the good times she had with Tykim, her regret grew substantially.

That regret was still present as she was pulled from her daydream when a truck horn sounded off. Tykim had changed lanes and apparently upset the tractor trailer driver as a result.

"You all right, Daquasha?" Tykim glanced over at her; she was staring out the window. "You ain't say a word since we stopped for gas."

"I'm okay, just thinking about some things."

"So how's your stomach? You still feel like you gotta throw up?"

"Naw, I'm okay."

"Keep that bag close by. That throw up don't always give you a warning when it's ready to ride."

"I got this," Daquasha wondered how long she could maintain this excuse. Surely, Tykim was going to start wondering why she was sick every morning. She was about to tell him, but decided to hold off a little longer, maybe when they got to Atlanta.

Tykim was about to spark up some good natured conversation, but he realized it was best to let Daquasha regulate the flow of discussion. He pulled back and went into his own world of deep thought.

The silence between them became long-standing.

Two hours flew by without a word spoken.

Daquasha saw they were now in Virginia. So far since leaving the Delaware hotel, she had sparked up only one cigarette and was struggling to keep her promise to smoke only four cigarettes a day and gradually reduce it to none. Looking at her watch, she saw she had at least two more hours before she could light up another smoke. She retrieved a stick of spearmint chewing gun and dunked it in her mouth.

Savoring the sweet tasting mint, she realized her unborn child weighed heavily on her mind. So many questions were demanding to be answered. She felt trapped, scared, confused and frustrated. How was she going to receive prenatal care while locked in this terrible situation? What was she going to do when her stomach started blowing up? What if she got caught and they put her child in a foster home? More questions started popping into her head so rapidly, she felt a hyperventilating sensation emerging, and so she shifted her thoughts to another topic.

Daquasha felt a hatred developing because Jamil suddenly formulated into her head. How could he try to kill her? That bastard assumed she would snitch on him! She was sizzling. Daquasha shook her head pitifully because he was wasting time trying to kill her when it could've been spent finding the real snitch. Despite Jamil's actions towards her, she sensed it was Kilroy behind it all. He hated her and the feeling was mutual.

Three hours later, Tykim stopped at a restaurant after crossing the South Carolina border. They ate a hardy meal, bought some snacks to take along with them, filled the gas tank and got back on Highway 95.

Five hours later, they pulled up in front of a driveway in front of a neatly groomed house. There were small bushes lining the walkway leading to the front door, and the trees in the back stood tall and intimidating. A row of similar built houses littered the whole block. There was a strong presence of a country vibe in the air. The sun was seconds from plunging into the western horizon.

Daquasha saw the red brick structure and the pretty flowers surrounding it made the place looked elegant and expensive. What kind of stick up kid was this guy with a house like this? He must be sticking up some real big places and some very big people in order to maintain a spot like this? Looking all around, Daquasha was surprised by all the beautiful houses in the area. This would be an excellent place to raise a child, she thought as Tykim got out of the Lincoln.

"Come on, let's go," Tykim headed towards the door.

Daquasha followed. The tingling needle like sensation from the lack of circulation in her legs was strong and very irritating.

Tykim pressed the door bell.

A short dark skin woman opened the door. Her eyes were sensuous and her hair was made up in a stylish bum. "Can I help you?" Her words were saturated with a southern drawl.

"Hey, Linda," Tykim gestured as if he was waiting for a huge hug. She looked just like all the pictures Nuke sent him when he was in Attica. "It's me, Tykim."

Linda opened the door all the way, scrutinizing Tykim closely. "Well, ain't this somethin'. Tykim! What you doin' down here, man!? Come on in." She ushered them inside and gave Daquasha a questioning look. "Nuke!"

She hollered towards the back of the house. "Hey, Nuke! Guess who's here!" She turned and spoke to Tykim. "It's sure nice to finally meet you in person. Go on and have a seat, y'all." She pointed towards the living room.

Daquasha and Tykim took a seat in the living room. The furniture was as courtly as the houses' outer structure, Daquasha noticed.

Nuke entered the living room. He was a light skinned, medium built brother with sneaky brown eyes, a short afro and was dressed in New York style 'hood clothing. He was drenched in gold necklaces, rings and bracelets. "Tykim! What up my main cousin!?" His southern drawl was even thicker than Linda's.

Tykim rose and gave Nuke a handshake and a hug.

Tykim waved for Daquasha to come to him. "This is Daquasha."

Daquasha shook Nuke's callous laden, sandpaper like hand. "Hi, you doin'!"

"Damn, Cuz, you rollin' real right with this fine little thang here." Nuke's eyes were filled with lust as they swept over Daquasha's body from head to toe.

"Easy now, Nuke." He unhinged Nuke's hand locked on Daquasha's. "This is the one I told you about."

"Oh, this is the one." He shook his head approvingly. "Daquasha, Yeah, I remember now. The way you used to talk about her all day when you used to come down here for the summer, when we was kids, damn right I remember." He spoke good naturedly to Daquasha. "Girl, I don't know what you did to my cousin, but he's strung out over you. It's a good thang you treatin' my cousin right. . . Y'all hungry?"

Daquasha looked at Tykim.

"You damn right we are." Tykim said, "We drove here from New York."

"Hey, Linda," Nuke said, "You heard our guests, they ready to eat."

Linda headed for the kitchen and rolled her eyes at Daquasha when she looked up at her. Tykim, Nuke and Daquasha all took seats.

Tykim leaned back on the sofa. "What's this shit I'm hearing, you tryin' to get back on the force?"

Nuke was perplexed. "Where the hell you hear that bullshit?"

"Aunt Sandra told mom's this." He lied. He just wanted to make absolutely sure Nuke was really living the life, and he wanted to hear it straight from the horse's mouth.

Nuke giggled under his breath. "Man, ain't a motherfuckin' police force in this country that'll hire my black ass. I ain't built for that cop shit anyway, and never was. I'm hard-core 'hood and I'm cool with what I do for a living."

Tykim nodded his head approvingly; he definitely liked what he heard. However, he wanted to activate a vein in Nuke's neck by talking about how he was kicked off the Atlanta police force for engaging in a get-rich-quick-scheme where he and two other cops had went on a stealing and robbing spree, taking things from suspects, victims of crime, vulnerable shops, stores and businesses, drug dealers, pimps, other cops and even the police evidence room, but decided to hold his tongue.

After they ate a meal prepared by Linda, which consisted of fried chicken, black eyed peas, brown rice, spinach, and sweet potato pie, Nuke was ready to talk business.

Sitting at the head of the table, Nuke said, "Linda, why don't you show Daquasha some of them jazzy new clothes of ours. I need to talk to Tykim in private."

"If it's business we talkin' about." Tykim touched Daquasha's arm. "Daquasha needs to hear it. She's down with this all the way."

Daquasha flinched. What the hell was he talkin' about!? She was about to comment, but her intuition told her to be easy.

Nuke smiled crazily. He was feeling Daquasha more and more with each passing minute. "Damn, girl, you all purpose, huh?" His smile faded as he cut his eyes at Linda. "I wish I had a woman who's a partner down with the real."

Linda sucked her teeth and rose from the table. As she headed towards the kitchen, Linda turned and rolled her eyes at Daquasha.

Nuke saw Daquasha's tight jawed response. "Don't pay her no mind." He chuckled. "She gets real jealous when competition come 'round her territory."

"You know what kind of work I'm talkin' about, don't-cha?" Tykim said.

"Shit, I been tryin' to get you to come down here and do some stick ups with me fo' the longest. Of course I know what kind of business you talkin' 'bout. I just hope you know I only do big time shit."

"So, how much we lookin' at?" Tykim said, "What kind of money we talkin' about here?"

Nuke smiled. "I got a real special job I been wanting to do." His excitement rose two notches. "Now, with a real live stepper like you, a person I knows I can trust, I'm goin' for this one." Smiling broadly, he added. "Daquasha, you ever seen how two million dollars in hard-core cash looks?"

Daquasha almost lost control of her calm composure upon hearing two millions dollars. "Naw, ain't never seen that much." Her fingers rotated the pinkie ring.

"Well, sit tight, 'cause we gonna be playin' with that kind of money real soon." It took Nuke four minutes to map out the robbery. "In two days, we gonna do our thang. I'm gonna call my man Cowboy over tomorrow and we'll fine tune this plan more thoroughly."

"Do you think it's safe for us to case a spot in a white neighborhood in broad day light?" Tykim had strong doubts about this whole plan. "If those Russian cats are holdin' like that, wouldn't it be safe to assume they got security people, both legal and illegal, all over that area?"

"This is an inside run, here." Nuke lit up a cigarette. "Cowboy knows where they holdin' the stash. He knows the whole area. This place is like a stash-house strictly for cash. Don't nobody supposed to know nothin' 'bout this place, so they don't waste money and time on real heavy security. They some arrogant mufuckas too. I been plannin' on hittin' these crackers for a good little while; I just needed four extra hands to hold me down. You and Daquasha make two, but we can make it work with what we got." Looking out of the corner of his eye, he saw Tykim's disturbed expression. "I know me and you Tykim can make up the difference."

Tykim gave Daquasha an expression which asked for her decision.

Daquasha nodded her head.

"Well, Cuz, we in." Tykim gave Nuke a high five.

Later that evening, after Daquasha and Tykim took a shower and were in the bedroom lying in bed watching TV, Nuke got on the phone and dialed a number. "Hello. Yeah, what's up Cee Cee. This is Nuke. I need you to call that dude from New York and tell him if he boost that price up 'bout five thousand dollars, he got himself a deal." After a moment, Nuke sighed in frustration. "Shut the fuck up! Just do what I said! I don't give a shit if he's my cousin. Money make the world go 'round, nigga. And when there's a toss up between that mean green and a old sorry ass cousin, guess what's gonna win every time?"

CHAPTER # 17

"Why didn't you just tell him, yes," Kilroy said calmly. He paced across the warehouse floor. "If he's Tykim's cousin, his allegations has to be accurate. We couldn't lose no matter what the price was."

Lunatic stared nervously at the floor. "He said he's gonna call back."

Devil-dog was leaning against a box-crate. "Next time we'll be there to talk to him personally. We'll even double the price. There ain't no way we won't get what we want."

"When is he gonna call back?" Kilroy picked up his suit jacket and put it on. "I hope it's some time soon."

"He didn't say," Lunatic said, "But Scram Jones got our number and he's got a three way. He's gonna connect us straight to him."

"For future references," Kilroy walked over to a table, picked up a hammer and began striking the head in the palm of his hand. "When one of you fuck up, I expect for y'all to tell me the truth."

Lunatic and Devil-dog felt a crippling anxiety rush.

The two machine-gun totting body guards came up behind Devil-dog and Lunatic, causing them to turn with frantic facial expressions.

"Why did y'all lie to me about the Queens run?" Kilroy continued striking the palm of his hand with the hammer.

Lunatic looked at Devil-dog with an expression which said, see I told you.

Devil-dog struggled to maintain his composure. "No disrespect, big papa, but what if you was in our shoes, and know no mistakes was allowed, wouldn't you have lied?"

Kilroy smiled as he approached Devil-dog. When he saw Devil-dog maintained his stern persona, his love for this stiff neck and rebellious worker grew more. He laid the hammer on the top of Devil-dog's head. "That's why I like you dog. You a thug ass nigga for real. And, yes, I probably would've lied, but I would've made sure I didn't get caught."

Suddenly, Kilroy swung the hammer and struck Lunatic on the shoulder. The blow was just hard enough not to break anything, but forceful enough to make him holler.

Kilroy tossed the hammer to the floor. "Now, next time, if I get the feeling I can't trust y'all." He locked eyes with Devil-dog. "Then I will have no use for you." He was about to give his bodyguard the signal to kill Devil-dog, but saw Devil-dog was smart enough to relax his eyes out of respect.

Only a fool sort to defy power when he wasn't in a position to do so, and Devil-dog's graceful head bow was the behavior of a wise man.

"Y'all can break out." Kilroy said, and watched Devil-dog and Lunatic shuffled away.

Kilroy headed for his office; his bodyguards followed. The fact that Jamil was making his own moves with the lawyer, Ron Cody, was gnawing at his patience. What the fuck, he didn't have confidence in his judgment?

Kilroy entered his office, took his jacket off, hung it up and took a seat behind his desk. Today was accounting day, and he sat behind his computer opening the appropriate files. As he analyzed the figures, Kilroy made a mental note in his head to pay Ron Cody a personal visit. All lawyer's had a price, and Ron was no exception. But there wasn't going to be any moves made without the top dog regulating the show, bet that!

£¥♥   £¥♥   £¥♥   £¥♥

Jamil entered the visiting floor and saw Brute with his leg crossed over the other. The cocky grin on Brute's face caused a flare of excitement to race through his stomach. As usual, the floor was filled with women and children visiting their incarcerated love ones.

Jamil took a seat. "Tell me something good, baby boy."

"You was right, Big Daddy. It ain't Danielle."

Jamil contained his jubilation. "What's her name?"

"Debra Holmes. She was Joe Rock-head's girl. I hear they got her under major police protection."

"Do you know exactly where she's being held?"

"Yeah, but I--"

"That's all that matters." Jamil's bowels felt weak from the anxiety that raced through his veins. Twelve dozen issues came to life all at once. Plus, his heart was a ball of flaming hot fire with rage and regret as his guiding forces. Thoughts of murder flashed across his mind. With a struggle, he neutralized the image of spraying Kilroy with Teflon bullets. Kilroy was his blood, it would be just like killing himself, he concluded. In his world, blood was truly thicker than mud.

"I think you should hear where they got her." Brute uncrossed his leg. "And how many cops they got looking over her."

"The floor is yours," Jamil had already formulated the run inside his head a day ago. He'd even had certain hitters on standby who he felt could handle this sort of job.

Brute spoke animatedly. "They holdin' her in a hotel on Soundview Avenue. There's a team of eight plain-clothe cops guarding her. I don't know how or where they're positioned, but I'm sure we ain't gonna be able to stroll up with a crew of hitters, blaze this bitch and just walk off into the moon light. Eight undercovers is a whole lot of security, Ja."

Jamil smiled inwardly as he realized he had been on point all along. His plan was going to need some minor re-working, but it had great potential for success. "This is a one shot deal. If we miss, my ass is out. Tomorrow my case goes to the grand jury, so we're gonna have to bring in top grade hitters."

"Shit, ain't we top grade hitters? Devil-dog and Lunatic is about as straight cheese as they can get. I ain't tooting my own horn, but I ain't no slouch either."

Jamil was moments from hurling a barrage of heart-breaking jokes designed to shatter Brute's well deserved confidence in his own abilities, but time was of the essence. "Yes, Brute, y'all are top grade. But this gotta be a different kinda hit. Listen carefully now. This is how we gonna do this run. . ."

£¥♥   £¥♥   £¥♥   £¥♥

The Royal blue van came to a stop on the corner of   Columbia Avenue. Nuke killed the headlights as he scanned the deserted streets. The elegant restaurant a half block away looked the way it was supposed to; quiet and no action lurking about. All the other shops and stores were closed, and the traffic was as dead as King Tut's tomb.

Daquasha's heart was about to beat itself out of her chest. Sitting on a crate in the back, dressed in a black skin-tight outfit, she was still asking, how did she allow herself to get involved in this madness. Twice she almost spun the ring right off her pinkie. She wanted to smoke a cigarette so bad the nicotine crazing sizzled with agonizing intensity. She saw Cowboy was almost as calm as Tykim. Cowboy was a Russian man with scary gray eyes and had a square jaw. He also had skullduggery written all over him. His crackling voice only served to magnify his wicked characteristics.

"Let's do it," Nuke said as he put his mask on. Everyone else did the same.

Daquasha and Tykim got out the back and rapidly headed towards the alleyway. Nuke and Cowboy stayed put so as to give Tykim and Daquasha enough time to cut across to get to the back of the building.

Daquasha was dead on Tykim's heels. They climbed two fences. When they arrived at the back of the targeted establishment, Daquasha saw a light over the door and the area looked very expensive.

Hiding in the bushes, Tykim got on his walkie talkie. "We in place. Fifty seconds and counting." He put the devise in his pocket and pulled the miniature Tech 9 Uzi. He turned and saw Daquasha had her Tech 9 in her hand as well. He started counting. When he hit fifty, Tykim was in motion.

Daquasha's knees trembled as she followed Tykim. They arrived and stood on the side of the door. Tykim quietly inserted the key they got from Cowboy. Daquasha flinched when the lock flicked open.

£¥♥   £¥♥   £¥♥   £¥♥

Moments earlier, Nuke and Cowboy moved swiftly down the street. Nuke saw everything was as planned. The streets were still empty and the lights inside the store were on. The Russian mobsters were secretly counting their millions they sucked from communities all over Atlanta and Nuke couldn't wait until that money touched his hands.

Nuke and Cowboy kneeled when they arrived in front of the restaurant. Cowboy pulled the key and silently opened the locks. He pushed the door open. Nuke rushed inside first with his trigger finger ready to get good and crazy.

£¥♥   £¥♥   £¥♥   £¥♥

In the back, Daquasha followed Tykim inside the restaurant. They were in a dimly lit corridor and the sound of a TV could be heard coming from the room up ahead. Suddenly, the two men they were planning to get the jump on started laughing. Daquasha suddenly had difficulty breathing. Tykim maintained his forward movement as if he hadn't heard anything. When they arrived at the room, Tykim stopped and turned to Daquasha with the Tech 9 raised in the ready, Tykim counted to three with his other hand.

Tykim rushed into the room. "Let me see your hands!"

Daquasha was seconds behind Tykim. As planned, she had her gun pointed at the man on the right side of the room. There were boxes and other warehouse type items scattered around the room. The two men had black hair; one was heavily bearded while the other was clean shaved.

"Put your fuckin' hands up!" Tykim's voice was soaking with seriousness. He moved towards the men as they raised their hands. Daquasha followed.

It took Daquasha and Tykim two minutes to bound the men with handcuffs and cover their mouths with tape. When Daquasha saw the two huge machine guns sitting next to the men, she trembled at the thought of the dangerous situation she was dabbing into.

£¥♥ £¥♥ £¥♥ £¥♥

In the front, Nuke and Cowboy entered abruptly, catching the three men dressed in suits off guard.

"Keep your hands up high!" Nuke shouted, changing his voice to sound high pitched.

Cowboy began handcuffing and taping the men's mouths.

A heavy-set Russian with red hair said, "There is no where to hide from the Russian Mafia. Leave now and all will he forgotten."

Nuke laughed as Cowboy began handcuffing the red beard Russian. Nuke rushed over to the red haired Russian and slapped him with the butt of the gun. "Well, I'm sorry to bust your bubble, but the Russian Mafia is getting had tonight."

Three minutes later, all the Russians throughout the restaurant were secured.

Daquasha and Tykim stood watch while Nuke and Cowboy went down into the basement to retrieve the money from a safe. While stuffing bills in a duffel bag, Nuke came across a black velvet bag of jewels.

Cowboy saw the black bag in Nuke's hand. His whole demeanor lit up with excitement. "That's from the Clairborne heist."

Nuke's eyes grew wide. "You mean to tell me these guys were behind that heist? The papers said 130 million dollars worth of jewels was stolen."

"Well, I guess that 130 million is ours now." Cowboy said, still pulling stacks of money from the safe and stuffing them into the bag. He really wanted to say all of it was his, but he would let his bullets do the explaining. He wondered should he kill Nuke right now? Naw, he had to stick with his original plan. He would kill them all, once they got away.

£¥♥ £¥♥ £¥♥ £¥♥

Meanwhile, a car with two Russian soldiers, who were making an unplanned drop off, drove pass the restaurant. The soldier in the passenger seat saw a black clothed figure inside the store move hastily out of sight.

"There's something wrong," The soldier said to the driver. "I saw something strange inside." He reached under the seat and pulled a compact Russian made sub-machine-gun from under the seat. "Park down here. We'll go in from the back."

The driver parked the car, retrieved an identical weapon as the one his partner possessed and they both exited the car.

CHAPTER # 18

The Desmont Hotel located on Soundview Avenue was a four story establishment with ten rooms on each floor. In room 3C, Debra Holmes sat watching the 11 o'clock news. Her emotions were filled with turmoil. Despite the plainclothes officer in the apartment with her and the other seven that were scattered all over the area outside, she was scared. Tomorrow she would tell a grand jury what she saw, and as a result, one of the city's biggest drug dealers would be indicted for three homicides. From what she heard, Kilroy and Jamil had stayed on top of the drug game so long because there was no one foolish enough to turn state's evidence against them.

"Excuse me, Ms. Holmes," The officer shouted from the kitchen.

Debra scurried out of the room and saw the officer putting on his coat.

"It's shift change," The officer said, "My relief should be here any moment. I need to introduce you to him."

"What happened to officer Hester?"

"Transferred to a new division."

Debra's heart jumped. Her nervousness resonated through her body.

"Relax, Ms. Holmes. Everything's under control. You're safe. I personally know this officer. He's righteous all the way to the bone."

Debra felt no relief from the officer's reassuring comments. She didn't know if it was her intuition or the jitters, but she was certain something was wrong.

Meanwhile, down the hall from 3C, an over-weight cleaning lady wearing a light green maids uniform approached. She was pushing a cleaning cart that had a raggedy wheel that made a whole lot of noise.

The officer seated in front of the apartment glanced up from the newspaper and saw the woman. He resumed reading the paper.

She stopped in front of the officer and said, "Excuse me, officer, I have to get inside here and clean up."

"Sorry Miss--"

The cleaning woman sprayed the officer in the face with an aerosol can. The solution instantly knocked the cop into a deep state of unconsciousness the moment the chemical touched his face.

She retrieved a key from her pocket and opened the door. With the spray can hidden in her left hand, the cleaning woman pushed open the door with her fat rump and quickly pulled her cart inside the room.

The officer inside rushed from the kitchen towards the door with his gun ready. When he saw the cleaning woman, he holstered his weapon. He remembered seeing this woman around the hotel. "Excuse me miss, the room is off limits."

sssssss

She sprayed the officer the moment he was five feet from her.

The officer was hurled into a state of triple darkness as he collapsed to the floor.

The cleaning woman pulled the silencer equipped 9mm from the cleaning cart and followed the sound of the TV.

Moments ago, Debra heard the cop's comment made to the cleaning lady. With terror racing through her mind, Debra sprung to her feet, looking around in desperation. She saw images of death dancing before her eyes. When she heard the cop's body hit the floor, she ran, picked up the portable radio and positioned herself on the side of the door, trembling as she heard the approaching footsteps.

The cleaning lady entered the room and saw no one. Suddenly, through her peripheral vision she saw movement.

BLAMM!

The blow to the cleaning woman's head seemed like it shook the whole room. The cleaning lady stumbled to the side, spun the gun, took aim and fired two shots. They both missed Debra. As she bounced off the wall, the cleaning woman saw her children lying in coffins; if she fucked up this run, it was made clear that's where they would end up. The cleaning woman charged at Debra and latched on to her shirt as Debra tried to flee out of the room.

Debra screamed when she realized the fat lady had grabbed her shirt, restricting her from running.

The cleaning lady aimed at Debra's back and her trigger finger was squeezing away.

SZK! SZK! SZK!

The first shot struck Debra in the lower back, cutting off her desperate screams. The cleaning lady shoved Debra away just as the second and third shots spun her around as she fell backwards to the floor.

The cleaning lady walked up to Debra and fired three more shots into her head. The gapping holes in Debra's skull and the missing chunks of flesh made her head look like a mass of unspeakable red gore.

The cleaning lady turned, about to leave and stopped suddenly. She touched the already growing lump on her head. She spun back around and fired three more shots into Debra's chest. The impact of the bullets made her body bounce.

Whistling an old down south tune, the cleaning lady exited the room with her cleaning cart and returned from whence she came.

£¥♥   £¥♥   £¥♥   £¥♥

Daquasha was the first to detect the noise. She was standing near a soda machine and waved excitedly to Tykim who was standing by the door leading down into the basement. Terror gripped Daquasha as the footsteps became louder. She shifted on her feet and got the gun ready.

Tykim saw Daquasha's disturbed look and knew there was drama on the way. He quickly tiptoed towards her and instantly heard the approaching men. The two men were whispering.

Tykim stopped at the corner, trying to get a feel of how many men there were and exactly where they were positioned. It sounded like two or three of them. He waved to Daquasha, gesturing for her to point the gun around the corner and start shooting.

She shook her head no.

Tykim was seething with anger. He angrily pointed his finger as if he was scolding her. Tykim wanted to gesture to her again, but the men were too close. Drawing deep breaths, Tykim stepped around the corner with his finger clamped down on the trigger.

SZK!--SZK!--SZK!--SZK!--SZK!

The two men's bodies jerked from the impact of the silenced bullets. One of the Russian soldiers squeezed off a wave of loud, nerve-racking machine gunfire that was aimed at the floor. After they fell, Tykim let up off the trigger and ran towards the two men. When Tykim was upon them, he squeezed off another wave of bullets, all aimed at the men's heads. Blood, flesh and bone was splattered, covering the immediate area in red.

Daquasha peeked around the corner when the shooting stopped. She saw Tykim rushing back.

Moments earlier, down in the basement, Nuke and Cowboy snatched the two duffel bags and frantically ran up the stairs. They both had their guns in the ready with Cowboy leading the charge.

Cowboy barreled out of the basement, Nuke was seconds behind him.

Cowboy moved towards Daquasha and Tykim. "Why the hell are you shooting without a god-damn silencer?"

"We had unexpected visitors." Tykim jabbed a thumb down the corridor.

Cowboy and Nuke hastily went to inspect the two bodies.

With a boot, Nuke repositioned the head of one of the fallen Russians to get a good look at his face. "You know them?" He said to Cowboy.

Daquasha and Tykim arrived standing behind the two.

Cowboy kneeled and checked their pockets. "Yeah, I know them. They work the eastside."

Nuke winked his eye at Daquasha and Tykim as he pointed his weapon at the back of Cowboy's head. "That's good, cuz you can join them--"

SZK!--SZK!--SZK!

The silence bullets tore through Cowboy's head. Blood and chunks of brain matter were sprayed all over the floor and walls. Cowboy landed on top of the dead Russian soldiers.

Tykim spoke calmly. "What the fuck is you doing--"

"He was gonna kill us all and take everything."

Daquasha spoke excitedly. "Don't y'all think it's time we get the fuck out of here."

Nuke kneeled and pulled the black velvet bag from Cowboy's pocket. He angrily mumbled under his breath because he didn't want them to see this bag.

"Looks like jewels." Tykim said as he picked up Cowboy's duffel bag.

The three ran towards the back of the restaurant.

Twenty minutes later, Nuke was racing the van down the highway. He looked at his watch. It was time to make that call. There was no need in putting off the inevitable, especially when his pockets were getting fatter in the process.

The first service station he saw, Nuke pulled in it. "I gotta make a call. I told Linda to make arrangements to have my assets frozen if I don't give her a buzz before 3 a.m." He laughed as he exited the van.

Nuke entered the store and went to the public phone. He dropped a coin in the slot and dialed the number. "It's yours truly. Add twenty gees to that and they're yours. . . That sounds good. They'll be at my house. . ."

CHAPTER # 19

Guzmon stood over Debra's bullet ridden body, holding back the urge to throw a temper tangent. A special kind of rage was boiling at the thought that Jamil was going to walk out of jail a free man if they didn't find Daquasha. He walked over to the officer who was inside the room with Debra. The cop was sitting on the sofa holding his head with both hands. He appeared to be more ashamed than in pain.

Guzmon took a seat next to him. He saw Armstrong interviewing the officer who was positioned in front of the door. Guzmon sighed and said, "I'm a little confused with a few parts of your story, officer. You said this over-weight cleaning woman entered the room?" He saw the officer nodded his head. "In light of your instructions, you didn't find this strange?"

"I--she--I saw her around the hotel, so I--when she entered, I thought she came to clean up the room."

Ten minutes later, Guzmon and Armstrong exited the hotel and got in their vehicle. They cruised down the Avenue in silence for several minutes. Guzmon sparked up a conversation.

"That son of bitch is gonna walk!" Guzmon slammed his fist on the dashboard.

"Don't throw in the towel too soon." Armstrong took his eyes off the road and laid them on Guzmon. "With a little ingenuity, we might be able to make something happen. There's always an ace in the hole."

Guzmon realized Armstrong's comment sparked an idea. He nodded his head, silently pondering the idea. "So, you feel like skirting the edge tonight?"

"Personally, I don't think we got much of a choice. It's worth the risk."

"Let's go for it." Guzmon felt an anxiety ridden vibe in the pit of his stomach. He hoped his luck was running high because if he and Armstrong got caught for what they were about to do, not only would their jobs be jeopardized, but so would their liberty.

Kilroy was pulled out of his deep sleep when the phone rung. He picked up the receiver. "Hello."

"Good news, big papa," Devil-dog said on the other end. "We found them. They in Atlanta Georgia. The cat says he's Tykim's cousin. He wants thirty gees transferred to account number 741-4341 and he'll give us the address."

"Good," Kilroy sat up, grabbed a pen and wrote down the number. "The money transfer is taken care of."

"Check it out Kilroy, we need a airplane ride down there. What's up, man?"

"Yeah, yeah, I got that. Go over to the strip, I'll send Sam over."

"I'll give you a buzz when I touch down. Peace, big papa."

£¥♥   £¥♥   £¥♥   £¥♥

Daquasha sat across from Nuke counting the stacks of money. Tykim sat next to her counting out loud. Her heart raced with excitement. Already they counted well over a million and a half dollars, and it looked like they were going to easily reach the two million mark. Daquasha thought she was dreaming, and twice she felt the urge to pinch herself.

Nuke suddenly started giggling. "Yo Tykim, don't you think it's fair I take Cowboy's cut?"

Tykim stopped counting and wrote down where he left off. "The rules say all survivors cut the catch right down the middle. Since it's three of us, we cut it in three ways and keep this thing movin'."

Nuke looked at his watch. He hoped those cats from New York got here soon. In another hour if they didn't get here, Nuke was planning to kill them on his own. All this talk about fuckin' with his money was really getting under his skin. "The jewels were extra. They weren't in the deal. And they probably fake any way. I should keep 'em."

Tykim thought about the issue for a moment. He knew from past experience that Jewels were traceable and the subject of a lot of headaches. There was a need for a reliable fence, and even if the jewels were worth a substantial sum of money, he was not a jewel thief and didn't know what he was supposed to receive anyway. Tykim hated being taken advantage of and didn't need any further hindrances. "Listen, Nuke, we counted 37 of those Jewels. I ain't got a problem with you taking the bulk of them. How you feel about that, Daquasha?"

Daquasha completed her 100 thousand dollar stack and then said, "I ain't got a beef with that, but what do you mean by the bulk?"

Tykim picked up a stack of bills. "I say Nuke should gets 27, me and you get 5 each."

Nuke wanted to burst out laughing. If they only knew. "That's cool. I think that's fair." In this moment Nuke was about to pull his gun and open fire, but he promised to give those New York cats the honor of pushing back

Tykim and Daquasha's wig. Plus, he wasn't into having the blood of a family on his hand. As long as someone else pulled the trigger, he could live with himself.

Linda entered the living room with a tray of champagne. She sat the tray on the table near the door and walked over to Nuke. She began messaging his shoulders in a seductive fashion. All this money was not only making her horny, but crazy as well. "How much longer?"

Nuke continued counting. After he completed his stack, he brushed her hands off his shoulders and said, "If you would stop distracting me, we'd be finished by now."

Ten minutes later, they completed counting. There was two million, 470 thousand dollars. Cut in three ways, Daquasha and Tykim each got 822 thousand, while Nuke got 826 thousand.

With a huge smile, Nuke rose to his feet clapped his hands together and vigorously rubbed them together. "God damn! It's time to celebrate!" He headed for the champagne tray with Linda behind him.

Daquasha remained seated as Tykim followed Nuke, who turned on the CD player, blasting a rap song by Cash-Rules and started pouring several glasses of champagne. She sensed something wasn't right with Nuke. All this partying seemed strange in light of the fact she insisted to Tykim that they hit the road immediately after counting the money, but Nuke demanded vehemently that they stay for the night.

After seeing all this money and those jewels, Daquasha was growing very nervous. Her uneasiness and intense apprehension was profound enough to make her not want to smoke a cigarette. She knew there was no rules of ethics for thieves, robbers, crooks, criminals and cut-throats, and when money popped into the picture, so did greed. A terrible combination that almost always lead to chaos. It was also apparent Nuke killed Cowboy solely to get his cut, and now that Tykim convinced him to split everything evenly, it was no doubt in her mind Nuke was plotting on how to get their share. Had he put up a stronger fight, she might have paid it no attention.

CHAPTER # 20

Guzmon and Armstrong sat in their vehicle watching Kilroy's warehouse. The glistening Milky Way over head twinkled with overwhelming clarity. The nervous tension resonating from the both of them vibrated the inside of the car. The silence only made the situation worse. They were out of their jurisdiction by at least fifty miles and two districts. A slip up could cost them everything.

Guzmon's conscience was telling him to pull back, but his heart demanded he move forward full speed ahead. Sitting on his hands while permitting a murderer to walk off Scott free was a matter of the heart, and therefore, he would let his heart regulate the situation. Plus, Guzmon's hard-on for Kilroy and Jamil took on a special kind of energy tonight.

For the hundredth time, the questions in Guzmon's head presented themselves, but tonight, they were saturated with the urge to be answered once and for all. Who the hell were they to even think they didn't have to grease his palms? Why was he sitting by letting them even think this foolishness? Just because they were paying off a few of those downtown big wigs didn't mean the uptown folks didn't deserve a piece of the action. Tonight, Guzmon decided he was going to begin the process of changing all that. He just wished he could share this newfound inspiration with Armstrong, but his inner voice told him that wouldn't be a wise move. Even though Armstrong was about as dirty as they came, Guzmon couldn't seem to reveal to anyone just how corrupt he himself really was.

Earlier, Guzmon snatched up one of his CIs (confidential informants), named Sharky, seeking information on how to find one of Kilroy's closest bodyguards. Sharky not only gave him names, places and the bodyguard's backgrounds, but also how much they were paid and who they were fucking. Sharky gave up all this information without Guzmon having to unleash one single punch in the face or a swift kick to the ass. He was glad ole Sharky was finally getting it in his head who was in charge around here.

Suddenly, they saw one of Kilroy's bodyguards exit the warehouse. It was Charlie Blue. The moon cast a gloomy streak of light over his tall, husky physique.

Armstrong started the car after Charlie Blue got in his red Porsche.

Guzmon forced himself to relax as Armstrong followed the Porsche. He was surprised by his sudden nervousness. He was powerless to conceal this response, since he knew what he was about to do was unequivocally wrong. Nature was taking its course.

Five minutes later, when they were in a deserted area, Armstrong turned and said, "You ready?"

"Let's do it." Guzmon pulled his gun, while Armstrong slapped the flasher on top of the roof.

The siren and flashing lights blared to life.

Armstrong spoke through the car loud speaker. "Pull it over."

Charlie Blue complied. Armstrong stopped about twenty feet behind the Porsche.

"Please step out the car and put your hands on top of your head."

As Charlie Blue did as he was told, Guzmon's eyes were searching the area. It was clear. He got out the car with his gun pointed. Guzmon rushed towards Charlie Blue's imposing figure. Armstrong was right behind him.

"Your under arrest," Guzmon handcuffed Charlie Blue while Armstrong kept the gun trained on him.

Charlie Blue had a snare on his face. "What the fuck are you fuckin' with me for? Where's your badge?"

Armstrong showed him his badge as Guzmon shoved him towards their vehicle. Charlie Blue resisted Guzmon's aggressive efforts as he was shoved in the back seat.

Guzmon struck him on the head with the butt of his gun. "Get in the fuckin' car."

After Charlie Blue got in the back, they pulled off. They rode in silence for five minutes.

Armstrong pulled the car on to a deserted back road, and headed down towards the underpass. When the car stopped, Guzmon sprung out the vehicle.

"I'm letting you know right now," Guzmon snatched the back door open and dragged Charlie Blue out the car. "We plan to get down and dirty with you. We wanna know what Kilroy is up to?"

"I don't know what you talkin' about," Charlie Blue said calmly. "Kilroy?! Who hell is that!? I don't know no damn Kilroy."

Guzmon laid an upper-cut to his stomach, buckling Charlie Blue's knees. "Did he kill that witness against his brother?"

Charlie Blue laughed in Guzmon's face and received a right cross to the jaw. The dozen or more blows to Charlie's mid-section and other extremities were inflamed with true malice.

Guzmon grabbed him by the throat and squeezed hard. "I'm prepared to do some real wicked shit to you to get what I'm looking for."

123

Armstrong punched Charlie Blue in the side, causing air to burst from his lungs.

Guzmon pounded his body repeatedly until Charlie Blue's knees started to give way to the weight of his big upper body. When Guzmon let the throat hold go, Charlie Blue snatched air into his lungs, breathing hard.

"What is Kilroy up to!?" Armstrong placed his gun on Charlie's forehead.

Charlie Blue laughed. "Suck my dick, cracker."

Armstrong stepped away and fired a shot. Just as he planned, the bullet breezed pass Charlie Blue's face and the powder burn covered his cheek. When he saw Charlie Blue trembling with terror in his eyes, Armstrong held back the laugh.

Guzmon pointed his gun at Charlie Blue's knee cap. "Be advised Charlie, we have no problem resorting to harsher measures. Shooting your big silly ass will be one of the options." He cocked the hammer theatrically. "Now, tell us what Kilroy is up to!? You talk, you walk! Play superman, and you die!"

Long sullen silence.

Guzmon shifted his footing and braced himself for the explosion.

"All right, all right," Charlie Blue sighed. It took him ten minutes to tell Guzmon and Armstrong all the things he thought they wanted to hear.

With some minor probing, they found out everything they needed to know.

Guzmon smiled. "How long ago did they leave for Atlanta?"

"About a hour, hour and a half."

Guzmon placed Charlie Blue back in the car and they sped off.

Several minutes later, Armstrong parked in front of the red Porsche. Guzmon got out the car, pulled Charlie Blue from the back seat and began uncuffing him. Armstrong stood next to Charlie Blue.

Suddenly, Charlie Blue took a swing at Armstrong. The blow was so monolithic, Armstrong was in dreamland before he hit the pavement. Charlie Blue frantically reached in the back of his waist and pulled a two shot derringer.

BOW!--BOW!

Guzmon fired two shots to Charlie Blue's chest. His body convulsed as he stumbled backwards and crashed to the ground.

"Shit!" Guzmon screamed. He was moments from panicking as he ran to Armstrong. "Wake up, Armstrong." When he saw his partner was out cold, Guzmon raced to their vehicle and retrieved the tube of smelling salt from the glove compartment.

When the salt was placed under Armstrong's nose, he woke up in an explosive fashion.

Guzmon helped Armstrong to his feet and leaned him against their vehicle.

"Did you have to shoot him?" Armstrong said, rubbing the lump on his cheek.

"He pulled a weapon." Guzmon pointed. The gun landed near the front of the Porsche.

"Well," Armstrong gritted his teeth. "I guess we fucked this up in a major way. Goddamn it! I hope you got money saved up because there goes not only our jobs, but our pensions as well...

£¥♥   £¥♥   £¥♥   £¥♥

Devil-dog, Lunatic and eight other men got off the plane. Three cars along with three drivers were waiting.

As Devil-dog headed towards the cars, he felt a great sense of pride; he was down with a team that had international connections and clout. Kilroy had all this popping with the mere snap of a finger and a bullshit phone call.

"Peace, my brother," Devil-dog shook the tall, slim black man's hand, who had dark bags under his eyes. "I'm Devil-dog."

"Drac," he said, his voice matching his sinister like features. "Kilroy said you was a piece of work. I see he wasn't lying."

Devil-dog was about to spazz out because he didn't know if the comment was intended to disrespect him or complement him. His fear and respect for Kilroy was the only forces that held him in check.

"Come on, let's go." Drac got behind the wheel as Devil-dog and his crew got inside the cars and sped away.

£¥♥   £¥♥   £¥♥   £¥♥

Daquasha was in the bathroom washing her hands. She just got finished taking a leak.

Suddenly, the headlights of moving cars slipped across the bathroom window.

Daquasha felt her whole body tense up. It was kind of late for cars to be moving around at this time of the night. She rushed to the window, stepped in the tub, climbed on the soap holder, saw three cars parked in front of the house next door and a group of men getting out of the vehicles. Devil-dog's face catapulted her into a frantic flee. Just as she was about to race out of the bathroom, Daquasha realized this could be Nuke's doing.

With casual smoothness, Daquasha exited the bathroom and hurried to Tykim. She whispered in his ear. "The dude from the junkyard is outside."

Tykim grabbed Daquasha and started dancing to the music. He slid over to the table where his gun was.

Nuke was talking to Linda. He looked up and saw Tykim heading for the table. Nuke realized Tykim was acting strange. He moved Linda out the way as he was about to pull his gun.

Tykim snatched his gun and spun with it aimed. "Don't do it, Nuke!" He moved rapidly towards Nuke who stopped in mid motion. Tykim took the gun from Nuke's waist. "Lay face down on the floor."

Nuke dropped to the floor.

Daquasha was frantically dunking the money into the two huge duffel bags.

"Hey," Nuke shouted as Tykim tied his hands with a towel he snatched from the nearby table. "What you doing? That's my cut!"

"Looks like you fucked that up," Tykim began tying Nuke's ankles. "How could you sell me out? I'm your cousin."

"What the hell you talkin' about?" Nuke said seriously.

"This ain't right, Tykim!" Linda said, "That's your flesh and--"

There was a thunderous explosion. The front door was tore off its hinges.

Tykim pushed Linda to the floor just as the silenced bullets tore through the nearby windows, tearing at the walls and the furniture.

Tykim rapidly crawled to the living room entrance and aimed at the front door.

SZK!--SZK!--SZK!...

All three of Tykim's bullets pounded a huge black man wearing a black leather jacket, causing him to jerk, flinch and stumble backwards into Lunatic.

In a kneeling position, Daquasha dumped the black bag of jewels inside the duffel bag.

Tykim got up and ran towards Daquasha just as more machine-gun bullets tore through the windows.

Daquasha pulled her Tech 9 as Tykim approached. When Tykim was a few feet from her, she tossed him one of the duffel bags.

Daquasha and Tykim barreled towards the back door. They both had a duffel bag in one hand and a 9mm in the other. Daquasha lead the way.

Tykim turned around as he ran and fired a wave of gunfire at the first man to enter the living room. The man stumbled backwards, hit the floor and caused his comrades right behind him to trip over him.

Daquasha quickly looked out the back window, saw it looked clear and open the door. She stepped outside. Her eyes tried to take in everything in every direction. The sound of crickets was heavy all around her.

When Tykim arrived, they charged towards the wooded area twenty yards away. They ran with frantic vigor, their legs working like the pistons in a high performance super engine. Tykim looked back and saw two men rushing out the back door.

Bullets whizzed pass Daquasha and Tykim just as they merged with the trees.

"Where we going!?" Daquasha was breathing hard, struggling with the duffel bag. She never realized how heavy paper money could be. "We need a car."

Tykim spun around and returned fire.

Daquasha was about to ask her questions again, but she felt a bullet breeze pass her. She turned and fired a shot. Suddenly, she saw the backyard of a house come into her vision. When she saw the motorcycle, she said, "Look Tykim, a bike."

Tykim turned his head and saw the bike. He ran towards it, increasing his speed. He hoped this was one of those bikes that could be hot-wired.

Tykim sat the duffel bag down and went to work on the bike with frantic haste. "Stand by that tree and keep shooting." He saw Daquasha obeyed as he fumbled with the wires connected to the bike's engine. When the wires were twisted together, he mounted the bike and kicked the foot-starter.

The bike started.

"Let's go!" Tykim revved the throttle and pointed the bike towards the front. "Grab the other bag!"

Daquasha grabbed the other duffel bag and jumped on the back.

Tykim hit the clutch and the bike jumped violently. It almost stalled. "Hold on to those bags real tight."

Just as the bike turned onto the road, Daquasha saw headlights approaching. She locked her arms firmly around Tykim's waist as he gunned the throttle. The bike jerked into its high speed take-off. The two cars that followed increased their speeds, the engines opening up with the sound of a collective roar.

CHAPTER # 21

Jamil sat next to his attorney, Ron Cody, struggling to hold back the anxious grin that tugged at his face.

The Courtroom was filled with family members of the victims. Jamil saw Brute sitting in the last row, dressed casually. Jamil hoped he wasn't underdressed for the occasion. His blue slacks and white Chinese collared shirt made him look like he was on his way to a party.

ADA Talbert, a mild mannered looking white man with striking blue eyes and jet black hair sat alone at his table. He looked shattered. Jamil wished he could have taken a picture of this beautiful, rare image.

"All rise," The court officer said.

The Judge, Hon. Stephen Folsom, entered the Courtroom as everyone rose to their feet. The Judge's premature balding hair style made him look like a rodeo clown who was suffering from hemorrhoids. Jamil sensed the Judge's pain-stricken expression was due to what he was about to do; cut him loose. He wanted a picture of this sight more than the ADA's picture.

"Please be seated," The Judge said as the crowded Courtroom obeyed his instructions. "ADA Talbert, are you ready?"

"Your honor, I have some very unfortunate news. The people have no indictment to offer this Court. Our only witness was murdered last night."

There were sniffling cries and angry whispers amongst the audience.

ADA Talbert continued. "We believe this defendant is responsible for Ms. Holmes' death. This was a--"

"Do you have proof of this?" The Judge said.

"Not at the moment, your honor."

"Then I advise you to refrain from that sort of talk in my Courtroom."

Ron Cody rose to his feet. "Your Honor, I move to dismiss the indictment for failure to prosecute."

"Motion granted," The Judge struck his hammer loudly.

As Jamil walked out of the Courtroom, he saw the vicious stares on the faces of all the victims' families. He instantly made a mental note to send out an investigator to accumulate the names and addresses of all the victims' family members. The look on their faces was serious business.

Brute rose and exited along with Jamil.

Ten minutes later, Brute was behind the wheel of an old creamy colored station wagon while Jamil was in the passenger seat.

Brute made a left turn. "I got some messed up news, Jamil. Kilroy sent Devil-dog and Lunatic down to Atlanta to deal with Danielle and Tykim. I would've said something, but you told me to keep everything on the DL."

Jamil gritted his teeth. "That's cool, you did right. Do they got an address of where they're at?"

"Yeah."

"Do you know it?"

"Yeah," Brute wondered where he was going with this.

"Take us to the airport." Jamil said, staring at the pedestrians on the crowded streets. "I hope you ain't got any plans. I need you to make this trip with me."

Brute was about to advise Jamil against this. He knew Kilroy wasn't going to appreciate Jamil intervening into this matter, but he quickly put a clamp on his lips because he wasn't about to get in the middle of two bulls locking horns. Plus, he knew Jamil was a loose cannon when his heart got mixed up with certain issues. In any event, he wasn't about to debate with the second man in charge.

£¥♥   £¥♥   £¥♥   £¥♥

Detective Guzmon's eyes were riveted on the station wagon as it turned on to the expressway.

From behind the wheel, Armstrong said, "You wanna try this again?"

"Don't plant any tempting seeds in the air. As pissed off as I am, I might just go there."

Armstrong saw a highway sign that said Laguardia Airport was ten miles away. "I wonder where he's going. Maybe we should pull back now."

"This case is still open," Guzmon said, "And we're the lead detectives. Bouncing a little out of our jurisdiction ain't gonna hurt nothing as long as we don't touch anyone. And especially if we don't tell anybody."

Armstrong shook his head. "Just make sure you don't get any crazy ideas with this guy. I don't feel up to cutting open anymore dead bodies and retrieving bullets."

Guzmon laughed. "The way your face looked when you slit that guy open and dug in his chest, I thought you were enjoying yourself."

Armstrong made eye contact momentarily. "I was trying to keep a leveled head, so we could get the hell away from there as quickly as possible."

Guzmon said, "I spoke with Danny. He said the fire concealed some of the circumstances. Since the guy had a track record as long as this highway, Danny said they could successfully write it off as gang related."

"It sure hurt to see that pretty car be put to the match." Armstrong sighed. "What a waste."

Twenty minutes later, Armstrong followed the station wagon onto the Laguardia Airport ramp leading to the parking lot. A minute later, he parked the car ten parking spaces away from the station wagon. They both watched Jamil and Brute get out of the car and head towards the Airport Terminal.

Guzmon and Armstrong looked on, irritated.

"This guy is going down there," Guzmon said, "He's planning to kill Danielle to make sure there's no one left to finger him."

"The way things are looking, I doubt if Captain Fletcher will allow us to make this trip."

"Well, I guess we gotta get creative in our endeavors to convince him." Guzmon went into deep thought. About a minute later, he smiled broadly. "Let's get out of here."

Armstrong saw the devious grin on Guzmon's face as he started the car. Moments later, Armstrong maneuvered back on to the highway. "From that look on your face, I assume the situation is about to get real heated. Just say the word, I'll be here, ready to get this thing poppin'."

£¥♥   £¥♥   £¥♥   £¥♥

Nuke sat at a huge dinner table with the Russians he'd just robbed. Devil-dog, Lunatic and Drac stood behind Nuke. Near the door were four Russian bodyguards who all had machine guns tucked in their waists. They made no attempt to conceal the fact they possessed military style weaponry.

Nuke decided if he couldn't enjoy that money nobody would. He also decided it would be a lot easier to track down Tykim and Daquasha with the help of an internationally connected group. These Russian cats had people in damn near every state in this country and they played no games when people stole from them. Nuke wanted those jewels back so bad, he'd kill anyone to get them. He was even thirsty for that two million and change worth of cash money. Nuke wanted it all. It would drive him crazy to sit around and not at least try to get all those riches back.

The red headed Russian, Ivan Putskoff, stared at Nuke. "Why does it seem like I know you from somewhere?" His foreign accent was very strong. "Have you ever worked for us before?"

Nuke almost panicked. He spoke in the strongest southern accent he could muster. "Nah, man, I don't know you. I ain't never worked for you." Ivan shook his head, still scrutinizing Nuke. "Well, we do appreciate you coming to inform us of these two robbers." He picked up the pictures of Daquasha and Tykim. "And you say Kilroy has big problem with them as well?" He looked at Devil-dog.

"Yeah," Devil-dog nodded his head. "They killed a couple of our peoples. And the bitch is snitching on Kilroy's brother."

"I heard of this Kilroy from several of my associates. They say he's good man."

Devil-dog saw Ivan's English was shot, but it was clear enough to be comprehended.

Ivan continued. "Tell your boss Kilroy we will join our forces to find these people. As for you Mr. Nuke, I will give you nice reward if we find them, say. . .ah. . .maybe five thousand dollars?"

Nuke wanted to tell him to stick it in his ass, but instead he just grinned and nodded his head.

"Now, we must make plan," Ivan said, "But, first you must meet the man who will be in charge of this whole mission." He waved to one of the Uzi totting bodyguards who opened the door.

In stepped a medium built white man who was wearing simple clothes. His face was even more simpler. It looked like he had a permanent smile on his face like the joker in the Bat-man cartoons. He was carrying a huge sack tossed over his shoulder, looking like a deranged Santa Claus, who just escaped from a maximum security prison.

Ivan continued, "Every one, please meet Boris."

Boris looked around the room at the faces. "I have one thing to say to all." His Russian accent was extreme. "If you have problem with following orders, you have option to leave right now." He gestured towards the door. A smile appeared when no one moved. "If anyone fucks up this run, if anyone jumps ship, if anyone becomes a rat, if anyone disobeys my order. This will happen to any and all violators." He dumped the contents of the bag onto the floor.

Eight human heads rolled from the sack, making hard disgusted thumps as they struck the floor, some bouncing and rolling about

132

indiscriminately. There were white, black, yellow, red and brown faces. Two were women and one was a child. They even looked freshly severed.

Boris spoke as he scrutinized the on-looking shocked faces. "All done by the hand of yours truly." He took a bow as if he was receiving applauds during a theatrical curtain call.

Ivan laughed when he saw some of the men's facial response. "Now, that that's out of the way, we shall discuss our plan. We should use all our resources. . ."

As Ivan explained how he felt the plan should be implemented, Devildog's cellular phone buzzed. "Excuse me y'all, I got a call." Devil-dog pulled his phone and moved to the corner of the room. "Hello,"

"Hey, Devil-dog," Jamil was standing at a phone booth inside the airport terminal.

Devil-dog's confusion was thick. "What's up Jamil? How you call straight out from a Rikers Island phone?"

"I'm home. The charges were dropped. Danielle wasn't the snitch. Listen up, I need you to do me a favor. Stay calm and pretend everything is still as is, but if you clash with Daquasha don't do shit to her."

"But, what about Kilroy he told us to--"

"Are you second guessing me motherfucker?!"

"No Jamil, I just don't want Kilroy spazzing out on us for not--"

"Didn't I say I'm giving you this order?"

Devil-dog relaxed. That's all he wanted to hear. "Sorry Jamil. I'm all ears, big dog."

It took three minutes for Jamil to explain what he wanted him to do. "Is there any way you can distract them until I get there?"

"I'll try my best," Devil-dog turned and whispered. "They stole two million and change from these cats and crazy jewels. They talkin' strictly drama."

Jamil's anxiety grew ten folds. "Where can I meet up with y'all?"

"I don't know right now," Devil-dog wanted to intervene into the groups planning session and ask where would they be headed, but knew that wasn't a wise move. "What I'll do is call you once we find out. Give me a call if you get here before I call you back."

"Remember, don't tell Kilroy shit if you talk to him."

Devil-dog smiled broadly. "No problem."

They both hung up.

As Jamil approached the boarding area, he wondered how was he going to explain all this to Danielle. There was so many things racing through his mind. Each issue seemed to feed off each other, compounding his pain and anger. His memory wouldn't give him a breather, since all his pass experience with the Russians told him this wasn't going to be a situation he could easily undo. Indeed, it was universally understood that when a person stole from the Russian mob, he didn't have many places to hide and the penalty was death for anyone who violated this rule, no exceptions what-so-ever.

CHAPTER # 22

Daquasha sat at a luncheonette table across from Tykim, eating a turkey and Swiss cheese sandwich. This establishment was located near the outskirts of Atlanta City. She was gobbling down her food as if she hadn't eaten in days. Trying to eat for two was serious business she was starting to realize. When her stomach growled, it felt like earthquakes rumbling through her whole body.

Daquasha saw Tykim's appetite was real slight. He was nibbling on his sandwich and seemed to have a lot on his mind. She saw the sun-rays dancing all over the interior of the Luncheonette. It was going to be a lovely day and this atmospheric circumstance was right in cohesion with her current mood.

After they escaped the two cars that pursued them for over twenty miles, Daquasha finally started to savor the thought that they had enough money to live very well for many years to come. Even the black bag containing the 37 Jewels she snatched along with the money had her all riled up. Those things looked too beautiful to be worth nothing as Nuke so snakishly put it.

Daquasha also noticed all this money and those jewels were transforming her. Maybe all this drama was a blessing in disguise after all. She felt this sudden urge to want to live every moment of her life all for what it was worth as if it was her last day on the planet. The saying, money changes people couldn't have been more accurate when placed side by side with what was going on inside of her.

Daquasha not only felt she could go cold turkey with cigarettes, but this new founded lust for living life demanded it. Somebody lied when they said money couldn't heal emotional, psychological and mental scars. She saw many wonderful things on the Horizon, and one of the things she wanted most was coming into view as a massive, heart soothing, dream come true image. It was so close she felt she could reach out and grab it.

Daquasha picked up her soda, took a sip and realized her shoulders were still aching profusely. She had two huge bruises on both her shoulders and her upper chest. Sitting on the back of the bike with both those heavy bags of money dangling from her shoulders was no small feat. During the ride, the pain became so extreme Daquasha thought she was going to lose one of her shoulders. It was clear if it wasn't for the fear of their pursuers catching and killing her, there would have been no way she could have endured this sort of grueling discomfort for so long.

"We gotta tighten the screws on our plan," Tykim said, "Now that we got us some real money, I think we'll be successful in our endeavors." He smiled at Daquasha.

"Ain't really much to tighten up," Daquasha said, "Since we're both fugitives from justice, we gotta find a way to get out of this country. Plain and simple. I thought we agreed to go to Mexico or any one of those South American countries?"

"Yeah, that's the long term goal, but what I'm getting at is we gotta find a way to get the materials we need to pull that off. I'm trying to figure out what State has a good counterfeiting ring in the direction we're traveling."

Daquasha realized exactly where Tykim was going with this. As she chewed on the last piece of her sandwich, Daquasha thought hard about Tykim's question. "I read a newspaper article a few months back. It said New Orleans had some of the most high-tech false ID rackets in the Country. They said the reason why this was happening down there is because some of the people doing this stuff were down with law enforcement."

Tykim smiled. "Well, I guess New Orleans here we come."

After they finished their meals, Daquasha and Tykim asked a waitress where could they find the nearest car dealer. They received the directions and landed at "Jerry's Car Dealer." Tykim wasn't choosy; all he wanted was a working vehicle durable enough to get them to New Orleans and then to Mexico. As result, it took them twenty minutes to purchase a navy blue Chevy Impala. Tykim gave Jerry six thousand dollars cash for the whole package, which included the car, full insurance, and temporary license plates. Since Daquasha had an extra set of false ID in her mother's real name everything was put in her name.

They drove in a south western direction for hours. Tykim was behind the wheel while Daquasha had a map laid open in her lap hurling directions and instructions whenever Tykim asked for them. The highways and byways were numerous, but once they hit Highway 85, things started to become less confusing. When the sun had set, they decided to make a stop. They had made it to Opelika, a small town in   Alabama. They stopped at a nearby store and bought two bags of groceries.

Carrying a huge duffel bag each, Daquasha and Tykim entered a shabby hotel and rented a room on the second floor. They paid for a 24 hours stay.

As Daquasha headed towards the elevator, she saw a woman dressed seductively and instantly knew this was a cheap hotel that catered to prostitutes and their tricks. Whether this was good or bad really didn't matter, since they were staying for a very short while. But the good thing was they could blend smoothly in with the general surroundings.

Daquasha saw the apartment looked clean and cozy. The smell of perfume soap fumigated the entire circumference. After Daquasha checked the rooms, she realized there was only one bed. This sight caused her evolving feelings for Tykim to take form once again. She struggled to hold on to her anger, but the memories were too strong. Daquasha hoped she knew what she was about to do because she decided to share the bed with Tykim tonight.

After they ate and took separate showers, they were ready for bed. As Daquasha expected, she saw Tykim had full intentions of sharing the bed with her and wasn't about to take no for an answer.

Tykim laid next to Daquasha and began massaging her thigh. He whispered. "Daquasha, you know I never stopped loving you."

Daquasha felt electricity run through her body the moment Tykim touched her. All the memories of her and Tykim's past sexual adventures bum rushed her mind. Her juices started to flow because she knew what was coming next.

Tykim sensed she had just given him the green light. If she wasn't in the mood, she would've made it known by now. "You remember when we was kids and all those times we said we would be together for the rest of our lives? Well, I don't know about you, but I meant that shit, Daquasha." He maneuvered his hand up to her breasts. When he saw she allowed him to do this, his dick snapped to attention.

Daquasha tried to tame her breathing without any luck. Her nipples suddenly became rock hard. She was ready to get it on, but wanted Tykim to initiate it all.

Tykim's hand traveled down to her vagina and he inserted two fingers. It was wet and extremely slippery inside. She open her legs while squirming in pleasure, and that told him everything he needed to know. Tykim rose and began kissing her.

Daquasha savored his wanting tongue. Breathing hard, she saw Tykim still knew where her gee spot was. As her hips began to move to a rhythm, she was thrilled he apparently hadn't forgotten the areas of sexual concern on her body. Thank goodness he was always considerate to her needs, she thought as her arms wrapped around his neck. Her tongue began to swirl around his with an urgency. She couldn't remember ever having sex with Tykim where there was a time he rushed through this delicate act.

As Tykim's fingers took care of business down-town and his tongue danced with her tongue, Daquasha began to compare between Tykim and Jamil. They both had their strong points, but what made judging who was the best a difficult task was they both made her come like crazy every time they touched her. Suddenly, Daquasha started trembling violently. The flashing hot organism sucked all the tension from her body as she spilled a juicy load onto his hand. She moaned and groaned under her breath.

Tykim pulled Daquasha's panties off and got on top of her. He grabbed his dick and was about to insert it into her watery tunnel.

Daquasha suddenly remembered she didn't know Tykim's health status and shoved him off of her. "You got a condom?" Breathing hard, she sat up right.

"Last year I got tested for HIV and all that stuff--"

Last year!? Daquasha tamed her breathing. "Listen, Tykim, I ain't been with you in years. People can get HIV and don't show no symptoms for weeks, months or even years." The safety of her child took center stage in her mind. "They call it the window period and I can't take no chances until we both put our cards on the table and make sure we--"

"Say no more," Tykim reached over, and grabbed a box of condoms. "Here they are." He opened the box and handed her one of the packs.

Daquasha looked at Tykim as if he was out of his mind. "Nigga, what I look like? Your fuckin' servant? You want it on, put it on your damn self." She tossed it back to him and felt her sexual appetite dribbling away. He had some fucking nerve.

Tykim excitedly ripped open the pack, put the condom on and began kissing her again. Daquasha's tight lips told him he fucked up.

Daquasha shoved him away. "I ain't in the mood." She laid down. She felt euphoric as a result of the nut she busted. She smiled because she got hers, but he didn't get his.

Tykim wanted to scream, curse and pound something. His dick was harder than cast iron and was throbbing with terrifying force. With a trembling struggle, he laid down and made himself relax. He wasn't about to give up. It wasn't in his character. He decided once she was asleep, he'd wake her up, catch her off guard like he used to do back in the days and lay this mandingo on her something proper.

After a moment Daquasha started feeling sorry for Tykim. The way he sighed it was obvious he wanted some of this pussy real bad. Her guilt grew unabatedly and her conscience reminded her that Tykim was putting his life on the line to save her. And she knew deep down inside he loved her. If he didn't, he wouldn't be going through all this hell for her. She rolled over and grabbed his dick.

Tykim was on top of her in a flash, kissing, massaging and taking his time. The plan was to put it on her like he'd never done before. Tykim went down on her.

Daquasha started screaming and hollering his name, while trying to crawl away from the awesomely powerful feeling. His tongue was as animated as a well greased machine.

Tykim played with her buttons in every way possible, flicking his tongue over her clit and wiggling it inside.

Daquasha dug her fingers into the back of Tykim's head as a river gushed from her. When he rose and mounted her, Daquasha felt his dick to make sure it was covered with latex. When he entered her, she thought she was going to explode again because he slid perfectly across her gee spot. She couldn't hold back her cries of pleasure as she wrapped her legs around Tykim's back.

Tykim pumped inside her. The deeper he went, the louder Daquasha hollered.

Five minutes flew by and the sweat poured from both their bodies. Fifteen and then twenty minutes slid pass; they were still going strong. By then, Tykim's knees were raw and his lower back and arm muscles were ablaze. Finally, they both exploded in unison and laid there holding each other. Their heavy breathing was harmonious.

Daquasha felt a tremendous wave of sleep swarm over her mind, but her whole being was in a state of sheer tranquillity. With drowsy eyes, she cuddled next to Tykim as he embraced her in his arms. She gently brushed her hand across his wash-board six pack. This was something he definitely had over Jamil.

Tykim rubbed her hand. "I guess this is the part where you spark up one of 'em cancer sticks." His tone was unmistakably filled with aggravation.

"For your information, I quit."

"I hope so, cause I'm about to put my foot down." He tapped her chin upward and gazed into her eyes. "I ain't never been into the business of letting people I love hurt and kill themselves." He kissed her and stared up at the ceiling. The night light cast shadows all over the room.

Daquasha savored those words as her finger-tips continued admiring his stomach muscles.

Tykim noticed the ring on Daquasha's pinkie finger. So this was the object she toyed with every time she got nervous or exited. Tykim grabbed her hand and kissed it. After looking closely at the ring, he remembered it. "Ain't this the ring you used to wear way back when we was doin' us?"

"Yeah," Daquasha's memories flooded her mind, but they surprisingly didn't spark any anger.

Tykim thought back, and it all came back to him. "This was the ring your brother gave you, right?"

She nodded her head propped against his arm. "Tareek gave me this ring on my birthday before he died. He saved up all his money he got from selling newspapers and from his allowance to get me this gift."

Tykim wondered should he change the subject. By the sound of her voice, he sensed she was eager to talk about it, so he egged her on. "It's obvious this ring means a lot to you."

"This is the only thing I own that I will never get rid of. Even when I had to pawn it when times got crazy, I would always come back for it. Tareek gave me this ring and made me promise to keep it forever."

The sudden sullen silence was loud and clear.

Daquasha squinted her eyes in shock when Tykim started rubbing her stomach. His gestures indicated he knew something was inside of her.

"I sure wish it was mine, Daquasha," Tykim felt a sincere pain in his heart. He wasn't into crying, but he truly felt that way right about now.

"What are you talking about?" Daquasha tried to sit up, but Tykim gently pulled her back into his arms.

"I know you're pregnant, baby girl," Tykim squeezed her close to him to reassure her it was all right. "The way you been throwing up and eating up everything are clear signs. I had two sisters that was having kids when I was a kid, remember? Plus, look at your tites, girl?" He massaged them. "They all swelled up." He was about to mention the fact that her pussy was unusually juicy and uniquely soft, a tell tale sign of pregnancy, but that would indicate he had hit a pregnant woman in the past. "I guess this baby is that creep ass nigga, Jamil's, huh?"

Daquasha felt totally awkward. "Yeah." She suddenly felt the urge to explain that this pregnancy just happened; it wasn't planned or anything. With an awkward struggle, she reminded herself that Tykim and her weren't man and woman at the time.

"Did he know you was pregnant when he tried to smoke you?" Tykim's tone was cold and callous.

"No. I never got the chance to tell him."

There was a long moment of silence.

Tykim kissed Daquasha on her forehead. "Don't worry, baby girl, I got your back no matter what happened in the past or what's going on now. We a team now and we gotta accept each other as is. When I said I'll love you to the end of time, I'm gonna show and prove it. I'll treat that baby as if it's my own."

Daquasha saw Tykim really did do some growing up over the years. "Tykim, thanks, Boo." She snuggled closer to him. "Tykim, I need favor."

"For you, baby girl, you can get a million favors from me."

"I need you to show me how to become a hit-man or hit-woman."

Tykim laughed. "Girl, ain't you somethin' A minute ago, you was callin' me all type of foul names because of my occupation. Now you want me to teach you this thang? Girl, you sho' is an enigma."

"Have you stopped to really look at our situation? We got professional killers looking for us. The police and probably the Feds too. We just robbed the Russian mob, and your fool ass cousin, who's an ex-cop. That's a lot of drama. I like life, and I ain't trying to get killed because I was caught off guard or not prepared. I gotta live for two people--me and my unborn child."

"Hey, now, I'm here to hold you down. I ain't playin' when I said I got your back--"

"What if something happens to you, and I'm left all alone?" She saw Tykim nodded his head. "My whole life has been nothing but fighting battles after battles, and I always knew the reasons I won most of those battles was because I was prepared for the storms I knew would always come. Whether it was emotional equipment or physical tools, I wasn't stupid enough to think I could fight and win without preparation and planning."

"Damn, baby girl, you sound like a philosopher or somethin'. Let me find out you been reading Sun Tzu's Art Of War on the down low."

"So what's up, you gonna teach me?"

"Damn right I am." Tykim reached over and kissed her with intense vigor. His Johnson rose into brick hard status within seconds.

"Hold up, now," Daquasha held Tykim back. Her voice was filled with drowsiness. "Now, I gotta fade out on you. I'm so tired, I feel doped up."

"Well, ain't this about a bitch." Tykim changed his voice, making it sound high pitched and woman like. "You fucked me and now you wanna go to sleep. You're so inconsiderate of my needs."

"Fuck you, Tykim," Daquasha tickled him under his wet armpit. She knew he was very ticklish and enjoyed making him squirm.

141

They both laughed while playfully wrestling with each other. Daquasha took it to the next level when she started bashing Tykim with the pillow. There was nothing like a good old fashion, down home pillow fight Daquasha concluded as Tykim bopped her in the head with his pillow. After a two minute workout, they settled down and both fell to sleep locked in a warm embrace.

£¥♥   £¥♥   £¥♥   £¥♥

Daquasha shifted her head on the pillow and the deep sleep disappeared. She opened her eyes and instantly saw Tykim was gone. Looking around the room, she saw it looked like the sun was either coming up or going down. She looked at the clock on the night stand and jerked out of bed. It was 6:10 p.m.

How could Tykim let her sleep the entire day away, she thought as she headed out the room. When she noticed the apartment was empty, she panicked. The first thing jumped into her head was that Tykim skipped out on her because she was pregnant. Tears were about to well up in her eyes. She rushed to the closet to see if he had taken the duffel bags of money. Daquasha snatched open the door. They were still there.

Daquasha repeatedly told herself to calm down and stop jumping to conclusions.

Suddenly, there was the sound of a key opening the door.

Daquasha went to the front of the apartment.

Tykim entered carrying two shopping bags. "So, old sleepy head finally came back to the world of the living." He smiled.

"Why you ain't wake me up?" Daquasha propped her hands on her hips. She was surprised Tykim had got rid of those corn-braids; his small afro made him look professional and intelligent.

"Girl, after all the shit we been through, don't you think it's time you start taking it easy."

Daquasha reprimanded herself for assuming Tykim abandoned her. She turned and entered the bathroom.

Twenty minutes later, they were exiting the apartment. The new clothes Tykim purchased fit her just right. Daquasha was surprised he not only knew her size, but also had her taste of clothing locked down as well. She also thought it was a wise move on Tykim's part when he brought two brief cases with combination locks for the money. Those two big crazy looking duffel bags made them look suspicious and streetish. She also liked the fact that Tykim purchased himself some casual, non thuggish clothing that were consistent with him carrying a briefcase.

The screams of a woman came from inside a room as they walked by. A man yelled, "I told you to get my money, bitch!" while striking the woman. Daquasha shook her head in disgust as she hit the button for the elevator.

Tykim frantically began checking his pockets. "Shit! I forgot the damn maps. I'll be right back." He jogged back to their room.

Just as Tykim entered the room, a light skinned black woman wearing tight blue jeans and a yellow blouse barreled out of the room where the screams came from. The crying woman was bleeding all over the place and was trying to smother her screams. A muscular black man with Jerri-curls and a goatee, wearing a white tank top tee shirt and had a metal clothes hanger in his hand, was wielding away at the woman while calling her bitch and demanding her to "shut the fuck up."

Daquasha felt a rage boiling at the core of her soul. "Leave her the fuck alone." She sat the brief case down and moved towards the pimp. His crazy looking eyes didn't scare Daquasha one bit, and so she continued towards him. "You're killing her, man. Be easy--"

The pimp sprung towards Daquasha with murder on his mind and malice intent in his bodily gestures. He moved like a black panther as he latched his hand around Daquasha's neck.

Daquasha scratched his face.

The pimp hollered, but maintained his grip around Daquasha's neck.

Daquasha started japping him in the face with a wave of jabs that were stiff, swift and professional like.

The pimp responded as if he wasn't the least phased by her attack. Still maintaining his locked grip around her neck, he began punching Daquasha repeatedly in the face. His grip tightened.

Daquasha realized she couldn't breath. She was about to panic. The pimp was definitely trying to choke her to death. She tried to scream for help while kicking, scratching and punching frantically. Tykim! Tykim! her mind screamed desperately, but those words wouldn't come out of her mouth. Daquasha suddenly felt her swings becoming sluggish. Then she just allowed herself to collapse to the floor.

Moments ago, Tykim heard a violent commotion in the hall as he found the maps. He headed towards the door nonchalantly assuming the noise was the pimp beating on his bitch. He exited the room and saw a man's back and a woman on the floor whimpering. The man was kneeled over as if he was striking someone.

Daquasha! The voice in his mind yelled when he noticed he didn't see her.

Tykim pulled his silencer equipped 9mm and ran at top speed down the hall. He kicked the pimp dead in his ass, sending him flying over Daquasha and into a baseball slide. When Tykim saw Daquasha trembling convulsively, he aimed the 9mm just as the pimp rose to his feet and hauled ass down the hall.

SZK!--SZK!--SZK!!

The first bullet hit the pimp in the upper shoulder. Simultaneously, the second and third shots hit him in the middle of the back. The pimp went headlong into another baseball dive, hitting the floor face first with agonizing force.

Tykim rushed to Daquasha with hysterical haste. When she started coughing and waving for him to help her up, he felt some relief. "Are you hurt?" He pulled her onto her feet. "Did he hurt you?"

"I'm okay," Daquasha said hoarsely while caressing her throat.

"What kind of hit-woman is you gonna be?" Tykim patted the 9mm tucked in Daquasha's waist. "Why you ain't use it, baby girl?" Through the corner of his eye, he saw movement. Tykim took off, heading for the pimp.

Daquasha tried to grab him. When Daquasha saw Tykim standing over the pimp firing silenced shots into the pimp's flinching body, she was instantly reminded of that night Jamil killed those three men. She saw Tykim rushing back towards her. He walked pass her and took aim at the blood covered woman who seemed to be drugged out of her mind.

"No!" Daquasha damn near tackled Tykim. "Don't kill her. She ain't do nothing; she's harmless."

"Daquasha, she's a eyewitness," Tykim turned and caressed Daquasha's arm. "If she talks, we'll never make it out of this State."

Daquasha looked panicked. Tykim was right. Damn it. They didn't need this shit. "We can't kill her. Hold up, I got a idea. Let's tie her up and drag him in the room. That should give us enough time to get some distance between us."

Daquasha went for the woman while Tykim ran towards the dead pimp. It took them several minutes to take care of business in accordance with the hastily concocted plan.

As Daquasha and Tykim exited the pimp and battered woman's apartment, utilizing the stairs instead of the elevator, they had no idea that two couples in near by rooms had already called the police. Both 911 calls were made around the time Tykim fired his first shot at the pimp.

CHAPTER # 23

Detective Guzmon hated airplanes. His loathing had nothing to do with him being afraid of flying per se, but it did have everything to do with the fact there were certain things that provoked this feeling. The food and the lack of roomy leg space were only a few of the things he really despised. Sitting in the window seat, he swept a clump of dandruff off his shoulders.

"Hey, take it easy there," Armstrong said, while waving his hand. He was reading a universal police profile manual. "I hope that stuff is not contagious."

"It's only dead skin."

"Well, flick that dead skin some where else." He picked up where he left off.

Guzmon pulled his handwritten notes from his pocket and began to read them. He was still amazed he and Armstrong were able to convince Captain Fletcher to let them take this trip down to Atlanta. Thanks to Jamil's hasty and suspicious activities, in conjunction with those airport surveillance tapes and documents showing Jamil traveled to Atlanta immediately after his release from custody, Guzmon was able to present a compelling argument in support of his position that Jamil was on his way to kill the only witness left who could identify him as the killer.

When Guzmon's eyes came upon the name John Cleveland, the special agent now in charge of investigating this case, he screwed up his mouth. He was agitated by the fact the Feds were now on the case; they received reliable evidence confirming that Danielle Lewis (AKA Daquasha Lawrence) and Tykim Hall had crossed State lines, were active fugitives of justice from the New York State jurisdiction and were engaging in additional, ongoing criminal activities in Atlanta, Georgia.

Right about this moment, Guzmon felt a surge of envy and jealousy. Guzmon never really had much control over his emotions. Jealousy and envy were the two emotions he particularly displayed weaknesses. From past experience he knew the FBI had far more resources and usually caught fugitives very quickly. He hated them for that because it made him and other State officials look incompetent when that wasn't the case. He sighed; if the FBI caught Danielle and Tykim before he did, that would mean he and Armstrong would be guilty of wasting precious departmental funds, substantial amount of man hours, and it would certainly kill his promotion. The urge to move faster made his heart pump harder.

Staring out the window at the clouds, Guzmon decided he was going to catch Danielle and bring her ass back to New York, even if he had to continue breaking some of the rules and bust open a million heads in the process. The quote: "The ends justifies the means" could not have been more accurate and true in this situation as far as Guzmon was concerned.

£¥♥   £¥♥   £¥♥   £¥♥

Jamil and Brute pulled the brown rental car into the lot of "Jerry's Car Dealer." From the passenger seat of this notoriously plain and simple looking vehicle, Jamil saw Devil-dog, Lunatic and Drac posted up near a red car, while a mob of white men (apparently the Russians) were prancing around the place as if they were running shit.

As Brute brought the car to a stop, Jamil saw Devil-dog approaching. About twenty minutes ago on the cellular phone, he had talked to Devil-dog and was informed that this was the place they were headed. With a heavy foot, Brute got them here in record time.

Jamil got out the car and gave Devil-dog a hug. After he was introduced to the rest of the underworld tracking team, Jamil pulled the Russian's crew chief to the side to have a talk with him. Jamil asked Boris how did they know Danielle and Tykim made a stop here at this car dealer.

Boris, who had sandy brown hair and a huge pimple laced nose said, "Our man Jerry here heard about our concerns and called us after he received our tab."

"There's a lot of places for a person to hide in a country this size," Jamil said, trying to encourage more dialogue. "How are we gonna find them if they go way under ground."

Boris laughed. "You full of jokes I see. I'm surprised you do not know about our way of doing things." He stopped and looked at Jamil suspiciously.

"Relax man," Jamil said politely. "I know how efficient you guys are when it comes to handlin' y'all business. I'll put it to you straight up. I need to know what is your plan of action in clear detail. I want to catch these motherfuckers so bad, and I can't afford any mistakes, nor can I waste precious time."

Boris's smile returned. "We have moles inside many police departments. And we have access to a radio frequency interceptor. We can pick up radio waves from all across the country. We also have people everywhere."

147

"But what if they don't touch any underworld folks? I hear they stole a lot of money from y'all. If they have money, don't you think they'll use it to their best advantage?"

Boris folded his arms across his chest. "It doesn't matter what they do. We have put out what we call a universal tab on them. Since they're running from the law as well, they might try to leave the Country. To do that, they will need fake ID, and identity change of some sort. That's why we are putting out a tab in Alabama, Mississippi, Florida, Louisiana, Arkansas, Texas and even Mexico. The tab is not complete yet because our people must contact tens of thousands of places." He laughed again. "You see, there is no place for them to hide or run."

Jamil nodded his head. He shook Boris's hand and was now glad he decided to play this thing real close. He walked over to Devil-dog and Lunatic and pulled them both to the side, out of hearing range of the others. "Listen Devil-dog and Lunatic, I need y'all to hold me down. Kilroy fucked up. We're gonna protect Danielle and kill Tykim."

Lunatic shook his head with terror on his face. "Yo, Ja, this is crazy man. Kilroy wants them both dead because they both responsible for killing five of us. I don't want no parts of disobeying Kilroy--"

BLAAM!

Jamil punched Lunatic in the face with an over hand right. The impact of the blow dropped Lunatic to the ground. Jamil began stomping Lunatic's head. "Nigger, I will kill you if you ever second guess my order!" He continued stomping and kicking Lunatic for a minute straight.

Devil-dog felt helpless. He wanted to save his right hand man, but that would be suicide.

The Russian's started laughing joyfully. Nuke admired Jamil's no nonsense behavior. Drac and his crew looked on with stone cold expressions. Black men fighting in front of white folk was taboo in their world.

Jamil reached down, grabbed a handful of Lunatic's shirt and jerked him onto his feet. Breathing like a deranged maniac, Jamil positioned his mouth inches from Lunatic's face and whispered. "I'll repeat your instructions. When we clash with them you are to protect Danielle and kill Tykim. Is that clear?"

Lunatic nodded with frantic force.

Jamil shoved Lunatic back to the ground and headed for the rental car.

When Lunatic hit the ground, he noticed a runaway tear had escaped his eye. As he struggled to his feet, he realized he was crying. There was no words to describe the level of embarrassment and humiliation he felt. Everybody was looking at him and he wanted to kill them all. He hadn't cried in years, but each time he did, he literally went on a suicide mission, killing that person responsible for making him cry and, in some cases, the person's whole family as well. He watched Jamil get inside the car. He smiled broadly because in that moment he decided to kill Jamil the moment the time was right.

£¥♥   £¥♥   £¥♥   £¥♥

Tykim's foot on the gas pedal kept the car steady at 50 miles per hour. This burgundy 1991 Cadillac coup deville they purchased in Auburn Alabama rode like it was floating on a cushion of air. The bumps in the road were virtually non-existent. As a safety precaution, Tykim decided to discard the Impala.

Earlier, as they raced out of the hotel in Opelika, they noticed there were too many eyes on them. In any event, they wisely concluded that it would be sheer stupidity for them to keep a car that might be linked to the dead pimp. There was no doubt the dead pimp would be found and the drugged out prostitute was bound to talk.

With the car radio turned on to a Mississippi black radio station called WKPF, Daquasha bounced to the beat. Even though she was sporting a black eye from the beating she took from the pimp, she felt in a half ass good mood. For the first time since this nightmare began, she started to feel good internally. Things were far from being favorable for them, but she had to force herself to find a way to bring some peace to her mind and inner being. If forcing herself into a good mood by thinking about the money and her and Tykim's new founded love would do the trick, then so shall it be.

Six hours later, the Cadillac pulled off highway 85 and on to the streets of New Orleans.

After covering ten miles into the city limits, Daquasha noticed they had entered a shopping district.

"I can make that stop here," Tykim said as he started looking for a parking space.

Moments later, as Tykim parked the car, Daquasha said, "You can handle this by yourself?"

Tykim hit the lever on the door. "You got jokes, huh? Just make sure you keep up that happy spirit, baby girl." He threw her a kiss, closed the door, and headed towards the grocery store that was in the middle of a Cleaners and a Drug Store.

As Tykim entered the grocery store, Daquasha saw a cop car turning the corner a block away in front of her. Her anxiety was turned on instantly. Daquasha fought to keep her eyes and mannerisms in a normal state as the police approached. When the cop car slowed to a crawl, while the two white officers inside scrutinized her, Daquasha's hand reached for the gun that was in her tote bag.

Inside the store, Tykim was stuffing food items into the small red plastic hand basket. So far, he had picked up sliced turkey and cheese, bread, pickles, Mayo, orange juice and a bottle of multi-vitamins. He headed for the cashier and saw the newspaper rack and snatched up one of the papers. He turned to the international news section, looking to see if he and Daquasha made it to the big time. After briefly scanning over two articles, he saw the head line "The World's Second Largest Jewel Heist Remains Unresolved." Tykim began to read.

When he saw the heist was in Atlanta, Georgia and mention was made about the Russian crime family's involvement, his eyes widened. He almost lost his composure when the article said the jewels were worth 130 million dollars. "Goddamn!"

Tykim looked around and saw his outburst caused the other customers and the cashier to look at him suspiciously. As he paid the cashier for the items, he saw the cop car out the corner of his eyes. He turned and saw the car had stopped next to the Cadillac. A lightning rod of terror gripped him when he realized one of the cops was talking to Daquasha while he remained in the car. He truly didn't know what to do.

Outside, Daquasha was surprised by her ability to speak calmly without a hint of nervousness. "Yes, officer, me and my husband are visiting."

"That's nice," The brown haired officer, who wore dark sunglasses in the passenger seat said, "But down here in New Orleans, we park our cars correctly. Tell your husband to keep that tale end tucked in." He was upset he couldn't lay down his pressure game since this gorgeous black girl was married and her husband was close by. Well, maybe next time. Boy did he love him that sweet dark chocolate meat.

The other officer, who had a fat face, said, "Take it easy with those slips and falls the next time." Slip and fall my ass. He wanted to wait and have a talk with her husband. "A pretty little face like yours deserve to be treated properly."

"I'll take it easy the next time, officer."

The brown haired officer said, "Since I'm in a good mood today, I'm gonna cut y'all a break."

"Thank you, officer," Daquasha gave him her best smile. "God bless you, officer."

The cop car pulled off. Daquasha and Tykim both sighed in relief.

£¥♥   £¥♥   £¥♥   £¥♥

Twenty minutes later, Tykim stopped at a red light and saw a street full of shabby looking houses. Further down the block, he saw a patch of tenement like buildings. In the front yard of one of the houses, he saw a sign that said, "Rooms For Lease."

"How's this area?" Tykim said to Daquasha.

She scrutinized the surroundings. There were a group of little black boys playing stick ball in the street. The entire scenario screamed ghetto. "I think it's all right."

When the light changed, Tykim turned right and found a parking space across from a raggedy house that had a small patch of dead grass and a frail bush in front of it.

As Daquasha and Tykim got out of the car, a fight broke out with the group of little boys. Two boys were pounding each other as the others rooted them on.

Tykim walked over towards the fight carrying a brief case. Daquasha tagged along wondering what Tykim was up to. She too carried a brief case.

"What y'all doin'!?" Tykim pulled the two apart. "Chill. Friends ain't supposed to hurt each other. Ain't y'all friends?"

"He's a cheater," The short boy shouted. "And he's a liar."

"Yo, mama's a cheater and a liar!" The taller boy blurted back.

The shorter boy angrily tried to get pass Tykim.

"Okay, okay," Tykim held him back with a small struggle. "I'll tell you what I'll do. If y'all two apologize to each other, I'll buy everyone as much ice cream as they can eat. And whoever apologizes first will get this twenty dollar bill." Tykim pulled the bill from his pocket.

When the two boys saw the money, their eyes lit up. The two started screaming and hurling apologies at each other while laughing, hugging and patting each other on the back.

Daquasha stood by smiling inwardly. Now she understood why her mother called Tykim an oxymoron; he was truly a healthy poison, and her moms apparently saw these attributes after only one long talk with Tykim.

Tykim laughed, as the two boys insisted he was the winner. They both started jumping up and down, trying to snatch the bill from Tykim's raised hand. "Chill, chill. hold up. Check this out."

The boys stopped jumping, now listening intently.

Tykim reached in his pocket. "I gotta admit, I think this was a tie. What you think, Daquasha?"

"Yeah, I think so too."

"Well, I guess y'all both get a twenty."

The whole group of boys cheered as Tykim gave the two grinning boys a twenty dollar bill.

"What about the ice cream you promised?" A little boy with biscuit cheeks said.

Tykim counted them all. There were twelve all together. He reached in his pocket and peeled off two fifty dollar bills from a huge web of money. "Who's the crew chief here?"

The boys screamed "Kasiem" as a light skinned, handsome kid stepped forward.

"Listen, Kasiem, make sure everybody gets as much ice cream as they want. When y'all finish, I want y'all to meet me back here. Okay?"

"Yeah, man." Kasiem said with his hand out.

Tykim gave him the bills, and they all raced down the street cheering happily.

Daquasha walked over and caressed Tykim's arm as they watched the boys running down the street. When the boys made a turn, Daquasha and Tykim headed towards the tenement building that had the "Rooms For lease" sign.

They had no problem leasing a first floor apartment in a building three blocks away from where they talked with the boys.

They entered the apartment and Daquasha did her usual inspections of the whole place. The smell of mold, mildew and old paint was thick in the air. It was clear the place needed to be overhauled as far as cleaning was concerned. Thank goodness they we're not staying here very long.

"Listen, Daquasha," Tykim said as he stood looking at a window. "I gotta hit the streets. I see our little friends are back." He saw the kids down the block waiting as he instructed them to do. "I gotta find us a connection for the identity change materials."

"Stop at a store on your way back and pick up some cleaning detergents or whatever else you can think of that'll straighten this place out for the time being. And don't forget we need some more groceries."

"I got that," Tykim headed for the door. "I'll be right back." He disappeared out the door.

A moment later, Tykim was talking to the boys again. He asked them how could he go about finding someone who sold things like guns. He knew if he found a gun dealer, that person could direct him to other illicit materials. The boys told him about a guy named Dezoe and where he could be found. Tykim followed their instructions, and as just they said, Dezoe had a small appliance repair shop on the other side of town.

Tykim entered the shop and saw Dezoe was a high yellow black man who definitely had European in his blood. His hair was nappy, but his skin was white through and through. Tykim approached. "How you doin' my brother?"

Dezoe looked at him tiredly. "Can I help you?" His southern drawl was heavy and very pronounced.

Tykim looked around suspiciously and lowered his voice. "I wanna buy some guns."

Dezoe locked eyes with Tykim, maintaining a straight face. "This is an electronics repair shop, not a gun store. Didn't you read the sign?"

"Listen, Bro," Tykim pulled a huge roll of money from his pocket. "I ain't the police. I'm living way on the edge and I need a few things."

Dezoe pulled a recording detection wand from under the counter. He saw Tykim's confused response. "Hold your horses. I'm just making sure." Dezoe scanned the wand over Tykim's body and looked at the monitor. "There's no such thing as being too careful." He saw there were no bugs or listening devises on Tykim. "What you looking for?"

"Well, I need a few guns and a full identity change for two, me and my girl."

Dezoe stared at Tykim for a moment. "How much you willing to spend?"

"Whatever it takes to get the best shit you got. The ID stuff gotta be good enough to get us out of the country."

"Well, I hope your pockets are quite deep because I'm a high roller when it comes to ID alteration. My prices range from 10 to 50 gees per person. I can clear you in every data base in the world."

"How fast do you work?"

"In an hour, I can have you in and out."

"I gotta pick up my girl, but first I wanna buy some hardware."

Dezoe showed Tykim an arsenal of some of the most high-tech weaponry he'd ever laid eyes on. Tykim purchased three super compact 9mm Uzis equipped with silencers, a professional marksman rifle with a night vision scope along with several boxes of bullets, all for seven thousand dollars. Tykim left an additional three thousand dollars with Dezoe as proof that he'd return. After assuring Dezoe he'd be right back with his girl, Tykim exited the shop.

Tykim raced back to the apartment, dropped off the new guns, retrieved a hundred and fifty thousand dollars, and raced out the apartment with Daquasha.

Tykim and Daquasha entered the shop.

"I want the top of the line ID change," Tykim said, as he opened the brown paper bag, showing Dezoe the money. "I'll give you a hundred grand."

Dezoe was practically licking his lips as he ushered Tykim and Daquasha towards the back of the shop.

As Dezoe was taking pictures of Daquasha, his phone rung. "I'll be right back." He headed towards the front of the shop. Dezoe picked up the phone. "Hello."

"Hey, Dezoe," Ivan's Russian accent was in full mode. "We have tab. Be on look out for black male and female." He described them both.

"Oh, shit!" Dezoe muttered loudly and then whispered. "They're here right now! They're buying the Executive line ID change."

"What!?" Ivan was filled with happiness. "Listen, if you kill them, I got twenty grand for you."

"Wait a minute, Ivan. You know that ain't my MO. I told y'all I don't handle heat like that. I sell that shit and that's it."

"Okay, okay, I understand. Can you hold them there for couple of hours."

"Be specific, Ivan. How long you talkin'?"

Ivan sighed because he knew his answer was ridiculous. "Five or six hours."

"Come on, let's be serious. Listen, I tell you what I'll do. I'll plant a homing devise in their documents. You can track them down when you get here. I'll get paid for making this sale and y'all get your targets. Bingo, everybody's happy."

"That's excellent. Dezoe, we won't forget this. Thank you." Ivan hung up.

Dezoe returned to the back of the shop and picked up where he left off. Daquasha instantly detected Dezoe's sudden change in behavior. He was acting too nice all of sudden; laughing and grinning as if he wanted to make certain they didn't change their mind about purchasing the fake documents. Whoever he spoke to over the phone apparently caused this change in attitude, she was sure of it. Watching Dezoe closely, she turned, rotated and twirled her pinkie ring.

Daquasha saw Dezoe hand Tykim a package containing documents ranging from driving licenses and military Service IDs to passports and public library cards. When Tykim counted off a hundred thousand dollars and gave it to Dezoe, she concluded Dezoe was probably acting that way because of all that money.

As she followed Tykim out the door, Daquasha determined she was once again jumping to conclusions and becoming paranoid. When she got in the car, Daquasha struggled with the bad vibe she was experiencing, but she squelched it after Tykim handed her the envelope and she closely examined all the professionally made materials. According to the documents, her new name was Janice Warner while Tykim's was Wallace Warner.

CHAPTER # 24

Detective Guzmon felt like a Tennis ball caught in the middle of a championship match. The moment he and Armstrong bounced off the plane and met the two Atlanta undercover cops (Kenneth Ball and Jackson Odell), they had to bounce back on a private jet bound for New Orleans. Guzmon was fastening his seat beat when Kenneth, a white man with sandy brown hair and youthful features, approached.

Kenneth took a seat across from Guzmon and Armstrong. "We're sorry about all this rushing, but we got a reliable lead on the suspects we're all after."

The small private jet began to move down the runway.

Detective Jackson quickly took a seat next to his partner, Kenneth and fastened his seat beat. Jackson was a muscle bound black man with an army style haircut and huge hands.

Within seconds, the aircraft was airborne.

Jackson looked at Guzmon with a icy cold expression. After a moment he said, "Again, we wanna welcome you guys to this joint investigation. There's a lot going on, and I think we need to bring y'all up to status." He pulled a small note pad and flipped a few pages. "The Feds have taken over this case, but the agent in charge, Mr. John Cleveland, has allowed us, including you guys as well, the courtesy of helping out wherever needed."

Guzmon shifted in his seat. "How are they so certain they're in New Orleans?"

"The Feds have a deep-cover agent involved in this case. Basically, when they get a lead on these perpetrators, it's forwarded to Mr. Cleveland."

Armstrong said, "I read this report you gave us." He gestured to Kenneth. "It says the FBI is also taking jurisdiction over all other extrinsic matters. What's the back story here?"

Jackson said, "There was a 130 million dollar jewel heist committed by a Russian crime family in Atlanta. The Clairborne Jewelry heist. The deep-cover agent was moments from cracking the case wide open, but in came those good ole New Yorkers and fucked up everything. In a nut shell, Mr. Hall and Ms. Lawrence stole the jewels from the Russians."

Kenneth added. "Now we're all locked in this big race to see who's gonna get them first."

Guzmon shook his head, amazed and furious at how Daquasha and Tykim were digging themselves into a remarkably inescapable and deadly corner. The realization that there was a very strong chance Daquasha wasn't going to make it through this alive, caused the acid in his stomach to bubble. But the piece of information that perplexed him and created some profound anxiety was the jewels. A 130 million dollars was a hell of a lot of money! Guzmon instantly realized it was apparent people would kill with a boldness not of this world for that kind of money. And personally speaking, Guzmon couldn't blame them, since he would have done the same under those circumstances.

£¥♥   £¥♥   £¥♥   £¥♥

Jamil stared out the window of the huge private jet that was transporting all ten of his men, Drac and his four men and five Russian soldiers. The aircraft was positioning itself to land on a long black landing strip somewhere in a swamp region in New Orleans. A similar jet had landed several minutes earlier and was carrying Nuke, and twenty other Russian soldiers.

The jet's landing gear made contact with the concrete landing strip. Jamil bounced in his seat. He admired the sophisticated nature of this jet. Jamil also saw the Russians really did have universal connections.

Earlier, as they approached the Mississippi border to check out a shooting believed to be connected with Danielle and Tykim, Boris got a call. He immediately pulled over, bringing the sixteen vehicle convoy to a stop. That was when Jamil found out Danielle and Tykim were currently in New Orleans. They had purchased fake IDs from an affiliate of the Russians. Boris made a phone call, did a U turn, lead the convoy to a private airstrip about five miles away from where they stopped and boarded the two jets.

As the jet moved down the runway, Jamil evaluated his current behavior. He was coming to terms with the fact he was pussy whipped, hooked, sunk and strung the fuck out. He giggled inwardly because ten years ago, this would have been unheard of. Suddenly, his mind reminisced of the day he decided to get with Danielle. He knew her for years, but she didn't know him. He even knew her real name was Daquasha Lawrence. His sorrow for her was what motivated him to go out with her. She had a fucked up life, and Jamil felt guilty and wanted to make amends by showing her a good time.

The inward bout of giggles returned as the jet came to a stop. To this day, even he still couldn't believe he started out trying to merely repay her for the pain he caused, and ended up getting his nose wide open and his heart trapped in a web of love that only grew with every moment he spent with her. Whoever said love was one of the World's greatest enigmas sure knew what the hell they were talking about.

Jamil got off the jet and headed towards Boris, who was talking to a group of Russians. Jamil saw five brand new vans all lined up. These cats had their shit together, Jamil reaffirmed internally, and the thought brought a severe case of doubt into his mind. Again he asked himself how was he going to save Danielle with this kind of pressure coming at her?

"Hey, Boris," Jamil said, "I need to see you when you're finished."

Boris nodded and continued talking to the soldiers. He was really into whatever it was he was explaining.

About five minutes later, Boris approached Jamil. "Hey, Buddy, what's up?"

"I know I'm probably over anxious, but I need to know are we gonna get some better guns? I can make a few calls and have an arsenal sent over--"

"Say no more," Boris headed over to one of the vans. "Come, come." He waved for Jamil to follow. Boris opened the back door of the van.

When Jamil saw the two gun racks containing an assortment of weaponry, his plan was instantly revised.

Nuke joined them and peer over Jamil's shoulder into the van. "Boy, is we gonna have some fun."

Jamil turned and realized every time he laid eyes on Nuke, he sensed something real foul about this cat. "Don't be breathing over my motherfuckin' shoulder no more."

Boris quickly intervened, cutting off Nuke's comment. "Okay, now, my friends. Let's take it easy. The last thing we need is team members fighting and killing each other. I would make y'all kiss and make up, but we got no time for that." Boris whistled to all the others and shouted. "Let's move out." He turned and said to Jamil and Nuke. "Whoever throws the first blow, will die."

Jamil pulled himself from the staring match and headed for the van he saw Devil-dog and the rest of his crew entering. He tucked a note in the back of his mind in the same fashion as a bookmarker is placed between pages; that cat Nuke was definitely on his hit list. Every time he sniffed the air when Nuke was around, he instantly smelled a rat and a great big ole one at that.

£¥♥   £¥♥   £¥♥   £¥♥

Daquasha and Tykim were on the roof of the tenement building where they had leased an apartment. Tykim approached the railing in tip-toe fashion as Daquasha followed. Tykim peered over the railing and saw the busy streets below.

"Let's set up here." Tykim sat the briefcase down, kneeled, opened the briefcase and began putting the high-powered rifle together. "Watch closely, try to remember the parts that go with each other. When we get in the apartment, you can put it together and take it apart until you can do it like you know the back of your hand."

When the rifle was assembled, Tykim laid a blanket out, positioned the rifle and got on his stomach.

Daquasha was next to him, mimicking Tykim's every movement. Her excitement was high and she couldn't understand why this was making her feel horny.

Looking through the scope, Tykim said, "What direction is the wind blowing?"

"This way," Daquasha pointed. "That means we gotta compensate by aiming at a spot a little off what we really wanna hit."

"That's right, baby girl." Tykim smiled, as he locked on a fat black man who turned a corner and headed towards them. "Here, Dee up on the fat guy coming this way."

They quickly changed places. Daquasha now behind the scope and Tykim next to her.

Daquasha saw the fat man in the scope. The cross marker in the lens landed on his right arm.

"If the wind fluctuates," Tykim said, "What do you do?"

"I try to shoot at a moment when the wind is in my favor. But if I have to shoot when the wind is bad, I compensate."

Tykim smiled. "Yeah, baby girl." He kissed her on the cheek. "That's it for now."

"I thought you said I could shoot something?" Daquasha maintained her position.

"Hey, now," Tykim was dead serious. "We ain't gonna be shootin' no innocent folks."

Daquasha pulled herself from the scope and beamed at Tykim. "I'm talkin' about shootin' a thing, not a person, man." She looked back in the scope. "You see that one way sign about two blocks away? I bet you I can hit the "E" in that sign."

"Do your thang, baby girl." Tykim dug in his nap sack, pulled out the set of binoculars and gazed at the sign.

Daquasha took aim and fired. The silencer made a muffled sound similar to a fat man passing gas. She saw when the bullet hit the sign, it scared a stray dog, causing it to haul ass.

"Well, well, my baby girl is a sho' shot, huh?" He said admiring the bullet hole through the binoculars. It wasn't a bulls eye, but it was excellent shooting for a beginner. By the look of that shot, he wondered if she was really new to this?

Daquasha felt gassed up. "I hit it!" She sounded like a child who just learned how to ride a bike.

Tykim rose to his feet. "Let's pack it up."

Moments later, in the apartment, Daquasha and Tykim was in bed having sex. Daquasha moved her hips to Tykim's gentle thrusting motions. Tykim was on top and began swirling his hips to their collective rhythmic endeavors. With electricity racing through her body, Daquasha realized her and Tykim were acting like they were high school teenagers again, having sex whenever the spirit moved them or whenever a bed was nearby.

"Yes, yes," Daquasha moaned as Tykim's pumping motions increased. The harder he pumped, the better the feeling became. The thrusting motions of his hips brought toe curling waves of pleasure through her whole body every time he penetrated her. Suddenly, the electricity fired through her body as she unleashed a glob of juices. She moaned in great delight as Tykim groaned along with her.

They held each other as their hearts thundered together. Their breathing sounded like two dancing buzz-saws singing in unison.

Tykim began kissing Daquasha while holding his position inside of her. After a moment, she felt his hardness slowly becoming softer. It was fading with each pulsating beat of his heart, but he continued kissing her with a deep passion.

Daquasha politely pushed him off of her. She felt like talking. Talking after sex was always an avenue for finding out what truly lied in the heart. If a man had no deep feelings for the woman he'd just fucked, it would reveal itself in how he talked to her after he got his rocks off.

Daquasha cuddled closely to Tykim with her hand on his chest. She could feel the rapid beat of his heart. A euphoric wave of good feelings came over her; she was finally going to get what she wanted. "Tykim, are you really ready to settle down?"

"With you I am. Baby girl, knock it off. You know I was always strung out over you."

"Family life ain't easy."

"Nothing worth having is ever easy."

"Time changes people and their views, and you ain't no exception to the rule. What's your views on family?"

Tykim thought about the question. Suddenly, he remembered a quote Daquasha had told him years ago. "I think. . .Family is everything."

Daquasha instantly saw what Tykim was doing. "I see ain't nothing wrong with your memory. I told you that's what my father used to say. Now we gotta see if it's really in your heart. I guess time will tell."

"Have you not heard that your word shall be born regardless to whom or what?"

Daquasha sighed impatiently. "That's the knowledge, knowledge degree, and you need to make sure you know and understand the answer, cause I do."

"If there's one thing about me, and I know you gotta know this, Daquasha, and that is my word don't fail, baby girl." He kissed her on the forehead.

"Yeah, okay. In the meantime, name some places in South America, where we could raise a family."

Tykim thought about the question only for a moment. "Venezuela, Guyana or Brazil."

"Guyana!?" Daquasha remembered she had a friend who was born in this country and used to talk about the place constantly. "What you know about Guyana?"

"I read about it in this travel magazine when I was in prison. There was this picture of this black couple. They was running on the beach. They looked so happy. I imaged it was me and you. Whenever I saw pictures of couples, I always thought about me and you."

Daquasha sucked her teeth. "Yeah, right. You ain't gotta stroke my ego and my heart. I thought I already proved I forgave you, so stop trying to lay all that grease on me." She tickled Tykim playfully just as he was about to respond.

"No, stop it!" Tykim giggled, while frantically trying to grab her hands. "You know I can't handle that, Daquasha." He laughed even harder as she warded off his hold. He grabbed and held on to her hands.

She broke away and tickled him again. His laughter made her feel good. It was the sound of sincere peace and harmony, something she hadn't seen, heard or felt in quite a while. She gave him a break and she saw he settled down. Daquasha felt she was now ready to ask some hard questions that were nagging at her curiosity for a while. "Tykim, what caused you to become a hit man? Of all the occupations in the world, why one where you kill people?" She sounded totally disgusted.

Tykim could've sworn he mentioned some of the reasons why he became a hit-man when they were at the hotel in Delaware. This time he would lay it all on her thick and uncut. "I don't know if I actually chose that line of work of my own volition. I would say it chose me."

Tykim held the silence for a moment. "What I'm about to say ain't got nothing to do with me greasing you, so don't even start assuming. The truth as the truth in my book. When I was in prison, besides thinking about you, all I dreamed about was finding that motherfucker who killed Tareek. I will never forget that voice and what he said just before he shot Tareek.

Tykim went into another short silent trance. "When I got out of prison, I vowed never to sell drugs again, and since drugs was the root of all my misery, I figured I could give back to the community by killing drug dealers and at the same time possibly find the nigga that killed Tareek. I only did hits against drug dealers or people connected in some way to drug dealers. And the only reason I took the hit against you is because it was so big and they told me you was the girlfriend of a big time drug dealer."

"What did this guy say before he killed my brother?" Daquasha inquired. She swept her fingers across his muscle laden stomach.

Tykim paused for a long moment. "He said japper, dapper, the smooth clapper. And then he just shot him." He left out the fact it was a pointblank shot to the head.

Daquasha squinted her eyes in confusion. "Japper, dapper the smooth clapper!?"

"Yeah, that's what he said. I guess it was some kind of ritual type word he would leave behind or something. Sort of like what serial killers do when they leave behind clues."

The silence filled the room.

£¥♥   £¥♥   £¥♥   £¥♥

Meanwhile, about twenty miles away from the tenement building Daquasha and Tykim were laid up in, Jamil was in the passenger seat of one of the vans. This vehicle was the third van in the convoy of four. Jamil's heart raced in his chest because he was just informed by Boris on the walkie talkie that they picked up a stationary signal. The targets were on the western side of New Orleans.

Jamil turned and gave Devil-dog the eye. When he saw his head nod, Jamil eased his stare over and laid his eyes upon Lunatic. There was something in Lunatic's eyes that told him there was going to be problems. His smirk seemed a little too bold. After years of surviving in the street, Jamil saw something in Lunatics eyes that made him very nervous.

As Jamil turned around facing forward, he wondered would it be a wise move on his part to keep Lunatic in front of him, where he could keep his eyes on him at all times.

£¥♥   £¥♥   £¥♥   £¥♥

Not too far behind Jamil and the four van convoy were Detective Guzmon along with six law enforcement vehicles. Special agent Cleveland and a mob of FBI agents lead the convoy. They were looking for the convoy of four vans. Special Agent Cleveland had received a call from his deep-cover agent informing him that they were heading west, but he was unable to provide additional specific details at the moment. However, he assured Cleveland that they couldn't miss the convoy if they saw it because there were two red vans and two black vans all moving in single formation.

£¥♥   £¥♥   £¥♥   £¥♥

Lying in bed, Tykim said, "Give me a run-down of the basic things you should know to be an effective cleaner?"

"Try to keep the element of surprise at all times. Aim for the center mass of the target. Heart shots are better than head shots. Know your weapon. Be mindful of the direction of the wind is blowing when shooting at a distance. Ah. . ." Her eyes squinted. "Ah, I think that's it."

"Nope. When you complete a hit, it dies with the target. Never discuss or talk about it ever again."

The silence was momentary.

"Tykim, who do you think is the most famous hit-man of all times?"

"That's kind a hard to say, since each time period had their top cats. Way back in the days around the medieval times, there were some Arab dudes called assassins. In the 1920's and 30's, there was Murder Inc. Then in the 40's, the most famous hit-man had to be this German cat named Skorzeny. But all and all, the CIA are the best cleaners in this day and age."

"The CIA!?" Daquasha was aghast. "I thought they were government agents who protect the country?"

"Yeah, that's part of what they do, but they just happen to be one of the most murderous agencies in the world. They don't kill petty ass street corner idiots either, they blaze Presidents of other countries, and big time cats surrounded by armies and shit. Straight up, they are some bad motherfuckers, when it comes to cleanin' up shit."

"Damn, I see you really did your homework." Daquasha suddenly jumped out of bed and headed for the radio.

Tykim savored the view of her naked body. She was truly a dream girl. His mouth watered as he gazed at her meticulously beautiful ass, her small waist and those perfect sized breasts. She was a bomb and a half. His dick pulsated back into attention.

Daquasha turned on the radio. The reception was bad. She turned the dial. Nothing happened. She went to turn the volume and knocked her purse to the floor. Suddenly, the reception came in clear. She squinted her eyes.

Daquasha picked up the bag and put it back on the table next to the radio. The reception went crazy again. "What the hell." She muttered out loud. She picked up the purse and stepped away from the radio. The reception suddenly came in clear. She moved towards the radio and the reception was bad again.

Tykim saw what Daquasha was doing and rose into a sitting position. He didn't want to believe it, but his instinct told him something was terribly wrong.

Daquasha frantically opened the bag, and pulled out the fake documents. She approached the radio and low and behold the reception went crazy again. She stepped away and it was clear.

A lightning bolt of fear and realization almost caused her mind to brain lock. Daquasha suddenly flashed back to the incident in the car:

"What's wrong with this radio?" Daquasha was turning the car radio dial. The distortion was as penetrating as an alarm. "I don't understand it. It was working just fine earlier."

Tykim said, "Let me try it." Keeping his eyes on the road, he played with the knob and got the same results. "I guess the radio is out of order." He turned it off, and they rode in silence.

"There's something wrong with that guy, Dezoe, Tykim. Did you see how he started acting after he came back from that phone call?"

"Nah, I ain't notice that. He seemed normal to me."

Daquasha pulled out her documents, scrutinizing them. She felt them with her finger-tips. She felt lumps in each document.

Daquasha snapped out of the reverie and raced for the bathroom while screaming. "They put bugs in these documents."

"Bugs!?" Tykim raced over to the documents and gathered them all. He raced to the window, looking out. He saw nothing. Tykim grabbed his clothing and started getting dressed.

Daquasha barreled back into the room with a single edge razor blade in her hand. She picked up a document and started slicing it at the corner, cutting it sandwich style. "Hurry Tykim, do what I'm doing."

Tykim grabbed two Uzis, cocked them and laid them on the bed. He followed Daquasha's lead.

Daquasha pulled a document apart and saw the device. It was a thin piece of wire. She saw Tykim had destroyed the document he was working on. "No, Tykim, don't cut the paper part. We're gonna need these documents."

Suddenly, Tykim realized what he was doing. "Fuck these damn documents!" Tykim ripped the whole document in half and threw it to the floor. "If these are tracking devices, we better get the fuck outta here in a god-damn hurry." Tykim snatched the document from Daquasha's hand. "Get dressed, hurry! We gotta get the fuck outta here!"

"But how are we gonna find more documents!?" Daquasha insisted.

Tykim ran to the closet, snatching out the briefcases. "We can find documents some other time. If we get caught by whoever planted them bugs, it won't be another time. Now hurry!"

Daquasha took off. She was planning on taking a nice hot shower, but that was now a long lost wish. As she frantically got dressed, she heard screaming car tires. When she heard a tremendous crashing sound (which was similar to two cars involved in a head-on collision) and saw Tykim grabbed the Uzis, her heart palpitated in her chest. But when she heard another identical crashing noise, she was almost paralyzed by a mixture of fear, dread and all other emotions synonymous with a natural response to impending doom.

CHAPTER # 25

Earlier, moments before Daquasha heard the crashing noise, Jamil was anxiously waiting for the signal while in the passenger seat.

Jamil looked at his watch. "Did you tell this nigga the time and place he was supposed to step up!?"

Devil-dog said, "I told him where we was headed. Just give it a few more minutes."

A moment later, the sound of screeching car tires filled the night. Then a tremendous crashing sound came afterwards.

Jamil peered through the windshield and saw the van in front of them slowed down suddenly to avoid crashing into the lead van.

Seconds earlier, Boris sat in the passenger seat of the lead van. He had a tracking monitor in his hands. The small box beeped loudly and the screen displayed two flashing lights; the stationery tracking device and the moving tracking monitor.

Boris spoke excitedly. "We're right on them. They're in one of these houses just up ahead."

The van rapidly approached an intersection. From his side-view, Boris saw the headlights of a fast moving car. Before he could get a word out of his mouth, the car struck the van. His head slammed into the passenger window upon impact. Glass and blood sprayed all over the front seat.

Jamil had saw the car collide into the first van, hurling the van into a vicious spin. The car continued on its way. The second van's tires screamed as the brakes locked and the rubber treads attempted to grip the pavement.

"Hit it!" Jamil shouted, grabbing hold onto the strap of the seat beat.

Brute's foot slammed down on the gas pedal.

BLAAM!

The van rammed into the back of the van in front of them, causing it to crash into the first van.

Jamil's head snapped forward. He instantly hoped this was enough commotion for Daquasha to realize she was in danger.

The van came to a stop when it slammed into a parked car.

Jamil screamed to Brute. "Get her back on track!" He unfastened his seat belt and pulled his Uzi.

£¥♥   £¥♥   £¥♥   £¥♥

Daquasha and Tykim rushed out the house with guns and briefcases in their hands. The moment their feet touched the black pavement of the street, they both turned and saw the huge collision about a block and half away.

As they got inside the Cadillac, Daquasha saw a van maneuvering around a black van and then headed towards them with urgent speed.

Daquasha was looking out the back window, shouting. "Tykim, a van is comin' at us! Go!"

Tykim hit the gas and the tires shrieked until the rubber caught hold onto the asphalt. The car jerked into motion.

£¥♥   £¥♥   £¥♥   £¥♥

Nuke was in the passenger seat of the fourth van within the convoy. The occupants of this vehicle watched in amazement as the first, second and third vans crashed and bounced off of each other.

Nuke shouted when he saw Daquasha and Tykim running across the street. "It's them! That's them right there!"

The van frantically maneuvered around the wrecked vehicles and the driver jettisoned the van down the street.

The six Russians in the back of the van got their weapons ready. One of the men slid the side door open as the van pursued the red Caddy.

£¥♥   £¥♥   £¥♥   £¥♥

Earlier, when Jamil saw Daquasha getting inside the red Caddy, and then the fourth van crept pass them, he started screaming at the top of his lungs. "Hurry up! Move this motherfucker! Come on, man!"

Brute threw the gear in reverse and slammed on the gas pedal. The van shot backwards. Brute hit the brakes, stopping the van with turbulent force. He slammed the gear in drive and the van catapulted forward.

Just as the van joined the high speed chase, Brute saw flashing lights several blocks behind them. Sirens could not be heard which meant the police were trying to catch them off guard.

Jamil had his Uzi ready as the van pursued the van containing Nuke and several Russians. Jamil sighed angrily because he didn't want them to get in front of him. His plan to act as a shield was completely out the window.

£¥♥   £¥♥   £¥♥   £¥♥

Boris was cursing profusely as he held a handkerchief on the cut on his head. He snatched up the walkie talkie. "Get those fuckin' back-up cars over here! Now!" When he saw the flashing lights, he started screaming, "Everybody out!" He rushed out of the van.

He saw approaching cars with flashers, but they were not accompanied by sirens. Then Boris saw three cars, his back-up team, turned the corner of the intersection and raced towards him. Boris shouted to his three soldiers as he headed for the cars. "Stay behind and hold them back."

The three cars came to a stop and Boris jumped inside the first car that arrived. They screeched down the block.

£¥♥   £¥♥   £¥♥   £¥♥

Daquasha shrieked when the machine gunfire battered the back of the Caddy. Two bullets shot through the back window and shattered through the windshield.

Both Daquasha and Tykim ducked in response.

Daquasha wanted to scream for Tykim to make the car go faster, but that obviously wouldn't help the situation.

Peering over the dashboard, Tykim made a vicious right turn. The tires screamed.

Car horns blared at them and pedestrians called them all assorts of foul names in response to their total disrespect for stop signs and lights.

After five miles of reckless turns and gas pedal flooring maneuvers, Tykim noticed the car suddenly started acting up. Every time he tried to floor the gas pedal, the car acted like it was going to stale. Tykim panicked as he looked at the dials on the dashboard. When he saw the flashing red alternator light, he screamed. "Shit! Fuck!"

Daquasha eyes were wide with terror. "What happen!? What's the matter!?"

"The god-damn alternator blew out!" Tykim started looking for a place to crash land the car, so they could flee on foot.

"The alternator!? How did that happen!?"

Tykim was too busy trying to think of a way to escape this situation to answer Daquasha. He saw a huge, four level parking garage up ahead. Using the garage as a means of escape was going to be extremely risky, but looking at the situation Tykim saw it was the only avenue available.

Minutes earlier, Guzmon saw the lead car turn on its flashers and increased its speed. All vehicles behind it did the same. Armstrong shrugged and followed their lead as the car radio came to life.

Guzmon picked up the receiver. "Guzmon here."

A voice crackled through the speakers. "The targets are just up ahead. Proceed in silence."

Guzmon said, "Specify which targets."

The voice said, "The four vans are up ahead."

"We're on your tail. Over and out." Guzmon sat the receiver back in its cradle.

Minutes later, Guzmon heard and saw the flicker of massive gunfire in front of them. The cars in front of them stopped abruptly.

The intensity of the flicking lights told Guzmon there were dozens of fully automatic weapons being fired. There was a symphony of squealing car tires as a few of the cars crashed into the back end of the others, while some vehicles collided with parked cars.

Armstrong had hit the brakes the moment the gunfire started, stopping the car with head jolting force.

Guzmon bolted out the car with his 9mm Glock and sought cover behind their vehicle. A bullet struck the door, and made Guzmon change his mind about immediately taking aim.

After a moment, Guzmon peered over the hood, trying to get a feel on exactly where the machine gunfire was coming from.

£¥♥   £¥♥   £¥♥   £¥♥

Tykim repeatedly stomped the gas pedal with frantic vigor. "Come on, you motherfucker!" He saw the garage was now at least two blocks away. The engine whined on and off as it coughed, sneezed, stalled and reawakened. "We gotta make a move, now!"

Daquasha peered over the back seat and saw the pursuing van was held up by a truck. "Turn! Turn right here!" Daquasha realized if they made a quick turn they might have enough time to flee into an alleyway or into a building before the van caught up.

The car's engine turned off and didn't come back to life just as Tykim hit the corner. Since the car was initially moving so fast, the tires squealed.

"Grab a briefcase," Tykim said as he strategically positioned the car, making sure it blocked traffic onto the two way street. He slammed on the brakes and flung the gear in park as the car was still moving. The car made a head jerking stop.

Daquasha and Tykim bolted out the car and fled down the street, leaving the car doors wide open. Both their hands were filled; Tykim had two briefcases in one hand and a gun in the other. Daquasha a had a briefcase in one and a 9mm in the other.

Daquasha saw a man entering a Tenement building up ahead. When she realized there were no alleyways or any space separating the block long row of buildings, Daquasha realized this man was they're only getaway. The street was too long to make it to the other end before the van would arrive.

Screaming car tires and a huge crash rung out.

Daquasha turned and saw the van had smashed into the Caddy. Daquasha turned back around and saw the man had the door open. "Wait! Help mister!" She saw the man hastily entered and slammed the door behind him. She instantly realized she should've concealed the weapon. She arrived and began banging on the door.

Breathing hard, Daquasha stepped back, aimed at the lock and fired two shots. Metal fragments dispersed everywhere. She pushed the door, but it didn't open. Why didn't it work!? It always worked in the movies.

"Move!" Tykim brushed pass her.

Suddenly, the sound of screaming car tires filled the night. The van was headed towards them.

Tykim kicked the door opened.

As they rushed into the building, machine-gun bullets ripped and tore at the pavement, nearby parked cars and the building walls.

Daquasha lead the way as she ran down the claustrophobic hallway heading for the back of the building.

Seconds later, they barreled out the back door and ran across a garden, squashing and destroying somebody's vegetables. They opened a gate and stomped across another garden.

Just in front of her, Daquasha saw the back door of another building that would apparently lead them to the next street over. Exhausted, she arrived and turned the knob. It opened and they raced inside.

Crashing through the front door of the apartment building like a pissed off tornado, Daquasha and Tykim fled down the street, heading for the garage.

£¥♥   £¥♥   £¥♥   £¥♥

Earlier, from the passenger seat of the van, Nuke screamed. "Watch out!"

BLAAM!

The van raced around the corner and crashed into the Cadillac.

Every one inside was hurled out of their seats, crashing into each other and the dashboard.

Nuke's head struck the windshield and his hand went to his head. He was dazed, but felt no blood. Looking through the windshield, Nuke saw Daquasha and Tykim running down the street. "There they go! Come on! Go! Go!"

The Russian man behind the steering wheel maneuvered the van around the Caddy and zoomed down the block.

Just as Nuke and another Russian man opened fire, Nuke saw Daquasha and Tykim had entered a building.

Nuke sighed, "Go down and cut around block. We'll catch 'em on the other street!"

£¥♥   £¥♥   £¥♥   £¥♥

Daquasha and Tykim's legs were pumping frantically. The briefcases in their hands flapped about wildly. Unsuspecting pedestrians, hysterically got out of their way. The garage was just up ahead.

Just as they were about a dozen yards from the garage entrance, they heard the van's screaming tires at a distance.

"Run, Daquasha! I'll catch up." Tykim slowed his pace, while turning around, looking for the van. As Daquasha made to the ramp and was rapidly ascending it, Tykim turned and saw the van had hit the corner like a stroke of lightning with it's engine wide open.

While still running, Tykim took aim and locked his finger on the trigger. All nine of his bullets ate at the windshield, causing the van to veer and sideswipe a parked car.

Tykim reached the ramp and saw a blue car headed down towards him. He continued up the ramp, procrastinating in his effort to get pass the car. The van was right behind him and he knew it wouldn't be able to get pass the car. This delay would give him and Daquasha a few extra minutes to get their shit together.

Tykim reached the top of the ramp, screaming. "Daquasha!" He turned and saw her running towards him.

£¥♥   £¥♥   £¥♥   £¥♥

Nuke was having a fit as he screamed and shouted at the blue car blocking their path into the garage. "Get the fuck out of the way motherfucker! Move!" He pulled his weapon, about to get out the van and open fire on this fool, but the car started backing up.

The driver of the van rammed into the front end of the car and speeded up its backing up process.

Jamil and his crew were dead on their behinds.

They sped up the ramp and stopped. Nuke and two Russians got out the van. Jamil and Devil-dog got out of their van as well. Boris arrived just as they were about to huddle up to discuss the situation

Boris sprung out of the car. "Are they in here?"

Nuke said, "Yeah, the dude is."

Boris looked at his soldier.

The soldier nodded his head. "Yeah, I saw him too."

Boris pulled his walkie talkie from his jacket pocket. "Cars two and three, I want you to surround this garage. Check every car that tries to leave very closely. Make some calls and try to keep the police away from here as long as possible." He disconnected and spoke excitedly to the others. "I want every square inch of this place checked; under every car, in every corner, no stone unturned. And we're not leaving until we find them. Let's split up." He started pointing. "Go that way." Boris said to Nuke and the two soldiers. "You go down there." He said to Jamil and Devil-dog. "And I'll go this way. You guys in the vans, block all the entrances."

£¥♥   £¥♥   £¥♥   £¥♥

Daquasha and Tykim cowered behind a car about a dozen feet away, peering at Jamil, Nuke, Boris and all the others. They were close enough to hear everything Boris said.

Daquasha could not believe the Russians, Jamil and Nuke all joined forces, apparently looking for them. She nudged Tykim and whispered. "That's Jamil right there." She pointed.

Tykim honed in on the Jamil. His clenched jawed expression tightened four additional degrees.

Daquasha was now on an emotional roller-coaster. The moment she laid eyes on Jamil she felt a strong vibe. The feeling wasn't hate, which is what confused her; she thought she was losing her mind because the emotion felt like love. She quickly shook loose of these crazy emotions.

Tykim whispered, "This is an example of a golden rule in action. A good hitter never leaves any eyewitnesses alive. I see your bitch ass lover boy here got that part of the program down packed."

After the Russian man, Boris, finished giving them his instructions and everyone took off, Tykim whispered to Daquasha. "I'm gonna hot wire a car."

Daquasha whispered back. "Didn't you hear them? They got all the entrances blocked. We can't just drive out of here."

Tykim ducked walked towards the nearest car as Daquasha followed. It was a green Hyundai. After he checked the car door and found it was locked, he whispered, "I know exactly what your saying. That's why I'm gonna use myself as bait so you and the baby can escape."

Daquasha didn't like what she just heard. His little plan didn't sound too thrilling to her at all. "I hope you're not telling me to leave without you."

"How else are you gonna escape," Tykim crawled towards another car. It was a black Toyota.

There was a noise, footsteps were approaching. Daquasha and Tykim hastily crawled to the back of the car, waiting for the person to pass-by.

Daquasha peeked around the car and saw it was Nuke and a Russian man. They both had huge weapons in their hands.

Tykim checked the car door. It opened. Tykim looked around. He saw what he was looking for. The air vent was about ten feet away. He exchanged briefcases with Daquasha, since the one she was carrying contained only the money. "Wait here Daquasha." He tiptoed to the vent, retrieved his pocket knife, unscrewed the grill, pulled it off, cramped the briefcase inside and put the grill back on. He returned to Daquasha. "Make sure you remember where I just put that briefcase. Look at this section very closely."

"Why are you doing this?" Daquasha was flabbergasted. "We're gonna need all the money we can get."

"I told you, the only way out of this is for me to use myself as bait. Those jewels we got in this briefcase here are what those Russians are looking for. I didn't tell you 'cause I ain't wanna put no unnecessary stress on you and the baby, but I read a newspaper earlier. The article said a huge jewelry heist went down in Atlanta. They described the stolen jewels and it said the Russians were the ones who did the heist."

Fiddling with the ring, Daquasha's heart rate increased because she always sensed these jewels were worth a lot of money. "How much are they worth?"

"The paper said 130 million dollars."

Daquasha suddenly felt a choking sensation. She instantly stopped toying with the ring. The shock gripped her mind. 130 million dollars!? Realization set in and the fear turned into instant terror. This state of anguish was also mixed with joy and a sudden powerful urge to get away so they could enjoy all that money. "So that's why these Russians are here? But how did they know we--" She answered her own question when she realized Nuke was with them. Nuke apparently flipped, went to the Russians and put all this shit on them.

"They want these jewels." Tykim was about to tell her they were not going to stop until they got their hands on them, but this fact was painfully obvious. That's why he knew there was only one thing for him to do. "Come on, get in the car."

Tykim slid in the car and Daquasha followed. It took Tykim three minutes to hot wire the car. The small Toyota's engine was very quiet. But as a safety precaution, he unfastened the wires, killing the engine. "When the area's clear, screw these red and yellow wires together and the car'll start. Head south. I'll meet you in that town in Guyana we talked about--"

"No, Tykim," Daquasha's anxiety was colossal. She couldn't do this alone. "We're a team. Let's see if we can get around this without splitting up. Everything has a solution, if you look for it. Maybe if we lay low for a couple of hours--"

A van turned the corner, causing Daquasha and Tykim to duck down out of sight. When the van passed by, they sat back up.

"Believe me Daquasha, this is the only way. These guys want those jewels and they ain't gonna stop until they get 'em. As long as I tell them I got their jewels, and if they kill me they won't get 'em, I can stall them long enough for you and the baby to get to safety. I'll find a way to get out of that situation when the time comes. Which is another reason for stashing that money in the vent."

"Nigga, is you crazy!? You talking about turning yourself over to them!? Fuck that shit, we're gonna find--"

He grabbed Daquasha's arm. "There's an army of these motherfuckers seconds from finding us, and we ain't got enough bullets to shoot our way out of this. If they catch us both and find these jewels, we're ass out. They'll kill us. The only thing we got going for us right now is you getting away with these fuckin' jewels. Now, stop beefin'. Just trust me on this one. When you leave, just remember, if you get caught then we're both dead."

Daquasha felt as if a ton of high grade doom was placed on her shoulders.

Tykim laid his gun in Daquasha's lap. He sighed, kissed Daquasha on her cheek, got out of the car and walked towards the corner.

Daquasha stared at his back. She watched carefully. Her eyes began to water. She was scared for Tykim. That voice in her mind told her they were going to kill him, and the guilt kicked in because this was all her fault. Tykim would die because of her. With a struggle, she tried to shift her thoughts to another issue without much success.

Suddenly, she saw two Russian men run up to Tykim with their weapons pointed. Tykim raised both hands in the air as they shouted and yelled at him. Daquasha flinched when one of the men struck Tykim in the head with the butt of a huge gun. Tykim collapsed to the floor.

About a minute later, Daquasha saw a mob of men surround Tykim. She gritted her teeth when she saw Jamil was amongst the crowd. Instead of rotating the pinkie ring she tapped it rhythmically on her knee cap.

Tykim struggled to his feet. "Yeah, motherfucker, I got your funky ass jewels, but they ain't here!"

Boris punched Tykim in the face, dropping him to the ground. "We want those jewels back." He looked around and spoke to one of his soldiers. "Where's the woman?"

Tykim said, "She ain't here. I dropped her off two blocks away when the car broke down."

Nuke started looking around the garage, his eyes scrolling across all the cars in the immediate vicinity. When he saw someone in a small car duck down abruptly, he smiled inwardly. He turned and got back involved with the interrogation of his sorry ass cousin.

At about the same time Nuke was looking around the garage, Jamil was doing the same thing and he too saw the sudden, frantic ducking motion come from a small foreign car about fifteen cars away.

Jamil interjected. "I think he's telling the truth. When we was chasing them, their car did break down. She probably got away."

Tykim was shocked by Jamil's voice. It sounded so familiar, but he couldn't seem to pin-point where he heard it before. Nevertheless, he was absolutely certain he heard that voice somewhere in his far off past.

Nuke chimed right in. "Their car broke down and they ran on foot. I ain't see the woman enter this garage. He was the only one who came in here."

Boris looked around at the faces of his soldiers. When he saw them indicate through their body gestures that Jamil and Nuke were telling the truth, he grabbed Tykim by the collar and yanked him to his feet. "Let's go." He pulled Tykim away. "My friend, you are about to discover why the Russians have become famous for putting fear in the hearts of all people in the criminal world."

As Tykim stumbled towards a red van, he wondered if he was doing the right thing. It was obvious this was crazy, but whether it was wise was up for debate. His doubt was so strong, he was about to make a break for it. Tykim was tossed inside the van and landed next to two machine-gun totting Russians. They grabbed him and tied his hands and feet.

The van screeched away.

£¥♥   £¥♥   £¥♥   £¥♥

Daquasha was trembling as she waited in the car. She wiped the tears from her face. Twice she glanced at her watch, and noticed only five minutes had elapsed each time. Her plan was to wait twenty minutes and then leave. Instead of turning the ring, she was now screwing it on and off her finger.

Daquasha sat behind the wheel staring at the area where Tykim stood earlier. She appeared to be in a trance. It never failed. She was alone again. Fighting as a solo artist. Her heart was once again shattered and pulverized into a fine dust that was blown away by a violent gush of wind. Her battered emotions were clouding her judgment and she knew now was not the time to succumb to them.

She had to be herself, be strong, firm and keep it moving. Tykim was built tough and to last, she told herself repeatedly, and knew if there was a way out of that fucked up situation, he would find it. At least that's what she was hoping and praying for. He had to make it back to her or else she would not be able to maintain her sanity. She couldn't lose him again.

Finally, she saw twenty minutes had gone by and she pulled the car out of the parking space, heading towards the exit. Staring at the vent where Tykim placed the briefcase of money, Daquasha embedded the image in her mind. The image was so penetrating it was as if a Polaroid picture was taken and the image was plastered inside her head.

As Daquasha pulled the Toyota out of the garage and on to the late night streets, from behind the wheel of a green Ford, Nuke screamed "Yes!" when he saw Daquasha. Alone and as happy as a faggot in boy's town, Nuke followed Daquasha. He got his gun ready and laid it in his lap to insure easy access.

As Nuke followed Daquasha, a blue Oldsmoble followed Nuke.

CHAPTER # 26

Detective Guzmon was squeezing the trigger on his weapon as the three Russians, about a block and a half away, rushed inside two cars. With tires screeching, the Russians fled the area with bullets still being fired at them.

For the past ten minutes, the two groups were engaged in an exchange of intense gunfire.

Guzmon and Armstrong rushed inside their vehicle as did all the other law enforcement officials. Armstrong sped off and got in line with the other cop cars that gave chase.

About half of the New Orleans police force arrived and joined in the high speed chase. The three men in their desperation to get away had ran over pedestrians, crashed into parked cars and proceeded as if there was not a single red light in existence.

Twenty minutes later, they arrived at an abandoned warehouse. The three men scurried into the establishment, still carry their machine-guns. The police instantly surrounded the entire building.

Guzmon got out his car and headed for Special agent Cleveland, who was already talking to Jackson, Kenneth and two New Orleans undercover cops. Armstrong was dead on Guzmon's heels.

Guzmon saw Cleveland was fuming.

Cleveland spoke calmly, but his demeanor was drenched with a smooth rage. "These guys here were a distraction. I don't know how I let them draw me into a chase of this magnitude."

Guzmon said, "Let's turn it into a positive. Maybe if he catch one of these shooters, they'll lead us to the others."

Everyone in the huddle turned and stared at Guzmon as if he had committed the ultimate sin.

Cleveland's patience was noticeably hanging on a very thin thread. "This is not New York. We don't apprehend culprits solely with the intentions of squeezing information out of them." He lied because he always did this sort of thing, but he never spoke about it in a public arena.

"I didn't mean it that way," Guzmon felt very self conscious. "I'm aware of the eighth Amendment--"

"These Russians are not into the snitchin' business." Kenneth said, "Most would die before they would talk."

Jackson said, "Simply put. Those extracurricular police tactics won't work with these particular perpetrators."

Meanwhile, as the army of police hovered all around the factory, the three Russians soldiers climbed down into a sewage drain and walked away (or rather swam away) as free as a fish in the ocean.

£¥♥   £¥♥   £¥♥   £¥♥

Daquasha drove down a deserted highway, pondering her next move. Question upon questions were formulating with each passing moment. She glanced at her rearview mirror and saw the car headlights were now rapidly approaching. She wondered if this was the same car following her about an hour ago.   The urge to increase her speed grew substantially as the headlights drew closer.

She decided to hold her head, stay in control and not panic. If it was the police merely trying to pass her, she surmised that any hasty response would draw unnecessary attention.

Daquasha noticed the car entered the opposite lane, trying to pass. She let up off the gas pedal to help speed up the process. As the car eased along side of her, Daquasha turned to see the driver of the vehicle.

BLAAM!!

The car slammed into Daquasha's car.

Daquasha almost lost control of the steering wheel as a result of the shock.

The car violently struck Daquasha's car again.

Daquasha saw it was Nuke inside the car. Her foot slammed down on the gas pedal, but he was still cruising next to her. She slammed her car back into Nuke's car. The crashing sound of metal against metal was terrifying.

Daquasha saw Nuke was aiming a gun. Just as Nuke fired a shot, Daquasha ducked and reflectively turned the steering wheel away from Nuke's car. Her vehicle went down into a slope and instantly picked up speed. Daquasha didn't realize she was screaming as the car bounced and bumped its way down towards what looked like a tree littered swamp. She tried to turn the steering wheel, but the car would not respond.

WHAAM!!

The car crashed into a tree.

Daquasha hit the bridge of her nose on the steering wheel and was punch drunk. Her mind was filled with a dark cloud that threaten to take her under.

£¥♥   £¥♥   £¥♥   £¥♥

Nuke slammed on his brakes when he saw Daquasha's car turn and descend down the slope. When his vehicle finally came to a stop after skidding for several feet, Nuke rushed out of his car and ran towards the slope. As Daquasha's car descended down into the dark swamp like area, Nuke saw the car was heading for a tree. Nuke laughed when the car crashed into the tree. He quickly descended the slope, heading for the car with his gun in his hand.

£¥♥   £¥♥   £¥♥   £¥♥

Daquasha shook her head to clear her mind of the pain. The gloomy cob webs began to subside. She grabbed the briefcase, pulled her gun and pushed open the door. The moment the door was opened, she heard the noise, but it was too late.

Nuke reached in and snatched Daquasha out the car. His hand grabbed her hand with the gun. Nuke twisted her wrist with savage force as Daquasha tried to scratch Nuke's eyes out. She screamed as the gun dropped to the ground.

Nuke caught Daquasha in the stomach with a tremendous upper cut. She knelled over like a broken-up pretzel. Her mind screamed, My baby! My baby! She was surprised a stomach blow was powerful enough to make her see stars.

Nuke saw the briefcase and knew he hit the jackpot. His excitement almost became unbearable. He grabbed Daquasha by the collar and pulled her up into a standing position. He whined up his fist, hauled off with an over hand right and connected with Daquasha's jaw.

Daquasha felt herself stumbling backwards. She landed hard and instantly noticed she was entering a dream state.

Nuke reached down, picked up the briefcase, sat it on the hood of the car, and tried to open the briefcase. He started banging the lock with the butt of his gun.

Suddenly, Nuke heard movement. When he turned, a fist caught him in the face. The blow knocked him silly. Nuke dropped his gun as he fell to the ground.

BOW!

Jamil shot Nuke in the leg. Nuke screamed as Jamil reached down and picked up Nuke's gun.

Nuke saw stars, flashing lights, moons and even suns swirling before his eyes. Although it was dark, the moon provided enough light rays for him to see it was Jamil. Nuke instantly realized he was in a very precarious predicament.

Jamil was tempted to rush to Daquasha, but dealing with Nuke was obviously much more urgent. In any event, he saw Nuke had only punched Daquasha and therefore knew she was probably knocked out cold. He decided to have a little fun with ole Nuke.

Nuke said, babbling. "Don't kill me, man. I'm a Federal agent. You know how much time they give people for killing FBI agents." Nuke pulled his badge. "See. If you let me live, I'll hook you up, man. I got crazy connections in Washington, man."

Jamil was surprised. "So all along you were a fuckin' pig. Who was you scoping out?"

"The Russians. They stole 130 million in jewels. I went undercover to find them. She got the jewels in that briefcase. Me and you can split the jewels two ways. Since I'm FBI, I can direct the investigation away from us. This is 130 million dollars, man."

"So, you're really FBI, huh?"

"Yeah, man. I'm with the deep-cover unit. So what, do we have a deal?"

Jamil walked over and kicked Nuke in the face. The blow was of a bone shattering nature.

Nuke shrieked in pain and started babbling again. "Wait! Hold up! No, man, don't--"

Jamil stomped Nuke in the face and grinded his foot, trying to mash Nuke's head into the ground. He felt something crunch under his foot, apparently Nuke's nose. Jamil flipped Nuke's semiconscious body over, cocked his gun, uttered a quote and fired a shot into the back of Nuke's head. Jamil took aim, said the quote again and squeezed off two more shots into Nuke's skull.

Daquasha could not believe what she just heard. She was awoke throughout the whole exchange between Nuke and Jamil. After Nuke punched her in the face and she fell to the ground, she decided it was safer to play dead than to engage Nuke in a fight or try to run from him. Nuke was an FBI agent!? That was truly an eye raiser, but what shocked her even more was that statement Jamil made. She couldn't find a way to make her mind accept what she had just heard. As her mind searched for a way to find logic in it all, her subconscious reaffirmed there simply was no rationalism to what she just heard.

Jamil walked over to Daquasha, kneeled and touched her face compassionately. "Danielle. Wake up, boo." He saw her shift. "There you go, come on, wake up." He helped her into a sitting position.

"Jamil!?" Daquasha could've won an academy award for her acting. "What are you doing here?"

"I'm here to protect you, baby," He helped her into a standing position. "It's all behind us now."

"How could you do this to me, Jamil?" Daquasha floundered over to the car and leaned against it. Her cheek bone throbbed with explosive pain. "You tried to kill me. Is that what you here to do, finish the job!?"

"Danielle, please hear me out, boo. I swear, I had no control over it. Kilroy wanted you dead. I tried to tell him it wasn't you who was snitchin', but you know how Kilroy is once he got his mind made up."

"But how could you let him do this to me!? I thought you loved me, Jamil. Is this the way you treat the people you love? You allow people with their own hidden agendas to fuck them around and try to kill them?"

"No, Danielle, that's not the way I do it. I do it by protecting them. Which is exactly what I did. I made sure Tykim was hired to do that hit because I knew he wouldn't kill you or allow anyone else to. I knew he was your childhood sweetheart. Yeah, I know all about it. How you and him broke-up, everything. I even know your real name is Daquasha Lawrence."

Daquasha realized Jamil was digging himself a deeper hole, but she was surprised he had hired Tykim and knew all about her background she worked so hard to conceal.

"I went through hell getting Tykim to take the hit against you, but I did it. And judging from the fact you're still alive and in one piece, I would say it worked just as I planned."

"That still don't excuse this. If you're the second man in charge of your crew, how could you let Kilroy gorilla you into even agreeing to this shit. Do you realize you could have killed me and your child."

Jamil felt a flash of anxiety. "My child!? What are you saying? Your pregnant?"

"Yeah," Daquasha felt a rage starting to develop. "That night all this bullshit started, I was gonna tell you, but I was waiting for the results. I told you I had a surprise for you. It was this."

"Yes, I remember, Danielle," Jamil went to her and hugged her. He kissed her neck, savoring the smell of her sweet body aroma. She was still so soft. "I'm sorry, Danielle. Please, you gotta believe me, I did everything I could to protect you. I would never hurt you, Danielle. That's why I'm out here. I wanna take you back and make everything right." He pulled from the embrace and caressed her hands. "I want you to come back home. I'll make everything right."

"I don't think you realize what you caused. I'm a fugitive from justice. They're looking for me for murders."

"I'll fix it all, Danielle. That means everything. Even that murder you had hanging over your head for years." He saw her surprised expression. "Yeah, I know about that night when that rapist attacked you in New Jersey and you killed his punk ass." The pride in his voice and bodily gestures were unmistakable. "Even though it was self-defense, the police turned it into something else like those foul mafuckas always do."

There was a long moment of silence.

Daquasha was hurled back to that dreadful night when she was returning home from work. It was a humid summer night and she was in a good mood because her tips were heavier than usual. She worked at a spot called Sweet Charlie's as a bar-maid and waitress. As she opened the door to her apartment, a black man with thick facial hair grabbed her, put her in a head-lock with his hand clamped over her mouth and shoved her inside the apartment. Daquasha fought him like a wild maniac, but he was too strong for her. Lying partially unconscious, the rapist ripped off her shirt and bra. As he began taking his pants off, Daquasha turned on to her stomach with her tote bag in her hands. The rapist saw her shapely behind and lost control. Daquasha inconspicuously pulled the 007 knife from her bag just as her shorts were ripped off and the rapist began licking and kissing her butt cheeks. The rapist turned her over and was greeted with the knife. Daquasha stabbed him thirteen times.

Shattered, scared, confused and alone, Daquasha fled to the Bronx. With a name change, now Danielle Lewis, Daquasha went underground. Too afraid to take chances working a legit job, Daquasha was forced to start working in strip clubs. The owners of such establishments didn't ask questions and paid reasonably well. Most of all, it was an off the books job. The first two clubs Daquasha worked at were too wild and raunchy. The women were nothing more than prostitutes with no principles, and the owners were slave drivers with pimp mentalities. Daquasha didn't last a week at those clubs, since she wasn't about to throw away her morals for a few dollars. When she arrived at the Paradise Lounge, it wasn't paradise on all levels, but the club was civil enough to maintain employment.

Daquasha pulled herself from the reverie. She locked eyes with Jamil for a moment and then turned away from the staring match. The night air was chilly, but it didn't fit the mood of her heart. She wanted all chaos, confusion and misery to be done and over with. Indeed, Jamil's offer was very tempting. But her heart was filled with warmth and Tykim was inside of that place in her chest that regulated sorrow, gratitude, and forgiveness. The thought of what those Russians were doing to him was creating an anxiety and a bone chilling fear. It didn't take a mathematician to conclude they would kill Tykim if they didn't eventually get their jewels back.

Jamil saw Daquasha was contemplating her decision too long. "Don't forget what you always say...Family is everything. Me, you and the baby is everything cause we family." He rubbed her stomach. "Don't break-up our family, boo."

Daquasha was touched by those words. Twirling the ring on her pinkie, Daquasha turned and made eye contact with Jamil. "What am I gonna do about the Russians? They're searching for me. Me and Tykim stole some jewels from 'em. If they catch me, you and I both know they're gonna kill me."

Jamil folded his arms. "Fuck the Russians. All we gotta do is give them their jewels back and they'll be satisfied. I guess those jewels are in this briefcase, huh? If you come home with me, I got this thing in the smash, nobody, not even the Russians will know it's you and I'll rig it up to look like you're dead. Can you feel me?"

"Yeah," Daquasha went into a silent trance. "I feel you." She suddenly felt her heart melting. It was not dissolving because of what Jamil said, but because she felt sorry for Tykim. She wanted to just go on with her life and let Tykim find his own way through this ordeal he put himself in. The tug-o-war match going on inside her was as furious as a hurricane and a Typhoon merged together. After a moment, she made her decision. Tykim had to handle it, he was on his own.

"Come on, boo, tell me what I wanna hear." Jamil moved towards Daquasha. He embraced Daquasha and kissed her on the cheek. "I gotta big surprise for you when you give me your decision."

Daquasha wasn't in the mood for anymore surprises, but based on what was going on she already knew what Jamil was planning. As Jamil leaned against the car, waiting for her to respond, Daquasha felt bad and guilty. After all the shit Tykim did for her, she was now going to abandon him as if he was a piece of garbage blowing in the wind. She had to do something or else her conscience would eat her alive. "I gotta rescue Tykim."

She blurted out the statement. "All the shit he did for me, I can't leave him to die like that."

Jamil felt like he was slapped in the face. He maintained his composure. "Well, who told his crazy ass to turn himself over to them." Jamil said sarcastically. "This ain't a wise move Danielle. The Russians ain't the type of crew you thump out with and call it a day. If we go to war with them, it'll be an everlasting one."

"Well, I'm willing to take that chance to save him. He put his life on the line for me, and it's only right I do the same for him."

Jamil always thought there was a chance this shit could happen; old lovers forced back together under life and death circumstances had the potential for reawakening old emotions, despite the fact one of the party members hated the others guts. Jamil was tight and was fuming because he felt it in his heart Danielle fell back in love with this chump, Tykim. "Danielle, what do you prefer to be called, Danielle or Daquasha?"

"What do you think?" Daquasha's tone displayed frustration. "You said you know my real name."

"Okay, Daquasha, I wanna ask you something I know I shouldn't because of the type of cat I am. But I'm gonna ask any way ... Did you fuck him?"

Oh, boy, here we go. Daquasha picked up her gun off the ground, tucked it in her waist and stared at Nuke's headless body. "What do you think, Jamil?"

"That's not an answer to my question. I asked you did you fuck--"

"Yeah, I fucked him! Is that what you wanna hear. And don't blame nobody for that shit but your fuckin' self. What else was supposed to happen! I'm thinking you're trying to kill me, he was protecting me against thugs, hit-men, criminals, the police and all kinds of--"

"Do you love him." Jamil said calmly.

Daquasha was becoming agitated. "What do you mean? Yeah, I love him as a friend. I love all the crazy shit he did to save me from being murdered--"

"Do you love him in a husband and wife sense?" Jamil hoped she said the right thing because he didn't want to flip on Daquasha. He did love her, but there was no way he was going to try to compete with another dude. She was all his or she wouldn't be anybody's.

Daquasha saw it in his eyes. The danger vibrated through the air like a violent radio wave. "No, I don't love him like that." Daquasha picked up the briefcase containing the jewels and the money.

185

Jamil sighed inwardly, but his inner voice was telling him to be careful, and to proceed with extreme caution.

Daquasha walked over to the car, snatched the door open, pulled the other briefcase (the one containing the sharp shooters rifle) from the front seat. With two briefcases in each hand, Daquasha headed towards the slope. "I'm gonna save Tykim. After that, I'll go back with you to New York." She waited for Tykim to say something. "I need you to show me how to become a professional killer. With all the practice you've had, I'm sure I'll be learning from one of the best."

"Boo, you must got ESP 'cause I was about to suggest you let me give you a crash course on how to bust your gun. I'm a little surprise Tykim didn't realize the need to pass on that type of valuable knowledge to you."

As Daquasha climbed up the hill, she said, "Now, here's the tricky part. I ain't giving 'em back those Jewels."

Jamil laughed. He decided the Russians were ass out of those jewels the moment Daquasha confirmed she had them. "That's my boo. Now, here's the even more tricky part. We gotta find a way to make them think we're giving 'em back without actually doing it."

Daquasha was about to reveal her plan, but Jamil's sudden interest in the Jewels changed her mind. If there was one thing she learnt a very long time ago, it was certainly the fact that money, greed and betrayal were synonymous and interchangeable. There was no way you could have anyone of the three without the others being present.

CHAPTER # 27

Tykim's whole body felt like it was on fire. Blood oozed from countless parts of his body, but the head injury seemed to hurt the most. He was blindfolded and was tied down to a wooden chair. The room smelled like piss and shit. Some of it was his, but most of it was some other poor fool who got caught up in this fucked up world. Tykim had lost track of time about a day ago. Or was it two days ago? The last thing he remembered was being struck on the top of the head with an aluminum baseball, and when he woke up, he was blindfolded and in this foul smelling room.

This was the first time in Tykim's life he felt true pain. It felt like he had a few broken ribs. He probably had a fractured skull and his ankle was sprain. They even violated him in ways he didn't think other human beings would even image doing to another human being. His whole body pulsated with agonizing pain. The dirty bastards did feed him. Whatever it was tasted like shit, and the more he thought about it, he realized it probably was shit. His rage was literally off the Richter scale.

The things they had done to him turned Tykim into a monster, a madman and a maniac. If he lived through this, he would kill and kill like he'd never done before. There was no grounds for any form of forgiveness for what they had done to him. Every time he passed out from the pain, he dreamed of killing Russians and anyone who even thought about sympathizing with them. The beautiful thing was, he really didn't know where the jewels were; even if he wanted to tell, there was no way he could.

Suddenly, Tykim heard the huge metal door open.

The Russian guy name Boris had entered the room. He was speaking in his native tongue. He was upset and there were several other men with him.

Boris snatched the blind-fold off Tykim's head.

Tykim's eyes screamed in pain. He saw the room was crowded. The Russian's appeared to be the majority. There were almost two dozen of them. He even saw a few of them up on some kind of watch-tower like scaffold. When Tykim saw Jamil and about a dozen other black men, he wanted to ask the brothers for some help. But his pride and ego quickly got in the way.

Tykim's eyes wandered around the room, taking in the surroundings. This place was very large; it was about the size of a dance hall. There were dozens of huge oil drums scattered about with sprinkles of huge wooden crates merged amongst them.

Jamil stared down at Tykim and wondered was he losing his damn mind. Here he was about to save the life of a nigga who had the potential to take his future wife away from him. The urge to kill Tykim right here on the spot was extremely powerful. If he hadn't given Daquasha his word that he would do his best to save Tykim from imminent death, he might have rigged up a way to have Tykim killed. Also, he couldn't get out of his mind the subliminal way Daquasha made it clear that if Tykim died, then she would even leave him. In order words, she put him under the gun.

Jamil turned and saw Lunatic beaming down at Tykim with a deep hatred in his eyes. The sight made Jamil nervous. He saw the need to give Lunatic an immediate and firm warning. "Be easy, Lun. This ain't the time or place to start fuckin' up."

Boris heard Jamil's comment. He walked over and stood next to Tykim. "Yeah, Jamil, you better make sure your little dog don't fuck with this here golden goose of ours." He stared down at Tykim. "You will talk soon. In a few hours, we will try new tactics. You like?"

A Russian soldier entered the room carrying a machine-gun. He stopped in front of the door and shouted. "Boris!" He waved for Boris to come to him.

As Boris turned and approached the soldier, Lunatic realized he couldn't take it any longer. Kilroy's instructions danced in his mind. The faces of Alley-bush, Two-face, Hector, Johnny B and Light all flashed across his third eye. Locked in a staring match with Tykim, Lunatic was starting to lose control. Tykim's eyes showed no fear and this was driving him truly insane. Lunatic pulled his 9mm.

BOW!

Just as Lunatic took aim and fired at Tykim's chest, Jamil kicked Lunatic's hand, causing the bullet to whiz pass Tykim's head.

The whole room was instantly hurled into a state of pandemonium. Within a fraction of a second, the room went up like a hydrogen bomb. Everybody panicked and started shooting each other. Misconception and twisted interpretations of the others' response were the universal consensus for the moment.

Devil-dog had pulled his gun as Jamil grabbed Lunatic's hand with the gun and started tussling with him.

Tykim had catapulted himself backwards, causing the chair to tip over backwards. It was evident there was going to be more shots fired, and he had no intentions of being in an upright position waiting to catch somebody's stray bullets.

Just as the first shot was fired, Drac and his crew thought the Russians were going to open fire on Jamil and his crew, so they opened fire on the Russians. The other Russians on the other side of the room saw Drac and his crew firing upon fellow Russians, so they started mowing down Drac and his people.

Boris had hit the deck as the soldier who called him over, did a dance of death when he took aim at Jamil and Lunatic, who were wallowing on the floor. Devil-dog's bullets were responsible for cutting this soldier down.

Jamil saw Devil-dog trying to take aim at him and Lunatic. Terror gripped Jamil because he realized Devil-dog was flipping on him. Lunatic was Devil-dog's ace number one partner, and it was evident who would get touched with his bullets. Massive gunfire was going off all around them. In a last ditch effort, Jamil reached for his 9mm tucked in the back waist of his pants.

BOW!

A shot rang out from Devil-dog's weapon.

Jamil tensed up, but he felt no pain. Lunatic's frantic struggling stopped instantly and his body went limp. Jamil turned and saw Devil-dog winked his eye at him with a crooked smile.

As Devil-dog attempted to approach Jamil, machine-gun fire cut Devil-dog down. Huge chunks of Devil-dog's flesh were flung everywhere. It looked as if he had imploded from the inside out and his upper body was ripped apart. The huge caliber bullets fired by the Russian soldiers were experimental slugs, and now they saw the damn things worked just as they were designed to.

Jamil's aim landed on one of the Russians responsible for killing Devil-dog. The man was hovering over a oil drum.

BOW!--BOW!--BOW!--BOW!

Jamil's trigger finger went to work. The first shot hit the Russian in the mouth, while the second, third and fourth all planted themselves in his upper chest. The Russian's already lifeless body stumbled backwards into a drum, bounced off it and fell crashing to the floor.   Scurrying towards a wooden crate, Jamil spun the 9mm with hysterical speed, aimed at the other Russian and unleashed four more rapid shots, two of which struck the target.

The gunfire seemed as if it would never stop and was coming from everywhere.

"Cease fire! Cease fire!" Boris screamed at the top of his lungs.

After a moment the room became as silent as a tomb. Boris remained on the floor, looking around at the massacre. He didn't get up until more of his soldiers came barreling through the door. They entered the room with mouths hung in shock and their eyes wide with devastating disbelief.

Jamil leaned against the crate and slid down into a sitting position. Staring at all the bodies, while shaking his head, he was almost as shocked as Boris's soldiers. He was furious beyond description. Looking closely at the disaster, Jamil saw he had lost his whole crew, all twelve men with one sweep of the hand. If he could bring Lunatic back to life, he would kill his stupid ass a thousand times over and over again, in ways that would put the Spanish Inquisition to shame.

Jamil sighed angrily because now an intricate part of his and Daquasha's plan had just disappeared. In fact, the plan couldn't work without his crew. And to make matters worse, he couldn't even get word to Daquasha to let her know the plan as they constructed was dead. He turned his head and made eye contact with Tykim.

They both held the stare. To both their amazement, there was no hatred in either of their stares. For lack of a better explanation, their expressions both conveyed a mutual respect for the other. Subconsciously, it would be fair to say, since they were the only two black men still alive in this room full of Russians, they innately knew they had better bury the hatchet. If not for the sake of their own survival, definitely for the subsistence of Daquasha.

"God damn it!" Boris yelled with both hands planted on his head as if he had a splitting headache. He paced angrily. "What the fuck happened!?" He started ranking. "You see, this is reason why I don't like workin' with niggas. I told you Jamil to keep that motherfucker on--"

"Boris!" A soldier shouted, handing him a cellular phone. "It's the woman with the jewels."

Boris's eyes lit up. He ran and snatched the phone from his soldier. "Hello, this is man in charge."

Daquasha spoke fast. "If you want your jewels back, I'll give 'em to you in exchange for Tykim. I want him in good health, not a single scratch or injury. Tonight at 12 o'clock, meet me at Lake Barataria shipping yard on the far west end. The jewels will be inside the old abandoned hangar inside a tool box in the back. If you try anything funny, your jewels are history." She hung up.

When Boris heard the dial tone, he tossed the cellular back. "We made contact. Tonight we get our jewels and be on our way home tomorrow." He looked at the dead bodies and screamed. "Clean this shit up!" He walked over to make sure Tykim was still alive. When he saw Tykim was alive,

Boris was relieved, but didn't show it. He reached down and snatched Tykim by the shirt collar with both hands and jerked him and the chair back into an up right position.

Boris patted Tykim's cheeks with both hands. "I see you have very good girl. She's exchanging you for jewels. But it's so so sad because we don't make deals when you fuck with Russian mob. The only arrangement is you die when you fuck with us."

As Boris stared at Tykim with clenched jaws, Jamil struggled into a standing position. He was so glad he heard those words roll off Boris's tongue. Now, if he could just come up with a workable back-up plan, when he brought the noise it would be all the more pleasurable.

£¥♥   £¥♥   £¥♥   £¥♥

Daquasha hung up the phone with Boris and entered the shipping yard through a tall metal gate. The road she walked down was ridden with huge pot-holes that looked like moon craters. She was on her way to the old hanger on the other side of this shipping yard.

Dressed in a black ninja like outfit with a matching backpack, Daquasha had the bag of jewels in one hand and a fully automatic Tech 9 in the other. A black backpack was flung over her shoulder. The sun was about to plunge into the western horizon and the atmosphere was inapplicable to her mood. She was scared, alone and determined to save Tykim. Although the weather was sunny all day, the night skies that were strong-arming its way into existence, seemed to look dreary and depressing.

Daquasha knew from her research this shipping yard had been out of use for quite some time. It was also in the boon-docks with respect to all the other new shipping yards; the closest sign of civilization was about three miles away. On Daquasha's left, were a bunch of dilapidated wooden rooming houses (or storage facilities) that resembled huge shacks. There were about two dozen of them and they consumed most of the yard. On her right, the five red brick factory like buildings were nothing more than burnt out shells and they collectively covered two city blocks worth of land mass. Over to her far left, were the freight docks and Lake Barataria, a huge body of water that spilled into the Mississippi River.

Increasing the speed of her stride, Daquasha looked up at the roof of the four story office building in front of her. By the monolithic nature of this structure, it was likely the headquarters and main administrative building when this yard was once a flourishing commerce facility. The hanger was right behind this building. The sight of the roof made her nervous, and she hoped Jamil's plan was the best way to approach this thing. The rapid disappearance of the sun only magnified this stress by an incalculable degree.

As Daquasha entered the hangar and headed for the tool box in the back, she realized her negative perception of the night was probably an over-exaggerated mental response. The night looked foreboding because her world was in a state of sheer turmoil. What went on inside a person usually determined the way that person viewed and responded to the outside, and this was a classical example of such a scenario. Daquasha placed the jewels inside the huge tool box. She'd been rehearsing this little routine for the pass two days and she still felt like she was leaving something of great importance out. Her instinct and that vibe in her heart was telling her she was overlooking a critical element in this very dangerous plan.

As Daquasha headed towards the entrance, she looked around and saw the place looked the way it was supposed to. She again looked up at the roof of the office building across from the hangar. This was the location Jamil said he would put some of his crew and she wondered if this was a good idea. Maybe this was the reason for that funny, indecisive vibe she was experiencing.

Daquasha exited the hangar to make a series of other preparations.

£¥♥   £¥♥   £¥♥   £¥♥

Detectives Guzmon and Armstrong sat at the hotel kitchen table, waiting for the phone call from Cleveland. They talked casually.

"I tell yah, man." Armstrong said, "I think we're wasting our time down here. I say we go back to New York and focus on that perp who just got caught with those 22 pounds of heroine. Finding someone willing to cut a deal against Kilroy is not an everyday thing. We need top seasoned officers handling that kind of thing."

"Captain Fletcher's not gonna allow anyone to fuck that up," Guzmon took a sip of the grape soda and sat the can back down. "Since we're already down here, we might as well play this hand out. From the way Cleveland sounded, there's something in the makings. I'm sure he wouldn't tell us to stay on standby and not come through with something."

Armstrong laughed. "After his deep-cover agent was found murdered gang-land style, and this whole operation has now turned into a complete disaster, he might be somewhere searching for a new job assignment."

They both laughed.

Armstrong continued. "I definitely agree with your assessment. If he don't come up with something, it would surely surprise me."

About a half hour later, the phone rang and Guzmon went and got it. "Guzmon speaking."

"Hey, I got some good news." Cleveland said, "In two hours, at 12 o'clock, the Russians are going to pick up the jewels. The woman you're looking for is supposed to be delivering them. According to my CI, the other culprit you're hunting, Tykim Hall, is being exchanged for the jewels."

"Exchanged!?" Guzmon was confused. "Was he kidnapped or something?"

"I would assume so," Cleveland said, "I need you guys to meet me at 743 Riverside Road within the hour. This location is about a mile from the target cite. We'll brief everyone on all the intricate details and develop tactical maneuvers."

"We're on the move as we speak. Later." Guzmon disconnected the line.

Moving with enthusiastic speed, Guzmon explained the situation to Armstrong as they raced out of the hotel room.

CHAPTER # 28

Daquasha laid on her stomach on top of the roof of the four story office building across from the hangar. She had a high power rifle with a infra-red night vision scope trained on the hangar. Through the scope, she saw the tool box containing the jewels. In her backpack there was the Tech 9, two handguns, and five boxes of Teflon tipped bullets. All weapons were equipped with silencers, including the rifle.

The quarter moon over-head cast a streak of light on the water just beyond the hanger. The lights attached to the building, and the hangar enabled Daquasha to see her surroundings much easier. The silence was as crisp and clear as a morgue during the witching hour.

Daquasha was scared and disoriented because Jamil's people's still hadn't showed up yet. He told her they would be here at least an hour before the Russians would arrive. It was obvious something went wrong. With fear raging through her veins, Daquasha wrestled with the reality that she had to do this all alone. When she tried to figure out what happened to Jamil's crew, her mind was swamped with too many negative thoughts and she would force herself to stop thinking about the issue all together.

To her surprise, Daquasha was still asking herself repeatedly if this was worth it. Several times she was about to back out, but the more she thought about the foul ass things those Russians were doing to Tykim, the more she decided to keep pushing forward. Her heart was beating so fast, twice she thought she was going to undergo a coronary attack.

Daquasha suddenly heard a moving vehicle. The noise was coming from behind her from the entrance to the shipping yard. With nervous stricken speed, she rose to her feet and raced to the other side of the building. In a crouching position, she peered over the roof railing. She saw rapidly approaching vehicles. Daquasha frantically dug into her backpack, pulled out the binoculars and looked through them. Her eyes almost burst from their sockets when she saw a ten police vehicle convoy. There were three police swat vans, two heavy artillery trucks and five unmarked police cars. Daquasha bolted back to her rifle, snatched it up and raced to the stairwell. She barreled down the stairs to the fourth floor.

Daquasha stood, looking confused and lost. What was she going to do!? She wanted to cry because it was evident the whole plan was now out the window. Don't panic! Don't panic! she repeatedly told herself. Daquasha raced down the dark hallway to the nearest office. She turned the knob. The door was locked. She continued down the hallway to another door. It opened and she rushed inside. Again she started pacing, trying to figure out what to do next.

£¥♥   £¥♥   £¥♥   £¥♥

Guzmon and Armstrong got out of the car as Cleveland shouted at the drivers of the trucks and vans. "Move them over there, out of sight."

The drivers of the trucks and vans pulled off, turning corners. Some headed for the back of the dilapidated rooming houses while others merged with the factories.

Kenneth and his partner, Jackson, approached Guzmon, Armstrong, four New Orleans cops, Cleveland and four additional FBI agents.

Kenneth said, "This is the building?" He pointed at the abandoned office building Daquasha was in. "I had no idea it looked like this. On second thought, I think it might pose some camouflaging issues. To use this as a base of operations without--"

"Pardon me, officer," Cleveland walked pass Kenneth. "Let's keep with our agreed upon plan. We all agreed to this tactical approach, did we not?"

Every supervisory official followed Cleveland towards the building.

Kenneth looked towards the entrance and noticed the sharp shooters had not entered the building yet. He had to stall them some more. "Wait a minute! Look at this here." He pointed at the Hangar as the group stopped walking. They all had impatient expressions on their faces. "If the targets are approaching from this direction," He suddenly saw the two groups containing six sharp shooters each running towards the office building. One group entered the building while the other group raced towards the rooming houses on the other side of the office building. "You know what? Never mind, forget it. Let's go."

They all resumed walking towards the office building.

Guzmon's alarms were ringing clean off the hook. Kenneth was up to something. Guzmon noticed Kenneth's behavior had even perplexed his partner Jackson.

£¥♥   £¥♥   £¥♥   £¥♥

Boris sat in the passenger seat of the moving van that lead the convoy of six other vehicles. There were two vans, two trucks, and two cars. Inside the van with Boris were Tykim, Jamil, and three Russian soldiers. Inside all the other vehicles were fully armed Russians. In total, there were twenty-two Russians, not including Boris.

Tykim's rage had continued to grow even though the beatings had stopped. The ill treatment left permanent scars on his inner being, and from the way things were going, it didn't look like he would acquire his revenge. The thought of dying without bringing Boris and his bitch ass soldiers along with him, caused more pain than the physical beat downs. He wondered what the hell was Daquasha up to? She'd had better know what she was doing, since these cats were playing strictly for keeps.

Tykim's vibes with respect to Jamil were mixed most of the times. It was apparent Jamil was down with the Russians. But on the other hand, he repeatedly detected Jamil was trying to communicate with him through his eyes. When Jamil saved his life during the shoot-out in the smelly room, Tykim initially thought it was because the boss Russian wanted to keep him alive, but Jamil's eyes were telling him it was another unrelated reason for the act. What really irritated Tykim was Jamil's voice. Tykim was still wrecking his brains trying to place that damn voice.

Jamil sat silently, wondering if there was a way to get a signal to Daquasha, informing her that the plan was dead? Every idea that surfaced was instantly neutralized when the reality of the situation came to light. There were at least two dozen Russians and they all were heavily armed. If Jamil pulled a stunt, it would spell the end of his life. He hoped those sharp shooting lessons he taught Daquasha were well absorbed because from the way it looked, everything was riding on her shoulders. If she didn't save the day, then all was lost.

£¥♥   £¥♥   £¥♥   £¥♥

The four sharp shooters ran up the stairs, heading for the roof. The sharp shooter at the back of the line, who's name was Gary Wilmore, pulled a silencer equipped handgun. As the group bolted out the stairwell door, and their feet crunched on the gravel of the roof, Gary opened fire on his comrades. The titanium tipped bullets eased through the protective helmets and bulletproofed vests as if they were nothing more than thin sheets of paper. One of the bullets had gone through two of the men. In fact, the bullets could have gone straight through armored tanks without the slightest difficulty.

Gary Wilmore was a Russian mole who'd been working for the New Orleans Police force for the past four years. Gary saw one of the fallen

196

sharp shooters moving and he took aim. The impact of the silenced bullet made the man's body tremble and flinch with excessive force.

£¥♥   £¥♥   £¥♥   £¥♥

The other group of sharp shooters, heading for the rooming houses, turned the corner of a building. The sharp shooter at the back of the line, who's name was Samuel Beckett, pulled a silencer equipped 9mm and opened fire on his comrades. The men tumbled to the ground like bowling pins coming in contact with a bowling ball.

Samuel's bullets missed the lead shooter, and the man spun around and squeezed off a ear shattering shot from the 30.06 rifle. Samuel raced behind the side of the building with his finger locked on the trigger and his weapon aimed at the man. He watched his bullets pound and shred the man's body. As the man stumbled backwards, Samuel was running towards him to inspect his work.

Afterwards, Samuel rushed over to the other side of the yard where all the vehicles were hidden and where four other Swat-team members were manning the radios, surveillance cameras and all other technical equipment. Samuel murdered them all.

£¥♥   £¥♥   £¥♥   £¥♥

Moments ago, the unexpected shot fired by the sharp shooter, startled Kenneth into a shooting frenzy. As the group walked down a long dark hallway, heading for the staircase, Kenneth shot his partner, Jackson square in the chest. This single titanium tipped bullet went through Jackson, and three of the FBI agents, dropping them all to the floor in a simultaneous fashion. Then Cleveland and Armstrong were struck down by the next bullet fired. The three New Orleans cops and a FBI agent attempted to run, but Kenneth's bullets were far more faster.

Guzmon dropped to the floor with his weapon in hand when he heard the first group of bodies drop. He turned, saw silent flames leaping from Kenneth's weapon and let off a thunderous shot. It missed Kenneth, but it did shake him up enough to force him to take cover inside a nearby room. As Guzmon sprung to his feet, he saw everyone except him was down. His instinct took control of his feet, and he ran for the stairwell about ten yards away.

197

Kenneth peeked out the room and saw Guzmon enter the stairwell. He pulled his special made communication device connected to the two rogue sharp shooters, Gary and Samuel. "Come in GW."

Gary pulled his device from his pocket. He was looking over the railing of the roof. "I read you."

"You got a stray coming your way."

"No problem." Gary disconnected the line as he headed for the stairwell door.

£¥♥   £¥♥   £¥♥   £¥♥

Daquasha was pulled out of her pacing trance when she heard a shot fired outside. The second shot fired downstairs inside the building catapulted her to the window. Staring out into the darkness, she saw nothing. The questions bombarded her mind as she headed towards the door. If these men were the police, who were they shooting at? The answer came and it made her even more nervous. The men Jamil said he would send were probably intercepted. Shit! She sighed angrily because everything was going wrong.

Daquasha peered out the door and saw the corridor was empty. She pulled back and glanced at her watch. It was 11:23. She had about a half hour to get in place, or to find a way to position herself so when those Russians arrived, she could go forward with the plan. But how were they going to escape with the police sneaking around?

She heard running footsteps coming from the staircase. Daquasha peeked out and saw a man barrel through the staircase door. The man was heading directly towards her. With wide eyes, she pulled back. She frantically dug in her back-pack and pulled the 9mm. She peeked out and saw another man rushed through the same door, chasing the fleeing man.

Daquasha saw the first running man turned with a gun in his hand. A ear shattering shot rang out.

Daquasha pulled her head back into the room.

Guzmon had saw Daquasha's abrupt movement. It looked like someone had pulled their head inside a room. Suddenly, he felt bullets whizzing past him and he reflectively dove to the floor. Guzmon started frantically crawling towards the room while firing shots at his pursuer.

Daquasha was about to close the door, but Guzmon held the door and rushed inside.

Guzmon was breathing hard as he rose to his feet and saw it was Daquasha. The shock was unmistakable. "What are you--" He saw

Daquasha was pointing a gun at him, but he instinctively knew she was not going to use it on him. Guzmon turned and peeked out the door. He pulled back, stuck his gun around the threshold and opened fire on the sharp shooter.

Several of Guzmon's bullets struck Gary, but didn't penetrate his head to toe body armor. Gary paused a moment, shook the pain away and the silent flames leaped from his rifle. He continued forward, not the least phased by the bullets.

Daquasha sensed this man had cop written all over him. She noticed he even smelled like a cop.

"Oh shit!" Guzmon muttered as he saw the man was still approaching. "This motherfucker's wearing body armor." He said out loud as he pulled from the threshold looking like he was about to panic.

Daquasha nudged her way pass Guzmon.

Guzmon moved aside and was shocked by Daquasha's aggressiveness. He was also moved by her tight fitting black outfit and the way it hugged her voluptuous body. Now what the hell do she think she's going to do?

Daquasha peeked out, found where Gary was positioned, stuck the gun around the threshold and fired four silenced shots without looking. One of the bullets struck Gary in the helmet, taking him off his feet. The slug easily went through the bullet-proofed plastic. The Teflon laced bullet worked just as Jamil said it would. Daquasha peeked out and saw Gary laid stretched out on the floor. She turned and faced Guzmon with her gun pointed. "Who are you?" She saw Guzmon was pointing his gun at her.

Guzmon ignored Daquasha and went to the threshold. He peeked out and saw the man was down. Guzmon couldn't believe what was happening. He turned and faced Daquasha. He'd been tracking this woman for the pass several weeks; now she stood face to face with him and he didn't know what to do. He shook loose of the indecisiveness. "I'm Detective Guzmon from the New York City Police Department. Ms. Daquasha Lawrence, I'm sorry to inform you that you're under arrest."

£¥♥   £¥♥   £¥♥   £¥♥

Boris saw the shipping yard come into view as he peered out the van windshield. "Slow it down." He said to the driver. "The insiders haven't made contact yet." He knew this meant Kenneth, Gary and Samuel hadn't cleared the entire area.

Jamil saw he had to make a move now or it would be never. He reached in his pocket and pulled out the hand-cuff key.

Boris said to the driver. "Stop here. We'll walk the rest of the way. By the time we get closer, our insiders should make contact."

As Boris got out the van, the soldiers man-handled Tykim up out of his seat.

Jamil grabbed Tykim's hands that were cuffed behind his back and slipped the key in his hand while pretending to be shoving him roughly towards the door. "Come on motherfucker, move your ass!" Jamil saw Tykim instantly grabbed hold of the key.

Tykim thought this was a trick of some kind as he stumbled out the van. He felt it was a key Jamil had just gave him. Tykim limped towards a tall chain-linked fence with the Russians on his sides and Jamil behind him. Now, he had to find a way to maneuver the key to open the cuffs.

The other men from the vehicles behind them got out and started running towards the back of the nearby rooming houses and the factory like buildings, apparently securing the area.

Tykim began fumbling with the key. He almost dropped it. His heart fluttered as he sighed inwardly. He told himself to clam down. Tykim tried it again. Thank goodness Jamil was directly in back of him, blocking his efforts from anyone coming up the rear. His heart sped up when the key slid inside the lock. He turned it. The lock clicked open.

£¥♥   £¥♥   £¥♥   £¥♥

"GW come in," Kenneth said into the communication device. "I repeat. GW come in." After waiting a moment without a response, Kenneth pocketed the device and headed for the stairwell. With his gun in hand, he looked at his watch and realized he was way behind schedule. He refused to call Boris until he was certain the area was in order. As Kenneth mounted the stairs two at a time, he called Gary a series of foul names.

Heading for the top floor, Kenneth knew the last shots came from that location by the way they sounded. When he entered the fourth floor and saw a body lying on the floor, he approached it with caution. He saw the Swat Police uniform when he was about ten feet away and he gritted his teeth.

He turned Gary's body over and saw he was shot in the face. Suddenly, he heard a voice. It was a woman's voice!? She was talking to someone. Then he heard Guzmon's voice. Thought you could get away, huh?

With his gun ready, Kenneth crept towards the room.

£¥♥   £¥♥   £¥♥   £¥♥

Moments earlier, Daquasha and Guzmon stood looking at each other. Daquasha lowered her Tech 9. "Wouldn't it be wise for us both to try to get outta this alive? From the way you came running in here, I don't think you in a position to be making enemies. If I wasn't here, you might be dead." Daquasha turned and rushed to the window. "What's your name, officer?"

"Detective Guzmon," He instantly noticed Daquasha's words made a whole lot of sense. Suddenly, Armstrong came into mind and the way Kenneth had killed him danced in his head in a vivid manner. Armstrong's wife, Carol, was going to be shattered; after all these years without Armstrong ever being hurt on the job, she assumed Armstrong was safe and immune from harm. The pain, anger and sorrow almost broke Guzmon in two. Pull it together he told himself.   Suddenly,   Guzmon   realized Kenneth was still out there somewhere. With a slight struggle, Guzmon concluded he had no choice but to join forces with Daquasha. She was absolutely right about getting out of this alive. And it should obviously be the first and foremost issue on both their minds. There was no doubt the Russians were on there way here; since they apparently had Kenneth and some of the Swat-police members in their pocket, this situation was now a very precarious one. "I guess you're right. Maybe we oughta put all that other stuff aside. Those Russians seem to have their hands in more places than any of us . . ."

As Guzmon spoke, Daquasha heard a noise outside the room. Suddenly, she saw the door behind Guzmon slowly opening. She raised the Tech 9. "Move!"

SZK!--SZK!--SZK!--SZK!. . .

Guzmon leaped away from the door just as Daquasha's silenced bullets ripped and tore through the door and the walls. In a sweeping motion, Daquasha held her finger on the trigger until at least half the clip was expended.

£¥♥   £¥♥   £¥♥   £¥♥

Moments ago, Kenneth arrived in front of the door as Guzmon was talking. Just as Kenneth was about to stick his arm inside the room with the gun, planning to open fire without rushing inside, he heard Daquasha screamed "Move!" Then, suddenly, he felt and heard the bullets tearing at the door and the walls. Had he known Daquasha had Teflon tipped bullets, he would've dove to the floor upon hearing Daquasha's scream. The bullets riddled his body, momentarily holding him in an up right position. His body hit the floor with a sickening thud.

£¥♥   £¥♥   £¥♥   £¥♥

Daquasha moved slowly towards the door. Guzmon was right behind her. She nudged the door opened, stuck her head out and saw Kenneth's bullet ridden body.

Guzmon peered over her shoulders. "Don't you know possession of Teflon tipped bullets are a federal offense?" He really wanted to thank her for killing Kenneth. "I see you're going all out, huh?"

"Is there any other way to do it?" Daquasha stepped out of the room and jogged down the hallway. Her back-pack bounced with every stride and the materials inside jiggled.

Guzmon was right behind her, enjoying the view.

Daquasha arrived at the stairwell and entered slowly. She raced up to the roof. She opened the door and was about to head for the side facing the entrance, but stopped when she saw the five dead Swat-police laid out on the roof. "Shit!" she muttered as her eyes rapidly scanned the area. It took seconds to determine there was no one else on the roof with them.

When Guzmon saw the dead cops, he felt his anger and pain increased ten folds. As Daquasha headed towards the railing, Guzmon realized he was about to become someone he despised and enjoyed hunting and arresting. But what surprised him was he realized he was going to enjoy every moment of it.

Tykim held the unfastened cuffs in place, waiting for whatever was going to come next. Suddenly, they stopped walking. Tykim saw Boris was stressed out of his mind.

"Where the fuck are they!?" Boris said out loud. "Durran, come here!" He shouted at one of his soldiers who was walking near the building. The man obeyed and jogged towards them. When he arrived, Boris said, "Listen, go check the area. If you see Kenneth or any of his workers, tell them I wanna see them right this fuckin' minute."

The soldier took off running.

Jamil shifted nervously on his feet. With a gun in each hand and a nap-sack filled with a mini-arsenal flung over his shoulder, Jamil's trigger fingers trembled. He hoped Daquasha saw them by now. But the fear was strong because Boris was apparently waiting for a signal from someone, which meant he had sent in a crew before they arrived. Jamil looked around and was reminded of the fact there were some areas he and Daquasha hadn't even examined closely because he assured her his crew would take care of all that. If Lunatic hadn't fucked up, he would've sent a couple of shooters to hold Daquasha down, but by now, she had to have realized what the deal was. He struggled against the thought that Daquasha wasn't going to make it.

As Boris watched his soldier running, he realized he was wasting a lot of valuable time. Kenneth had to have taken care of business by now, he surmised with confidence. He saw two of the empty police vehicles in the back of one of the factory like buildings, and no police officers on foot, which meant they were neutralized. Also, two of his soldiers had told him they had found a few dead police bodies. Maybe Kenneth's communication devise was malfunctioning or something, Boris told himself.

Boris looked at his watch. It was 11:50. Boris made up his mind, it was show-time. Boris pulled his communication device from his pocket and spoke into it. "Listen up everyone. Groups A and B, come to me. Groups C and D, stay with the plan. We're going in the Hangar." He pocketed the device and moved towards Tykim with his gun pointed at his head.

After Boris grabbed Tykim, placed the barrel of his gun to Tykim's head, he started walking down the pot-hole ridden road as two of his soldiers pointed their weapons at Tykim as well.

£¥♥   £¥♥   £¥♥   £¥♥

Earlier, Daquasha peered through her binoculars and saw Jamil, Tykim and a mob of Russians. Oh, shit! She saw they were slowly entering the shipping yard.

With frantic speed, Daquasha began preparing her rifle, trying to remember all the stuff Tykim and Jamil had told her. She screwed the long-range scope and the silencer onto the rifle, got on her stomach, and peered through the infra-red scope. When she saw Tykim covered in a greenish glow of light, she paced her breathing. She slowly moved the rifle, bringing everyone in the immediate area into focus. Suddenly, she saw the entire group stopped walking. One of the Russians spoke to a man, who took off running towards the building she was on top of. He had a weapon in his hands. A moment later, she saw six more men come from the nearby buildings and joined the group containing Tykim and Jamil.

"I know you don't think I'm gonna standby while you commit murder in my presence?" Guzmon was kneeling next to Daquasha. He didn't know if he was serious or joking, due to the way his words sounded.

Daquasha continued what she was doing. "You wasn't beefin' when I saved your ass a minute ago."

"This is crazy." Guzmon mumbled out loud, peering over the roof railing as he saw the running man, despite the darkness. Guzmon's mind began reevaluating this current situation; several wonderful prospects suddenly emerged. Maybe this isn't as bad as it seems. Yeah, this might be something worth breaking a few rules for.

Daquasha counted all fourteen targets in her sights, but she knew there were many more. She wondered why hadn't the police clashed with them yet? There had to be other police, since she saw the whole fleet of vehicles with her own eyes. As Daquasha positioned the cross in the lens upon the chest of one of the men standing next to Tykim, her finger trembled. She wondered if changing the plan to start shooting now was a wise choice? Jamil and Tykim had better be ready because this was the way it was going down. She was hoping and praying they were prepared. She drew a deep breath and was about to pull the trigger.

Her finger stopped like screaming car tires locking on concrete. She saw Boris grabbed Tykim and was now moving towards her. He had his gun to Tykim's head. The two Russians on both sides of Tykim had their weapons pointed at him as well.

"I can't believe I'm going along with this." Guzmon said.

Daquasha looked up at Guzmon. She wanted to tell him to shut the fuck up. She spoke casually, without ill-will. "Well, you should've stayed in New York." She looked back into the scope and saw with terror they were moving towards the hangar. Maintaining her position, she realized she was going to have to move the rifle and that the original plan was back in effect. She wanted to take the shot and set this thing off, but there were too many guns pointed at Tykim. If she hit one of the men, the others would open fire on him. Shit! She held the position as they walked past the building.

£¥♥   £¥♥   £¥♥   £¥♥

Samuel Beckett heard the noise coming from the roof of the building. He looked up and detected movement. Then he saw a man running towards the hangar. It looked like Durran and he was about to call to him, but Samuel heard a man's voice up on the roof. Samuel had been trying to make contact with Kenneth and Gary without any luck. Policy and procedure told him they both were dead. Whoever that stray was, the one he overheard Kenneth telling Gary to catch, had to be responsible for killing them both. It was conclusively confirmed that they both were dead since they all agreed to meet here and if someone didn't arrive by the designated time, it was to be concluded that he was dead. Therefore, Samuel knew they both were dead.

Samuel decided to put the final touches of the clean-up phase into effect. He had planted explosives all through the shipping yard, on all the police vehicles, inside the factory like buildings and inside some of the room houses where he had dragged the dead police bodies. The only locations left were this four story building and the hangar.

Samuel entered the building and found the stairwell. He positioned a bomb on one of the steps near the second floor. He turned on the detonator, but didn't activate the timer. Samuel rushed to the basement, found the main beams. There were eight of them. He planted a slab of C4 (plastic explosives) along with a small detonator attached to the explosive to each beam. Each detonator had built-in timers all set for the same time.

As Samuel posted up on the main floor of the building, he activated all nine detonator and timers. Each device registered 5 minutes and, in unison, they all began the count down.

£¥♥   £¥♥   £¥♥   £¥♥

With frantic speed, Daquasha jumped to her feet, startling Guzmon. She hastily gather the rifle, ran to the other side and positioned the rifle. She laid flat on her stomach, peered into the scope, and followed the group of men as they continued towards the hangar.

"You got some heat with a silencer?" Guzmon was rummaging through her bag. "Ain't no sense in me sitting around missing out on all the fun."

Daquasha turned her head and saw Guzmon rambling through the bag. "I think you should let me handle this." She wretched the bag out of his hands. "I don't want you shooting the wrong people."

Daquasha positioned the tool box in her sights, making sure when Boris found it, there would be no doubt, she could do her thing.

£¥♥   £¥♥   £¥♥   £¥♥

Boris moved towards the hangar. He saw the tool box and his excitement rose. His eyes scanned the area. He waved to the two soldiers nearest to him, signaling them to check the area out.

They raced ahead of them and entered the hangar.

Boris would have told Kenneth, Samuel and Gary to do this, but 130 million dollars was too much money to trust anybody with. He told them just what they needed to know to get their part of the job done, no more, no less.

£¥♥   £¥♥   £¥♥   £¥♥

Jamil tagged along, realizing they were fucked up. There were simply too many of these Russians. He was sweating pounds of sweat in anticipation of shots suddenly ringing out. He saw the reason why Daquasha didn't open fire was because there were three guns pointed at Tykim. When Jamil saw Boris break away from the group and moved rapidly towards the tool box, while one of the other men took his aim off Tykim as he looked around the area, Jamil saw the window of opportunity had suddenly opened. Please, Daquasha do it! he muttered to himself. Come on, boo!

Just when Jamil thought all was loss, he saw the man who had his gun pointed at Tykim's head flinch from the shot right between the eyes.

£¥♥   £¥♥   £¥♥   £¥♥

Seconds earlier, Daquasha's arms, fingers and neck were screaming in pain as she followed the group with her eye planted to the scope. She was afraid to even blink an eye out of fear of missing the chance to set it off. A wave of nervousness welled up in her chest when she saw two of the Russians ran head of the group and entered the hangar.

Then the whole group stepped beyond the threshold. They were inside the hangar. Every muscle in Daquasha's body tensed up. Damn it! All three of them still had their weapons aimed at Tykim.

Suddenly, Daquasha saw Boris walk away from the group. Then she saw one of the men moved his weapon as he turned around, looking at the interior of the hangar. Bingo!

Daquasha pulled trigger. The recoil was remarkably non-existent, but the noise was even more non-existent. She saw the man in her scope jerk with tremendous force and fell to the ground. As instructed, Daquasha started picking off as many men as she could while Tykim and Jamil moved with frantic speed.

£¥♥   £¥♥   £¥♥   £¥♥

Jamil was in motion the moment he saw the Russian's body jerk and collapsed to the floor. Inconspicuously, Jamil shot the other Russian next to Tykim in the back. He then hit the deck as did Tykim. As they were on the floor, Jamil crawled over to Tykim and handed him one of his silencer equipped 9mm. The bullets from Daquasha's rifle were raining a beautiful rhythm with excellent results. Numerous Russian soldiers, both inside and outside the hangar were dropping like flies caught in a room fogged out with Raid.

Tykim felt like a death row prisoner released from a capital punishment sentence. He snatched the gun and started firing at Boris who was already fleeing for cover behind the huge tool box. He spun his aim and cut loose another wave of bullets.

Tykim sprung to his feet as Jamil was firing upon the Russians who were completely caught off guard. He even cut down two that tried to enter the hangar, but he wasn't certain if it was Daquasha's doing.

Jamil ran towards a huge barrel as Tykim followed him. Bullets whizzed pass them just as they arrived near the barrel. They both returned fire. A moment later, they noticed the entrance was cleared and raced out of the hangar with Boris firing shots at them. They turned the corner and disappeared.

£¥♥   £¥♥   £¥♥   £¥♥

Daquasha was firing silenced shots at the men rushing towards the hangar. She saw Guzmon had grabbed one of her silenced Tech 9s, ran to the other side of the roof and joined in the frenzy. After hastily reloading her rifle four times, Daquasha saw she had done just about all she could do and Jamil and Tykim were out of the hangar. She jumped up, hastily packed up the rifle and fled towards the stairwell with Guzmon behind her.

Daquasha entered the staircase running at top speed. The plan was to hit and run, and that's exactly what she did thus far. She bolted down the stairs as if the building was on fire. A sudden noise came from downstairs and she put on the brakes.

Breathing hard, Guzmon said, "What's the problem?"

"Shhhh!" Daquasha said, straining to hear the noise again. Her breathing was heavy. She pulled her 9mm as she moved slowly down the stairs, trying to be as quiet as possible. She saw they had made it to the second floor.

Suddenly, Daquasha realized the noise was a beeping sound. It was coming from the flight down. She saw a box, and instantly detected it was the source of the beeping. Just as she arrived, Guzmon rushed in front of her and went to the box.

Guzmon's heart flinched when he saw what the box was. "My God! It's a bomb!" Guzmon saw the digital numbers counting away. Terror gripped him when he saw they had one minute and two seconds before it would detonate. "Let's go!" He was about to bolt down the next flight of stairs.

Massive machine gunfire rang out. The bullets blew humongous holes in the stairwell walls. A dust cloud as thick as tear gas instantly appeared.

Guzmon pulled himself back up the stairs. "We got less than a minute before it blows!" He was beyond a state of panic.

Daquasha raced back up the stairs. It was evident the person shooting downstairs was going to prevent them from getting out through that route.

"What the hell is wrong with you!?" Guzmon followed her more so out of confusion and desperation than anything else.

Daquasha barreled through the second floor door. She ran to an office, checked the door. It didn't open. She ran for another door.

"We got about twenty seconds!" Guzmon shouted and realized what Daquasha was doing. He checked a door and it opened. "Right here! Right here!"

They rushed inside and saw the window.

Daquasha ran to the window, looked out and saw a heap of trash down below. There were sharp metal objects and a spectrum of deadly things that could easily kill them if they landed on them.

"We got ten seconds!" Guzmon said calmly. "It's this way or nothing. Move!" Guzmon ran and leap towards the window.

"Jump far out--" Daquasha tried to warn him, but he crashed through the window.

Daquasha ran to the door, did an about-face and bolted towards the window.

KABLAAM!

The explosion was so awesome, it shook the land and everything on it for a distance of a mile.

£¥♥   £¥♥   £¥♥   £¥♥

Boris was savoring the beauty of the 37 jewels. They were all here. Each one looked as they did weeks ago after Boris and several other men stole them. The huge explosion shook him out of his trance and into a flee towards the side door. He wrestled it open with a good struggle. Several explosions followed behind the first. He was furious with Kenneth because he still hadn't made contact and already he was implementing the clean up phase. As Boris stepped outside, he pulled his device and spoke in a frantic tone.

"Chopper, come in!"

"Chopper here." A man with a high pitched voice said through the device.

"It's time."

"I'm on my way."

Boris disconnected and ran towards an empty lot.

£¥♥   £¥♥   £¥♥   £¥♥

Jamil and Tykim were positioned behind a building when the explosion went off. Seconds before the blast, they both saw Guzmon crash through the second floor window. Then upon impact of the explosion, they saw another person, Daquasha, being hurled out the window as if she was shot from a cannon.

As Tykim and Jamil raced to Daquasha, they heard additional explosions and saw the whole building started coming down. It seemed like explosions were going off everywhere. The whole shipping yard was going up. When they arrived, they saw Daquasha was unconscious. Tykim and Jamil argued over who would carry her away.

Guzmon struggled to his feet. He was partially covered in rubble and was flinching with every explosion. Suddenly, Guzmon saw the rogue swat-cop (Samuel) moving towards Tykim and Jamil while taking aim. Guzmon pulled the weapon he got from Daquasha and opened fire while screaming.

"Get down!"

SZK!--SZK!--SZK!--SZK!...

The bullets from Guzmon's gun ripped and pounded Samuel before he could get off a shot.

Simultaneously, Jamil and Tykim spun around with their guns ready and saw the man who jumped out the window moments before Daquasha was shooting at a man dressed in police swat-clothing. They both were about to open fire on Guzmon, but it was evident he had saved their life. They both concluded he wasn't a foe and didn't pull the triggers on their weapons.

Tykim and Jamil resumed their argument over who would carry Daquasha. Tykim gave in and Jamil scooped her up into his arms.

Just as they rushed away, Guzmon followed them, limping and hopping along. "Is she all right?"

Tykim and Jamil turned with impatient expressions, but continued moving.

"Me and Daquasha were on that roof," Guzmon said, still following. "We were working together up there. Thanks to us, y'all asses are still alive."

Jamil nor Tykim said anything as Guzmon tagged along.

Jamil realized Guzmon's face looked very familiar, but couldn't place the face. By the accent, it was evident he was from somewhere up north. He shook loose of the thought. This guy just saved their life, and if he helped Daquasha while she was on the roof, then he had to be a friend. Maybe he jumped ship on the Russians.

Two minutes later, they all were on a speed boat, breezing away from the shipping yard.

Jamil was behind the wheel while Tykim and Guzmon sat staring at each other. Daquasha was lying propped against a box with Jamil's jacket acting as a pillow.

Daquasha suddenly woke up. She started coughing and Tykim went to her.

Tykim embraced her. "Daquasha, where you hurting at, baby?"

"My head," She massaged the back of her head. She looked around and saw Guzmon. "Detective Guzmon, what are you doing here?"

"Detective Guzmon!?" Jamil and Tykim both said at the same time as they both pulled their weapons.

Guzmon raised both hands. "Easy fellas. I'm not here to break any balls."

Suddenly, two police helicopters flew pass them. Daquasha, Tykim and Jamil all looked up in terror. They all looked at Detective Guzmon as if he was responsible for the helicopter's appearance.

"Why the fuck did you come with us?" Tykim maintained his aim. "What are you here for?" He smiled wickedly. "I know not to arrest us."

Guzmon laughed. "Well, actually no. I was--"

The sound of rapid approaching boats appeared. They all turned their heads and saw five police boats racing towards them. Panic drenched their minds.

Daquasha had daggers in her eyes as she stared at Guzmon. "Oh, so, this your plan?"

"What are you talking about!?" Guzmon said as the boats drew closer. "I'll tell you what. Y'all cut me in on those jewels and I'll clean this up."

Daquasha was aghast, but she had to play out this scenario. "We gave them back in exchange for Tykim."

"Well, I guess you might as well start shooting because I'm either in or y'all going down."

Jamil laughed. "Now I know where I know you from. You're the detective who was investigating my case. Grimy Guzmon. Uptown's finest and slimiest."

The boats drew closer.

"You better make up your mind," Guzmon said nonchalantly.

Daquasha, Tykim and Jamil looked at each other. They each nodded their heads reluctantly.

Daquasha said, "You got a deal. You get a million dollars--"

"Five million," Guzmon said, "non-negotiable."

There was a moment of silence.

The police boats' spotlights were turned on. A man's voice boomed from a bull-horn. "This is the New Orleans police. Bring your vessel to a stop."

Jamil complied, bringing the speed boat to a stop.

They all hastily agreed to Guzmon's offer.

The five police boats surrounded them.

Guzmon showed the fellow cops his badge and told them they were sight seeing. Guzmon also told the cops he rented the boat and Daquasha, Tykim and Jamil were his friends. They asked about the explosions and Guzmon informed them that they had heard and saw them, but that they were many miles away at the time the explosions went off. Since the police boats were in a hurry, on their way to the shipping yard, the interview lasted only a minute or two, if that.

As the five police boats pulled away, and Jamil got the speed boat moving again, Guzmon saw Jamil's evil grin. He instantly realized he was playing a very dangerous game, and wondered was he playing himself into a premature grave. Something inside of him was talking to his inner being.

This voice told him, his greed was going to be the cause of his demise, but his lust for that mean green was a far more powerful emotion, and it insisted he play the hand out for all it was worth.

CHAPTER # 29

Daquasha stood in front of Guzmon, screaming at Jamil. "No! We made a deal! He saved us back there! It proves he's straight cheese. I'm not gonna let you kill him."

They were on a boardwalk. The waters just beyond were mellow and non-threatening. It was about 2 o'clock in the morning and the place was deserted.

Jamil put his gun down, his arm rested in a sagging fashion. "Listen, Daquasha. This motherfucker is one of the foulest cops in the Bronx. He came down here to arrest us all. He has set-up crazy cats from the 'hood, robbin' and killin' dudes. He's a cold blooded snake, who can't be trusted. I bet you when we get back to New York, he'll hunt us down like dogs!" He stared at Guzmon. "What, you tryin' to steal all the jewels for yourself motherfucker? Is that what you want?"

Tykim had his gun in his hand with his arms folded. "I don't trust cops. I gotta agree with Jamil. I say we smoke his ass and keep it movin'."

"If you kill him, then you gotta kill me," Daquasha stepped up in Jamil's face and stared him straight in the eyes. "That means our baby as well."

Jamil shifted on his feet. He grunted as if her comment struck him in the gut.

Daquasha walked over to Tykim. "I'm asking you to hold me down, Tykim. Can you do that? I think he's gonna be straight up with us. I say we let him live." She winked her eye at Tykim.

Tykim was confused by her eye winking trick. He didn't have the slightest clue where she was going with all this, but he was certain this meant to play along. "Well, I guess you're right, Daquasha. I'm holdin' you down, baby girl. If you want him alive, then he'll stay alive."

Daquasha and Tykim looked at Jamil. Guzmon had on puppy dog eyes as he too stared at Jamil.

"Fuck it!" Jamil threw up both hands in defeat. "He lives."

Daquasha walked over to Guzmon and pulled him to the side. "Listen, detective. I hope you're not gonna turn me into a liar. Are you gonna bust us the first chance you get?"

"Of course not," Guzmon lied. "I would never do something as foul and evil as that. I just want a piece of the action. I've been working my whole life trying to make ends meet, and what do I have for all these years of busting my damn ass? A jive ass pension and a bunch of fuckin' headaches that could kill a hardheaded mule in a minute. Don't worry, you cut me in, I'll hold you down."

"Detective, I need you to wait over there," Daquasha pointed at the bleachers. "I have some private business to deal with."

Guzmon nodded, walked over to the bleachers and took a seat.

Daquasha turned and walked towards Tykim and Jamil. This was the messed up part. As she approached, Daquasha saw they both had that look on their faces and they both knew it was time to choose. If there was a way she could keep them both, she would probably try it out, but neither Jamil nor Tykim was going for any of that. It was sad because her mind was made up a few days ago when she received that nasty little surprise, and there was nothing anyone could say to could change it. Yeah, there was gonna be a broken heart, but, hey, it's just a feeling. He'll get over it sooner or later.

Daquasha stood in the middle of them, staring out at the dark waters. She waited for one of them to spark up the conversation.

Tykim coughed loudly. "Listen, Daquasha. We was a team for the past two weeks, we been a team when we was kids, let's stay a team, baby girl. He can't love you like I will, bet that. With this money and them jewels, we'll be one big happy family. Let's keep this thing goin'."

Jamil gave Tykim the mad screw face. "All I have to say is, keep your promise, Boo. Remember, what you said that night I saved you from Nuke?"

Daquasha knew exactly what she promised him, and there was no need to repeat it.

Tykim felt terror forming because Daquasha didn't refute Jamil's allegations. "Oh shit. So you breaking out on me, huh? And you been planning this shit all along." Tykim felt choked up, but he refused to show any weakness in the presence of another man. "Well, ain't this about a motherfuckin' bitch! What's wrong with you, Daquasha? This nigga tried to murder you and now you gonna walk off with him? A man can't love a woman he would try to kill."

There was a moment of silence.

Jamil was smiling. "Maybe you need to be brought up to status. I hired you because I knew you wouldn't let anything happen to Daquasha. My brother wanted her dead, so I did what I had to do to protect her." He gave Daquasha a firm embrace and kissed her on the forehead.

Tykim felt foolish because it all suddenly made sense. That was why this hit was so god damn big. It was also true that there was no amount of money anyone could've paid him to kill Daquasha. And if he had to risk his life to protect her, there wouldn't be the slightest hesitation on his part. And he would do it again and again, and would enjoy doing it each and every time. "So what's the deal, Daquasha, you goin' back to New York with him?"

Daquasha nodded her head. She struggled to keep the tears back; she felt sorry for Tykim, but she loved Jamil and her child should be with its real father. With a loud sigh, she forced the crying sensation back. "I'm sorry, Tykim." She began turning the ring on her finger. "I'm sorry." Daquasha hugged Tykim and kissed him on the lips. "I love you too, but in a different way."

Tykim was as hot as a furnace. He locked eyes with Jamil. The thought of killing Jamil was hovering heavily in his mind. He saw Jamil cracked an arrogant smile and Tykim literally almost lost it. Tykim turned, stared out into the dark watery horizon. He was shattered and was now struggling to maintain his dignity, pride and honor as a stand up brother who took no shit from anybody.

Jamil walked over to Daquasha and gazed into her eyes. The urge to fuck with Tykim's head was strong. He had to make sure Tykim knew who's girl Daquasha was, and the perfect way to accomplish this, suddenly came into his head. "Daquasha, remember I said I had a surprise for you?" Jamil grabbed Daquasha's hands, kneeled and got on one knee.

Ah, shit! Daquasha felt a stream of tension roll down her spine. "Yeah, I remember."

"Daquasha, will you marry me?"

Daquasha turned away, unable to maintain eye contact with Jamil. Why the fuck did he pick a time like now to do something like this!? She decide to go with the flow, but was furious because Jamil was rubbing salt into Tykim's wounds. When Daquasha felt Jamil's grip tighten, she said, "Yes, I'll marry you."

Tykim sighed loudly. There was blood in his eyes. The rage was truly blinding. He turned, gazed into Daquasha's eyes for a moment and headed for the black four door Dodge Daquasha and Jamil had stashed as a getaway car.

They drove off. During the ride, no one besides Guzmon said anything. It took twenty minutes to arrive at the train station where the jewels were secured in a public locker.

After Daquasha and Jamil retrieved the jewels, they all went to a secluded area and split them up. Daquasha, Tykim and Jamil got 12 jewels each, while Guzmon got one, but it was the biggest one of them all and was visibly worth far more than 5 million dollars.

An hour later, they all were at a bus depot. Guzmon had got on a bus and had gone his way. About a dozen men who worked for Jamil and Kilroy stood-by, watching and body guarding Daquasha and Jamil. Now it was time for Daquasha and Tykim to say their good-byes.

Daquasha approached Tykim as Jamil stood watching closely. She was twirling the ring on her finger. "I'm sorry, Tykim." She gave him a strong hug. "Thank you for being there for me. Thank you for saving my life, and thank you for being a true friend." She gave Tykim a kiss and could feel Jamil staring a hole in the back of her head. She let go of the kiss, but maintained the close embrace. "I forgive you for what happened to my brother. It wasn't your fault. I'm sorry for all the pain I caused you." She pulled away from the hug. She grabbed both of Tykim's pants pockets and pulled him to her. "Please say something, Tykim."

Tykim stared into Daquasha's soft brown eyes. He held this position for a moment. Looking away, he saw Jamil acting like he had rocks in his jaw. "Well, I guess it was all in the cards, it wasn't meant for me to have you. You take care of yourself, baby girl. And always remember, I love you." He kissed her and looked up at Jamil. "You got the best jewel a man could ever have, Jamil. Make sure you treat her like what she is, a precious jewel."

Jamil gave Tykim a raised clenched fist salute. "Mo' power to yah, my brother. Believe me, I know how to treat a jewel." He was about to say, maybe if you treated her like a jewel when you had her, maybe you wouldn't be going through this.

Tykim gave Daquasha another glance and walked away.

Daquasha shouted at Tykim's back. "Don't forget that Georgetown dream. I hear the beaches in the fall are fabulous."

Tykim turned and waved at her.

Daquasha was about to shout her statement again, because Tykim acted like he didn't hear her. "Don't for--"

"Come on, Daquasha." Jamil latched on to her arm and gently pulled her along.

As Daquasha headed for the car with Jamil's arm wrapped around her shoulder, and the mob of bodyguards hovering around them both, she realized she should have made her last comment while they were embracing each other.

CHAPTER # 30

Tykim got in his new car. It was a black, simple inconspicuous looking Honda Dualnute. As time progressed, he realized he was beyond shattered and couldn't believe after all he did for Daquasha, she was giving him the boot. She chose Jamil over him. He started feeling inadequate and began beating himself up. Maybe he really was a hard person to live with. Maybe he was the type of individual who didn't deserve a strong black woman. Maybe he didn't hit it right. Maybe Jamil had a bigger dick than his and his tongue game on the downtown tip was probably tighter. Maybe his mandingo wasn't the real deal after all. Whatever it was, she apparently felt Jamil was the best man, and his heart was hurting.

As Tykim started the car, he realized he had to get focused. He was far from safe. There was plenty work to be done before he could even entertain the thought of allowing his heart to get in the way. It was evident when the Russians found out they got shammed it was going to get as hot as a blow torch flame. There will be bloodshed as high as the knees, and that ain't no bullshit. Tykim pulled the car onto the streets of New Orleans and struggled to think of pleasant things, like how was he going to spend all this money.

Keeping his eyes peeled for anything suspicious, Tykim cruised down the highway. He had to pick up that money from the garage vent and then he could be on his merry way. Where should he go? Mexico, Venezuela, Brazil? He didn't care where it was as long as it was out of the good old US of A. But common sense indicated Mexico would have to be the first stop on his way out of the country. He was tired, worn out and his whole body was in great pain from the injuries he received from the Russians. There wouldn't be any sleeping or even a moment of rest until he was in the safe zone. He just hoped Jamil was thinking along the same lines, since Daquasha was technically still a fugitive, and it was universally known that the Russians' reach was very long and they didn't give up easily.

Tykim raced inside the garage. And as bold as he wanted to be, Tykim got out of the car, left the door open, went to the vent, unscrewed it open, snatched the briefcase, jumped back in his car and sped off.

Twenty minutes later, Tykim was on Highway 85, putting major distance between him and New Orleans. Next stop, he determined would be Houston Texas. The thought of sending his three sisters and their countless kids some money, crossed his mind. With some apprehension, he decided this would be one of the first things on his agenda when he settled down. Even though they all shitted on him fiercely when he was bidding up north and when he was released on Parole, this time he would be the better being. He would bless everyone of them and shock the living shit out of them in the process. Sort of like killing them with kindness. If Daquasha could forgive him and even Jamil after all the foul shit he did to her, Tykim figured he could do the same for a bunch of broke ass, foul-spirited family members who had done just about everything in their power to make his life miserable.

"Love is love when the heart overrules the head." Tykim remembered this quote made by an old, gray haired prisoner named Attitude Jake when he was in Attica. In fact, this was a popular phrase amongst the older prisoners, but sadly, Tykim never really understood what they meant by it and wasn't interested enough to try to find out. Now, he sensed he knew what those old timers were talking about, because after this ordeal he was surprised he suddenly felt in a giving and sharing mood that was straight from the heart. The urge to show some love was vivid and intense. Two weeks ago this sort of thinking would've been sheer lunacy. He guessed money really did have the power to change people in surprising ways that weren't always negative.

Five hours later, he arrived in the ghettos of Houston. After an hour of asking around, he found a man named Dog-bone who was able to provide him with fake ID at a very reasonable price, $500; and was able to guarantee him the documents were good enough to get him across the border. After purchasing the documents, Tykim was back on the highway.

Popping caffeine pills by the bottles, Tykim stayed on the highway, eating away miles upon miles, until finally he saw the border tolls. Trembling like a scared puppy, he pulled his car in line behind an old Ford pick up truck. It was late night, the time was about 11:30, yet the toll booths looked quite crowded. However, the traffic coming into the US borders was much larger than the traffic going out. Moments later, he pulled the car to a stop in front of the border patrol officer in the toll like booth.

"Papers, please," The officer said with his hand stuck out.

Tykim handed the cop his papers. He repeatedly told himself to relax and be easy. Everything was going be just fine. Tykim kept his eyes on the cop as he banged down his stamper, played with his little computer and read information on the screen.

"Visiting or leaving permanently?" The man asked Tykim without looking at him. He was reading the screen.

"Visiting," Tykim said, suspecting the permanent stay answer might cause some suspicion.

The officer stopped reading and slowly turned his head as if Tykim had said the wrong thing.

Tykim felt a flash of terror sweep over his whole body when he saw the officer's facial expression.

The officer started looking around for someone. He was noticeably excited. He picked up the phone, turned his back and whispered into the receiver.

Tykim strained not to panic. His hand slid towards the gun. He started looking inconspicuously at the surroundings. He couldn't seem to control the wide eyed expression on his face. In an instant, he saw if he opened fire he would be doomed. There was no where to run and he was boxed in with cars in front and back of him. There were at least a dozen border patrol cars laying in the cut as if they were itching for some drama. Through the side view mirror, he saw another officer running towards the booth.

The officer in the booth spoke in a changed voice that was firm, serious and saturated with stereotypic police mannerism. "Excuse me, Mr. Jones, I need you to put your hands on the steering wheel."

Tykim turned and saw a evil smile on the officer's face. The crippling thought of going back to prison caused his eyes to water. He came this far, just to fall victim. He was a few feet away from crossing the border, but yet, so far from acquiring this freedom. He let go of the gun and put his hands on the steering wheel. There was no need in committing suicide. With some luck, he might be able to wiggle his way out of this jam without spending the rest of his life in prison. That voice in his head assured him this was highly unlikely, but it couldn't hurt to engage in wishful thinking.

The other officer arrived, breathing hard. "Hey, Mr. Jones." He smiled broadly. This officer had stringy blond hair and sounded like a nerd who got high off of glue and other dangerous chemicals.

Tykim turned and looked at the man with a shocked facial expression. What the hell is this!? This didn't look like the type of drama he was expecting.

"Hey, guy," The blond haired officer said smiling. "That interview you had on the radio about white guys in the rap industry was really awesome, man."

The officer in the booth laughed explosively. He changed his voice to sound serious. "Put your hands on the steering wheel, Mr. Jones." He laughed, making chortling sounds. "I got you good, didn't I? Say, when you come back to the States, why don't you ask one of them big time producers you work with to hook me up on one of them funny TV shows?"

219

The officer with blond hair continued. "I tell you, Mr. Jones, you did a awesome job."

Tykim sighed and started laughing. "You liked it, huh?"

"Yeah, guy, you are really the shit, man."

Tykim stuck his hand out the window and shook both officers' hands. He changed his voice to sound like a nerd. "I'm glad you enjoyed it. Thanks for supporting me. I love you guys. I really do. Hey, you mind if I go now?"

"Of course not" The officer in the booth handed Tykim back his papers. "But first, you gotta give us an autograph for Christ sakes."

Smiling broadly, Tykim signed two pieces of paper with a surprisingly steady hand. "Have a good night, guys." He hit the gas and waved happily. It instantly felt like a thick cover of distress was pulled off of his suffocating body.

Two hours later, Tykim was in a hotel room. As he was getting undressed, he was still reminiscing about the two nerdy border patrol officers. He wondered who was this guy Mr. Ronald Jones? For him to develop such a following was rather surprising to Tykim. Damn, was that one hell of a scare. Tykim pulled his pants off and turned them upside down, about to shake them.

PLICK!

A ring fell from the pocket and hit the floor. Tykim kneeled and picked it up. "What's this!?" He saw it was Daquasha's ring. The one she said she got from her baby brother. How in the world did this get in his pocket!? Boy was she gonna be tight when she found out she--

The realization stuck him like a slap from King Kong Bundy. She put it there. And she put it there for a reason. But when? That obviously didn't matter. What counted was she put it there. He found a seat as his mind rewind the last time he saw her. Just as that moment flashed across his mind, Daquasha's statement about the ring took over his mental facilities. She had said she would always come back for the ring, no matter where, what or how it left her possession. Tykim's stomach turned queasy. She was coming back to him. That's why she put it there. She was telling him she was coming back. He rose and started pacing.

Tykim stopped pacing. But how was she going to find him!? After a moment, realization struck again. Her very last statement appeared in his mind. He flashed back to that moment. Daquasha's pretty face danced in his mind. She said, "Don't forget that Georgetown dream. I hear the beaches in the fall are fabulous."

"Yeah!" Tykim shouted. He hastily got dressed and raced out of the hotel room to find a map of South America.

£¥♥   £¥♥   £¥♥   £¥♥

Boris, Ivan and three of the heads of the Russian mob sat at a huge table as the jewel appraiser examined each of the 37 jewels.

Boris was about to lose control. The way the appraiser responded after examining the jewels didn't appear to be in accordance with what he expected. The white haired English accent having man appeared to be upset by the jewels. Boris thought back and realized he might have made a series of hasty and catastrophic decisions.

For the first time, Boris thought, what if they switched the jewels and replaced them with very convincing fake ones. They could've found a way to get the jewels copied and then put them forth as the real thing. Oh no! it can't be, he tried to assure himself inwardly as his fear was slowly transforming into terror. For a 130 million dollar fuck up, death would be the only penalty. No ifs, ands or buts about it. Death would be as guaranteed as taxes are in America.

Boris wiped the runaway trickle of sweat from his nose. The palms of his hands were as damp as rags soaking in a puddle of water. He saw Ivan was almost as bothered as he was. At least Ivan didn't have to worry about getting the ax, since he was the big man's baby brother. Boris, on the other hand, was nothing but a brother-in-law to Ivan, which meant blood couldn't save his ass.

"I am so very sorry to inform you gentlemen, these jewels are nothing more than colored glass. But, I will say the cutter who shaped and molded these imitated jewels did a rather convincing job."

Boris looked around the table with pleading eyes as the appraiser was escorted out of the room. Boris wanted to scream the word "NO!" as loud as he could, but he knew that wouldn't help. In fact, he knew there wasn't anything, any force, any object or any person in the world who could help him right about now.

£¥♥   £¥♥   £¥♥   £¥♥

Guzmon pulled his blue Chevy Nova in front of the Sheepshead Bay Tenement building and killed the engine. He pulled the jewel from his pocket and looked at it. Five million dollars, he muttered to himself. Maybe even more. He needed money so bad. His wife was in the hospital with a rare kidney disease, and the health coverage was all but expended. His side work on the street wasn't coming in correctly. His two daughters were both in college asking for money every five minutes.

Five months had past since Guzmon acquired this jewel from Daquasha, Jamil and Tykim. Deep down, he knew it was a little too early to try to sell the jewel, but the damn thing was burning a hole in his pocket. He'd also been searching for Daquasha and Jamil. They said they were returning to New York, and Guzmon had full intentions of relieving them of those jewels. So far, he had no luck finding them. It was like they vanished from existence. But sad for them, Guzmon decided long ago, for that kind of money, he would search for them until the sun burned out. The word on the street was they both were dead, but he knew that was a rumor designed to facilitate their plan.

Guzmon stuffed the jewel in his pocket, got out the car and strutted towards the building. After two presses of the second floor buzzer, Guzmon heard Joe Ammanati rumbling down the steps. Joe was the Gozzolli crime family jewel expert, who owed Guzmon a few favors. Joe opened the door.

"Hey, Guzmon." Joe said, his fat face, triple layered chin and super sized beer belly jingled like jelly. "We're all waiting for you."

Guzmon entered. "Look like you lost a few pounds, Joe."

Moments later, Guzmon entered the second floor apartment and saw the two jewel appraisers. Joe said there would be only one and Guzmon's alarms started ringing. "What's with the extra?"

Joe pulled up a seat at the huge table. "Let's all have a seat. They're both good, Guzmon." Joe sat and everyone followed. "This is a big deal here. The buyer has a right to bring a set of extra eyes. If I was paying five million, I would probably want ten extra eyes." Joe laughed at his own joke, but only Guzmon joined in. The two jewel appraisers maintained their cold and callous expressions.

Joe said, "Guzmon, this is Michael and Peter. This is Detective Guzmon."

Guzmon shook Michael's hand first. He was a middle aged, blond haired man with blue eyes. Then he shook Peter's hand. He was tall, had brown hair with matching eyes, and a serious acne problem.

Guzmon suddenly felt another alarm go off. These guys looked more like harden thugs than intellectuals.

Peter said, "Well, let's get this show on the road."

Guzmon pulled the jewel from his pocket and sat it on the table.

Michael picked it up and pulled a jeweler's eye piece from his pocket and examined the jewel from almost very angle. He muttered oohs, huhs, and aahs during his two minute observation. "This is very good."

Suddenly, Peter sprung from his seat and shot Joe in the head. The impact of the bullet hurled Joe backwards, causing him and the chair to crash to the floor.

Michael was less than two seconds behind Peter and had his gun pointed at Guzmon. "Put your hands up, Detective." His accent changed suddenly. He sounded explicitly Russian. "And do not make me repeat myself."

Peter rushed over to Guzmon, grabbed him by the collar of his coat, yanked him on to his feet. His accent suddenly change from perfect English to clear Russian. "One down. 36 to go." He took Guzmon's gun, hand cuffed him and lead him to the door. "You will tell us where you got the other jewels."

Michael came along side of Guzmon as they moved down the stairs. "We know what you did to Daquasha, Jamil and Tykim. Yeah, we know all about it."

Just as they reached the ground floor, Peter opened the outer door as a truck pulled up in front of the building. Peter smiled wickedly. "You killed them and took all the jewels for yourself."

"You got it all wrong!" Guzmon struggled against being dragged to the truck. "They're not dead! I was about--"

Michael slapped a strip of black tape over Guzmon's mouth and they whisked Guzmon away.

CHAPTER # 31

Tykim sat at an elegant outdoors lounging table nursing a drink. The full moon over-head cast a smooth glow over the Guyana beaches. The rolling waves of the ocean splashed on to the sandy beach and brought with it a cool evening breeze that was clean, crisp, calm and cordial; it was even comforting after the intense 90 degree heat that battered the region all day long.

This little routine Tykim was currently engaged in had become a ritual several months ago. This particular resort was the most expense vacation spot in Georgetown, Guyana. About a half mile away, Tykim had purchased a comfortable beach house that had a outdoor pool in the back. Every couple of weeks, Tykim would visit the two nearby resorts to see if any new visitors had arrived.

It was December 13th, and with less than two weeks left before the fall would vanish and the winter season would take over, Tykim was beyond discouraged. Last month he started second guessing his whole approach to this thing. Doubt loomed in every crevice of his thinking process. There wasn't one single analogy that came to mind that held the same energy and vigor as that day he found the ring and discovered Georgetown was in Guyana and had a beach.

Tykim raised the glass to his lips and sucked down a huge gulp of the exotic tasting drink. The alcohol was strong, just the way he liked it. The fruity taste blended perfectly with the liquor. The buzz he was feeling at the moment wasn't strong enough to make him overlook the fact he played himself again. The more he reexamined the situation with the ring, the more he realized Daquasha probably gave him the ring merely as a way of leaving him with something for him to always remember her by. Simply put, she probably had no intentions of coming back for it.

Tykim finished the drink and was now ready for another one. He waved to the pretty chocolate complexion waitress. When she looked over at Tykim, he shouted. "Two more of the same." He raised his glass. She smiled at Tykim and nodded her head.

Tykim sighed. Yeah, he played himself again. He guessed he wanted to be with Daquasha so bad, his mind was making up imaginary circumstances and scenarios. There was a name for that sort of delusional behavior, he realized. He couldn't recall what the name was, but looking at the situation, it was apparent he was suffering from it. Suddenly, his thoughts shifted. What if the reason she hadn't showed up was because she was dead? This thought brought too much anxiety, and Tykim quickly thought about something else.

When his two drinks arrived, Tykim chugged one down. He decided to move on in about a mouth. Maybe he would go down to Brazil or somewhere deeper into South America.

"Hey, my friend," A jet black skin man dressed in a Hawaii shirt and blue shorts said to Tykim.

Tykim looked up. He noticed the man looked and sounded African. "What's up, Bro?"

"You mind if I cop a seat here? Maybe we could have a drink together?"

"Help yourself," Tykim gestured with his hand at the seat across from him.

The man sat down. "My name is Allan. I'm visiting from Nigeria."

"Tykim," He stuck his hand out and Allan shook it. "I'm basically visiting also."

They talked for five minutes about a bunch of mundane things; at least that's what the topics were from Tykim's perspective. Twice Tykim thought Allan was acting strange; he was looking and acting as if he was waiting for something to happen or he was expecting someone.

Suddenly, Allan sprung to his feet.

Tykim was not only shocked by the abrupt nature of his action, but also by the gun he had in his hand.

Allan said, "Mr. Tykim Hair Trigger Hall, you're under arrest."

Tykim felt faint. He rapidly blinked his eyes as if he was seeing an illusion. His mind refused to believe this was happening and it rebelled by blaming it on the alcohol in his system.

"Put your hands where I can see them," Allan's tone was as deadly as snake venom.

Tykim wondered could he grab his gun before Allan pulled the trigger. He struggled not to let the alcohol talk him into committing an act of suicide. With a teeth clenching reluctancy, Tykim slammed both his hands on the table.

Allan rushed around the table, found Tykim's 9mm, and tucked it in his waist. Allan returned to his original position and sat back in the seat.

Tykim and Allan sat staring at each other; no one said a word for what seemed like several minutes.

Tykim heard laughter in back of him. It sounded like a woman. She was welling good naturedly. Tykim kept his eyes on Allan, wondering what the hell was he going to do next. When Allan started laughing along with the woman somewhere in back of him, Tykim thought he was buggin'.

Tykim heard the laughing female's voice drawing closer. She was now almost right upon him. Tykim turned his head and saw a black woman. She was carrying a baby. Tykim was about to scream, "Daquasha!", but the woman's face. It wasn't Daquasha's face. His eyes were wide with confusion, anticipation, hope and distress.

"Damn, Tykim. Close your mouth." Daquasha said.

Tykim jetted out of his seat. It was her. "Daquasha, baby girl, you came." He grabbed her arm. He wanted to kiss, hug, caress and embrace her, but she had the baby in her arms. Her sweet smelling perfume sparked up his hormones and made his nature rise. "What happened to your face?"

"Plastic surgery," Daquasha was already planning how Tykim should look when he got his face remade. She said to Allan. "Mr. Morgan, thank you very much."

Allan walked over to Tykim and handed him his 9mm. "Nothing personal, Bro. It's just business." He patted Tykim on the back and walked away. Allan turned and shouted to Daquasha as he continued walking. "I'll send you my bill for my services before the week is out."

Daquasha had a huge smile on her face as she sat down in Tykim's seat. She sat the baby on the table.

Tykim pulled the chair Allan was sitting in close to Daquasha and sat next to her. "Boy or girl?" He played with the baby's tiny hand.

"Oh, no you didn't!" Daquasha's voice was sassy and filled with indignation. "I know you ain't go there. What you tryin' to say, my son ain't got masculine features?"

"Naw, I ain't mean it like that. You know I would--"

"I'm only jokin'." Daquasha touched his arm. "His name is Tareek." She smiled proudly. The mere mention of that name made her feel good. "Look, don't he look like Tareek?"

Tykim looked closely. "Yeah, damn sure do." He guessed it was all in the mind of the observer because Shorty did have some of his daddy's features as well.

"I see you still lookin' good." Daquasha caressed Tykim's hand. "I ain't gotta ask if you been takin' care of yourself."

"And that goes the same way for you, Boo. That face job fits you all the way. But keepin' it real, I like the old look better."

"Me too. But, I didn't have much of choice in this matter. Hey, where's my ring?" She stuck her hand out. After Tykim dropped the ring in the palm of her hand, she put it on, twirled it as if she'd been craving to do this for quite some time and continued. "Let me bring you up to par. The Russians, and the police all think we're dead. Even you." She smiled.

"Even me!?" Tykim shifted in his seat, he definitely wanted to hear how she pulled this off. "Go ahead. I'm listening."

"Me and Jamil made it look like Guzmon killed us all and stole all the jewels for himself. We found three bodies similar in weight, height, age and ethic background as the three of us. The bodies were burnt beyond recognition and we paid the medical examiner to confirm the dental records. After we started a vicious rumor on the street, word got to the Russians. They investigated and it all checked out. Guzmon, as I suspected from day one, couldn't wait to cash in that jewel. He tried to sell it, and the Russians snatched his greedy ass."

"So, that's why you was so obsessed with keepin' that foul ass chump alive?" Tykim wanted to give her a hug.

"Yeah, I'm just so glad it worked out the way I was hoping and praying it would."

"So, are you here to stay or is this temporary? I know Jamil can't possibly know about this little visit of yours."

"Well, where he's at now, I don't think he cares. Jamil met with a very unsuspected and gruesome demise. He was poisoned."

With eyebrows raised, Tykim said, "How did that happen? Who smoked the infamous and notorious Jamil Nevez?"

"Japper, dapper the smooth clapper." Daquasha saw Tykim's startled eyes display deep confusion.

"What are you saying? That's the quote that cat said just before he killed your--" Tykim saw Daquasha nodding her head.

Daquasha said, "I guess this was a classical example of that saying, that which is in the dark will some day come to light. And it proves Tupac knew what he was talkin' about when he said revenge is the sweetest joy next to getting pussy. But for me, it was the sweetest joy next to getting some dick."

"It was him!?" Tykim saw Daquasha nodded her head again. As the shock slowly settled in, he noticed her eyes becoming misty. "How did you find out it was him?"

Daquasha told him about the incident in New Orleans when Jamil made the statement twice just before killing Nuke. Daquasha shook her head as if the mere thought of that incident had crumbled her heart totally. She continued. "As a way to make sure it was him, I asked a couple of

227

Jamil's workers who handles his Brooklyn spots. All five of them said Jamil personally gorillaed about thirteen of those spots. That spot you had was one of them. All this happened the same year Tareek was murdered."

"You know what, baby girl?" Tykim's memory bank began rearranging, recalling, and repositioning a series of information. "I knew I heard his voice somewhere before. Now that you pin-pointed it, yeah, it was him. It was that motherfucker Jamil who killed Tareek."

There was a very short moment of silence.

Tykim saw Daquasha needed some cheering up. "Damn, baby girl. Look like you done fucked around and turned into an all American black widow. Shit, I might have to seriously reconsider whether I wanna roll with you, Boo."

Daquasha laughed along with Tykim. "Stop, frontin'! You know you wanna get with this. As hot and juicy as these skins is, you wouldn't pass this up for 130 million dollars."

They laughed even harder, the sound was harmonious.

"Well, that's enough of that," Daquasha rose to her feet. "We got too much catching up to do to be pondering the past."

Tykim grabbed Daquasha. "And the first order of business is to tighten up our little family here, cause family is everything." He kissed Daquasha with a deep passion.

In the shadows, near the resort terminal, a white man looked on. He pulled a high-tech night vision camera from his tot bag and started taking pictures of Daquasha and Tykim.

THE END

About the Author

Divine G is the founder and owner of Divine G Entertainment. He is a four-time PEN American Center award winning writer and the winner of the 2008 Tacenda Literary award for best play. He has been quoted by the United Nations and the New York Times.

Divine G recently produced, directed and starred in his debut short film consisting of a scene from his novel, Enigma of Love, which is currently being entered into various film festivals internationally. The film's trailer can be reviewed at http://www.imdb.com/video/demo_reel/vi69708057/

He is currently employed as a carpenter for Lil Wayne on his 2013 AMW tour and is also hosting his own Internet Radio (The Divine G Show), which can be reviewed at http://www.spreaker.com/show/the_divine_g_show

Discover Other Titles by Divine G:

Enigma of Love (Kindle Edition) -   http://www.amazon.com/Enigma-Love-Divine-G-ebook/dp/B00C1Y13AY

Money Grip - http://www.amazon.com/Money-Grip-1-Divine-G-ebook/dp/B00BWEU92W

Money Grip 2 - http://www.amazon.com/Money-Grip-2-Volume/dp/1481924451

Baby Doll - http://www.amazon.com/Baby-Doll-Divine-G-ebook/dp/B00D55MZYQ

The Canarsie Connection -
http://www.amazon.com/s/ref=nb_sb_noss?url=search-alias%3Daps&field-keywords=Canarsie+Connection+by+Divine+G+paperback

No Other Love - http://www.amazon.com/s/ref=nb_sb_noss?url=search-alias%3Daps&field-keywords=No+Other+Love+by+Divine+G+paperback&rh=i%3Aaps%2Ck%3A No+Other+Love+by+Divine+G+paperback

Upcoming Novels from Divine G

TGONG
(In bookstores Spring 2014)

Rayhiem Jones loved his community (Nubia Gold) so much he was willing to do whatever it took to clean it up. But he never thought his efforts to rid the community of drugs would cost him ten years in prison for a murder he did not commit. After finding out Jose Rodriguez (J.R.), the leader of Supranova, a vicious drug gang, had framed him for the murder, and upon his release from prison, Rayhiem is unable to simply put an H on his chest and handle it. Driven by a series of incomprehensible, reoccurring, life-long dreams, Rayhiem formulates a group that specializes in shutting down drug houses called . . . TGONG.

TIME-JACK
(In bookstores Spring 2014)

Calvin Thompson spent countless years mastering the field of Time Travel Technology and just when he is finally about to become the first official time traveler, a jealous co-worker, Eric Seabright, sends him back in time to the year 1831 in the deep south at the height of slavery.

With 4 months to make it to a Backlash zone (a safety component within the Time Machine that may transport him back to the future), Calvin struggles to overcome slavery, futuristic hit-men, and the demons inside of him that will not allow him to love and appreciate the people who are indispensable to his survival, his humanity and the victory of his journey.